TIDAL STARS

A SCI FI FANTASY RETELLING OF THE LITTLE MERMAID

E. M. RENSING

ALSO BY E. M. RENSING

The Heliosphere Trilogy

The Lighthouse of Kuiper

The Ariums of Earth

The Cathedrals of Mars

The Abiota Series

Source Code

Unity Code

Numina Code

Domain Code

Virch Code

Anyon Code

Historical Gaslamp Fantasy

The Scholar the Seer and the Outlaw Fae

Sci-Fi Fairytale Retellings

Engines of Winter

TIDAL
STARS

E.M. RENSING

ACT ONE
SHALLOWS

CHAPTER ONE

Unara had no fear of the sea.

It was life itself on this blasted world. Jailer and guardian. Cradle and cage. Joy and sorrow. The beginning and end of all things.

It was early yet, only the brilliant white-blue face of Brynhildyr having risen over the eastern deserts. Her light filtered down through the water column, the harshness of her rays softened by the endless dance of the waves above. Playing through the rich upper waters, then falling down, down, down. Down into the blackwater. Into the endless night of Thalassa's heart.

It was—

"Unara! Spear it!"

Her sister's shout brought her back to the present. To the moment.

To the eye of the kraken, locked on to her with murderous intent.

Unara struck out with her trident, raking the tip across the thing's vulnerable side. It thrashed, dark ink streaming out into the water, all attention on her now. Mission accomplished. Unara urged her akker backwards, the thing jetting away as fast as it could go, instinct as much as command driving it out of the killing black.

But even wounded, even half-blinded, the kraken was faster. Much faster. It came on hard, tentacles slapping the water in front of it, attempting to...

"Drown your foes!"

Glaeva. She'd gotten above it, broad-bladed fishing spear in hand, hanging for a moment, her brilliant purple hair streaming around her, backlit by the suns above.

Then she dived.

Straight through the kraken's arms, too fast for the befuddled thing to grab. She drove her blade into the creature's primary appendage and her akker arced up, gliding into a broad barrel roll that dragged both Glaeva and trident with it, all the way around the tentacle's base.

It was an effective strike, but a dangerous one, bringing the rider far too close to the main beak. With an adult kraken, it wouldn't have worked at all.

Unara zoomed back in under the monster, lying back in the saddle, trident braced against the akker's back. Timing was everything with this. Her path would take her under the monster. Closer, closer...now.

She lifted her spear, dragging the blade the full length of the creature's underside. One second, two, three, and then it was over. Her akker was propelling her past the flailing tentacles. Glowing blue blood spilled out into the water.

Blood and ink.

On her back, Unara had a good view of it. Ink, expanding like a summer storm cloud. The wounded kraken screeched in rage, even as other tentacles—far larger and plated with hard, knobby growths —flung up through the ink clouds to grab it.

Glaeva pulled up alongside Unara. Her own akker had circular wounds all over it from the kraken's suction cups. She was whooping.

Unara just gritted her teeth and tried not to think about what was happening behind her.

The princesses swam hard, letting the water pull every trace of blood out of their armor. Finally the screeching stopped. The waters stilled. The morning's calm resumed.

"A good fight, sister, a good fight." Glaeva's words were proud, but her face pale.

Unara glanced back over her shoulder at her sister. Glaeva was suffering, but Unara was too. Her heart was hammering in her chest. She felt like there was an iron band around her ribs. It was her lungs, she knew. Her lungs were all wrong. But she couldn't show that. Couldn't let any hint of it slip. At least she wasn't as far along in the transformation as Glaeva was, only hanging on to her ocean-born body by the most meager of genetic threads. "The shoal took care of it, at least."

"You need...to learn to...enjoy it more."

"What?" Unara retorted, more heat in her words than she intended.

"The battle-joy, sister."

Here was a lecture Unara had gotten her entire life. She had always hated it. "What's to enjoy about being eaten by a kraken?"

"It was a juvenile. And besides, you're the one who wanted to go out to the seamount," her older sister replied, and pulled up her akker, body shifting uncomfortably in the shell-saddle. "Let's stop for a moment. I need to catch my breath."

"Do we need to surface?" Unara asked, concerned.

Glaeva waved her away. "Stop fretting. I'm not that far gone yet."

A conch blast sounded in the distance, strong and pure in the midmorning waters. Unara's heart sank, even as Glaeva smiled.

"Looks like Father sent a search party for us." Glaeva patted her braid. She had plaited it back against her skull in one big pile for this, and the fight had pulled some of it loose. "He shouldn't worry so. These seas aren't going to claim my life. Not today."

Unara sighed and swam back to her own mount. "I know that conch, sister. Father didn't need to send anybody."

"Hush," Glaeva said, but her smile grew wistful.

"Why don't you tell Father about him?" Unara asked quietly.

"You know why," Glaeva said sharply. "I can't show favoritism during the kaupang. If we were to announce anything now, it would be seen as nothing more than the delegate from the Drift Clans attempting to secure his people a better position."

"Everyone knows you and he—"

"Everyone? No, you, you know, Unara, and it's none of your business, either. Besides," Glaeva told her, voice lowering, "we don't know if I'll make it back to the sea after this."

Unara shook her head. "Of course you will."

"A man such as Jarl Dryagr deserves a woman who can swim the currents with him, not some broken thing left on land like coral washed ashore after a storm."

"You know he wouldn't care," Unara said. "He would probably pull on legs to join you under the sky."

"What an insane thing to do. Give up the ocean? I wouldn't marry a man who would do that for me."

"There are more powerful forces than the ocean."

"Not on this world, little sister." Glaeva gathered herself, straightening in the saddle. "He and I have waited this long. We can wait another week."

And on they swam.

They met the man near a grand arch, the rock covered with wild titanocoral. The polyps, which could grow as big as a man's fist, were all asleep right now, only the ends of their colorful tentacles waving gently in the soft current. It was indeed the Drift Clan, streamlined and silver, the forms of ones who lived far from shore where speed was favored over all other factors.

"Princesses," Jarl Dryagr said, a lithe man whose tail and hair were both the color of sunlit water. "I smelled kraken blood. Feared the worst."

"Hardly, Jarl Dryagr." Glaeva sniffed, tucking a bit of hair back into its braid. "If we can't handle one juvenile kraken on our own, we don't deserve to call ourselves ocean-born."

"Kraken are dangerous, regardless of the size," the Drift Clan lord replied. "I am grateful to see both of you safe and sound."

Glaeva nodded, as if his concern was beneath her consideration, and patted her akker. The cephalopod flopped one tentacle back to return the gesture, catching her on the shoulder. She laughed and patted it again. "You always like a good fight too, don't you?"

Dryagr smiled himself. "What are you doing this far from the palace reefs anyway?"

"Out for a swim," Glaeva replied. "Before tonight. And you?"

"The same," he said easily. "It is different for your clan, I think. You live in these waters. I was eight before I first saw land. It is hard enough being enclosed in the bay. But the thought of walking out under the sky..." He trailed off.

Glaeva smiled at him, one of her warm, generous smiles. "Strange, I agree."

"It is how humans were meant to live," Unara offered quietly.

He snorted. "It is not how Hildra wishes us to live, not on this world. Now, Princesses, may I extend my protection for the swim back to the palace?"

Glaeva laughed. "You're as winded as me, Jarl Dryagr. What good would you be in a fight right now?"

Dryagr grinned. "Never underestimate the power of a beautiful woman on a man's resolve, my princess."

"I would never underestimate you, Jarl Dryagr," Glaeva replied, voice growing soft.

Unara resisted the urge to roll her eyes at her sister's flirting, but an opportunity was an opportunity. She seized it. "Why don't you go back with him, Glaeva?"

"And miss my last day with my sister? Hardly."

"I have a few more crevasses down here I want to check for

pearls," Unara said, "and I wouldn't want either of you to be late for your appointments with the gene-priests."

"Pearls?" Dryagr had an amused expression on his face. "Surely your father has enough pearls stockpiled in the palace to satisfy half the galaxy."

"These are for me," Unara replied quickly. "I'd like to barter for a few incidental things. Trinkets, jewelry, nothing of consequence."

"And how are you planning on doing that? It's not as if we can invite the off-worlders down to the boundary pools."

"Not without Father ordering them executed after," Glaeva said with a slight smile, "and then what good would the pearls do?"

Dryagr laughed at this. Unara tried not to react.

It was maddening, this many people on the reef, in the palace. No privacy, no freedom of movement. The princess had tried to slip away this morning, but her sister had caught her and asked her where she was off to. Unara hadn't exactly lied when she told her sister she was off to harvest pearls: she did have a few more seeded mollusks that she needed to inspect.

But she had other things, more important things, that she needed to accomplish. While her sister's presence already made that difficult, Dryagr's would make it impossible.

"One of my friends in the Stone Clan offered to make the barters for me," Unara said, taking a risk, dangerously close to the truth. "After we review the initial offers together, of course. I am told that the lesser tradesmen often attempt to undercut the value of our goods. And even cultured pearls command a high price off-world. The highest margin commodity for them, kilo for kilo."

Dryagr shook his head. "I am glad I have only our regeneratives to worry about. How do the shore clans keep track of so many trade goods? Fish and nacre plating and pearls and all the rest."

"It is a great burden, but Unara has helped me organize the accounts," Glaeva replied. "She has a good head for these things."

"Is that so?" Dryagr said, considering Unara for a moment.

"Well, perhaps I shall consult with you as well before finalizing any transfers."

"I would be happy to help, Jarl," she replied. "But perhaps after I…" And she pointed down, hoping he would take the hint.

He laughed. "Of course, of course. Princess Glaeva?"

Glaeva laughed. "Don't miss the ceremony, Unara! I wish to see you before I depart."

"Of course, sister," Unara said.

Glaeva smiled at her one more time, then urged her akker forward, next to Dryagr's. Their mounts jetted out quickly. Soon they were nothing more than streaks, fading out into the distance.

Unara waited until she could no longer see them, then sagged.

Turning her akker around, she headed back to the north.

She was late for her own appointment, and being late for that would mean being late for the ceremony later, and being late for that would almost certainly mean censure. Discovery, even.

She'd risked too much. She couldn't afford exposure now. Not now, when everything was almost done.

THE SWIM WAS PAINFUL TODAY. Even mounted, tucked into the living shell-saddle of her akker, Unara could feel the strain. The fight had only exacerbated it.

The changes Unara sought were slow but ongoing. Progressive. Her tail, her lungs, everything she had been born with, had to change. She wasn't deep here, only twenty meters, but she could still feel the weight of the water column pressing down on her. It was daylight above, and yet there were still shadows in the reef that her eyes wouldn't now pierce.

There was a creeping unease beginning to grip her, a foreign fear, some deep instinct being stirred awake in the back of her brain.

Unara tried to ignore it.

This was still her world.

Everything was fine.

The waters were slightly cooler right now, a sure sign that the planet was very nearly at apogee. The Thalassan System was a complex one, a trinary star system whose central bodies were so tightly packed it was a wonder that anything could survive at all. But survive the Thalassans did. Thrive.

Even if being bound to the water was the price.

Unara didn't know what the first colonists on Thalassa Prime must have thought of it all. Any records had long since been corrupted, and her people's current stories gave it no thought. They were the people of the seas now; they were the ocean and the ocean was them. What did it matter how the first humans on the planet had felt?

They had adapted.

What would it be like? she wondered. All her life, she had been one way. Hair the same shade as the titanocorals at night under the great moon Hildra's light. Skin burned bronze by the sunlight of the continental shelf. A tail longer than normal human legs, scales the color of a tide pool at midday.

But that would not be for much longer.

What would it be like to see the off-worlders when they came? To walk among them? Be—

A noise.

They banked as one, the akker moving the position of its jet, Unara swinging her tail out to arrest their momentum, knife out. If this was an eel or a placoderm or, seas forbid, another kraken...

Unara was breathing hard, half-altered lungs desperately trying to still pull oxygen from the water. Breathing hard, staring out at the blackwater. They were close to it now, five meters above a narrow shelf where the cliffs fell away into the darkness.

Unara had never been much of one for the stories of the skalds, sung to the sounds of drum and harp during great clan gatherings. But still, the blackwater was a place avoided by her people, the source of horrors both imagined and all too real, a place Thalassans only ever went in force, and even then, only at great need. Only the vents were safe havens out there in the darkness, and even those, even those...

The akker underneath her was changing color rapidly. No longer a mirror of the reef around them, it was taking on a deep and dangerous red. It uncoiled its two longest tentacles from their own protective sheaths, edged with titanium blades.

Unara looked around, scanning for threats. Her eyesight was beginning to shift noticeably now, her ability to pierce the shadows somewhat compromised. She wondered if she was imagining things. If her altered brain was interpreting things wrong.

Her hearing was unchanged, at least.

Something was there.

But when it didn't show itself, Unara relaxed. The currents were pushing her off course. She had an appointment to keep. She sheathed her knife and settled back down in the saddle.

She was wasting time.

THE GENE-HALLOW UNARA sought soon came into view. These facilities were ubiquitous throughout Thalassa. They varied wildly in design, their functions ranging from practical to esoteric. The entire economy of the world revolved around the art of genetic manipulation. The gene-priests here, the gothi of the guardian moons, were the foremost practitioners of that craft.

Unara approached cautiously.

Passing through a massive ridge of titanocoral, her akker navigating the narrow confines carefully, Unara emerged into the gene-hallow's outer halls. This was a vast but shallow pool, barely more than fifteen meters deep, brilliant with the fierce midday sunlight. As was tradition, a coral carving of the gene-hallow's patron moon stood proudly in the middle of the pool, so worn by tide and time its features were indistinguishable. The place was teeming with fish, small hardy things braving the light to gobble up the algae blooms forming on the rocks. The akker grabbed a few of the fattest and slowest of these, bringing them to its beak.

"Must it feed here?" somebody all but sighed.

Unara smiled and hit the akker gently with the back of her hand three times. A signal to dismount. The muscles that helped hold her in the saddle released. She slid free.

The muscles of her tail were sore.

"It has been a long journey, Gothi Strygr," she replied.

There, in the middle of the deep well of light, by a large outcropping of titanocoral grown to resemble a pavilion, was a very old Thalassan. His hair was gray, his scales milky-white. When Unara had first come to him, six years ago now, she had wondered if he would live to finish their work together. But he was no more frail now than he had been then.

The regeneratives that the off-worlders sought so fiercely served a practical purpose here on Thalassa: knowledge was best preserved at its source. Wise men and women, important men and women, the ones who held the clans together and guided them in Thalassa's dangerous seas, were worth keeping alive. Gene-priests like Gothi Strygr might live for centuries.

"Your akker is taking advantage of my gardens, Princess," the gothi replied. "A breed like that shouldn't need to eat but once every two days."

"It's hungry. We had a fight with a kraken out there," she replied. "I can pay you for the fish. My pearl collection is here after all, honored gothi."

"Honored. Ha!" The old gothi shook his head. "Old and forgotten, that's what I am. Do you know, you're the only member of the royal family to visit me since the last Sunwrath?"

Her smile became a bit more fixed. They had this conversation every time she came. "Yes, I believe I have heard that before."

"Your father is a shrewd man, Princess, and I know he's making the right choices for our people, but to not visit me, one of his most dedicated servants, for the past twenty-three years has been quite the blow, let me tell you."

"Gothi Strygr," she said gently, "the ceremony for the delegates is happening at twilight. I cannot miss it. I don't have much time."

He smiled at her, then waved for her to follow. "You never have much time, Princess. It does not help that you are late today. Are you ready for your final infusion yet?"

"No, not the change. Not yet," she said. "There are too many eyes watching me at the reef. When we do it, it must be quick."

"This is not good, dragging it out like this. But we shall see what we can do."

He swam slowly into the shaded inner chambers of the gene-hallow. The walls glowed with soft light, reef fish swam through the coral formations, anemones swayed in the slow current.

As he always did, the gene-priest stopped at a small alcove, allowing Unara to deposit her latest addition to her pearl hoard. She undid the lid of the clamshell chest, taking in the contents. It was substantial, the careful work of the past decade. She hoped it would be enough.

She drew out the pearl she had retrieved from the seamount. It had been worth the risk. Bigger than her fist and a deep purple-blue, it was the equal to anything her father had in the treasury.

"Beautiful," Gothi Strygr commented. "I should have had you bring me a tissue sample from the bivalve that made it. That's a rare color to come by."

"I wouldn't risk hurting the poor thing," Unara told him, and placed it carefully into the chest. With it went a handful of smaller pearls, gleaned from the same field. She had waited as long as she could to harvest all of them. Larger pearls commanded higher prices; she just hoped this would be enough. "I seeded another pearl in it. For my sister someday." The princess closed the chest and, with a gentle flick of her tail, swam on. "I know this has been a huge risk for you, taking me on as a patient, but—"

"Four hundred and twenty years I facilitated the greed of Thalassa," he replied, giving her a considering look. "New regenerative compounds for prolonging life, new breeds of nacre mollusks for the off-worlders to do whatever it is they do with them. Never has anybody wished to go out there and understand the rest of humanity. I am happy to help you."

"It is not about greed. My father worries what the off-worlders would do if we refused to trade."

"Yes, that's been a fear for a very long time," the gothi said, leading her into the treatment space. "But what could any of the trading houses truly deploy against us?"

"They could bombard us from orbit," Unara said.

"To what end? They would only destroy what they come here for in the first place. These humans of the trading houses care about money, profits, young princess, and nothing else." He smiled at her, an unpleasant expression. "And lest we forget, we exist entirely at the moons' pleasure. It is doubtful that any of them would allow such a destruction of their ecosphere to take place."

Unara sighed. Gothi were geneticists and bioengineers, yes, but they also had other functions, religious functions. It had always seemed a bit ridiculous to her. "What could the moons do?"

"What can't they do? What don't they do?" he chuckled. "They give life and take it. What else is there?"

Unara shook her head. "Humans exist elsewhere in this galaxy, far from either."

"None like us," he replied proudly, and gestured at his table. "Now please, if you will, Princess..."

She settled down in place, letting Gothi Strygr arrange the straps and tubes and all the rest around her. Unara watched him work for a few moments, listening to the surf crash in the upper layers of the gene-hallow, waiting for the first needle to slip in, for the coolness of the next dose of serum to hit her veins.

She closed her eyes. Imagined the stars.

So close now.

She was so very close.

CHAPTER TWO

Karl Gyes, designated lord negotiator, merchant prince, wayward son, stood on the observation chamber of his family's interstellar trader, the *Vanatar Deep*, watching the bright blue planet grow in the darkness beyond.

A strange world, Thalassa Prime. It was not a system he himself would have recommended for colonization, had he been the one to find it. Protocol would have ruled it out as safe for human settlement. Trinary star systems were tricky things even with the best of stellar configurations. But here, the F-type main sequence star, Thalassa 1A, was an absolute monster. Even though the system's three rocky worlds orbited the smaller G- and M-type binary pair, that larger star guaranteed that Thalassa Prime was only inhabitable by the barest of margins. And the conditions in the void were hardly any better. Unpredictable solar winds, treacherous orbital conditions thanks to its mass of moons, a location relatively close to the galactic gulf...nothing worked in this world's favor.

And yet, human life persisted here.

And not just persisted, either. Thalassa Prime was one of the most strategically important worlds in the Spiral.

The observation chamber was a fist of reinforced glass punching out of the *Vanatar Deep's* hull, twelve meters wide. It was almost perfectly spherical with a single ringed walkway set about two-thirds of the way down from the top of the sphere and connected to the rest of the great craft only via a thin, telescoping passageway. There was no gravity here. At full extension, it felt like floating in a sea of stars.

Under normal ship operations, the chamber sat inside a hollow within the outer hull, enclosed fully and protected by a series of huge shutters. It could be deployed like a balloon, far above the ship, either for receptions or private conversations or to take more accurate visual star readings. Right now, Karl had the passageway extended only a little way. Just enough to get a full view of the planet without the *Vanatar's* bulk interfering with his line of sight.

Since his recall to the main fleet, Karl had come here often.

Now, he watched the main landmass just begin to rotate into view, calm, peaceful. It seemed strange that so many resources were expended on this place. A world that should not have been at all. A world that—

A noise behind him. The sound of somebody clearing his throat. Karl sighed and turned, the magnetic locks in his boots making the movement slightly harder than it should have been. "What do you want, Captain Thorsen?" he asked.

The man who had been behind bowed a little, hand on his chest in salute. "I've been sent up here to ask you to come down to the bridge. Something about it being too dangerous up here." Captain Thorsen's expression didn't waver. "After what happened to your sister, I believe your father is feeling...protective."

"If he's worried, he shouldn't be. We've been decelerating from the system's edge for three days and are currently on an orbital inser-tion trajectory, are we not?" Karl said, looking back down at the planet. They were close enough now that the largest of their competitors' ships were now just visible. Sunlight glinting off the hulls, points of light moving against the star field. "If the windows cannot handle the strain of in-system flight, then they have no place on a Gyes vessel."

"It's not the strain. The moons present an extreme hazard to navigation, I'm told."

"My father thinks a moon is going to fly through the observation bubble?"

"Your father requests your presence on the bridge, milord."

Karl sighed. Turned. Attention fully fixed on the other man now. House Gyes, like most of the other Trader Houses, maintained a private military as part of their overall organizational structure. A necessary precaution, given the state of the galaxy. Captain Thorsen had been assigned to Karl as his personal bodyguard upon his return to the fleet three years ago. He was a bull of a man, large and imposing, with a shaved head and an understated sense of humor that poked out around his professional bearing.

Generally, Karl liked him. But his presence was a constant reminder of what Karl had lost by returning here: his freedom. A bodyguard was one more layer of protection, control.

"Are you really going to insist upon that ridiculous mode of address?"

"You are my lord, aren't you?" Thorsen replied.

"We've been friends since we were children, Mikkel, running around the halls of this ship together after lessons," Karl reminded him.

"Yes, but you were always the son of Lord Gyes, and I the son of sergeants from the House Guard," Thorsen said seriously. "Besides, your father said I had to be more formal for the kaupang."

"So you're what, practicing?"

Thorsen shrugged.

With one last look back outside, Karl disengaged the mag-locks in his boots. "If my father is looking for me, I shouldn't disappoint him," he replied, and pushed free of the catwalk, his momentum carrying him expertly back down to the passage.

Karl had been born on the *Vanatar Deep* and spent most of his life in the void. He was at home here in the endless night in a lot of ways. And yet, looking back up at the observation chamber, with the great shutters drawing closed and the passage telescoping back into the hull, he felt trapped.

BACK IN THE main spaces of the interstellar trader now, the two men headed for the command deck. It wasn't far. Unlike the explorer frigate Karl had not long ago commanded, trader craft were concerned more with efficiency of propulsion than physical protection; the command bridge was not buried deep but placed near the outer skin of the craft.

"Such a strange world," Karl said.

"A hostile one. How anything survives here is beyond me," Thorsen grunted.

"Aren't you curious about it, Thorsen?" Karl asked.

"Only so far as I need to be in order to keep you safe." Reaching the bridge doors, Thorsen laid his palm on the scanner. A light dinged green, the locks disengaging. "Curiosity is not rewarded here. And remember, we shall be competing against a dozen other Trader Houses that will descend to the surface looking to strip this planet of every shred of wealth they can shove in their holds."

Karl shook his head as they stepped inside. "We shall prevail. Against whatever is waiting down there."

<Nacre armor is what is down there, my son. Now come here and tell me what you think of this world.>

"Of course, Father," Karl said, and strode across the deck to meet his lord, his father, his jailer, glittering in holographic light.

LORD VILHELM GYES had ruled their House for over three centuries, Standard. Some of that longevity was due to the vagaries of interstellar travel, relativistic speeds and hyperspace transit interfering with the natural flow of time. The rest of the difference was made up by regeneratives, compounds found here on Thalassa Prime and fiercely sought after by all of human space.

Once, Lord Gyes had retained the mind and body of a man in his late forties, a powerful figure in the realm of interstellar commerce, a giant of trade.

Once.

Now, a glittering projection showed a man in the prime of his life. Tall, strong, dressed in the ceremonial uniform of Lord Negotiator. The face was indistinct but the stance, the posture, the movement, Karl was assured, was a perfect analog for the man his father had once been.

A technological ghost, still commanding one of the largest trading fleets in the Occidental Spiral.

How Karl hated living in the shadow of that thing.

The figure was standing in front of the largest of the command bridge's windows. Thalassa Prime hung before them, turning slowly against the harsh light of its suns. The glass of the window displayed read-outs of every kind, features on the surface or other fleets in orbit mapped out.

Karl ignored the projection of his father as it pretended to examine the planet before them. All the information present on the window would be pushed directly through his father's neural links. The projection was a pantomime, a reminder to the crew, an overcompensation. A way of demonstrating that Vilhelm Gyes was still in command, despite his current...condition.

"What impressions would you like from me?" Karl asked.

<Anything you wish to say, my son.>

Karl considered this carefully.

He had been to all the briefings, read everything he could get his hands on. Thalassa Prime was an ocean world, over eighty percent of its surface covered with water. A few volcanic island archipelagos scattered away from the single supercontinent that straddled the equator. The eastern side was battered by storms; even now, during this period of relative calm that marked Thalassa Prime's orbital apogee, rotating cloud systems obscured that coastline from view. The interior was bone-dry, parched, bare desert, too far from the sea for rain to fall. In some places, even now, temperatures there could rise over fifty degrees during the day. But it was the radiation from the system's stars that rendered the interior abiotic; Thalassa 1A baked the desert clean.

Thalassa's human population made their living on the western coast, but how exactly, nobody knew. It was theorized that they had vast underwater habitats, but nobody knew for sure. No off-worlders had ever been invited into such places, and scans were impossible; something here interfered with even the most sophisti-cated surveillance technology. It was attributed to the chemical composition of the water, but then, how did sunlight penetrate so readily? All of Thalassa Prime was a mystery.

"It seems a simple world, Father," he finally said, "but I suspect it is anything but."

A laugh sounded across the bridge. His father's holographic form smiled.

<It was this world that required me to take up residence in my current quarters,> his father said.

"Yes, Father. I am aware," Karl replied stiffly.

<Anything else you wish to know? Trillions of kroner are at stake, my son.>

"We have an entire star system's titanium in the holds," Karl said. "I could buy half of the Caledon Sector with that kind of wealth."

Another laugh. <Indeed. I have great faith that this year's kaupang will be even better than last.>

"I'm sure it will be, Father. They can't poison you twice."

For a moment, silence fell across the operations floor.

Then his father's projection looked at him. <Step into my chamber, Karl.>

"Lord, I did not mean—"

<My chamber. Now.> And as if to punctuate the seriousness of the command, the holographic figure blinked out.

Behind him, a set of discreet doors slid open.

Several of the bridge staff were staring at him now, although most were scrupulously pretending to work. Karl sighed. What a stupid thing of him to say.

Karl's eyes struggled to adjust to the light as the doors slid shut behind him. His father's personal quarters. It was dark in here, only a few recessed floor lights and the glow of medical equipment offering any illumination.

Attempts had been made once—before Karl's time—to dress up the life support tank. It was skinned with a fine fretwork of brass and steel, given the kind of nautical detail found on the finest ships of the Rikstag Sector.

But even that finery didn't hide the truth inside.

Karl caught a glimpse of himself, a reflection in the glass, super-imposed over the form within. They had the same height, the same strong build, the same pale skin, faded from lack of sunlight. They'd once had the same gray-blue hair. The same dark eyes. Karl knew this. He had seen photographs, paintings, all his life.

But now Lord Vilhelm Gyes was a ruin of a man, face pitted and sunk, skin mottled dark red from sores, every bit of fat long since used up. His eyes were hidden behind a visor now, his shaved scalp dotted with interface ports. He floated in a tangle of wires, tubes, and support filaments. He could still move his limbs but rarely did. Such things, Karl was told, were painful.

There were medical staff in here, always staff. Three of them today, the bare minimum. Normally, they would be tending to the machines that kept old Lord Gyes alive, but right now, they were on their way out. Two human women and one alien.

"Don't you need to stay?" he asked, slightly alarmed by this.

The human women didn't answer him, but the alien stopped. Looked at him, the blank mask of her face giving nothing away. Karl had encountered a handful of feii over the years. Their environmental suits varied wildly in design, keeping only the bare minimum of humanoid features and sharing nothing in common except those blank eyes. Feii were said to have a strong ability to influence both space and time, but who knew the truth?

Eyr, her name was, and Karl had always found her presence uncomfortable.

"Your father wishes to converse with you alone," the feii told him. "Be quick. The poison in his body is insidious and slips back into his bloodstream when I'm not here to hold it at bay."

And before Karl could protest further, the doors slid shut, locking the two Gyes men away together.

<You speak out of turn, my son,> his father said now. The words here came from speakers set into the tank, softer, less augmented, than the voice on the bridge. Attempts had been made to make it sound like a natural human voice, but it had always sounded false to Karl.

"I meant no offense."

<If you cannot think before you speak, then perhaps I should send someone else to handle this year's negotiations.>

"Father, forgive my attempt at humor. I can handle the negotiations."

<This Thalassan exchange is what the wealth of our family has been built on.>

"I understand that we must—"

<Do you? Do you imagine that the forty years it took to empty that minor star system of its titanium came cheaply? The future of House Gyes is tied to our success here. If we fail, we face bankruptcy and dissolution.>

"I understand all of this, Father," Karl said. "We have talked of nothing else for the past two years."

<Perhaps I should have started sooner. I do not see a serious trader in front of me now.>

"I am sorry for any shortcomings I may possess," Karl said, bitter now. "We both know I did not wish to come back from the explorer fleet. But I am loyal to this House, to you. I have no desire to see this fleet broken up and sold off to our competitors. I want—"

Something chimed. An alert. Karl fell silent as a new voice broke into their conversation.

<My lords, I am sorry to interrupt.>

It was the bridge. Karl frowned.

<Report, Captain Andresson,> Lord Gyes replied.

<The surveillance probes have found something potentially problematic among the assembling trader fleets.>

"And what is that?" Karl asked.

<Vessels bearing Suyarii identifiers and hull configurations.>

Karl's blood ran cold. He looked back at his father. The old man hadn't changed position, but inside the tank, one hand was clenching into a fist.

CHAPTER THREE

Unara's heart was racing a little too fast as her akker dived through the lower gate of the bay's barrier wall.

The Palace of Sun and Water's Meeting was a grand affair, worked into the cliffsides of Oceanfall Bay over the course of a hundred generations. Grown of the finest titanocorals, the upper levels gleamed a brilliant white under the harsh Thalassan suns. Under the water, smaller corals had long since colonized the outer walls, lending a rainbow of color and texture to the original titanium-reinforced curves. The palace spilled down the cliffs for hundreds of feet, tumbling out across wide, flat rock shelves above.

Every kaupang saw it expanded, repaired, improved.

That was made possible by the structure she was swimming over now. The bay gates were vast and complicated things, wrought from stone and titanium, capable of damming up the one-hundred-and-sixty-meter gap in the towering bay cliffs, turning the bay beyond into a deep pool nearly four kilometers across at its broadest point.

Few things on Thalassa were purely mechanical, and the bay gates were no exception. While the barrier itself was unliving, the muscles that moved it possessed a beating heart and rudimentary brain. Tucked away into caverns deep within the cliffs, the gate organisms were difficult to rouse and moved only at the command of the king. The gates were only ever closed after the kaupang was complete, to effect repairs and make changes on the palace.

Such undertakings were the work of lifetimes.

She nodded to one of the human guards, an ocean-born with a short tail adapted for close-quarters combat. He nodded back and paid her little heed. The entire palace guard was used to the princess's comings and goings.

Looking up, she could see the daylight fading above. That wasn't good. The ceremony of transition was always held at night under Hildra's watchful eye. That moon would be rising soon. Unara would be expected.

The infusion had taken longer than she had expected and affected her more than she had anticipated. The bones in her tail were rearranging, nearly to the point of division now, and it ached. Any base set of genes could only be twisted so far from its original plan, and humans were no exception. The adaptations that allowed the ocean-born to survive in Thalassa's ocean were the absolute limit of how far the genome could be altered. Forcing the human body back into a baseline configuration was a tricky, difficult process.

Some people claimed it was magic. Others, the eldritch power of the guardian moons, Hildra chief amongst them.

Unara wasn't sure she believed that. Surely, if there was magic involved, it wouldn't hurt so much.

Normally, she left her akker out on the reef to feed and rest, but not today. Today, she overshot the paddock reefs, heading straight under the shield coral, toward her chambers in the upper palace.

The akker didn't complain. It wasn't a true organism, not like the fish and coral of the reef. Akkers were closer to machines, biolog-ical vehicles whose underlying genetics had been taken from cephalopods. The combination of mobility, protective shells, and intelligence provided the perfect base pattern for all manner of craft.

The Drift Clans bred versions capable of housing entire families, floating platforms from which they worked the surface waters far from shore. The reef clans grew akkers like Unara's own, fast and agile, capable of hunting the armor-headed sharks that lurked in the huge sea columns. Small akker, functioning as drones, helped maintain the health of the northern kelp forests or were employed by the ice clans to flush prey into the open during the winter.

Now, Unara's extended a tentacle to gently help her out of the saddle. She gave it a pat, then whistled for it to go hunting. She watched it swim away for a moment, then turned with a flick of her tail, swimming back to her own chambers.

The line between animal and machine here on Thalassa, Unara thought, watching it swim away, was a fine one indeed. What would it be like to live in the world of the air-breathers? Where all machines were made of silicone and steel?

Thinking about the world beyond her own was a nice distraction from the pain. Her body had stiffened during her ride back, and fresh movement sent flares of pain up her spine. But she couldn't afford to be distracted by it right now. Unara was late.

She dived down through her window into her own chamber. This part of the palace was more titanocoral than rock, worked into fluid, flowing curves. The delicate bone-white walls were planted thickly with sea-flowers that glowed with blue bio-light. Normally a place of peace and relaxation for her, she barely even glanced at it. Instead, Unara feverishly thrashed about, throwing her dive knife aside, shucking off her lightweight armor, digging through a clamshell chest, looking, looking for—

<You need this, Princess?>

The voice almost gave Unara a heart attack, and she nearly banged her head on the lid as she extracted herself from her search. Floating there in her room was a slender sky-born woman in full dive gear, braided hair streaming out behind her like a tail, used air bubbling out from her breathing regulator. In her hand she had Unara's court finery, gauzy silks and beaten gold bracelets.

"Vaelyn," Unara acknowledged, hand over her heart. It really did feel like it was going to explode out of her chest. That next infusion couldn't come soon enough. She reached for her clothes. "What are you doing here?"

The other woman pointed a finger up at the sky. <We had an appointment at half tide this afternoon, remember?> Her voice was amplified by a small speaker-conch integrated into the regulator.

Unara cursed internally. By the blackwater. "I forgot. I was late out of here to go see the gothi and—"

<How's it going?>

"Hurts," Unara said, pulling her dress over her head and working on the straps. Her fingers were shaking. The material was sliding everywhere. "Like it always does. These holding infusions are awful."

Vaelyn shook her head and moved forward, helping Unara tie and buckle the dress into some semblance of order. Even with the dive-suit gloves on, she had more dexterity right now. <Are you sure you want to go through with this? It's not too late to back out if you—>

"Are you still willing to help me find passage off-world?"

<I've got the dossiers on all the Trader Houses,> Vaelyn replied. <I think I've narrowed it down. I was going to discuss this with you today. I've requested to be assigned to the House I feel is most promising.>

"Good," Unara said, and ran her fingers through her hair.

<Want me to help you braid that?>

"No time," Unara said shortly. She glanced at herself in the room's mirror, then looked around at the mess she'd made. "I have to go. Pick this up for me, would you?"

<Your command, Princess.>

Unara nodded her thanks and with a flick of her tail, was off again, through the interior doors and into the depths of the palace.

VAELYN SIGHED as she picked up Unara's armor.

Thoughtless. As usual.

It wasn't that the princess was a nasty person, nor was she unpleasant to be around. When Vaelyn first set her sights on making friends with King Aegyr's youngest daughter, she had expected her to be thoroughly disagreeable. Unara was not. Indeed, under different circumstances, Vaelyn might have considered her to be a real friend.

Under much different circumstances.

Right now, Vaelyn worked quickly, tidying up the mess that Unara had left behind. It wasn't like the princess to be late, and it certainly wasn't like her to be forgetful. For years, Vaelyn had been helping her. Teaching her Standard. Passing along every scrap of information Unara requested about the off-worlders. There was much in the sky-side records that was not duplicated in the ocean-side archives.

The ocean-born had never been very curious about anything above the waves.

Fools.

Perhaps if they did care a little more, if they did turn even slightly more of their attention to matters above their own waves, then none of this would have been necessary. But they didn't care. Not about the off-worlders. Not even about their own sky-born population.

Vaelyn's clan was not numerous. A few thousand at the most, scattered between Oceanfall and the forge islands. They were the castoffs, the failures, the ones the guardian moons, with Hildra as their chieftain, had rejected.

Due to the extreme nature of Thalassan genetics, the ocean-born adaptations didn't always breed true, or didn't always hold, or wouldn't reform, in the case of the ocean-born who came ashore.

At least, that was the story Vaelyn had grown up hearing.

Her own parents were unknown to her, her lineage and clan a mystery. She had been surrendered at the palace as a newborn, a child born to the sky. No tail, no lamellae folds in her lungs, no nictitating membranes to protect her eyes from the seawater.

But just because the people of the Stone Clan had been rejected didn't mean they were forgotten.

Oh no. The ocean-born always had use for them.

Even on a world like Thalassa, where nothing survived for long on the surface, certain things had to be done on dry land. Forging glass, for example, or maintaining the landing fields for the kaupang.

No matter how much the skalds sang of their importance, no matter what fine words King Aegyr spoke at shared feasts, the sky-born were an exploited clan.

That was the truth that Vaelyn had learned.

That was the truth that had been shared with her, her and many others among the Stone Clan, a truth that required action.

And act she would.

If she could prove herself this kaupang, if she proved true, then the ultimate freedom would be hers. Not trapped in this narrow strip of land, not bound to the service of a building, of all things, but free to explore the endless expanse of Thalassa's oceans.

No boundaries, no restrictions.

No more slavery.

She threw Unara's things into a trunk and flipped it shut. It wasn't like the princess was going to need them anymore anyway.

Besides, Vaelyn had to be in the Hall of Transformation as well.

The Hall of Transformation was set high in the palace, not placed back in the stone of the cliff but grown entirely of titanocorals well out into the reef. It was the largest of all chambers within the palace and quite shallow, the roof only three meters below the surface of the waves at low tide. These vaults were comprised of the shield corals above, held up and supported by many smaller columns rising from the floor here, another ten meters down. The floor was paved with polished granite taken from the interior deserts of Fjorgyn. Tapestries swaying in the currents were of the finest sea-silks. Statues stood in their niches, personifications of the world's many moons. And in the center was a great grand dome, an exquisite structure of glass and gold filigree that held an airspace large enough for a hundred to stand within, connected back to the upper levels of the palace by a long tunnel and fed by a mechanical ventilation system whose outlets were high above the clifftops above.

Here, the two worlds of Thalassa could meet in equal dignity.

At least, that was what Father always said.

In other places, grand halls like these were built all the way up to the surface, walls designed to capture wave action and oxygenate the interior waters. Here, with the roof of the hall cut off by the shield coral cap, fresh currents had to be brought in through a complex set of sponge tunnels. It worked, but the sponges did take what they needed along the way, and thus, the currents were not as rich as they could have been.

One of the many limits of organic structures.

But Thalassa had no other options. Building underwater was exceedingly difficult, all the more so because of the sheer impossibility of extracting mineral resources from Fjorgyn's hostile deserts. Concrete was impossible to manufacture at any appreciable scale and metal forging was likewise difficult. The rich seawater ate away at almost everything anyway.

Unara had heard that the air-breathers had grand ships the size of cities, all built entirely from metal. She had always wondered what such things would look like.

Soon, she promised herself, she would see for herself.

All around her, the water was filled with the soft conversations of dozens of people. Every major clan, along with several coalitions of smaller ones, was represented here today. Unara's father may have held the title of Ocean King, but it did not make him the direct dictator of the world. Every clan here on Thalassa conducted their own trade negotiations. Under his direction and guidance, of course, but Thalassans were fiercely independent. The only real rules were the ones that benefited them all.

There was a riot of color in the hall. Most clans refined their genetic patterns to not only adapt to their environments but also distinguish their clan from all others. There were the garish Reef Clans, marked by flamboyant tail markings and complex hair braiding. There were the Ice Clans, cold blue and purple and white, stout forms bulked with extra fat as protection in the chill winter waters. There were the Drift Clans with broad fins made for long-distance cruising and silvery coloring, nomads who spent generations tending vast krill herds and hunting the largest deep-ocean beasts, who only ever saw solid land during the kaupang. And at the far end of the hall was Lady Hethra, chieftain of the Abyssal Clans. Alone. Apart.

She caught Unara looking at her and smiled back.

It was an expression as cold as the depths.

Unara shivered

"Daughter. I was beginning to worry. Did Vaelyn find you?"

It was her father, swimming up in his full ceremonial regalia, with two of his personal guards trailing behind. Three hundred and twenty-four years had he led the people of Thalassa, and he was still as strong as ever. Lean, broad-shouldered, and completely in command. His presence was like a maelstrom. Even Unara felt his pull.

"Yes, Father," she said. "I'm sorry. Glaeva and I were out hunting and..."

"Your hair is a mess," he said quietly, leaning in.

She ran her fingers through it again. "Better?"

He grunted, but before he could answer, a trumpet sounded.

The delegation was arriving.

Far from the triumphant parades that followed the defeat of a rampaging kraken or a chieftain's marriage, the procession of the trade delegates toward the water-lock was an almost funereal affair. At this point in their transformations, most of the delegates could no longer swim well. Many struggled with breathing. A few were borne in by attendants on palanquins, while others relied on family or their clan gothi for support.

Only Unara's sister was moving on her own, and even she had a breathing apparatus with her, swimming alongside like a tame hunting shark.

It was the same future that awaited Unara, if she persisted. Her conviction from earlier in the day felt false; her palms were clammy.

Get through it, she told herself, *get through it and—*

Her father swam forward, the delegates and their assistants arranging themselves in a rough semicircle. He set the butt end of his trident down, the soft sound of titanium knocking against the granite floor enough to pull every set of eyes in the hall to him.

"I shall not be long," he began, "for I know you all suffer. Years you have spent preparing for this day. I have walked under the sky myself three times before, and I can tell you, what you are about to experience is a profound shift. But you are the best of your clans, here to represent your people in the upcoming negotiations. Be strong, be fair, be wary. The off-worlders will seek to dazzle us with their wealth and power, but what is any human against the might of the ones who guard us?" He gestured upward with his trident, where the soft glow of the guardian moon Hildra was just beginning to filter down through the evening waters. "We are the people of the ocean. Don't forget that up there."

"For the ocean," everyone murmured. Unara was glad it was growing dark. Her face was burning with a sudden and unexpected shame.

Then the king moved aside, sweeping an arm out. "Glaeva, daughter, will you lead the delegates through the boundary, as you will lead them above?"

Unara's sister pulled the breathing mask away from her face. Highly oxygenated water gurgled away into the soft currents. Her lips were blue, her voice thick. The time of change was close. "By your will, Father," she said, and replacing the mask, swam forward.

The others followed.

At the sound of the water-lock doors closing, a few quiet cries were heard. Trade negotiations were so important that clans often prepared their delegates from early childhood for the task. Some clans engineered children specifically for this purpose. Others held competitions to select the best candidates. Delegates were held in great affection by their clan. In them rested the hope of a half century or more of hard work.

And this transformation was temporary, but not without risk.

One of Unara's sisters, Dryfa, had pulled on legs a century ago and never returned to the ocean. And even that was not the worst that could befall someone undertaking the change.

There were Stone Clan waiting in the water-lock in dive gear. No gloves. This was delicate work. These were the gothi of the sky-born, the doctors and medical staff that would oversee the final stage in the transformation.

They worked quickly, laying the delegates out on tables, hooking up tubes and placing breathing gear on standby. Glaeva was the first to lie back, followed by almost two dozen others.

As the minutes ticked by, some of the assembled ocean-born began to drift away. It was a slow process, even now. It would likely be hours before tail separation began, but it could happen at any moment, so everything had to be—

Then.

Screaming.

Screaming.

Inside the water-lock, Glaeva writhed in her restraints. Her tail, the purple of a stormy sunset, was beating hard against the table, knocking itself apart. The water frothed, streaked dark as squid ink.

Father rushed for the water-lock. "Get this open!" he roared, beating on the surface, and two of the Stone Clan inside rushed to the controls.

It was too late, though. It had been too late from the moment the needle was put into Glaeva's arm.

Everyone outside the room stared in horror.

Soon, all that was left of Unara's sister was a cloud of drifting scales.

CHAPTER FOUR

"What did the water analysis reveal?"

Father was angry. Unara didn't need to look at him to know that. His rage seeped out into the water. To anger him further was to invite disaster. Everyone knew that.

The silence that followed his question spoke volumes.

And so, it was family that spoke up first.

<It will show nothing, my jarl.>

The king's eyes turned to the sky-born who had spoken. Unlike the others, clustered on the other side of the wall in this shallow audience chamber, this air-breather was in the water with them. No dive gear, just a breathing hose and face mask and voice emitter. He floated in his own corner in a slightly elevated position. Nobody took offense at this. The vantage point was necessary.

"Skald Hakon, you speak out of turn," Father warned.

<I do not believe I do, great King Aegyr. I was there to observe the great care they took with the samples taken from the water-lock. My job is to record the history of this family, after all, with most exacting precision, and I can tell you without a shred of doubt, they found nothing.>

The king turned his attention to the palace's gene-priests. "How is that possible?"

Gothi Injyr drummed his fingers on the table. "The princess's DNA, of course, was badly damaged by the time we were able to stabilize a sample, but our best patterning models indicate nothing foreign in her system."

"So you are saying this was nothing more than catastrophic biological collapse?"

"That is the case, my jarl," the gothi replied.

Father got up, swimming pensively to the window overlooking the reefs beyond the palace walls. "You are the best gene-priests on this planet. How could you make a mistake like this?"

<Jarl, if you please,> one of the Stone Clan gothi began, speaking through the conch set into the boundary wall, <even with the best prior patterning, there is always the chance of missing something that—>

"Not on my daughters!" King Aegyr roared, whirling around again. The current from the movement buffeted all at the council table. "A missed allele, a forgotten amino acid sequence, some failure in your entreaties to Hildra, and you have killed her!"

Silence once again fell in the room.

"They speak the truth to you, King Aegyr," another voice said, speaking up, soft and quiet as the sea floor. "I saw nothing that would lead me to believe there was foul play involved. I am sorry, my jarl, but sometimes these things do happen. I remember another princess, Dryfa, having a bad reaction to the change as well."

A murmur went up around the council chamber.

Father turned a baleful eye on the one who had spoken. "What are you implying, Lady Hethra?"

"I imply nothing, my jarl. I state facts only."

Father rubbed his temples. "We have the off-worlders' ships in our lower orbits already. Their landings start the day after tomorrow. Glaeva was not only representing these reefs but our entire people. Who do I put in her place? Jarl Dryagr?"

The Drift Clan chieftain and delegate, outside the barrier in the air now, shook his head. His skin had lost most of its silver tint with the change, but his hair was still a brilliant blue, his expression stoic. "I am senior, that is true, but I cannot lead these negotiations, my jarl. Put me up against a swarm of kraken before taking on the off-worlders in such a way."

There were a few faint smiles around both sides of the glass, but they were brittle and short-lived.

"It must be one of you. We have less than a day to get somebody on the surface," the king said, looking at the trade delegates outside in the air.

Nobody would take the offer, Unara knew. Her clan, holding Oceanfall as it did, had long-standing exclusive contracts with both House Gyes and House Amaro, and then only for what supplies were needed to maintain the palace. Glaeva's primary duties would have been oversight, deconflicting issues between clans, handling disputes, ensuring disagreements didn't grow into feuds, that every-thing remained as peaceful and profitable as possible. There was no time for detailed, personal negotiations in all of that. To accept the role of lead negotiator was to put one's own clan at a severe disad-vantage.

"Father," Unara said gently. "I am willing to take Glaeva's place."

Another murmur went up, louder this time. King Aegyr waved a hand wearily, bringing it up to rub his temples. "Absolutely not."

"I can speak Standard. I am already your trade representative among the clans here in the ocean. I am—"

"That is the key. Here. In the ocean," Father said. "You were not trained for Glaeva's task."

I have a better mind at finance than she did, Unara thought, but did not say it. "I can do it."

"You would never survive a rapid transformation."

She could have. She would have welcomed it. But Unara could not bring herself to say it. There was a reason she had been hiding all this from him and even now, she feared what he might do to her.

<With respect, my jarl,> Yvan said from the air side of the chamber, <Lady Hethra has an expedited process available to us now. I undertook my own transformation in less than a week without any pain.>

<It was the same for me,> Dryagr confirmed. About half the other delegates nodded.

"It is true," Lady Hethra said demurely, the king turning his attention to her. "My clan has found ways of late to shorten the process."

"To less than twenty-four hours, for a girl who has had not a single drop of preparation?" King Aegyr said and shook his head. "No. Not Unara. I will not lose another daughter to this foolishness with the off-worlders."

"I thought it was you who insisted that we deal with them in the first place," Lady Hethra replied coolly.

"The kaupang is a tradition not so easily discarded. We Thalassans honor our word," Father said. This was met with nods of agreement. Many of the assembly thumped their chests or beat their tails in the sand. Father cracked a small smile. "Besides, we always need the contents of their holds." Her father nodded, beard moving with him, and spread a hand. "Gothi Injyr, I want a full assessment of Lady Hethra's new process as quickly as it can be made."

"Of course, my jarl."

"But who among the ocean-born will use it?" Lady Hethra asked and smiled at him.

WETSUIT AND AIR tanks slung in the pack over her back, Vaelyn hurried back through the palace tunnels. Her hair was still wet from her rendezvous with the princess earlier, starting to stiffen with salt. It was a sensation she'd lived with all her life; nobody on Thalassa paid much heed to things like that. But tonight...tonight, her skin itched.

Watching Glaeva come apart had been...

Well.

Thalassa was a hard world, a hard world for everybody, but much worse for the sky-born. Vaelyn had lived her whole life in these sea cliffs; it was one of only a few such settlements on the entire planet. They grew no food on the land, the sky-born population dependent on the ocean, harvesting and hunting on the reef, where there were a thousand ways to die. Creatures, certainly, for the rapid evolution of the ecosphere had led to organisms developing many ways to kill prey and predators alike, but other dangers as well. Decompression sickness, if one dove with a tank and surfaced too quickly, or being trapped in a crevasse or caught by a clam and drowning, if one free-dived with a single breath in the lungs. Storms. Currents. Even some of the plants here, or the coral, would kill the unwary swimmer.

And then, once the sky-born were done with that, Vaelyn thought bitterly, they had to come back here. To these caves. Sure, there were a few fine buildings that clung to the cliff faces, but those were mostly ceremonial, only used at night and not at all in the years leading up to Brynhildyr's Wrath. They hid from the suns in the shadows, in the darkness of these hollows, living in rooms lit by blue bio-light lamps, stained from decades of kelp-wood fires, the fresh air channeled in through breather sponges reeking of sea-rot. Clinging to existence the way their distant ancestors had, before they found a home under the waves.

Vaelyn longed for release from it. Not that she wanted to walk freely under the sky—here on Thalassa, that truly was a death sentence.

She wanted what had been promised.

She wanted the ocean.

"Easy there, my girl!"

Vaelyn came up short, stopping only just in time. So lost in thought was she that she had just very nearly collided with somebody. She blinked, holding on to her bag almost defensively when she saw who it was.

"Honored Skald Hakon," she stammered. "I am sorry, I didn't see—"

The clan historian waved it aside with his usual ease. "It's been that sort of day, has it not?"

She nodded, and he cocked his head, the strip of braided hair that sat along his scalp shifting a little. Despite being sky-born, Skald Hakon was one of the few in the Stone Clan who retained the coloring of the ocean: dark green hair and brilliant violet eyes. He could see in the dark as well as any of the ocean-born, it was said. But then, a lot of things were said about the skald.

"Where are you off to this time of night?"

"There's still maintenance left to do in the aquariums," she lied, casting a hand out in the direction of the ocean gates. "A few things have been left in the pools that we need to get cleaned up."

Skald Hakon sighed. "I suppose it is too much for us to ask our guests to pick up after themselves," he said. "Would you like some help? I should like an opportunity to get back in the water after this miserable evening."

"No, honored skald, I'll take care of it," she said, cursing herself. "I think... I think I should like to be alone right now."

He nodded, his expression thoughtful, sad. "Losing Princess Glaeva is a hard blow. She would have no doubt been a good queen someday."

"King Aegyr would have had to step down first," Vaelyn replied, a bit more acid in her words than she had intended. She scrambled to recover. "I mean, I meant no disrespect. He's just...always been king."

"Three hundred and sixty-seven years without a male heir or son-in-law who can pass the trials," Skald Hakon replied, still thoughtful, and shook himself. "But you need to get going, yes, I know. I know. Get it done. The landings will begin at dawn. I don't think any of the off-worlders shall be down at the pools so early, but let's not risk an incident."

She hesitated, thinking about the screams from Princess Glaeva again. "Why the need for all this secrecy, anyway?"

"What do you think they would do to this world if they knew about our...adaptations? If they knew we were confined to the ocean here? Might they not attempt to subdue us, rather than treating us as equals and partners?"

"You really think they would attack this world?"

"I think humans, ocean- and sky-born both, love violence," he told her.

Vaelyn thought about that all the way out to the pools.

THE PALACE'S upper levels clung to the cliff faces inside Oceanfall Bay, but on the ocean side of the cliffs, other structures lay deep.

Waves and wind, over the long ages, had worn the cliff face away here into a series of broad bowls, little bays that mimicked the larger bay to the east. The cliffs plunged to great depths below the water, but above the water, things were somewhat different. Up here, the cliffs gave way to a broad, rocky shore. Tide pools stretched out for kilometers along this outer coast, and on their outer edges, tucked into carefully cultivated titanocoral formations, lay the aquarium-mansions.

Some were open at the top to the air, while others were capped off fully with great glass and titanium finials. Each contained many millions of liters of water, the largest nearly two hundred meters in diameter. Different environments from across the coast were simulated here, from the frozen north to the warm and turbulent equatorial reefs, transplanted flora and fauna flourishing inside, just as they would have in their own biome.

Glowing plankton in the pools made it easier to see; Vaelyn

hadn't dared bring a lantern. That would have drawn attention from anybody still in the vicinity.

For the past few weeks, the place had been bustling. Reunions. Competitions. Hunts. Feasts. The months leading up to the kaupang were a rare opportunity for the Thalassan ocean-born to gather en masse. These mansions were used as accommodations for anyone visiting from distant waters; Thalassans tended to adapt themselves to regional conditions, after all.

But of course, the more people in the Oceanfall reefs, the more risk of discovery by the off-worlders. So many of the ocean-born had already departed. Visiting clans and the local population both, going home to distant waters or temporarily relocating to the Fjallnar Reefs, fifty kilometers to the south. By squid-boat and crustacean-palanquin, a parade of color, of singing and chanting and conch-blasts, bio-lanterns set out as lures or warnings for the reef's larger predators. Much of the local animal life had either fled or been consumed over the past few weeks—such was the impact of hundreds of additional humans and biological constructs on the area —but it was coming back now with a vengeance, hungry.

Those who remained, mostly the elderly, women with children, and those critical for the trade negotiations, would not be staying in the outer pools. Instead, they would retreat under the shield coral within the bay, concealing themselves from the air-breathers above. Or, such as with the Drift Clan, they would hide in akker-habitats in the depths and the dark of the outer waters.

Wherever they found shelter, the ocean-born would hide until the off-worlders were gone again. And for now, the grand aquarium-mansions were mere tourist attractions.

Vaelyn passed through the complex quickly, taking the above-water walkways out toward the northern tip of the cliffs, almost to the mouth of the bay. The catwalks gave way to a cut stone path. Her pace slowed. This was a dangerous way to come, only possible at night and low tide, when wave action was at its weakest.

Finally, she found what she had been looking for. A small grotto, barely large enough for a person to stand in but quite deep, running back a good twenty meters into the cliff. Vaelyn slipped in.

She had been coming here for years.

Vaelyn laid her bag out on one of the few dry spots in the far back of the grotto, quickly pulling out and laying out her dive gear, doing her pre-entry check. It was route, routine, natural as breathing. She adjusted the tank on her back, positioned the breathing regulator in her mouth, and slipped into the water.

Below her, a tunnel of water fell away into blackness.

Vaelyn swam down.

Glaeva. Poor Glaeva. Vaelyn had liked her. Even if she had never been all that fond of the royal family as a whole.

But things would change soon. Things were already changing now.

Vaelyn followed the subterranean tunnel, swimming carefully so as not to damage her air tanks. Even sky-born Thalassans spent much of their lives in water, and Vaelyn was accustomed to cave-dives. This tunnel still gave her the creeps. It was like descending into some netherworld: it was kept deliberately dark to avoid discovery, and it was far too deep and twisted to safely free-dive. You had to know what you were looking for to find it, and you had to be prepared for it.

Finally, though, up ahead there was a soft glow, and Vaelyn swam for it gratefully.

She emerged from a narrow crack into a wider cavern. It was a natural space that had been expanded by construction crab at some point; nobody had ever bothered to conceal the claw marks on the walls. It had a fine sandy bottom, as did so many of the ocean-born's spaces, and the shimmer of light on the surface in one corner betrayed the presence of an airspace up above. That led up to a water-lock that itself led back into the palace proper, although that path was rarely used.

This place had to be kept secret.

In the center of the underwater cave was the only source of light:

a grand column of cooling sponge, filled with glowing bladders. The sponge pumped chilled water across the rubbery kelpskin bags, keeping the contents at an optimum storage temperature. There were treatment chairs down here too, three of them, and all the associated equipment and gear and wires and tubes necessary for administering the contents of those bladders.

Someday, she knew, it was going to be her turn to lie down in one of those chairs, have a breathing mask slid over her face and a needle pushed into her arm and—

A sound behind her.

Vaelyn whirled, dive knife out. It wasn't impossible for some monster from the reef to have worked its way in here, a reef eel or octopus or some other such...

"Jumpy tonight, are we?"

Heart hammering, Vaelyn lowered her knife. <Lady Hethra,> she said, bowing her head a little, the stream of bubbles from her regulator disrupted. <I didn't realize it was you.>

Vaelyn had never known how to feel about the chieftain of the Abyssal Clan. Lady Hethra was strange-looking, even among the ocean-born, gray and red and unlovely. But she had always been good to Vaelyn, generous if not kind, and she was the preeminent gene-weaver on the planet, and she alone cared about those Thalassans doomed to walk under the sky.

Her words gave Vaelyn hope.

Vaelyn gave the abyssal ruler her loyalty in return.

"Tell me you aren't getting lost in the palace rumors about monsters stirred up from the bottom of the sea," Lady Hethra said now, her smile somewhere between fond and mocking. "Such foolishness I hear below the waves."

<No, milady, of course not,> Vaelyn said, and tucked her titanium dive knife back in its sheath. <It has just been a...difficult night.>

"Yes, yes, of course it has," Lady Hethra said, waving it away. "King Aegyr is quite distressed. Do you know what he asked me to do for him? Help him pull legs back on! Can you imagine? Unara offered to go instead, of course, and of course, he says he won't sacrifice another daughter."

<That seems noble of him,> Vaelyn replied.

"Noble? Ha. Selfish! If he loses Unara after losing Glaeva, he loses all possibility of a successor, which would no doubt spark a clan war," Lady Hethra said. "And that does not fully accomplish our aims, now does it?"

Vaelyn hesitated. When Lady Hethra had first come to her, all those years ago, the promises had seemed too good to be true. All she had required, Hethra had said, was a little help. Just a little help, with just a few things.

"Do you think I had you befriend his youngest daughter for nothing? No! I had you feed her selfishness, Vaelyn. They always were a terribly selfish family. And it will be their downfall."

Vaelyn nodded, thinking again about Unara's dismissal of her, back in her sleep chamber. <I know.>

"Vaelyn, I tell you, as high gothi of the depths, I hear the whispers of the ocean, and she is not pleased with us. The high-water clans loyal to Aegyr think only of themselves, stripping the planet of her wealth, her life, enslaving your clan in order to facilitate it. Freedom! Vaelyn, freedom is the birthright of every Thalassan, and you cannot have it while confined to this handful of cliff-dwellings, however grand they might look."

<I know, milady,> she said, uncertain.

Lady Hethra tilted her head. "I hear a question in there, Vaelyn."

By the waves and water, there was no hiding anything from this woman. <But Glaeva...> she began, and trailed off, looking around, not sure how to articulate her thoughts.

But Lady Hethra just put a hand on Vaelyn's shoulder. "You wonder what will become of you if you take the treatment from me. It is a fair question, Vaelyn. And do not worry. This"—and she indicated the column—"will work its magic for you just fine." She chuckled. "Glaeva is dead because she needed to be. It was not an accident."

Vaelyn was glad for her breathing regulator. She couldn't keep the shock from her face. <But, milady, she... What?>

"She is dead because I needed her to be."

Vaelyn's mind spun. <But milady, you said nothing to me and I am coordinating for you here in the palace and—>

"I said nothing in order to spare you, Vaelyn. If you had had prior knowledge of it, might you not have reacted differently? Might not King Aegyr have noticed? You could very well be in an interrogation pool right now, had I told you."

Vaelyn felt like an idiot. <Of course, milady.>

"Do not worry about the details, Vaelyn. All shall soon be revealed. All that I have planned shall soon come to pass. All shall be made whole."

<I understand.>

"Good. Now, thank you for meeting me here tonight. My instructions to the rest of your compatriots are simple: the work must be completed on schedule. That goes for you too. Give Unara anything she wants. But be careful. Tell everyone to be careful. With the kaupang about to start, things will become very complicated."

<I understand, milady.>

"I swear to you, Vaelyn"—and Lady Hethra's hand squeezed down on Vaelyn's shoulder with bruising force—"the first moonrise after the kaupang's end will see King Aegyr and all his house laid low, and your people returned to the sea, the way you were always meant to be."

Vaelyn eyed the column. What would it be like, she wondered, to be out in the ocean with nothing between herself and the salt water? To be one with it? To finally be whole?

<I look forward to that.>

"Then serve me well over this kaupang," Lady Hethra said, her voice as cold as the waters from which she came, "and you will have your reward."

CHAPTER FIVE

"Are you here to complain at me, Captain Thorsen?"

"Far be it from me to order you around, milord. I'm ready to depart whenever you so choose. But I would feel better if we took the armored lander down instead of this delicate thing."

Karl barely glanced over at his head of security, continuing on his stroll along the upper hangar deck, his casual inspection of *Gylfy's Delight*, his transatmospheric explorer craft. He'd had to lay aside his more comfortable shipboard uniform for the formal trappings of House Gyes. The ornate high-collared jacket was stiff, inflexible, rendered more so by the internal cooling system hidden in the lining. "You're a worrier, Thorsen, always have been."

The other man, dressed in his dark blue and gold formal uniform as well, sighed. "You aren't worried enough, milord."

"His lordship will be fine." And that was the *Gylfy's* pilot, Henrich Alfir. The man had been with Karl for the past ten years, a highly skilled voidsman and utterly loyal to the House. "Atmospheric conditions are favorable. Weather events unlikely."

"This ship is—"

"Tougher than she looks, Thorsen. Or are you questioning my qualifications?"

Karl ignored them both and stepped over to the edge of the landing platform, staring off into the hangar bay's depths.

Interstellar trader craft were more akin to cities set loose in space than anything else. And even by the standards of the Trader Houses, the *Vanatar Deep* was a massive thing.

Eleven kilometers from prow to engines and nearly two kilometers wide, the *Vanatar* was the heart of the Gyes fleet. The command section was relatively small, with functions like Engineering, Command, and Medical, as well as the crew's living quarters, crammed into less than a tenth of the craft's overall bulk. The engines and fusion generator took up a fair bit of room, as did the hangars and armories for the private military that House Gyes commanded. But the purpose of the *Vanatar* was cargo hauling, and the majority of the ship was given over to that.

The space Karl stood in now was a huge open space that ran clean through the center of the *Vanatar*. Cargo could be flown directly inside, then off-loaded to any of the many segmented cargo compartments that ringed the space. Some compartments were used for general cargo, but others had been specially engineered for specific trade goods. Secondary engines in those compartments powered thousands of stasis fields, necessary for transporting everything from edible delicacies to regenerative compounds.

Cantilevered platforms of all sizes hung from the sides of the great hollow space, landing and maintenance platforms. Entire workshops and supply warehouses were nestled in as well, every spare space between cargo holds utilized in some way. Massive cranes and manipulation arms were mounted to the walls of the space at quarter-kilometer intervals.

In less than two weeks, Standard, every machine, every crew member, would be working feverishly to move hundreds of tons of material from the surface into the proper holds. For now, trade goods were being pre-positioned in their landers. Metal was the most common thing requested by the Thalassans in trade; pure gold, platinum and titanium were all present on the *Vanatar* in obscene quantities. Entire solar systems had been devoured over the centuries to facilitate the Thalassan trade.

Is it truly worth it? Karl wondered to himself. But he already knew the answer to that. "The Suyarii," he muttered to himself.

"The Suyarii presence here is both unexpected and unwelcome," a voice said behind him. "And one even I did not foresee."

Karl turned and found himself staring into the face of his father's feii healer. He eyed her warily. "More warnings? I have had enough of that from people who know what they're talking about. I do not need it from my father's jailer."

"I am the only thing keeping him alive," Healer Eyr said with that infinite patience of hers. "I would think that you would be grateful for that."

"He is in that tank because of you. Fifty-seven years now, because of you."

"There was no other way to save his life," she replied evenly, and cocked her head. The gesture, while simple, was disturbingly inhuman. The neck of the suit she wore bent too far to the side.

"What do you want, feii?"

"As I said, to give you a warning. The same warning I would have given your father before he set foot on the surface here for the first time, had I been able."

"What do you mean?"

"This world rejected the feii. It should never have been settled by humans. There are dangerous powers here, and the Thalassans know it. Those powers, I fear, are stirring again."

"Cryptic," Captain Thorsen said. "If there's a threat to Lord Gyes's life here, can't you be clearer about it?"

"All is occluded in this system. The solar winds block more than hyperspace communications and scramble more than realspace transmissions. They obscure the currents of time as well. Perhaps that is why regeneratives from this world are so effective."

Thorsen rolled his eyes. "Can you at least tell him not to take this pleasure craft down?"

Healer Eyr looked between them, something glowing deep within her mask, but didn't speak for some time. "No," she finally said. "I will not tell him that, Captain Thorsen." And she looked to Karl again. "Have you heard the story of the end of House Remia?"

"They've been gone for at least two hundred—"

"Two hundred and twenty years of your Standard years, yes," the feii said flatly. "They went extinct here."

"How?"

"They landed a biology team on the east coast. They said nothing to the Thalassans about it, and the Thalassans said nothing to them. That particular team never made it back to its fleet."

"That's one group," Karl said, not sure what the feii was driving at.

"House Remia had a few problems loading cargo. Caused delays. They were still in the system when all the other Houses departed. One fleet, still in orbit around a world with thirty-three moons. Two major, thirty-one minor," Eyr said. "But when the kaupang came around again, there was no fleet. And only thirty-two moons."

Karl looked at her askance. "Are you saying the Thalassans flew a moon into the Remia fleet?"

"This is a world of secrets, Lord Gyes. You'd do well to remember that."

A loud hum filled the hangar bay; Karl turned to look. The *Gylfy's* main propulsion had just been brought online, her crew conducting an engine check. But when he looked back to ask Eyr what she meant, she was already gone.

Karl shook his head, heading back to where Thorsen and Alfir were arguing.

Infuriating creature.

"Considering what happened to Lord Gyes the last time the House was here," Thorsen was saying, "I think you'd be—"

"Enough of this," Karl said, shutting it down with a wave of his hand. "All *Gylfy* here needs to do is get us down to the surface, eh? Not host a multi-week mapping expedition. Pilot Alfir, do you suppose you can handle that task?"

"Exquisitely," the old pilot said.

"See?" Karl told Thorsen and turned to head up the boarding ramp. "It's fine!"

UNARA WATCHED the landings from the Hall of Dreams.

It was even more amazing than it had looked in her books.

Not that her opinion was widely shared.

Every Thalassan not busy with other tasks had crammed in here for a view of what was going on up above. The Hall was a round amphitheater a hundred meters across, a bowl carved deep into the bedrock, isolated from the rest of the palace. Ledges ringed the outside edge, coral railings serving as anchor points for anyone in the water. An enclosed gallery, up near the top of the space, provided the Stone Clan access to the space as well. And below, housed in a highly controlled environmental chamber, a dreamer crab.

Widely cultivated on Thalassa, such crabs had a specially adapted ventral ganglion that, once severed from basic motor functions, could be expanded and reprogrammed to handle anything from genetic modeling to tide tracking.

This one, however, was not employed as a bio-computer. Instead, its dorsal ganglion had been heavily manipulated to accept and process data from the palace surveillance drones. These smaller crabs were simple but powerful, each hatched from the altered crustacean down below and capable of sharing their vision with the mother organism.

Such creatures represented the absolute limit of Thalassan bioengineering; psychic linkages were incredibly difficult to attune and maintain. As simple as the crabs were, their altered neural systems overloaded quickly; life expectancy, once activated, was measured in days. Three crops of the creatures, grown to maturity in the vast rock pools around the palace over the past two years and held in reserve, would be needed to cover the entire kaupang.

Unara was grateful for their sacrifice now, for the sight that the crabs revealed was utterly fascinating.

The dreamer crab down below controlled a vast assemblage of specialized bioluminescent larvae. Through a combination of water currents and silent commands, the dream-mother shaped her offspring into a swarm that gave shape to the events up above.

And so the assembled ocean-born watched as the detailed outlines of spacecraft, cast in living blue light, descended en masse to the surface of their world.

Unara was amazed. The ships were of all different designs, a testament to the vast variety of humanity that surely existed beyond their world. These weren't the huge craft, the monsters that would later land at the loading zones of the western coast upon the conclusion of trade negotiations. No, these were smaller, landers meant to ferry key personnel and supplies down to the world's surface.

There was a great deal of murmuring among the assembled Thalassans, as well as laughter and snorts of derision.

Unara didn't care.

Some of the craft she recognized; these ships had been seen time and time again and were part of the historical record. House Amaro, the Royal Caledon Expedition, Fleet Rigura, Delegation Njeri. But there was one landing on the outer edges of the fields, almost beyond the range of the water-loving surveillance drones, that she didn't recognize.

She swam up to one of the ocean-born skalds, positioned on a platform rather above the plane of view. It wasn't Hakon, not today. He was above, in the air, alongside the king.

"Princess," the poet-historian acknowledged, inclining his head slightly, eyes still fixed on the scene below.

"I know I am interrupting your weaving of memory, Skald Firi, but I—"

"Was curious, I know," he said, finally turning away from his task to look her over. "When are you not, Princess?"

"I am sorry, I—"

He waved a hand, causing a small group of floating larvae to swirl out of position. "You are going to pester me until you get your answer, so go ahead and ask."

She looked back down at the scene. Another ship had just appeared, lit up with soft biological blues, the real thing having just come into range of the surveillance drones now. Other ships were already on the ground and disgorging their passengers. So great was the scale of the landing fields that even in the huge Hall of Dreams, those people getting off their ships were represented by only scant handfuls of larvae, tiny glowing points against the vastness of the landing craft.

"I recognize many of these ships from your songs, Skald Firi, but that large one there is unknown to me," Unara said, pointing.

"Yes," he said, "that particular hull configuration has not been seen here before. At least, not as far back as the stories tell."

"And that one?" she asked, pointing up at the craft that had just started to descend.

"That one is not spoken of in the official songs either, but I recognize the hull configuration. A new ship from an established House," Skald Firi replied. "At least, that is my read. I shall consult my counterparts for their opinion on the matter. Interpretations can vary between us, you know."

"What House do you suppose it belongs to?" Unara asked.

"The House Gyes," he told her. "Now, enough interruptions, Princess. I must watch so that future generations may know."

Strangely unsatisfied, Unara still nodded. Hakon would have chatted at length with her about it. "Thank you for your time, Skald Firi."

Unara swam back down to the lower viewing level, imagining what it would be like to walk among those giant machines, bigger even than the biggest krakens.

Soon, she promised herself. Very soon.

Her chest ached, her lungs protesting. She rubbed her chest absently, thinking. She desperately needed to move into the final stage of the change, get out of this limbo she had been in for the past several weeks. One infusion to restart the transformation process. Another to take the final step.

Father. Father had been the reason she hadn't done it. He had been planning on watching the kaupang quite closely, both from this room and through the reports of others up on the surface, Glaeva and Hakon and all the rest. And he had told Unara he wanted her there with him.

Except he was walking under the sky now and could scarcely pay attention to what his daughter was doing in the water at all, much less demand her constant presence. And besides, it was unlikely she would run into her father up on the surface anyway; the ocean-born Thalassans spent as little time as possible around the off-worlders.

If she could get up there a few days early, if she could hide in the market streets and avoid her own people, she could negotiate her own deal, secure passage with the best House under the best of conditions.

Glaeva's death, as hard as it was to even contemplate, had just increased the chances of her own plan succeeding.

When these ships departed for the stars again in ten days, she was going with them.

Unnoticed by anyone, Unara slipped from the Hall of Dreams and went to find her akker.

Even so close to the sea as they were, the air was bone-dry at the moment. Bone-dry and blazing hot, thanks in no small part, she knew, to the ships all around them.

She was standing at King Aegyr's side, out on the surveillance platform atop a high tower at the heart of the landing fields. The fields were huge and empty, planed flat by huge machines kept in hangars cut deep into the great bounding cliffs. The desert groaned under the feet of so many spaceships. The heat of their engines boiled the air, and thus, landings happened during the coolest part of the day.

"An astonishing sight," King Aegyr told her quietly. "Your clan has done a most impressive job in maintaining these fields."

She couldn't meet his eyes. "It is most impressive, milord," she replied softly. "A once-in-a-lifetime sight."

The king paced around the platform. The rest of the ocean-born who had undertaken the change for this had been too skittish to come up through the tower. Understandable. It was common knowledge among the Stone Clan that the ocean-born were often terrified of heights in the open air.

Vaelyn wondered if King Aegyr was afraid. He didn't seem to be. But then, there was the way his left fingers were gripping his right wrist behind his back, the slight tension around his mouth.

Perhaps he was afraid and merely hiding it.

"How do you see me, sky-born?"

Vaelyn flushed, embarrassed. "My apologies, King, I did not mean to stare."

"I did not ask for an apology, Vaelyn, but an answer."

"I am...not used to seeing you like this."

"I am not used to it, either," he said. "It's been over a century since I've done this. But with Glaeva gone..."

"I understand, my jarl," she replied, and hesitated. "Why...why did you call me up here with you?"

"I am assigning you to Lord Gyes to be his escort, as you request-ed," he replied. "Securing the resources of that House is critical to not just my own clan, but the planet at large, and there was a great deal of trust broken when last he was here. I trust you will make him comfortable."

"I shall, my jarl. It is an honor," she said honestly. This was a fantastic development, even though she didn't quite understand why Lady Hethra had wanted her to do this.

"When you see him today, extend my deepest apologies for his poisoning when last he was here."

She nodded. "I will."

"I am glad to see his House back on our world." The king stroked his beard. "Ah, there we are." And he pointed. "The last lander."

Looking out at where the king was pointing, Vaelyn frowned. "I don't recognize that hull configuration from any of my briefing material," she replied.

"Nor do I, but there is usually a newcomer or two every kaupang. It doesn't matter. We shall see if they are worthy to be here. If not, we shall ensure they do not return." He turned away from the window and headed back inside, inside to the crowded command room filled with Stone Clan operators working to deconflict the air space and ensure all landers made it safely to the ground. "Finally, I can leave this damn platform."

THEY DESCENDED the surveillance tower with speed, down the spiral staircase in the interior, cut in imitation of a conch shell from the living rock. King Aegyr may have said he just wanted a discussion, but he had to lean on Vaelyn for support on the stairs several times. She couldn't help but wonder if he had brought her along specifically for this.

The tower sat near the western edge of the landing fields, a tall spire of rock standing all alone on the vast plain. A broad concrete avenue led through the center of the landing field, sweeping down to the market gates of the palace like a white river, but starships lay all around them. They were huge, far larger than Vaelyn had been expecting, and it lent weight to all of Lady Hethra's arguments.

These things did not belong here.

The delegation was waiting in a pavilion set up on a high dais near the base of the tower, comfortable chairs and huge ewers of water placed on low tables. None were sitting, but all were drinking water, looking out at the ships with expressions that ranged from interest to disgust.

"How are we finding this today?" King Aegyr boomed, striding toward them confidently. No tremors. None of the faltering steps she had seen on the tower steps.

What was it taking from him, she wondered, to maintain this legged form? And after so short of a transformation process as well?

The trade delegates all looked to their king. Attempted some form of the bow they might have used underwater. They were all clumsy. Here, their grace was stripped away from them.

"It is terrifically hot," said Lady Ragnyr, the stout representative from the northern ice floes. She was sweating profusely, fanning herself with a broad leaf of dried kelp. "And quite dry, my jarl."

"It's the landers," the king said. "They burn the moisture from the air. At this time of day, this time of year, there should be fog out here."

"Is there nothing that the off-worlders do not make worse with their presence?" snorted Yvar, another of the delegates. His long hair, the dark green of kelp, was braided back against his scalp and shaved along the sides of his head. He was a last-minute replacement, if Vaelyn understood correctly. His cousin had been trained for the role but had been killed on the journey here to Oceanfall a few months ago. There had been a number of such unfortunate happenings among the delegates. Lucky for them all, Vaelyn thought to herself, that Lady Hethra's new infusions worked so quickly.

"Peace, Forest Clan," Jarl Dryagr replied. "It may have escaped you, Yvar, but the kaupang is the only source of metal we have. And how else are you going to repair your towns destroyed by the hurricanes last year?"

"I hear the sneer in your voice, Drifter. But we do not all ride the currents in akker habitats. Imagine, spending your entire life up the ass end of a squid."

Several of the other delegates chuckled. Vaelyn looked at the king. He wasn't paying attention, eyes fixed on the landing fields and their massive ships, settling now like dead sharks on the abyssal plain.

"We do not need the resources of the stars as much as the rest of you, that is true. But we honor our contracts, both with the off-worlders and with the abyss," Dryagr replied levelly.

"The abyss is almost as bad as the air-breathers," Lady Ragnyr said, still fanning herself.

"Without the abyss and their careful work with the hydrothermal vent fields, none of us would have the precursors necessary for the gothis' work, and then where would we be?"

"They hide away from all of us. How can we trust such a clan?"

Dryagr shrugged. "They do not hide from us. They are merely adapted for the depths at which they live. It pains them greatly to come too close to the surface, even in pressurized akker-craft."

"Then how is it that Lady Hethra swims among our kin, even now, in the palace reefs? I have spent the last few months here just acclimating to the water temperatures," Lady Ragnyr protested. "What manner of gene-craft does she possess that allows her such rapid ascension and why does she not share it with the rest of her clan? Why does she send no delegate to this kaupang?"

"Lady Hethra does share her skills. She helped the king, did she not?"

"That is not what I mean. She is hiding something!"

"They trade little with the off-worlders," Dryagr replied, "so I am authorized to handle such negotiations for her."

"Yes, but even you surely must agree—"

"This is not the time for clan disagreements," King Aegyr said, cutting off the argument. He used his spear to point out at the space-craft now powering down all around them on the field. "This is not the time to renew old grudges or start new blood feuds. The outsiders are here, and they must only see unity. This kaupang keeps the off-worlders contained, focused, fighting amongst themselves for what little we are willing to grant them. There is no space for division. By Hildra, we keep our secrets."

"Exactly my point, my jarl," Dryagr said. "We stand with you as one people, united, as they will not be."

"No," the king said, smiling a little. "And we shall all profit from it."

Everyone laughed.

Vaelyn looked around at her fellow Stone Clan, all the escorts for the kaupang. They were handpicked by Lady Hethra, placed here by the work of many years, utterly loyal to the cause. Not one of them gave any hint of what they were thinking. One of them, Leyli, a good friend, smiled a little.

Vaelyn wondered if they felt the same sense of irony she did right now. The only way to save their world, protect their secrets, was to stop this. End these kaupangs. The scale of this landing only reinforced that for Vaelyn. Permitting this was flirting with disaster.

It had to end.

CHAPTER SIX

"I would like to say again, we should not be doing this. You should have allowed me to perform a sweep first."

"Why? Does it look like there is anyone around to stab us with poisoned knives?"

"You never know, milord."

"Relax, Thorsen. You have your rifle and I have my sword and everything's fine."

Walking into the broad streets of the upper palace, it struck Karl that Thalassa Prime was one of the strangest worlds he had ever encountered.

Gylfy's Delight had been built for planetary mapping and observation; its bridge had offered an unparalleled view of Thalassa Prime upon their descent. He had stood before the great windows the entire way down, watching the blue waters grow closer and closer.

It was pristine in a way that few inhabited worlds could be. No smog of industry, no sprawl of buildings. Everything did lie under the waves and within the rock, of course, so perhaps it was just as unpleasant and crowded in there as any other planet, but somehow, Karl doubted it.

He ached to grab his survival pack, pull on his trusty old boots, and get lost in this world. Just himself and the wilds.

That was no longer an option. Not here, nor on any other world. It chafed.

But at least there was this strange palace to explore. If one could call it a palace at all. It was more akin to some ancient ruin, like the tomb-cities of Gyptan Beta or the sprawling alien architecture of Akroti Gamma. The silence, the empty porticos, the lack of life.

He commented on this to Captain Thorsen now, who just laughed. "No life? Just you wait a few hours when everyone gets organized. Then this will all be wild."

"Exactly why I wanted to see it now," Karl replied, looking around.

A broad avenue, paved with white stone, had led them from the landing fields, around a promontory of rock carved into an approximation of a control tower, and down onto a gently sloping shelf on the cliff. Pavilions rose up along either side of this main thoroughfare, with little byways threading off between, leading to smaller structures. Courtyards that overlooked the water. Doorways that led back into the cliffs.

None of these structures were particularly tall, fifteen or twenty meters at the most, but they were quite impressive. Hints of architecture from across the Spiral could be seen: the flying buttresses of Caledon, the delicate spires of Merovingia, the soaring columns of the Hellenic League, but all subtly twisted out of their original forms. Organic, flowing, and all bone-white. Every major Trader House had one, places to conduct business, rest, hold receptions and balls and whatnot.

Such things were quite serious here, Karl's father had told him. House Gyes had a ten-person staff whose sole responsibility was to design, set up, and manage their pavilion. They had been working on it for years now, and today, they would have command of all of House Gyes's planet-side personnel, assigning them to any and all of the myriad tasks required by such an endeavor.

Only the House military was spared, but most of them would be on guard duty or surveillance, and they would be assisting with the movement of goods into the pavilion anyway.

Karl had seen photographs and holographic models of the place all his life but had wished to see it now with his own eyes, before it filled up with whatever it was his hospitality team intended to install.

"This city is a marvel," Karl commented to Captain Thorsen as they continued down the avenue. "Do you know that they grow these structures? From corals, no less."

"I was not aware, milord," Captain Thorsen said, still looking around. The man was almost twitchy.

"Really, Thorsen, didn't you read the briefing packet?"

"I was more concerned about the disposition of the Suyarii fleet, milord."

Karl was concerned with that as well. "Have we deployed our surveillance drones yet?" he asked, dropping his voice.

"Not yet," Thorsen replied quietly. "Whoever their commander is, he knows what he is doing. The Suyarii anchored in a high orbit, away from everyone else, very elliptical, retrograde. Reaching it without detection will be quite the challenge."

"A problem for later, then."

"Indeed, milord," the captain said, and then turned, rifle coming up to ready. Karl paused beside him, hand on the hilt of his own sword.

From the shadow of a pavilion, a crustacean the size of a fist stood, waving its front claws in the air.

"So something does crawl up out of the ocean here," Karl mused, and then looked at his captain. "Thorsen, lower your gun."

"Why's it here?" he asked.

"You need to relax, Thorsen."

"The Suyarii are here, milord."

"Well, that's not the crab's fault, now is it?" Karl asked. "Come. I want to see this place before it fills up with people."

No thanks to Thorsen's unnecessary fussing, they reached the pavilion safe and sound. It was built in proper Frederiksborg style, with steep rooflines, towers capped with complex dragon spires, ornately curved detailing, and grand colonnades with great open windows between them. The solid walls were few and the sea breeze drifting through carried the bracing scent of mineral salts. Thalassa Prime's ocean was thick with dissolved iron, carbon, silicon, and other elements eroded from the continent.

"A lovely place," Karl commented as they headed for the main doors.

"I suppose," Thorsen replied suspiciously, as if he were being asked to walk into the mouth of some giant sea creature.

"Captain, relax!" Karl laughed and clapped him on the back. "It's a building. It is not going to devour us!"

"I don't trust this place," Thorsen said. "If these things are built from coral, how are they up here in the open air?"

Karl waved that away. "Consider the cliffs all around us, and the narrowness of the bay's mouth. If one dammed that up, it would be possible to flood this entire place, grow the coral that way."

"Then how do they bring the water in?"

"I don't know," Karl admitted. "But I should like to find out. What a fascinating place this is."

Thorsen shook his head, about to answer when a trumpet blast caught them unawares. Karl and Thorsen exchanged a look, then hurried back outside.

It was a procession, a crowd, a flood of humanity. Laughing, singing, walking alongside wooden wagons loaded high with all manner of household goods. Women mostly, silk overdresses tucked up into leather belts over their kirtle skirts, so colorful against the bone-white of the pavilions that it almost hurt Karl's eyes to look at them. Servants in slightly more subdued livery pulled the carts. Live off-world animals were strictly banned from the surface of Thalassa

Prime, and powered conveyances were only permitted by the Thalassans for the purposes of loading and unloading cargo, after negotiations were complete. Everything here would be accomplished by raw manpower. It cut down on pollution, yes, but it was all quite noisy.

"So much for peace and quiet," Karl muttered.

"Caledons," Captain Thorsen sighed, and re-slung his rifle again. "Should have known Lord Willam would be the first to get his people organized."

"What is that with them?" Karl asked, pointing to the largest of the wagons they were dragging with them. "It looks like a roasting spit."

"It smells like a spit," Thorsen agreed, shading his eyes for a better look. "And two wagons full of wood to boot. What are they planning on doing? Roasting an entire whale while they're here?"

"Thalassa has few aquatic mammals," Karl replied absently. "Something about the sunlight during the summer months being too severe."

Thorsen shook his head. "Ah. Perhaps Lord Willam brought a dead Caledon boar in stasis. You know how he is with his feasts."

Karl shook his head. "We're a hundred light-years from the nearest star system. One would think we would enjoy local customs instead of dragging our own along."

"Politics are your problem, milord," Thorsen replied. "But every major trade conference I've seen involves this kind of showmanship."

Pageantry. Politics. Karl had a headache from it already. "Does it work?"

Thorsen snorted. "On the Thalassans? Who knows what they value?"

"They value titanium," Karl said with a sigh. "And that is what we shall give them."

THE OCEAN WAS UNSETTLED that afternoon as Unara swam to the gene-hallow.

She couldn't quite identify the source of the problem. But she could feel it. In the currents. In the creatures, moving all around her. Perhaps it was just the ships, she told herself, the heat, the wind of their descent, not felt on Thalassa for over half a century.

Or perhaps it was just her. That sick feeling in her gut just a physiological response to water pressure and her own shifting biology and her sorrow over her sister's death.

Even her akker's own skittishness was incidental, a product of the slower pace she was forcing it into today.

That was it.

That was all it was.

And yet, Unara could not shake the feeling that something was amiss in the reefs.

She felt guilty about this, coming out here today. But her father's absence—regardless of the terrible circumstances around it—was an opportunity she couldn't pass up.

She reached the gene-hallow as Brynhildyr slipped below the horizon. And as she reined in the akker and set it loose to go hunt, she felt as if she was being watched.

Noises behind her, like crabs shifting in the sand. She whirled around, knife out, straining to see in the darkness.

"I hope that's not for me."

She turned back around, hair drifting around her, blade up. "Gothi Strygr," she said, heart hammering painfully in her chest now. "I thought I heard something out there."

"No doubt one of my many watch-fish, trying to flee. They don't like your akker, you know."

She smiled and resheathed her blade. "I am sorry about that, Gothi."

He nodded. "I heard about your sister. Terrible business, that. She was a good woman. Bright future ahead of her."

Unara bit her lip. "Yes, she was." And then she thought of something. "How did you hear about that?"

"I hear what the moons whisper to me," he said, chuckling a little, pointing up at the surface of the water. "It was quite the surprise to all of them."

"I don't think the moons saw it, Gothi," she said when she'd caught her breath a little. "It happened under the shield coral."

"Do you think such a little thing stops one such as Hildra, or Rota, or any of the rest of them? Thalassa turns under their watchful eyes. It rises and falls to their dance."

Unara wasn't in the mood for his ramblings just then. "Truly, you know them well, honored gothi, but I've come here to inquire about—"

"Another maintenance treatment?"

"No," she said. "The next step."

"Ah," he said, and rubbed his chin. The old gene-priest had a pensive look on his face. "Everything we have done up until now may be reversed. But with this, my princess, you cannot move back from the edge. You must find the land, or the water will kill you."

"And how would that be any different from any other day on this world?" she asked, impatient. Impatient with these unexpected dramatics. Impatient with the entire process.

Perhaps the old priest didn't understand.

There had never been any going back.

But at least now she had the space to act.

"Princess..."

"I'm not backing out now," she told him firmly.

"Then let us get started," he said, and offered her his hand.

CHAPTER SEVEN

Twilight in the market streets of Thalassa was as boisterous as the morning had been silent.

Karl wasn't sure he liked the transformation.

While preparations were still underway in the trader pavilions, including his own, an impromptu party had sprung up in the main market square. Food, wine, and entertainment from across the Spiral was represented, with different types of music mixing with the sounds of conversation and laughter.

Utterly ruining what would have otherwise been a beautiful afternoon. The largest of Thalassa Prime's suns had already set, and without its brilliant white-hot light, the world had descended into a half twilight, shades of red and purple coming out to play on the bone-white buildings, turning the shadows a most interesting deep blue.

"Sixteen of the usual players are here," his father's chief financial advisor was saying as Thorsen and three of his men made them a path through the crowds. That was Henriet Branner, head of accounts for the past century. She had waited longer than most to begin regenerative treatments and appeared to be a whipcord-thin woman of nearly fifty, serious and uncompromising. She had come with the rest of the household delegation. "I count three new Houses replacing Inez, Semanov, and Harrin."

"And what happened to them?" Thorsen asked.

"I've spoken to the chief financial manager for one of the replacements, MacKennan. They bought Inez's share in the kaupang for twenty-point-six billion, adjusted for—"

"Void above. That much?" Karl asked.

Branner shrugged, the heavy material of her House jacket dampening the movement somewhat. She eschewed the full skirts and elaborate headdresses of the Rikstag Sector female elite. Her uniform tonight was very similar to Karl's own, albeit cut for her far slimmer build. "I agree, it doesn't leave them much margin. But if a House can hang on through its first kaupang, there is considerably more profit on the next one. Tiber also bought in, although that seems to have been an action by the Aragon Sector's ruling family. House Inez didn't secure sufficient nacre plating for their navy last time, it seems."

"What about the Suyarii?" Thorsen asked, still pushing them a path through the crowd. A pair of half-drunk Alamani gave him a once-over and then moved out of their way. "How do we know they didn't just attack House Semanov's fleet and get the coordinates here?"

Brenner ran a hand through her short silver hair, shaking it out. With the landings over, the humidity had become fearsome. "What difference does it make? I haven't caught the name of their head negotiator yet, but no doubt he'll be good. They all are."

"Good enough to get Lord Willam laughing," Karl muttered, and nodded up ahead of them.

At the center of the square, under huge trees planted in improbably small pots, a group of traders was gathering. It was their destination as well, an informal reception of sorts, held jointly by Lady Amaro and Lord Willam. The former had donated the trees and a ten-piece chamber orchestra, while the other was handing out tankards of ale from an oversized barrel, chatting with a man in Suyarii dress as if the two of them were old friends. The trees were strung with lights, giving the whole scene a cheery, almost rustic air.

"Don't be fooled by Lord Willam's joviality," Branner told Karl quietly as they approached. "He cut his teeth fighting the Suyarii in the Ishtar system, four hundred years ago. There's no love lost between his sector and their empire, and he holds the title of knight commander back home. Even at his age, that comes with expectations."

Karl nodded. He knew Lord Willam's disposition. "You think he'll start a war here?"

"The Thalassans don't care what we do to each other, as long as they get their titanium," she told him. "Look at what happened to your father."

A guard at the edge of the gathering stopped them. Thorsen approached, official House seals in hand.

"What about Lady Amaro?" Karl asked Branner quietly.

"House Amaro is going to be concerned that their trading position with the Oriental Spiral will be undercut by the Suyarii's presence. They do a great deal of business across the star-gulf," Branner told him, voice low. "Lady Amaro is a practical woman. Her response to this will no doubt be to drive a harder bargain for regeneratives. Our response, young Master Karl, should be to deal harder for nacre plating, see how much of the excess harvest we can scoop up. The Thalassans won't be dumb enough to offer Semanov's orders to the Suyarii. But regardless, the price of everything will be going up this kaupang. We shall have to trust in our surpluses to make up the difference."

In front of them, Thorsen shook hands with the House Amaro guard, who stood aside, his pike gleaming.

"Ah, Karl, young Master Karl, I was wondering if it would be you here today!" Lord Willam boomed, waving as they approached. The wily old Caledon was the oldest trader present, sustained by the vagaries of interstellar travel and a steady course of regeneratives. To look at him, though, he seemed to be a man in his late fifties, rather rotund with a full beard. Between that and the colorful hose and doublet he wore, he cut something of a comedic figure.

Karl knew better.

He forced a smile and held out a hand in greeting, stepping away from his own entourage. "Lord Willam, it is good to see you again."

"What's it been, twenty years?" Lord Willam asked.

"Twenty-three, Standard. I was a boy when we visited your estate on Caledon Prime."

"Yes, yes, well, everyone is a boy from my perspective," the old Caledon laughed. "And look at this lovely little forest we have around us tonight, eh? You shall have to thank Lady Amaro in person for it."

"My father told me she had exquisite taste," Karl agreed, looking around. "This is very nice."

"She's been growing these trees with the help of a feii arborist. Cost a fortune. But she wanted everything to be perfect." Lord Willam leaned in, pointing over at a tall, slender woman with jet-black hair and an outrageous wine-red silk gown in the very latest Venetian style. "She's dying, you know. Her body started rejecting her regenerative treatments this year. Happens to the best of us, I suppose."

"Indeed. Regeneratives work magic, right up to the point where they fail," said the Suyarii next to Willam, voice dripping with irritation. "Perhaps our chemists can stabilize what yours clearly have not been able to."

Lord Willam gave the newcomer a genial smile. "Ah, I almost forgot. May I introduce Prince Imran of House Balat. He is a newcomer here, like you, young Karl, but lacking any previous ties to this world."

The Suyarii lord was dressed in the manner of his empire's elite: long kaftan, full trousers gathered near the ankle, sash, and high-crowned cap. His mustache was perfectly waxed and shaped and his hair short and dark. "Imran is fine," he said in lightly accented Standard. "I am grateful for everyone's kind welcome."

"Yes, yes, well, the shipwrecked are assured safe passage, you know," Lord Willam replied, still genial. One of his servants handed him a tankard of ale and he waggled it at Imran. "Are you sure I cannot offer you a drink?"

"I don't indulge in such things," Imran said, still cool.

The tankard was plunked down into Karl's hands instead, ale sloshing up over the wooden rim. "You then, my boy. You look parched."

"Thank you," Karl said, taking a sip to be polite, then another. It was excellent. "The humidity here could choke a horse."

"It is like this at home," Imran said. "Ocean and desert."

"Our hosts all dwell beneath the waves in great sealed habitats," Lord Willam replied. "Fascinating world, even if they'll never let you see most of it."

"We are grateful for what little we can see," Imran replied. "I thought we would never leave the interstellar dark."

"So you were adrift?" Karl asked.

"Yes. My fleet was on its way to the trading system of Temasek when we encountered the Semanov fleet in hyperspace. The collision left both fleets crippled."

"Lady Ruiz was killed in the initial collision, poor thing," Lord Willam added.

Lord Imran waved that off. "Indeed, as were many of their personnel. But the remaining family bid us come with them. Said it was the only safe harbor for a hundred light-years. We have been limping this way for the past five years."

"Pity Lady Semanov died before you reached us," Lord Willam said.

"Yes. A terrible shame. She was a lovely woman."

"Did none of their ships survive?" Karl asked.

"Not one, tragically. We have absorbed most of their crew into our own now."

"Undoubtedly," Lord Willam said, and for a moment, the mask of geniality slipped. There was pure, unrelenting hate in the man's eyes. But it was gone by the time Imran looked at him again. He grinned widely. "You have nothing to worry about, Lord Imran. It will be good to have some fresh competition here this year."

"I admit, finding the mysterious source of Occidental regeneratives makes the loss of life in my fleet almost worth it."

Lord Willam's face twitched, and Karl was about to step in again when a pair of trumpet blasts tore through the growing revelry.

"Ah, at last," the Caledon trader said. Imran lifted an eyebrow. Willam smiled at him. "Our hosts emerge."

The gates at the end of the broad square swung open, and through them stepped the Thalassans.

From his position beside Lord Willam, Karl had a good view of them. There were two groups, it seemed. One boasted a riot of color, all shades of the rainbow represented in both skin tone and hair. The other was paler, more gray, muted. But all wore outrageous clothing, fish leather and sea silk and nacre armor that had clearly been custom grown for the wearer. All carried weapons. Knives, mostly, but a few spears and tridents as well.

At first, the Thalassans appeared to have nothing in common. But as they approached, Karl thought he could see a few similarities. Most were lean, all with broad shoulders and long fingers, and there was a distinct otherworldly quality to them. Like they didn't quite belong here, walking in this world.

It was, Karl thought, like looking at a group of feii.

But that illusion was quickly shattered as the Thalassans reached them. The oldest among them, a man with a full beard and nacre plate over his tunic, strode right over to Karl's position.

"New faces this year, I see," he announced in a surprisingly resonant voice. "And old. Lord Willam, are you still alive?"

A ripple of laughter moved through the assembly. Lord Willam raised his tankard. "All thanks to you, old friend!" He gestured broadly. "Everyone, may I introduce King Aegyr, our gracious host and the administrator of this fine system, not to mention the brewer of some of the finest regeneratives anywhere in the galaxy.”

The laughter was joined by a smattering of applause. A few of the Thalassans smiled as well, but they didn't join in the clapping.

King Aegyr looked around. “It is good to see you all. My people are assembled, your letters of trade approved, working spaces assigned. May this year's gathering leave us all richer!”

There was a cheer, and that, it seemed, was that. The king vanished but the rest of the Thalassans stayed behind, dispersing out into the crowd.

“You gentlemen will forgive me,” Lord Willam said, indicating one of the Thalassan men, taller than the rest, “but I have business with the jarl over there. Drift Clan, you know.”

Both of the other traders nodded, and Lord Willam fetched another tankard, moving away from them.

“Jarl,” Imran mused after the Caledon was gone. “Is that a name or a title, I wonder?”

“A title, I think,” Karl said. “Many of the terms here bear linguistic similarities to Rikstag, my sector's language.”

“Then we are that close to Rikstag here?”

“We are close to nowhere here, Lord Imran. But this world does seem to have been originally settled by colonists from my sector.”

Imran nodded. “A fascinating world,” he said. “With fascinating company, I think.”

“I am sure we all have much to learn about each other this week,” Karl said drily. “If you'll excuse me, Lord Imran, I think I have had enough of Lord Willam's hospitality for one night.”

“A pleasure meeting you, Lord Gyes.”

“And you.”

Karl wandered then, saying hello to a few of the other traders before drifting out of the square entirely to the edge of one of the ocean-facing courtyards.

Karl hadn't seen a sunset—a true, proper sunset, while standing on a world's surface—for at least two years now. He stared out at it. He wanted another ale. He wanted some peace.

There was an exclusion zone around the palace, wasn't there? One kilometer out to sea, one kilometer inland, ten kilometers up and down the coast.

Enough space to watch the sunset without disruption, wasn't it?

With one last glance back at the setting sun, Karl turned away, headed for the landing fields.

What good was bringing his old exploration ship along if he didn't do a little exploring?

Unara had always loved the sky.

Skygazing was not an uncommon practice on Thalassa. But it was a limited practice. The movement of the suns drove the seasons, while the moons' dance across the sky was the core component of the gene-priests' work. It was formalized, ritualized, guided by ceremony and tradition, facilitated by great telescopes or viewing halls, glass and metal and living coral serving as mediators.

Almost nobody came to the surface to look for themselves.

What was there to know? everyone always said.

Unara, on the other hand, had been doing this since she was a little girl. Since before she was old enough to understand she wasn't supposed to.

Always on her stargazing expeditions, Unara was forced to take a breathing apparatus. The gene-craft that allowed the Thalassans to extract oxygen from seawater without gills or other significant alterations was one of the greatest achievements in the genome. One of Hildra's many gifts to her people. But it did preclude breathing air.

Unara sucked water through the mask now, wondering what it would be like when she could take her first real breath.

Out here, under the sky, she could almost taste it.

She had finished the penultimate infusion a little while ago but hadn't been able to relax in the gene-hallow's halls. The feeling of water rushing through her nose had nearly sent her into a panic during the infusion process.

"It's your brain," Gothi Strygr had told her, tapping his temple. "Hildra's gifts suppress an innate fear of drowning. This is a good sign, a sign that your nervous system is preparing for the change."

She'd glanced at the bag, the silvery-white serum inside pumping into her veins one drop at a time. "I didn't expect this," she replied, feeling her chest beginning to lock up.

"Nobody does," he chuckled. "But the brain, the brain, you see, had to be adapted as well, when Hildra took us in. Now don't fret. Another twenty minutes and this bag will be done. You can take a swim then. Shallower water usually helps."

But Unara hadn't opted for the shallows. She'd come all the way up, into the tide pools. The water was over the top of the corals here now, Rota's tide waxing. The dark moon hung in the sky now, barely visible, a silhouette against the stars.

Just a little bit longer, she told herself. Just a bit longer, and she would see it from space, instead of this wet perch. Out there in the peace of the stars, the great silence she longed for.

All would be well, Unara told herself, fin flipping in the shallow water. All would be right. Father would have more children, if he still could, or pass the crown to Jarl Dryagr, or something.

It didn't need to be her problem.

Thalassa wasn't her problem.

And then a star moved in the sky.

CHAPTER EIGHT

Karl stood on the bridge of the *Gylfy's Delight*, marveling at the shoreline around him. The cliffs were taller here, more rugged, with great arches carved in them, falling away into the dark twilight waters. There seemed to be another broad bay up ahead, just within the permissible zone for flight, and Karl had directed the crew to take them there.

"A lovely sight," he commented to nobody in particular.

"Fine indeed, milord," Pilot Alfir replied. "Lovely. Almost as nice as the seas on Gidden-Taurus Three."

Karl laughed, remembering that expedition. Beautiful world, completely unsuitable for human settlement. "Better, I'd say. You can actually step outside here without an environmental suit."

"Well, that was a young world," the pilot replied with a nod. "This is older. Still a bit too young for the maturity of its ecosphere, but one can attribute that to the Thalassans, I think. Forced evolution, I'd warrant."

Karl nodded, only half listening. The suns had set, but light still lingered, casting the western sky in deep purple. To the east, one of the planet's moons was rising. Hildra, he guessed, based on the silvery tint to its glow. From orbit, it had been gray.

"How many of those things are there here?" he asked Alfir softly.

"Moons?"

"Eyr was telling me something about it."

"Ah, yes, the moons are problematic here. All pulled in from other parts of the system, it seems. The two largest ones are well set in their orbits, but the mess of smaller ones..." Alfir trailed off. "They're said to move and shift between orbital paths, sometimes quite unexpectedly. Hazard to navigation, those things, like a flock of birds menacing an atmospheric flyer."

"You make it sound like they're alive, Alfir."

His old friend shrugged. "I've seen stranger things, but not by much."

"Endless ocean and sentient moons," Karl said, and raised his voice a little so the crew could hear. "It is good to see a new world with all of you again."

That got a chorus of soft acknowledgements. Karl knew they were as delighted as he was to be taking this little excursion. He felt somewhat guilty about bringing *Gylfy* and her crew back with him from the expedition fleet, but it had seemed only fair at the time. If his father was going to finally burden him with the mantle of Lord Negotiator, he at least wanted something familiar around him.

A selfish choice, and one that didn't best serve the House. But Karl hadn't cared at the time he received the summons. Still didn't really care.

He stared out at Thalassa. "Beautiful world," he muttered to himself again.

A noise, soft and wet behind him, like a damp rag being dragged across the deck plates. Karl turned, confused, and caught the briefest glimpse of something gray sliding into the main piloting console. "Alfir!" he called, making for it.

But it was already too late.

UNARA STARED in horror as the star grew. Huge it was now, detail obscured by roaring flame, falling to the ocean.

It seemed almost serene, cast in slow motion, hypnotic. But it was falling fast, falling into the bay, and Unara realized what was about to happen.

Waves.

Unara saw the first of these, a huge crest of white foam coming straight for the tide pools. With only seconds to spare before she was dashed to death on the rocks, she wriggled down, back into the bay proper, swimming for deeper water.

Her body was compromised, her lower half in the midst of its own painful transformation, and she couldn't get up the speed she needed quick enough. Unara was knocked back hard, caught in the undertow.

She was saved from the rocks by slick tentacles catching her by tail and arm, arresting her momentum. Unara looked up to see her akker, bright blue with concern, white spots rippling down its side as its double jets fought to hold their position.

Then, the next wave caught them both. Unara was torn from her mount's grasp and thrown backwards once again. Instead of rock, however, she slammed into one of the great nursery sponges that dotted the gothi's domain. These were effective synthesizers of all manner of esoteric compounds, and the water around her was stained red and black and purple with the sudden release caused by the collision. She gagged; the taste was indescribable. Unara fought both sponge and akker to get free of the noxious chemicals.

And as she cleared the plume, she finally saw it clearly, the thing that had struck the bay.

A spaceship.

It was a spaceship.

The craft must have been fatally wounded; the fires were all out and it was sinking, sinking to the bottom of the bay. Running lights along its hull illuminated the underwater world, dancing between the huge coral outcroppings and scaring away the creatures who always came out at night. And against that light, Unara thought she saw shadowy figures moving, dark shapes detaching from the coral and walking, unhurried, toward the craft.

What should she do? What could she do?

Nothing. Nothing without revealing herself. Without totally destroying the careful masquerade that her people had always performed for the rest of the galaxy.

But then she caught sight of something, a blue and gold device branded on the side of the spacecraft, illuminated by its own dying light.

The crest of House Gyes.

Her clan's chief trading partner.

Her primary choice for off-world passage.

The akker was on edge, its attack tentacles out, blades glinting in the unnatural light. Unara snapped her fingers at it, however, and it responded immediately, arcing up into position for her to grab the saddle. She swung herself in and urged them into a dive.

Maybe there was something more valuable than pearls she could offer House Gyes.

By the time she reached the ship, it had already settled at the bottom, right on the edge of the great sea cliffs here that dropped off, down into the blackwater. The water here was at least fifty meters deep; not normally a problem, but with everything reordering itself inside of her by the second, her limbs felt sluggish.

The depth appeared to be a problem for the craft as well. Sections of the smooth metal were dented. Even as she watched, a rear window cracked, then collapsed, caved in by the weight of the water. Air bubbles streamed out of a thousand wounds. Lights along the hull were beginning to die. A ship made for the vacuum of space could not handle the relatively low five bars of pressure here.

Unara hesitated a moment, staring at it, wondering what it was that she could do here, what she was even thinking, and then she saw them.

Figures.

Coming out of the darkness.

They were bipedal, she could tell now, two arms and two legs, misshapen and twisted, a corrupted vision of humanity's original form. There was nothing like that in Thalassa's seas; no creature, no gene-wrought creation of the Thalassans, nothing but—

"Draugr," she breathed.

It couldn't be. Stories, stories, only stories. They were metaphors, poetic personifications of the ocean's wrath that existed only in the skalds' sagas. They weren't real.

Except—it seemed—they were. They were scaling the hull now, clawing their way up toward windows and hatches and there—the entire back end was cracked apart. The craft settled, falling back slowly, and bodies drifted free.

Unara reached for her fishing spear only to find it missing. Cursing, she pulled her knife out of its sheath.

She reached the back of the ship at the same time as one of the dark figures. But before she could do anything, the akker already had it, tearing it apart with a few quick strikes of its blades.

Unara left her mount to monitor the ocean floor and peered into the interior of the spacecraft. There was a small, tight room here, very much like a water-lock, and a long hallway beyond. There were such things on these craft, air locks, to protect against the vacuum of space. Why was this one open? Had the water pressure damaged it?

"Stand guard," she told it, rapping the order on the shell.

The akker obliged, bristling, tentacles wide and stained deep red.

And, biting back a sudden rush of fear, Unara forced herself into the craft.

The royal tutors had been reluctant to give out any information on the off-worlders, but even as a child, Unara had been curious. Vaelyn had been quite helpful, passing Unara anything and everything she asked for.

So Unara knew a few things about spaceships. Off-worlder structures were built entirely by mechanical means. Straight lines, clean angles, simple intersections. The pattern seemed to hold true. Here, she found herself in a long corridor, a few meters high and broad, with rectangular doors set at regular intervals. The strangeness of it was both fascinating and unsettling, the space barely enough for her to swim in.

But where would the off-worlders be? And could she even get them out alive?

Then, movement, there, behind her. Unara whirled around, facing another pair of the strange creatures. She lashed out, swimming circles around their slow-moving forms, dropping them both. Dark blood poured out into the water in great billowing clouds, then reeking foam as the things fell apart. Behind her, she heard the akker screech.

More were coming. This was a problem. The blood would soon bring in sharks.

If there was anyone alive here, she had to find them quickly.

"Hello!" she called frantically, swimming deeper and deeper into the craft, calling out in Standard. Her voice would travel far down here. Hopefully, it would travel through the metal bulkheads in addition to the water. "Hello! Is anybody here?!"

Then, a reply. Banging, pounding. Coming from a broad set of doors at the end of the hall.

"Who's there?!" somebody yelled in Standard, their voice muffled by the thick metal.

Unara hesitated. "A friend!" she yelled back as loud as she could. "How many are you?"

"Six! We have Lord Gyes here with us!"

More movement. A rotten smell, carried on the currents. Unara looked up into the darkness of the craft. Figures moved above her.

"How do I open the doors?"

"You can't! Emergency overrides are in place. We are attempting to launch life pods, but the controls won't respond! If you can make it to—"

And it was then that the first draugr got a hand on Unara.

Five of them, there were five of them, dropping down on her in a space as tight as the intake chamber of a ventilation sponge. Barely enough room to move, no room to fight properly, they pawed at her, broken claws raking her skin.

Unara panicked. Lashing out hard, she managed to catch one with a stunning blow from her tail, stabbing her knife through the eye socket of another. But the blade was stuck, and the creature seemed unbothered by the injury. She tugged, frantic, trying to get her knife free. It was the only thing that saved her. The momentum of that movement swung her up, head down and tail up, hair streaming out around her.

Up the hallway-shaft.

She turned and bolted, swimming as hard as she could, zipping past other draugr crawling out of other rooms, other holes. Several dropped on her, but with speed, she was able to throw them off, shooting out into the open water once again.

Arresting her ascent with a hard braking turn, she looked back.

Her akker wasn't at the entrance. It had dropped, engaging with a knot of draugr-things coming up over the edge of the underwater cliffs in a cloud of ink and sand. It was furious, she could tell, its blood up, but beyond that, she could see little of what it was doing.

The bigger problem was the spaceship itself; the craft was balanced against the edge of the cliff, stable for the moment but clearly precarious.

And the hull was crawling with draugr now, like deep-sea crabs coming to harvest the fallen body of a dead kraken.

Unara scanned the craft. It had windows, she could see that. Perhaps there was a window that led to the compartment where the air-breathers were—

There.

Hanging on the edge of the cliff, a great bubble of glass, lights flashing inside.

Unara dived back down, ignoring the discomfort flaring in her body now. The pressure was catching up with her altered body. She couldn't linger at this depth for too much longer.

She reached the window in just a few moments. Inside, she could see that the compartment was indeed filling up with water, air-breathers rushing about back and forth between stations, clearly yelling out to each other.

Unara pounded on the glass with a fist. The nearest air-breather, a woman, looked up from her console and started. Unara couldn't tell how much of her they could see; there were still lights on in the compartment and the sea around her was pitch black, so perhaps not much. She held up her hands, hoping it would signal them to give her some kind of sign.

The woman yelled again. A man in blue and gold hurried over, peering out into the darkness and then pulling back in shock. Unara put a hand on the glass.

"What can I do?" she yelled, unsure if the sound would carry through here.

He gestured to the right, back along the side of the spacecraft. Unara looked. The entire side of the craft was wedged in against a huge outcropping of coral, the hull bent and scraped. She realized that must be where the life pods were. She looked back to the man, shaking her head and holding her hands together. "Nothing is launching from there," she told him, hoping her meaning would be clear.

The water moved.

Her akker was alongside her now, still on high alert, bleeding from a dozen small wounds along its arms. In the light from the cockpit, the blood glowed a brilliant cobalt blue.

She followed its eye. The draugr were coming.

The man stared at her for a moment more, then hurried back, grabbing the man in the ostentatious outfit. He and a half dozen others were at the doors now, objects in their hands. Guns, Unara recognized. Energy weapons. Those wouldn't do any good down here. The ostentatious man shook his head.

Everyone on the command deck was staring now. Unara was confused, but then the man in blue pulled out something. A gun, she realized.

Started firing at the window.

Unara pulled back, confused at what was going on here. Everyone else in the command section began firing as well. She could only imagine the noise. But then she realized what was going on. They weren't trying to kill her. They were trying to break the glass. Break the glass, open a hole, so she could save the man in the ostentatious outfit.

Somebody inside fell, a massive wall of water rushing in, and then the dark shape of the draugr were among them. The man in blue kept firing, keeping the other man between himself and the window, even as the air-breathers began dying.

The window, stressed to failure by the barrage of energy, finally burst open. Water rushed in, knocking everyone still standing down. The akker grabbed Unara again, jets fighting hard to hold them both in position, but even with that, she only barely avoided being sucked through the hole or getting caught in the huge burst of bubbles. The last of the air-breathers' life-sustaining atmosphere was escaping to the surface.

It was a sacrifice made for the one man in the ornate coat.

The least Unara could do was honor it.

The hole they had made was barely big enough for her to squeeze through, but she managed. Scales scraped off her tail as she forced herself through. A body bumped into hers: one of the air-breathers. The man in blue was scrambling against a pair of draugr; the doors had been breached. Unara tried to reach him, but then the water filled with red blood, and she knew there was no hope.

The man the others had died to save was face-up in the very last pocket of air, in the furthest corner of the room. The draugr were headed for him, moving faster now, hands reaching for him. Unara delivered the hardest stuns she could, banging her tail against the cold hard consoles as she did. Fresh pain flared through her. A hand caught her fins and then released; she felt the coiled tentacles of her akker slide around her.

Leaving the fight to the altered cephalopod, she grabbed for the man. "Take your last breath!" she yelled, yanking on his jacket.

Under the water, she saw his chest expand.

Good enough.

She pulled him down.

The man swam with her, clumsy and slow in his clothing, but he was clearly struggling. Then the akker wrapped an arm around him, tugging. Between them, they got him out of the window, but a draugr almost grabbed him, and by the time Unara had dealt with that—a precious four seconds, lost— his eyes were closed and his hands limp.

But his heart still beat. She could feel that through the material of his thick jacket.

So Unara slung his arm around her shoulder, grabbed her saddle with the other, and got him to the surface as fast as the akker could swim.

GETTING him back to shore was significantly more complicated than getting him up to the air.

Only the lack of wave action saved him. With the ship settled deep below, the bay's waters had calmed once again, smooth and still as a rock pool at high tide. Still, Unara's body ached from the fight. Her lungs burned, and the off-worlder in his sodden clothing was heavy.

The akker had gotten them to the surface at least, jetting up there as fast as it could, Unara holding the off-worlder in the saddle. But the akker wasn't built for surface travel and neither was Unara.

The man had hit his head hard on the window glass on the way out and hadn't woken up yet. This meant Unara had to hold his head steady above the water with the last of her failing strength, dipping her own head every few seconds to gulp more seawater herself.

By the time she got him to shore, the narrow sandy beach that ringed the bay, nearly half a kilometer from where the craft had gone down, she could barely move.

Still, she pulled him out of the saddle and as far up on the beach as she could.

The akker had to pull her back into the waves.

Lying just below the water, Unara let the soft little nighttime waves crash over her, lifting her head now and then to take in the man she had just saved. Who was he?

Somebody important, she thought. The other people in the spacecraft had clearly been trying to save him, him over their own lives. Dedication like that was admirable, she thought, and felt a surge of guilt for not having been able to do more for them. They had been brave.

The man was breathing.

At least there was that.

She held her position in the quiet, lapping waves, taking a few deep gulps of sand-gritty seawater, considering her options.

A missing spacecraft was surely a notable event. Somebody would eventually come looking for him. The beach here was wide and sandy during low tide, and a good bit of it was still dry. But the tide was coming in, and in a matter of hours, this would all be under-water. She didn't know how long it would take this man to wake, nor if she would have the strength to hold him above water if the tide covered the sand before then.

As concerned as Unara was with the off-worlder from House Gyes, she had herself to think of as well. She needed to get back to the gene-hallow. She needed to finish out the round of infusions or her body would start to destabilize for sure. Catastrophic biological failure. Just like Glaeva.

Unara glanced up at the silver form of Hildra above. "Could you be bothered to help?" she muttered.

And then, a light. Lights overhead, streaking across the beach, sweeping toward the man. Unara pushed herself further out into the water, out from the shallows, taking refuge behind a large outcropping of rock, trusting the shadows to hide her.

The bright beam landed on him. From the ocean's darkness, Unara watched as the craft landed and a group of people rushed toward the man from Gyes.

One of them, Unara saw, was Vaelyn.

Satisfied her friend wouldn't let the man die, Unara pushed all the way back out into the deeper water, slipping down into the nighttime ocean of Thalassa.

She needed to get back to the gene-hallow.

CHAPTER NINE

"Thank you."

"Anything for House Gyes, Captain Thorsen. Besides, I shudder to think what old Vilhelm might order you to do to me, should I refuse to help his son."

"I don't think I'd take an order to eliminate your House, Lady Amaro. Not without a very good cause."

Laughter then. Vaelyn tried to ignore it. She didn't feel very much like laughing herself.

The two off-worlders were sitting in large, padded seats on either side of the small craft's upper observation deck, a finely wrought bubble of glass with an unobstructed view of the night sky. The captain in his blue and gold formal uniform, the trader in her priceless silk gown. Lady Amaro was completely composed, seemingly without a care as to how her voluminous skirts were wrinkled in the narrow seat. The captain, on the other hand, was miserable. No wonder, Vaelyn thought grumpily. A housecarl who lost his jarl was hardly worth the nacre he was paid in.

The flyer they were all on was about the size of a large maintenance submersible, albeit one with a far more aerodynamic shape and without a back water-lock. It was almost all window, with only the barest bit of solid floor and some exposed ribbing to hold it all together. Atmospheric travel only, Lady Amaro had told Vaelyn.

It was a novel experience, but one that Vaelyn couldn't enjoy. She could only imagine what King Aegyr might say when he inevitably found out. She would have to tell him, of course. She would have to tell him about all of this.

Or at least, all of it she could.

Vaelyn had not really been enjoying the party out in the market square. Too loud, too chaotic, too many people. Even the Stone Clan, crammed as they were into the caverns and air-habitats of the palace bay, enjoyed solitude, space. The desire for such things ran deep in the Thalassan heart, both in and out of the water.

But solitude was not hers for the next week. She was supposed to watch Lord Gyes, watch him very carefully.

Finally, after searching the entire market square, Vaelyn had retreated. Out to a quiet courtyard with a view of the sea. Her heart ached, looking out at it. So close. They were so close now. A week, and surely, she would finally be able to go home.

Something nudged her foot. One of the crab drones.

Frowning, she'd moved her boot out of the way, hoping the creature would scuttle on, take its little spying eyes somewhere else. Before somebody down in the Hall of Dreams spotted her and decided she wasn't working hard enough.

But that didn't happen. Instead, the crab's eyes and shell flashed blue with bio-lights. An adaptation the crab drones weren't supposed to have. Frowning, Vaelyn knelt down to get a closer look.

The crab moved, hard front claws dragging on the ground. The streets between the pavilions were paved with a layer of fine gravel and soft sand over hard rock, the same stuff that covered the floors of Thalassan buildings everywhere. Vaelyn had always hated the stuff, wondered why they couldn't just sweep the rock smooth, but the traditions of the ocean-born often overrode common sense.

The crab wasn't just moving, she realized.

The crab was writing.

Gyes?

Swallowing hard, not sure if this was Lady Hethra's influence or not, Vaelyn shook her head. "Haven't found him yet."

In air. In water. Find him if alive.

"What do you mean?"

Star-akker go do—

But that was it. The crab stopped moving halfway through the sentence, ventral cortex no doubt burned out by whatever Lady Hethra had been doing to the thing. Vaelyn stared down at it, trying to figure out what it meant. And then it clicked for her.

She'd kicked the crab over the edge of the cliffs and rubbed out the message, then hurried back to the party.

She had to find the Gyes delegation.

A few desperate questions to the off-worlders finally got her pointed in the right direction: a small knot of men in blue and gold uniforms, near the northern edge of the party.

"And you did search the pavilion?" one of them, a hulking man with a shaved head, was saying, clearly exasperated, then noticed Vaelyn. He straightened, schooling some of his concern off his face. "May I help you, Lady...?"

"Vaelyn, just Vaelyn," she replied. "I am to escort your House during your time here. I was hoping to speak to Lord Gyes."

"He's not here. We're trying to figure out where he got off to."

"Ah." She thought about that for a moment. "Would he have a... a flying ship?"

The big man looked at her for a moment, then went pale. "Go out to the landing zone," he ordered one of the men. "Run!"

It turned out that Lord Gyes had indeed taken the lander.

And nobody knew where he was.

Every House was only permitted one craft capable of atmospheric flight while on the surface. With *Gylphy's Delight* missing, House Gyes had nothing with which to conduct a search. Lady Amaro had volunteered her own flyer.

And Vaelyn had made sure she went along.

"What do you think happened?"

It was Captain Thorsen, the big man from the market square. Talking to her right now, Vaelyn realized with a start. She pulled herself out of her miserable reflection. "I don't know."

"Craft don't just fall out of the sky."

"I don't know."

"Most likely it was some kind of explosive device," Lady Amaro said. "Something or someone did try to kill Vilhelm last kaupang."

"None of this feels right," Thorsen muttered, and ran a hand back through his short hair. "How far are we from the edge of the exclusion zone, Vaelyn?"

She glanced out the side of the flyer. It truly was a marvel being up so high. Like walking along the clifftops, but here, she was looking back at the coastline. Vaelyn had never seen her world laid out for her like this. Thalassans had no use for the sky. The ocean, it was always said, was humanity's rightful place. But for a moment, surrounded by all that wonder, she thought she understood Unara just a little bit better.

"Not far," she said, and pointed up ahead. "That bay is the end of what we allow off-worlders to visit."

"I still don't see anything," Lady Amaro said.

Captain Thorson muttered something unintelligible under his breath and headed forward, presumably to go talk to the pilot.

With him gone, Lady Amaro's gaze fell fully on Vaelyn. "Stone Clan, I see," she said lightly, and at Vaelyn's confusion, she laughed. "Six of your clanswomen have escorted me over the centuries. I always ask for some nice young man instead, but I never get one."

Vaelyn smiled, despite the situation. "Leyli, your escort this kaupang, is a good friend. She'll take good care of you, milady."

"Ah yes, that famous Thalassan hospitality," Lady Amaro said. "Warm and friendly, but everything concealed. I wonder every time I am here, what are you hiding in these waters?"

Vaelyn swallowed. "Nothing you'd like to see, Lady Amaro."

"Well, hopefully young Karl isn't down there. Vilhelm will have me skinned alive."

Vaelyn wondered if that was a joke. She couldn't tell. But then something shifted unpleasantly in her gut, responding to some movement of this air-akker. But Lady Amaro just smiled, leaned back in her seat. "Ah, descent at last. Let us go see what they've found, eh?"

Vaelyn, by her own insistence, was the first out of the craft. She wasn't sure what to expect out here, but she wanted to get eyes on it before any of the off-worlders did. Just as a precaution.

Nothing. She saw nothing.

Nothing...until she spotted a blue and gold form sprawled out on the beach.

She ran over to him, more sure-footed in the soft sand than the House Gyes troopers in their heavy boots. Dropping to her knees beside him, she felt for a pulse.

"Don't," he gasped weakly. "I'm fine."

"You look half-drowned," Vaelyn told him, confused by what she was seeing. This man looked not much older than her. Strong features, no sign of regenerative use in his eyes. Bruises on his face, wounds on his knuckles. He'd been through some kind of fight. But against what? And where was his ship? "I do not think you're fine."

The off-worlder blinked up at her, like he couldn't figure out what he was looking at. "Monsters," he panted. "There are monsters down there."

"Yes," she said. "I know."

But then Captain Thorsen moved her back, gently but insistently. She stepped away, allowing House Gyes to tend to their own lord. She looked out over the water.

What had happened here tonight?

And what did Lady Hethra know about it?

FINALLY FORCED TO ADMIT DEFEAT, Unara sank down to the ground, ran her fingers through the sand of the gene-hallow's devastated upper hall.

Gone.

Everything was gone.

She had retreated from the surface, down here, to find the place devastated.

Every piece of equipment broken, every serum spilled, every vat broken. All the food stores; what wasn't stolen or eaten was being busily consumed by scavenger fish. Even her own treasure was missing, the clamshell chest gone.

She could guess what had happened. Signs of the draugr were everywhere. That strange blood, the scent of their bodies that she had smelled on the spaceship. But not bodies. Not Gothi Strygr's. Not theirs.

There was nothing left.

And beyond the grief for the gothi, Unara had a more fundamental problem now.

She had taken the penultimate infusion.

There was no turning back now.

Unless the alterations were supported, encouraged, completed, her body would go to war with itself, her organs would fail, tumors would erupt, and she would die.

But how was she going to manage that?

Go to Gothi Injyr? At the palace?

There was no chance he would keep her secret. Father would find out, and Unara didn't want to know what her father would do to her then. Would he even let her come back to the sea? Or would she be cast out, forced to finish the transformation and then be trapped forever with the Stone Clan?

Losing both the sea and the stars was an unbearable thought.

But if she did nothing, she would most certainly die.

She looked around the dead gene-hallow and despaired.

CHAPTER TEN

There was water on the floor. Here, in the damp and cold of the palace's lowest halls, in the old tunnels, the tunnels that most of the time, were abandoned.

The tunnels that connected directly to the abyssal delegation's manse.

Some effort had been made to tidy up down here, seeing as how Lady Hethra was in residence. The algae had been swept from the walls, the palace's ventilation system extended through new offshoot arteries to ensure the air remained breathable. Unlike most of the rest of the palace, this living network of tubular air-hardened sponge wasn't hidden behind the walls and decorative paneling. No, here it was out in the open, sprawled through the tunnel like a kraken seeking food.

Vaelyn tried not to look at it.

She preferred coming down here with an air tank and a breathing mask. At least then she wasn't imagining some giant beaked maw around every corner waiting to devour her.

She knew the way well and barely needed the lantern she'd

brought with her. Dodging the puddles and the broader protrusions of ventilation arteries, she made for her destination.

One of Oceanfall's forgotten boundary pools.

There were dozens of these places scattered throughout Oceanfall. Built in natural grottos, they were a place where water and air could meet, where the ocean- and sky-born could talk without need for a wetsuit. They were all similar in construction: a precautionary water-lock, an open-air space consisting of a ledge above the waterline and a viewing window with a speaker-conch below. Unara and Vaelyn had been meeting here for years now. It was little used by anyone else, so far was it from the main bulk of the palace, but it was perfect for their needs.

And Lady Hethra's today, it seemed.

Vaelyn sealed the water-lock behind her and headed down into the viewing pit. Lady Hethra was already here, floating just on the other side of the glass. At the bottom of the stairs, Vaelyn took a respectful knee.

<You're late.> Lady Hethra's voice was scornful, even while modulated by the speaker-conch.

"A lot is going on, milady. I don't want to anger King Aegyr by shirking my duties to Lord Gyes."

<Lord, ha!> The abyssal chieftain's voice echoed from the speaker. <He is a boy, barely worth the carbon that he's knit from. But his father! Now there was a man worthy of the title lord, odious as he was. But they keep resisting my attempts to kill them, no thanks to that feii witch their House courts.>

Vaelyn looked up at that, startled. "A feii?"

<Yes, the feii came down in a lander late last night. With permission, if you can believe it. An indulgence from King Aegyr.> Lady Hethra swished her tail angrily.

"I thought the feii weren't allowed on the surface."

<Aegyr has ordered it confined to the drop-craft. Still, its presence may help our plans>

"Milady, I had hoped to bring you the news about Lord Gyes

myself, but it seems you already know everything I do and a great deal more besides. Why did you want to see me?"

<Unara will need some attention in the morning. Her gene-hallow was destroyed, after all.>

Vaelyn blinked. "What?"

<A trifling matter but one that we shall take advantage of. Find her before she does anything stupid, like talk to her father.>

Biting the inside of her cheek, Vaelyn tried to keep her body relaxed. Lady Hethra was exceptionally good at picking up the smallest clues about...

<This bothers you. Why?>

"What does Unara have to do with anything, Lady Hethra?"

<Do you think I had you befriend her, tutor her all these years for no reason at all?>

"No milady, but—"

<Her desire to leave the planet, on its own, is enough to merit her death.>

"I understand that, but—"

<But nothing, Vaelyn. You must understand, we are attempting to overthrow the ruling order here on this world, are we not?>

"We are. To ensure a better life for everyone. But Unara—"

<Unara is a daughter of the ruling clan, is she not? And look how flagrantly she attempts to violate one of our most sacred traditions. Nobody leaves this world. Not even a princess.>

And that, Vaelyn thought she understood. "So you've had me help with all of this in order to delegitimize King Aegyr?"

<Exactly,> Lady Hethra purred. <It's all foolishness, of course. Hildra and Rota and all the rest are hunks of rock in orbit, my girl, nothing more. Do you suppose they will pull on fins, like in the skalds' tales, and come down to swim among us? Will they save us? Punish us? Of course not. But the notion of it is something that will resonate with the other clans. Let them see what is to come as punishment for the royal family's decadence and failure.> And Lady

Hethra put a hand on the glass between them. <And believe me, this is punishment. Just not of the...celestial kind.>

Vaelyn nodded, absorbing that, trying to wrap her head around it. "And Lord Gyes?"

<A simple infiltration organism, programmed to do exactly what it did: work its way into his craft's mechanisms and take it down next time he was in the air. I didn't expect it to be so soon, and I didn't expect to be there. Immaterial to our larger plans, Vaelyn.>

She hesitated. "He said something to me about monsters."

Lady Hethra swished her tail, impatient. <Immaterial, Vaelyn! Find Unara and send her to me. And stay close to Lord Gyes. That is what I require of you now.>

Vaelyn bowed her head, questions still rolling through her mind. "Yes milady."

UNARA AWOKE that morning in the middle of the ruined gene-hallow, sunlight streaking down from above. Her tail ached. Her hair was full of sand. It had been an unpleasant night, sleeping here on the sand. She had been in no condition the night before to brave the reefs. She hoped she could manage it that morning.

Working a knot out of her berry-red hair with her fingers, she swam slowly out to the main courtyard. Her akker wasn't there and for a moment, she feared the worst. But forcing herself to remain hopeful, she whistled and waited, still working on her badly tangled hair.

After a few minutes, the akker turned up, a giant reef jack in one of its lesser tentacles.

The swim back to the palace was difficult. Her lungs weren't processing the oxygen from the seawater properly but were still not ready for air. She had to stop every so often to catch her breath.

Her akker was on edge too, posturing at every little movement, avoiding the deep shadows. She didn't blame it, not after the events of last night. And while it was no longer bleeding, it was still wounded. It would require attention from the gothi when they returned to the palace, but what would she tell them?

We were attacked by draugr?

It sounded insane even to her, and Unara wondered if she had been mistaken. But it wasn't her real problem, and she gave it little thought.

What was she going to do about her transformation?

She could not stay as she was. She could not. Already, the discomfort in her muscles was growing. More than mere fatigue from the battle, she ached. She was hours overdue for her final injection, and with this kind of rapid metamorphosis, hours mattered.

She could not stay in this in-between state. Her own gene-code was not yet fully replaced and would reassert itself fully in a matter of days. Then her own biology would go to war with itself, killing her.

What other options were there? The palace gothi were out of the question. Another gene-hallow? There were precious few of them that were independent, and any that were even within a month's swim had already turned down her initial entreaties years ago. A gene-hallow pledged to the service of another clan? The potential for political fallout there was too high. Direct confrontation or blackmail. She couldn't risk that, either.

Leaving her family behind was one thing. Leaving them in danger was quite another. She had never wanted to hurt anybody. She just wanted to see the world beyond this endless sea.

And Unara had no desire to die. Not now when she was so close to her goal.

But who should she sacrifice? Herself or her clan?

She had still not arrived at a satisfactory answer to that question by the time she dragged herself back to the palace. She sent the akker off with directions to report in to the healers and curled up in her sleeping hollow, utterly exhausted. A few hours of sleep, she decided, just a few hours and she would be better able to face whatever was coming.

Except before she could drift off into painful, uneasy dreams, there was a knock at her chamber door. The sound sent a thrill of fear through her. Her father had found out, she thought wildly, her father had—

No. How would he know?

With a flick of her tail, Unara was out of her hollow and drifting over to the door, laying a weak hand on its release.

But instead of her father or the palace guard, out in the hallway was a familiar figure, wrapped in a wetsuit.

"Vaelyn," Unara sighed with relief.

<Oh thank the moons, you're alright,> her friend said, swimming in. <When I saw where Gyes's ship went down last night near your gene-hallow, I feared the worst.>

"The ship didn't touch the place," Unara said, and hesitated.

<But?>

"It's gone. Totally destroyed, everyone dead and everything lost."

<Gone? How?>

"I—" she began, and hesitated again. "Vaelyn, there were draugr there."

Vaelyn recoiled, a huge stream of bubbles escaping her regulator. <That's impossible.>

"I swear, it was draugr, as sure as I swim now. There's no mistaking monsters like that. Either the stories are true—"

<Doubtful.>

"—or somebody's made something that intentionally looks like our monsters and released it into our seas."

<Who? One of the trading houses? How would they know our stories?>

"I don't know," Unara admitted, feeling drained. "I saw two-legged creatures, slow-moving with human features, swarming the downed spacecraft. I killed several of them. They were attempting to breach the last air chamber when I pulled out the man who was there and—"

<So you're the one who saved Lord Gyes?>

"Lord Gyes?" Unara asked, a little stunned now. Lord Gyes was an old man, possibly still injured from his poisoning last kaupang.

<And good thing you did. I am not sure who would have spoken for his House here if you had not saved him,> Vaelyn continued, shaking her head. <There seem to be a lot of tensions between the off-worlders at the moment, and without the leading House present at—>

"Vaelyn," Unara said, cutting that off. She had no wish to get lost in some air-breather political intrigue at the moment. "Vaelyn, I took the penultimate infusion yesterday."

That pulled her friend's attention firmly back. <Unara, you need your final dose. You'll die!>

"What am I supposed to do? If I go to anybody here in the palace, it will get back to my father, and if I go to another clan, that'll just cause other problems with—"

<Lady Hethra.>

"What?"

There was a long pause before Vaelyn spoke again, and when she did, the words sounded grudging. <Lady Hethra. Unara, she can help you. You know she can. She's one of the best gene-wrights in the entire ocean. Look what she did for your father.>

Despite her need, Unara felt a chill run through her at the idea of asking Lady Hethra for help. The people of the deep were a breed apart, and Lady Hethra had never been particularly friendly with any of Unara's clan. And at any rate, it was still going to another clan for aid.

But when she mentioned all of this, Vaelyn brushed it aside.

<Unara, don't worry about it. You know the Abyssal Clan doesn't participate in the kaupang directly. She's just up here to keep an eye on things. And she takes her oath as a healer very seriously. If you are in distress, I am sure she'll help you.>

"But—"

<But nothing, Unara. Your body will start breaking down, and soon, if you don't do something. She'll take care of you. No ques-

tions, no price. Trust me. Everything...everything shall be alright.> And she held out a hand. <Come on, I'll even help you get over there.>

"You have to have other, better things to do this morning."

<Lord Gyes was still unconscious when I left the drop-craft. A sleeping man doesn't need an escort,> she said, and waggled her gloved hand again. <But you do need help, and soon.>

Unara recognized a lifeline when she saw it. "Thank you," she said sincerely, taking Vaelyn by the hand. "You're a good friend, Vaelyn."

<Come on,> Vaelyn said. <Let's get you out of here.>

Unara was shaking all over by the time she made it to the abyssal manse.

Lady Hethra's domain was not anywhere near the prime regions of the palace. Instead, it was out on the very tip of the bay's end where the cliffs dropped straight down into the blackwater, out on the north side of the bay, far distant from the rest of the palace.

Something about it reminded Unara of the battle she had fought the night before, and she shivered looking at it.

But there was nowhere else to go, so on she swam.

Vaelyn did have appointments to keep up on the surface, but she had done what she could before leaving. She had gotten Unara out of the main sections of the palace, calling back her akker and getting her in the saddle. But that was all she could manage, she said; she was needed back at the Gyes's drop-craft.

Unara was grateful for the akker. Her tail wasn't working right, the bones in it prepared for that final reconfiguring, and she doubted she would have been able to make it on her own. But here, her akker could take her no further. She slipped from the saddle, giving her akker one last pat, before swimming down to the gates.

"Who goes there?" a pale-skinned guard with the tail of a snail-fish challenged her.

"Princess Unara," she gasped. "I must see Lady Hethra."

A fishing spear went up, blocking her way. "King Aegyr has no authority in this house."

"Please," she said. This entrance was deep, almost a hundred meters, and her body was struggling to draw water into her lungs. Her heart missed a beat. "Please, I—"

"Stand down," she heard a voice call from inside. Unara looked up in time to see Lady Hethra swimming toward her. "Can you not see the princess is in distress?"

The guard's face twitched in surprise. "Milady?"

"Let her pass," Lady Hethra said, reaching out a hand and pulling Unara closer in, like she was helping some newborn babe. "Don't worry, my dear. You are among friends here."

CHAPTER ELEVEN

"So far, we do not see any ill effects from your rapid ascent to the surface, Lord Gyes, and we are not anticipating any kind of ongoing health issues. However—"

"Fantastic. Let me out of this thing."

"Milord, I and the human medical team still have a few more tests we need to run and—"

"Now, Eyr."

Karl only had the faintest recollection of how he had come to be here. An impact on his ship. Falling out of the sky. A great rush of water against the hull. Screaming, dying, and then—

Cold. He'd been cold, sand gritty under his hands. And the sense of a woman, beautiful beyond measure with a sadness as broad as the sea, watching him.

And then, nothing.

Then he'd woken up in this enclosed pressurization vessel. Staring into Eyr's blank, impassive face. Karl's nerves were frayed, and the last thing he wanted to be dealing with was her.

Through the hyperbaric chamber's speakers, his men had explained what had happened. He'd listened, getting angrier and angrier. The *Gylfy's Delight*, gone. Pilot Alfir, his old friend, gone. A dozen crew members, gone.

But he had survived.

Somehow.

Eyr stared at him for a moment more and then bowed her head. "As you will it, Lord Gyes. Open the chamber."

It took a few moments for the chamber's lock to disengage and the medical staff to pull the door open. Karl strode out as soon as he was free, looking around at them all. There was fear in their eyes along with relief. They were scared for him, he realized, and something clenched up in his gut.

All his life, he had been raised with the expectation of leadership. Of one day stepping out from his father's shadow and donning a title for himself. Once, he had hoped that would be as the Lead Navigator of the expedition fleet. More recently, that had turned into Lord Negotiator. He had been tutored for as long as he could remember in what it was to hold the lives of other people in the balance. But he had never really felt the weight of that concept before; he'd never had his entire crew die on him.

His mouth felt suddenly dry, and something must have shown on his face, because two of the medical staff stepped forward, reaching for him. "I'm alright," he said, waving them back as he tried to think of what to say. "Thank you for your diligence."

Branner, who was also there, sitting on a stool off to one side, nodded. "We would do nothing else, milord."

"Thanks are still in order, I believe," Karl said to the financial expert. "Have I missed our first meeting with Aegyr's delegation?"

"You have not, but Vaelyn has rearranged the schedule for you," Branner replied, utterly nonplussed by his appearance.

"Vaelyn?"

"Our Thalassan escort. She went out with Captain Thorsen last night. I think she was concerned for you this morning."

Karl shook his head. "House Gyes always takes the first meeting with the king. We have quotas to fill for nacre plating. I cannot allow another House to bid for those first. Branner, wait outside. We shall head to the trade chambers together as soon as I've dressed."

The silver-haired advisor raised an eyebrow but said nothing. Just bowed and turned away. The medical staff likewise scattered.

Eyr stayed behind.

"I don't suppose it would do me any good to order you to leave," he said wryly, making for a side table where a House uniform had been left for him.

"Indeed not, milord," Eyr replied. "Your father bid me care for you and that is exactly what I shall do."

Karl stripped the medical gown off, wincing a little. His back and legs were littered with bruises, it seemed. It hurt to move. He started to pull on his trousers. "Do we know what happened to the *Gylfy*?"

"No," Eyr replied, flat.

Karl's undershirt came next, followed by his jacket and boots. "Do the other Houses know?"

"Milord, I am concerned only with you."

Karl grunted and started working on his jacket's buttons. "Could you look, see what happened to me last night?"

"You mean, back through time?" Eyr asked. Karl nodded. The feii's blank mask shook slightly. "I will do it if you so command, but would not advise it, milord. I am not especially skilled in temporal manipulation and—"

"People are dead, Eyr. They were my crew, my friends. I want to know why."

"Such things may only be undertaken once. Don't waste your one opportunity on my meager skills."

Karl sighed and scrubbed a hand through his hair. The medical staff had washed it, at least. He felt no grit of salt there. "I suppose the past can wait. I need to go save the future of the House first. Are you going back up to orbit now?"

"No, not right now. Your father is stable enough," the feii said. "I plan on staying. In case any further harm befalls you, milord."

He nodded back. "I don't know why you're loyal to my family, Healer, but I appreciate it."

"See? As I said. No attempt to understand."

BRANNER WAS WAITING for Karl as he stepped back out into the hall. Captain Thorsen was with her as well, with half a dozen House Guard.

"Really?" Karl asked, tearing his thoughts away from the strange conversation, waving a hand at the show of force. "Captain, is this necessary?"

"You almost died last night, milord," Thorsen replied.

"There isn't anything you could have done about his ship going down, Captain," Branner said, and adjusted the short shoulder cape she was wearing. "We would have lost you too."

"Yes, but why did it happen at all?"

"Questions for another time," Karl said, and nodded to his bodyguard. "I am sorry I gave you the slip last night, Captain Thorsen. I won't do it again."

Seemingly mollified, the captain nodded back.

"Now, let us head down to the trading halls. I would hate to think that the Suyarii have already bargained away the planet's entire wealth while that damn feii had me in a glass bubble."

Even Thorsen smiled at that. But as they set off, Karl was still wracked with doubts.

What had happened last night?

And, more importantly, how had he survived it?

THE ABYSSAL MANSE ran deeper than Unara had imagined. The place seemed far more expansive than it had always seemed from the outside, burrowing into the rock of the cliffs, its halls flowing down, down, down.

Every meter they descended felt like a brass band tightening around her chest.

"Painful, I know, to take one such as you this deep," Lady Hethra told Unara at one point as they approached another shaft. "My apologies, Princess, but with the exception of the main reception hall at the entrance, everything lies further down. We build as deep as we can, even so near the surface as this. It is painful for most of my clan, being in the shallows."

Unara nodded and focused on breathing.

There was no use trying to get a sense of what the manse truly looked like. It was dark, lit only by small bioluminescent creatures that floated freely in the water, strings of lights that turned and twisted in on themselves. At one point, Unara brushed close to one and got a better look.

"Siphonophore," Lady Hethra explained, swimming back to her. "Practically immortal, you know, although I have altered them to withstand these lower pressures. And we have to feed them, of course."

Unara reached out for it cautiously. The creature didn't move on its own, simply drifting away from the current off the motion of her hand. "I thought even the Abyssal Clan would have light in their dwellings."

"Why?" Lady Hethra asked. "We must embrace our world, same as any other clan. I had all such things removed from our places a long time ago."

Unara thought about that, living forever in the dark, and shivered. "Then how does anybody see well enough to hunt or flee predators?"

"There are other senses more valuable than sight in the deep oceans," Hethra replied. "Come. We're wasting precious time."

Unara took one last look at the siphonophore, hanging there in its circle of illumination, and followed the abyssal chieftain further into the eternal midnight.

Despite Lady Hethra's statements about light, the small gene-hallow at the end of their swim was well lit and comfortable, with a treatment chair and breathing apparatus set up in the center. Lady Hethra helped Unara over to the chair. Unara sank into it gratefully, pulling one of the straps over her. Everything ached.

"Now," Lady Hethra said, fixing the breathing apparatus mask over Unara's face, "tell me everything."

So Unara did. In between deep gulps of super-oxygenated water, she told Hethra about her longing to see the stars, about her plans to leave with the trading vessels, about the treatments she'd had and the progress she'd made. Lady Hethra listened intently, taking a few vials of blood as she did so.

"And you aren't sure what transformation protocol they were using?" Hethra asked as she placed the vial into a strange piece of equipment on a side table.

"It was a custom design," she replied.

"Yes, yes, of course. While there are, of course, vast similarities between even the most disparate individuals, the nuances of a patient's genetic code do require a great deal of customization," Lady Hethra said, "and I would imagine that committing yourself to the air forever is a much more challenging task than allowing one's unaltered human genes to assert themselves temporarily."

"What do you mean?"

"Don't worry yourself about the details, Princess. I'll soon have your transformation set to rights." Something chimed on the table, and Lady Hethra referenced a small, enclosed screen. "Ah yes. As I feared."

Unara took another deep gulp of the oxygenated water before asking, "What is it?"

"I'm afraid that your gothi was not handling this properly, Unara. There are irregularities in your new gene-code that should not be there. If you had received your last infusion, it's extremely likely that you would have suffered profound and systemic organ failure, or at the very least, rapid and fatal tumor growth." Lady Hethra looked at the printout again. "Yes, yes, this is a problem, Princess."

"Truly?"

"Yes. I can comprise a report for you, if you would like."

The revelation crushed Unara. She thought she had been so diligent about it, so careful. "I trusted him."

"Trust given in the hope of what one wants may often lead to disaster," Lady Hethra said. "I can fix most of this, stabilize you, but I cannot be sure that there will not be consequences. In fact, I am certain there will be consequences."

"Like what?"

"I can't be entirely sure. I'll need better genetic modeling than what I have here to get a full idea." Lady Hethra set the read-out aside. "Unara, it pains me to see such shoddy work performed on the daughter of my king. Will you allow me to fix this for you? Give you what you deserve?"

Unara felt something clench up in her gut. A warning, maybe. But she shoved it aside.

"Yes."

Lady Hethra smiled. It seemed a strange expression on her dour face, like it didn't quite fit. Her teeth were slightly too long, her lips too thin. It was the expression of a shark come in to feed. "Excellent," the abyssal chieftain said. "I'll prepare my dive akker."

"Dive akker?" Unara asked.

"This space is for treating my people who have depressurization sickness or need a quick adjustment to their own surface adaptations while here. It is not set up with the specialized equipment we'll need for a full and final transformation," Lady Hethra replied, and that strange smile broadened. "We shall have to go deeper. To my gene-hallow back home."

Gripping her mask a little tighter, Unara asked the question, already knowing the answer. "Into the blackwater?"

"Yes."

ACT TWO
DEPTHS

CHAPTER TWELVE

Descending the back ramp, Karl noticed a woman standing there. Thalassan, from the look of her—she wore some sort of skirt that resembled a fish's tail, and her gray skin and red hair was decidedly not human-standard. Her face was familiar, though, and he stopped as he approached her.

"I know you," he said. "Did I meet you yesterday?"

The woman inclined her head slightly. "I helped pull you from the beach, Lord Gyes."

"Ah. Of course. Forgive me. And you are...?"

"Vaelyn," she supplied.

It was a lovely name, he thought, for a lovely woman. But judging from the look on her face, Karl didn't think she would be receptive to such a comment. "You are my handler here?" he asked instead.

"I am your liaison, Lord Gyes," she said, and hesitated. "You should have met with me earlier. I would have warned you of the danger you were putting yourself in, venturing out that far."

"Do you know what happened?" he asked. "Some kind of weapon or something we couldn't detect?"

"Perhaps," she said. "It was not authorized by the king, if that is what you are asking."

"That's a good thing. Considering I am going to see him now, I should hate to think he tried to kill me twelve hours ago."

Again, she paused. "Lord, I did rearrange your appointment with—"

"Any alteration in Lord Gyes's schedule could be interpreted by the other Houses as a weakness," Branner said firmly. "We do not accept starting negotiations on such a footing."

"But after last night, surely—"

"It's better to be considerate of the House than the man," Karl told Vaelyn, and at her confused expression, he smiled a little. "I'm fine, but my chief financial officer here might murder me herself should we fail to finalize our outstanding contracts with King Aegyr."

She nodded. "Then I will accompany you."

The entourage set off again. Thorsen and his security detail. Branner and her herd of assistants. Karl felt vaguely embarrassed as they headed down to the palace. It was ridiculous, being accompanied so.

But then, he mused as they reached the market streets, the Gyes delegation was reserved compared to many of the others.

Every Trader House present had worked through the night to establish their pavilion. Banners flew from every spire and hung from every window. Market stalls selling everything from Alamani sausage to Zanzib jewelry had been set up in every free nook and cranny around. House Amaro had brought out more of its splendid potted trees. The Hellenic delegation under Negotiator-elect Hektir had carted in a massive fountain carved in the likeness of their ocean deity, a man with a fish's tail, surrounded by horses with fins for ears.

Karl stopped there for a moment, smiling a little at the fanciful thing. Vaelyn, on the other hand, crossed her arms, glaring at it balefully.

How did the Thalassans feel about this chaos being dragged into their quiet city of coral and stone? Karl wondered if anybody had ever bothered to ask them.

"It's Hellenic," he told her softly. "They have strange beliefs, but their artistry is exquisite. Look at this, worked from a single piece of Achillan marble."

"What is it supposed to be?"

"I believe it's their sea god."

"They think the sea is male?" she asked, incredulous.

Karl shrugged. "Maybe it is on their worlds."

Vaelyn sniffed.

"Sir, we should proceed to the palace," Captain Thorsen murmured, leaning in. He was more heavily armed than usual today, although the casual observer wouldn't have noticed. The House Guard escort, on the other hand, was attracting all kinds of attention. "It's not safe out here in the open."

"We should go, milord," Branner added. "They'll be waiting."

"Of course, of course," Karl said with a sigh. "Lead on."

At the end of the main market square was a set of strange doors. Wrought of stone and rounded, they were five meters tall and covered with delicate veins of what looked to be carved nacre. Stopping to touch it, Karl was surprised to feel how warm they were.

"It's the control organism," Vaelyn explained, gesturing at the walls surrounding the doors. "It lives in its saltwater housing in here and guards the entrance, opening and closing the doors at need."

"It is alive?"

"In a manner of speaking," she said, and led them on.

A second set of doors lay a few meters from the first. Drains and the mouths of pumps lay in carven stone housings in the space.

"Water-lock," Thorsen muttered, leaning in at Karl's side.

"So they do flood the bay," Karl agreed softly, and followed Vaelyn inside.

From the water-lock, they stepped out into a wide atrium, perfectly round, with a high dome above. The cupola had been visible from outside, rising on its round lantern base from the rock, but inside, it was far more intricate. A double ring of columns ringed the central space. The first ring supported the main tambour, where a complex series of buttresses were braced against the rock and allowed light from above to stream down. The second, wider ring of columns ran around a wall, doorways cut between them into the rock. One side of the ring was open to the sea, broad, bright windows overlooking the bay. There was no glass, and a fresh breeze blew in off the water.

But it was all strangely nondescript. Pillars, domes, vaults, balconies, stairs. None of it had any sense of design, of style. It was a world of white shapes, added to or subtracted from each other. No attempt at adornment, no frescoes or wall hangings or even furniture to fill the space. There weren't even any signs of coral growths here, as if all had been smoothed away.

"Tugs at the senses, doesn't it?" Branner commented quietly as they walked.

"Who builds something like this?" Karl replied in kind.

"We don't seek to impress you with our wealth," Vaelyn said. "This is not a rich world."

"The gold in our hold might say differently," Captain Thorsen said, deadpan.

Vaelyn brushed that aside. "What good is gold against the typhoons of Sunwrath, Captain? What can titanium ingots do against the kraken swarms that devour entire clans?"

"Perhaps we may judge your wealth by the richness of the ecosphere here," Karl said. "Your oceans are a wonder, from what I have read about them."

She cocked her head, as if trying to determine whether or not he was joking, but then looked away again. "The king's hall is just ahead," she said. "I shall see if we may maintain the original order."

They soon reached another set of doors, similar to the palace's main gates in every way but scale: these were smaller, only three meters high, and the webbing on them appeared to be made of pure titanium.

A pair of Thalassan guards in brilliant nacre armor stood at either side of the gate, wicked-looking spears in hand. In front of them was a small cluster of off-worlders, talking softly amongst themselves in a language Karl didn't know.

The Suyarii.

"Ah, Lord Gyes!" Lord Imran said, waving a friendly hand. He was dressed rather more formally today, his coat dripping with medals and pearls looped through his turban. "It is good to see you. Have you recovered from the night's ordeal?"

"What ordeal is that?" Karl asked mildly.

"Your spacecraft sinking, of course. Have you been able to determine a cause?"

"No questions," Thorsen grunted, attempting to step forward, but Karl held him back.

"You must forgive my bodyguard," Karl said. "We were unaware that news had spread so quickly."

"Ah, yes, well, I know about it from orbital surveillance. Perhaps the word of your unfortunate accident is spreading rapidly amongst the other Houses," Imran said with a smile. "They haven't seen fit to share such things with me yet."

The doors opened again. Vaelyn was back.

"The king will see you first," she told him, and nodded to the Thalassan standing slightly to the side of the Suyarii group. "Your lord will have to wait."

"And why is that?" Imran asked, a hint of arrogance creeping into his previously friendly tone. "I was told I could see him today."

"First among equals, milord. The Thalassans honor their word and their history," Branner replied coolly.

"And what history is that?"

"House Gyes discovered this world nearly fifteen hundred years ago," she replied, and turned her back on the other trader. "Thank you, Vaelyn."

"Lead on," Karl said, turning the conversation with Imran over in his mind even as the doors were opened and his small delegation stepped inside.

Darkness.

There was nothing but darkness down here.

Unara had been to the blackwater. Once. Only once. Her father had been inspecting some of the deepwater mollusk beds and had taken his daughters along with him. Those beds lay south of the palace reefs in a place where the continental shelf dropped off precipitously to the upper abyssal plain, three kilometers below. Not so deep in relative terms—in places, the Drift Clans said, the ocean was eight kilometers deep—but enough to require the use of dive craft.

Things grew slowly at that depth, but the pressure was significant, enough to change the composition of the shells that the mollusks formed, perfect for incorporation into starship shielding. Food was likewise scarce there, and despite the fact that the mollusks did receive supplemental nutrition, they were spread thin: each animal had a fifteen-meter radius of empty sand around its location.

Unara had been eight, and marveled over how the small mollusks, barely bigger than her fist, would eventually reach a market size of three meters.

"We seed this field with the expectation that it shall be ready not by the coming kaupang, but the one after it," King Aegyr had told his daughters. "We plan for the future here on Thalassa. All things serve the next generation."

Looking back, Unara supposed he was trying to make some kind of point about clan and legacy. But as a child, the only thing she had really noticed was the emptiness. That vast, barren plain, utterly empty.

She had never wanted to see it again.

"Nervous, Princess?" Lady Hethra asked.

The deep-diving akker was far from a comfortable thing. It was similar to the grand akker that were used for long-distance journeys on the reefs: interior compartments, powerful suction jets, trailing arms covered in delicate suckers. But unlike the reef-bound models, this one's interior was segmented into three separate compartments, nestled inside of each other. For the pressure, Lady Hethra had explained as she had ushered Unara into the space. But even that would have been alright, had the akker not been entirely transparent.

Only a double layer of bioluminescent cells—one on the outer skin of the akker and another inside, in their pressurized compartment—gave any indication of separation from the sea outside.

It was unnerving.

Or maybe that was just her brain going a little haywire as old genetics battled the new in her nervous system. The breathing apparatus that Unara was having to rely on now wasn't helping her anxiety, either. Somehow, having to suck super-oxygenated water out of a mask, while still surrounded by the sea, made her feel like she was drowning.

"You're looking nervous," Lady Hethra said now. She was settled into a hollow in the akker's fleshy interior wall, stroking the command column next to her. This contained a not-insignificant portion of the akker's nervous system, Unara knew. The training and guidance of such massive bio-craft as this was an art form, one passed from generation to generation. Piloting one could take a Thalassan decades to learn. To see anybody handle it so casually was a strange sight.

"I don't think I have been in an akker such as this," she said, hoping her fear wasn't showing. "It is...curious."

"It is that," Lady Hethra agreed. "But pigments are not necessary for the protection of flesh, down beyond the reach of the suns, and many creatures look like this."

"So you do this to honor the animals of your section of the sea?" Unara asked.

"Not entirely," Lady Hethra replied. "We do it for practical reasons as well. All the better to see with."

See? Unara almost asked. What was there to see down here?

But then, as if she had heard Unara's thoughts, Lady Hethra leaned forward and pointed. "Ah," she said. "Here we are."

WHILE THE PEOPLE of Thalassa often lived in isolated communities, sometimes separated by many hundreds of miles, the Abyssal Clan had a few production sites relatively close to Oceanfall. Thalassa was a young world and still quite volcanically active; the deep sea vents were scattered far and wide across the ocean floor near the shores of Fjorgyn. Here, in the heat and the pressure and the utter darkness, the Abyssal Clan synthesized many of the compounds vital to the world's fabled regeneratives. The blackwater may have held much terror for the Thalassans, but it was essential to not only their star-trade, but their very way of life.

This place, however, wasn't the site she had visited with her father on their last diplomatic excursion. Or if it was, she did not recognize it.

They had come down about five years ago, bearing gifts, in order to deliver a fresh load of pressure-rated glass and discuss progress on a few important compounds. Back then, there had been an entire city built from stone and titanium, glass and shark-bone, sprawled out around the knees of a vast vent field. Even with the best of Thalassan gene-craft, the vent fields lay at a thousand meters or more, well past crush depth for an unchanged human body, and they were brutally hot. The people here employed both pressurized habitats and specialized akkers for survival.

But even with that, the city had been bustling. Akkers darting through the huge vent columns, performing maintenance or harvesting freshly synthesized compounds or scaring away the crabs that might disturb the bacterial culture mats. Outer patrols looking to scare away any kraken or blackwater sharks that might roam close, looking for prey. The pressurized structures glowing with thousands of lights, like blue stars in the night sky. The people had been gray, cold, strange, but their welcome had been warm.

None of that seemed to be here today.

There was no city. Or at least, there was no city that she could see; all was dark below them.

Lady Hethra's akker did have light within it, and now that light was directed outward as well. So Unara got a clear view of the vents. The columns reached high, built over the centuries from the minerals condensing from their flow. Some were dead, but many remained active. Shimmering smoke poured from the living chimneys, and all manner of strange depth-adapted creatures clung to their sides.

But no people. There were no people anywhere.

"Life began here, you know," Lady Hethra said, interrupting Unara's thoughts. "Down here in the depths."

"The sagas say otherwise," Unara replied. The akker was swimming through the columns now; the scale of them was staggering.

"What do the sagas know? Even the best of them only go back to humanity's arrival on this world," Lady Hethra said dismissively. "Nobody wonders. Nobody bothers to look. That is the problem with this world, my dear princess. Nobody asks the real questions, so nobody ever gets the real answers. Life began here in the depths, a long time ago."

Unara held the breathing mask to her mouth, staring out at the smoking columns, wondering where Lady Hethra was going with this conversation.

"Long before the meddlers came," the abyssal chieftain continued in a sing-song voice, "like that feii bitch currently in the employ of House Gyes, the ocean had already given birth to its chosen children. Back then, volcanic activity was much stronger. Vent fields such as these were found everywhere. But the feii did not care about the depths, did not care about the ocean's true children. So they enslaved Rota to stabilize the axial tilt. The volcanic activity died down. The vent fields retreated. The epipelagic zone began to dominate, showering the depths with its filth. All was disordered."

"But we fixed it," Unara said, confused as to what Lady Hethra meant. "Hildra and the others, they fixed it. They brought balance to things."

"Yes," Lady Hethra said, stroking the command column. "Yes. Hildra and the others."

Unease was rippling through Unara now. "How do you know this, Lady Hethra?"

"About the depths?" The other woman's red tail flicked slightly. "I looked, Unara. I wondered, and I looked. Our people are so busy fighting the sharks and the kraken and the suns that nobody has time to care about anything else. But we are a species of explorers, Unara, of scientists and adventurers! I honor our species by uncovering these truths about our world! And you, you have that spirit in you. It is a rare gift among Thalassans and one of the reasons I wish to help you."

Unara didn't know what to say. "Thank you."

Lady Hethra just smiled that strange smile again. "Don't thank me yet, Princess. This shall be extraordinarily painful."

Unara knew that the water outside had to be unbearably hot; the fluid issuing from the grand chimneys had to be well above boiling. And indeed, they skirted the smaller columns for a while before approaching what looked to be an entire underwater seamount, covered in individual vents.

Carved into its side was a pressure lock.

At a few taps of the command column, the akker jetted around, working its way around the lock.

"A failed island," Lady Hethra explained as the craft maneuvered. "It grew and grew but the lava subsided. And now it is mine."

Unara eyed it warily. She knew, coming down here, that she

would have to exit the akker eventually. But being faced with it now was unexpectedly daunting. "The pressure inside is survivable?"

Lady Hethra laughed. "Of course. This is where my clan comes before we ascend to the surface. Even I have to undergo certain adaptations before visiting your reefs, Princess. But I will admit, I did have to have it adjusted for your comfort." The lights inside the compartment flared. "Ah, here we are. Seal achieved. Princess, will you follow?"

Unara stared through the transparent akker toward the doorway. It was open, but nothing inside was illuminated. It was darkness like she had never seen, and something about it made her quite nervous. It was more than the lack of light. Something was wrong here. Wrong.

But her lungs were screaming at her now and her heartbeat was erratic; she didn't have much time. It was either this or death.

She nodded. "I will follow."

Lady Hethra smiled. "Then we shall give you your legs."

"That settles three of our primary accounts. Prices are slightly above ideal, but nothing that eats into our reserves. Now, if you consider the figures in column gamma here, you can clearly see that the barter rate for—"

Karl held up a hand. Branner stopped talking immediately, laying her tablet down on the table. "Something wrong, milord?"

What wasn't, today?

His audience with the king had been short, almost perfunctory. The Thalassans, it seemed, didn't care to stand on ceremony. A few little trinkets were exchanged. Metal samples were handed over to be analyzed. A handful of words were spoken.

"I apologize for dropping a spacecraft in your ocean, King Aegyr," Karl said.

The king waved it away. "You weren't eaten by anything, so we shall consider it a victory. But we must see about getting the spacecraft out."

"I would like to see where it is before you raise it. If that is possible."

"It might be," the king conceded. "But for now, please know I am glad the son of my old friend is safely walking back under the sky."

"Friend?" Karl smiled. "You only see us every fifty-seven years."

"The time and tides have no bearing on such matters. He has proven himself true more than once, and I honor that. The only force on this world stronger than water is a man's word to those he values." Then King Aegyr nodded, whispered something to one of his attendants, and walked away.

And that was that, it seemed.

As strange as the initial meeting was—they hadn't even talked about standing contracts, nor surpluses—Karl couldn't let himself worry about it. Branner said it had gone well, and he trusted her judgment. Besides, there were at least four other clan delegations Karl had needed to talk to that day.

Almost everything Thalassa sold to the greater Spiral was biological in nature, and therefore subject to some changes. Sometimes new nacre formulations didn't turn out right, or an entire reef of regenerative precursors might get wiped out in a storm. In the case of severe impacts, there would be a scramble between Houses to determine who could snap up their full quota while leaving the others with only partial fulfillment. The weather had been kind since the last kaupang, it seemed, and there was a bumper crop of almost everything on offer.

It should have all been so simple. Father always made it sound simple.

This was Karl's first major round of negotiations. Today had been exhausting, and these were only the preliminary overtures. He had withdrawn back here for something to eat and a chance to regroup.

Now, he gave Branner a weary smile. "We've been at this for almost ten hours now. I need a break."

She folded her hands on top of the tablet, careful, like a cat minding its claws. "Milord, we have very little time here on the surface of this world. Every second matters."

"I understand that."

"And in that very little time, we have at least eight different entities with whom we must review current contract fulfillment and negotiate new—"

"I understand," he said, a little more forcefully this time. "But I need a break from the ledgers. Just for a little while. So, without bringing up numbers, what's the main focus for tomorrow?"

She glanced down at her tablet again and shook her head, silver hair falling down around her ears. "We have to talk to the Forest Clan, milord."

Karl rubbed his temples. "We need their nacre." It wasn't a question.

"Absolutely, milord. It's essential. Our contracts with the sector naval forces alone—"

He waved his hand. She stopped. "Any idea why the Forest Clan refused our meeting today?" They were the only major Thalassan trading partner who had not opened their doors immediately when Karl's delegation had stopped by. Even Vaelyn couldn't get him an audience.

"I should know more tomorrow once my people have a chance to report in tonight," Branner replied.

Every House, as far as Karl knew, utilized intelligence operatives during trade negotiations like this. The Thalassan kaupang was short, chaotic, and highly lucrative. Finding out what deals the other Houses were making, watching their movements, trying to push them subtly in one direction or another, were all common tactics. Mercifully, Branner was in charge of that aspect of things.

Karl nodded, then got up, pacing over to the window. They were in one of the smaller chambers on the upper floor on the seaward side of the pavilion. Twenty meters below, the ocean lapped at the base of the cliffs. The water was calm right now, as still as deep interstellar space. The tranquil blue stretched for nearly a kilometer in all directions, the cliffs encircling it like a girdle.

Branner came up alongside him. "The last two times I was here, my team worked sixteen- to eighteen-hour days. As House representative, you set the terms with the clans, but we follow up on all the details."

He smiled at her. "Don't take this as a repudiation of your work, Madame Branner."

"I don't," she said, and nodded. "Don't worry about the numbers right now, milord. I'll make sure they're correct. I'll have my team start working on what we've already discussed, let you enjoy this glorious view in peace."

"Thank you," he told her.

Karl stood at the edge of the balcony for a while longer. An easterly breeze was picking up, blowing through the fine silk curtains his people had hung yesterday. He closed his eyes for a moment, wishing he was anywhere else on this strange world.

"Lord Gyes?"

He started a little, turning to see Vaelyn there. She opened her hands apologetically.

"I am sorry," she said. "I didn't mean to startle you."

"It's alright," he said. "I've just been a little jumpy today. Almost dying will do that to you." And he smiled, trying to let her know it was a joke.

She didn't seem to pick up on it, though.

"This is a prime view of the bay," Vaelyn observed, her pale face raised to the setting suns. "Your House holds a favored position."

He nodded down to the water below. "That looks quite light there. Is the bay so shallow?"

She smiled slightly, inclining her head. "You know water?"

"I spent a year on Caledon Prime during my schooling," he said, and at her blank expression, added, "The ocean world seat of Lord Willam's people, if you have met him."

"I am familiar with him. Almost as favored a trade partner as House Gyes," the Thalassan woman told him. "I did not realize his world was like ours."

"I don't think any world is like yours," Karl replied.

The faint smile that was on her lips vanished then, and she sighed. "This is true. The bay here isn't so deep, maybe fifty to sixty meters in some places. But what you are seeing is the shield coral, a feature ubiquitous to reefs in these latitudes."

"Shield coral?"

"It grows in the upper layers of the reef and thrives under heavy light. Its structure is somewhat translucent, and it filters out the harshest of the solar radiation. During the years of Brynhildyr's ascendence, it grows rapidly and begins to darken. By the months of Sunwrath, it will cover this entire bay, protecting all below it from the majority of the solar radiation."

"Sunwrath?"

"The period of perigee," she said stiffly, "when our planet is at its closest point to all three suns."

The way she was forced to switch back and forth between tribal norms and more accessible explanations, Karl could see, was unpleasant for her. "So it's a bioengineered life-form?" he asked.

She hesitated before answering. "It was...guided, you could say, but the original organism is one of the few remaining that predates human settlement."

He nodded, looking back down at the water. Translucent it might be, he thought, but it obscured anything below. "What lies under it?"

"Hildra's world," she replied. Karl raised an eyebrow, and Vaelyn's smile was back. "The ecosphere, I suppose would be the correct word in Standard." She pointed up, up at the faint outline of a huge moon. "Rota's reign alone was chaos, her colossal tides battering the western coast here as surely as the great storms tear at the eastern. It made life anywhere near the continental shelf almost impossible. Only in the depths could creatures cling to existence. Our ancestors called for aid and the other moons came. Hildra is their chieftain. She and her clan balanced Rota's influence, calming the seas. Together, they hold the power of life and death over all of us."

Karl digested that for a moment. "You speak of the moons as if they were aware of their role in all of this."

"They are at the heart of our understanding of our world," Vaelyn said, and she looked distracted again, almost irritated. "The story I just told you is what the skalds sing. I know the technical history. This was not the original destination of the colony fleet. There was some kind of accident with the main ship, and it was forced out of hyperspace during Sunwrath. They limped along, bleeding air, until they found this world. But the oceans were wild. Huge tidal swells made settling on the coast nearly impossible, while the interior was entirely inhospitable. Many died, and the rest lived in terror."

Karl nodded.

"The first colonists in desperation sent the last of their space fleet out into the asteroid fields to capture a body large enough to counteract Rota's pull on the oceans. The mission took years. Many of the crew died along the way. But Hildra was found and gravity-towed into her present position, dragging the others along with her." She paused for a moment. "I suppose to a House like Gyes, with so many resources at its disposal, that sounds foolish."

"Not at all." Karl shook his head. "Colony development is a fraught enterprise, and the people who go on such journeys can be endlessly inventive. Good people."

"You speak as if you know them firsthand."

"I trained as a navigator and pilot in our House's expedition fleet," he told her, and at her blank expression added, "The portion of our business that seeks out new systems for human settlement."

"So there are still new worlds to be discovered?"

"Endless worlds," Karl replied, and hoped he didn't sound bitter.

For a moment, Vaelyn didn't speak. She picked at an invisible speck of dirt on her sleeve, watched the curtains blow in the wind, fiddled with her hair, before she said anything more.

"I did come with news."

He sighed internally. "Please tell me the Forest Clan doesn't want to meet tonight."

"What? No." And she frowned. "I still have not received word from Jarl Yvar about a meeting time. But the king did say I could take you to your ship."

"Excellent," Karl said, some of his weariness lifting at the idea of getting to see more of this fascinating world. "When can we leave?"

"Immediately, if you wish."

"Oh, I do. I do."

CHAPTER THIRTEEN

"A machine?" Karl asked Vaelyn as they stepped into the subterranean grotto.

She had led him through the palace, going further and further down, leaving behind the strange organic flow of Thalassa's architecture, venturing into this chamber which had to be entirely natural. And in a large pool at the far end bobbed a small vehicle, streamlined like a reef fish. A clear acrylic bubble set into the body held seats for two people.

Vaelyn just shrugged, making for the vehicle. "We are not savages here, Lord Gyes. We know the art of mechanics, even if we don't often choose to practice it."

The submersible, once Vaelyn opened the bubble and they were able to climb in, was small but surprisingly comfortable. The smell, on the other hand, took a little getting used to. The seats had been grown out of some kind of seaweed and stank. Sitting there, watching Vaelyn go through her pre-launch checklist, Karl concluded that his current set of clothes would need to be incinerated after this was all over.

He considered the thickness of the canopy above them. "This

does not seem like it would withstand high pressures," he commented.

"It's only rated for two hundred meters," Vaelyn said absently.

"I hear many varieties of nacre mollusks are grown in deeper waters than that."

"As you said," she replied, still without looking up, "this is not biological. It is just for expeditions such as ours here. If we were to go out to the blackwater, we would need an akker."

"An akker?" Karl asked, fascinated.

"A squid boat, an organic ship," she said awkwardly, as if this was a piece of information that had escaped her without her permission.

"I'd love to see one."

"No, you wouldn't," she told him flatly, and tapped something in the control panel. The submersible jerked, then began slowly descending. Cut free of its docking clamps, Karl figured.

And down they fell. Back into the Thalassan sea.

THE REEF here was unlike anything Karl had ever seen.

After a short journey through an underwater tunnel, they emerged out of the cliff face into a world utterly alien to the void-raised trader.

They had emerged outside the bay, on the ocean side of the cliffs. The nighttime ocean danced with light; from corals clinging to the rock face around them, from vast anemones waving in the currents, from creatures, small and large alike, floating like stars all around them. Through it all swam other sea life, hunting and hiding, flitting away from the submersible's running lights, or coming close to bite at them. The cliffs continued here, dropping down into darkness, but the submersible stayed close, close enough for Karl to take it all in. A vertical garden, as vibrant as the surface world was dead.

"It's beautiful," he commented to Vaelyn.

Her face was set in a hard, blank expression. Whatever she was feeling, she wasn't giving it away. "This reef is badly degraded by the landing fields above. It takes decades to recover after the kaupang, and as soon as it does, it is injured again by the next kaupang."

"How?" he asked, incredulous. How did the rest of Thalassa Prime's oceans compare if this, here, was degraded?

"Industrial runoff," she said. "After your ships all leave, the storms will come. The aftereffects of the atmospheric disturbances. Rain and wind wash off engine residues into the seas. It is most concentrated here."

He thought about that. While fusion engines kept the largest ships warm and mobile in the void, many craft, including the transatmospheric cargo lifters, still needed liquid fuel. "But you have strict emissions regulations for any ship landing here."

"Even so, it's not enough."

"Then why not just build an elevator?" he asked. "One of those could—"

"No," she said.

He looked around some more. "Is the concern for pollution why you use biological vehicles?"

Vaelyn frowned. "A fringe benefit, perhaps. Now, enjoy the view, Lord Gyes. It's a two-hour trip to where your ship went down."

The reef grew deeper, the outcroppings of coral taller and further apart, canyons in the underwater landscape. Vaelyn took them down through one of those, diving precipitously. Soon, the light around them faded to an eternal dusk, the water filtering the sunlight from above, and Vaelyn switched off the cockpit lights.

Other lights came out. Blue and white lights, rippling in the ocean depths around them.

"Lantern squid," she told him, "migrating to the surface to feed. I have swung out away from the cliffs. We are close to the edge of the continental shelf here, and the currents are too strong for this little craft. We're traveling over about a thousand meters of water here."

In the soft illumination of the bio-lights all around them, he saw her mouth was pinched. Nervous, he thought. "Is it unusual on Thalassa to travel over deep water?"

"Not without caution," she said, but would offer no more details about it. She didn't speak again for a long while.

Karl settled in to watch the squid's vertical migration. Seeing so much life, after how barren the surface was, was quite the revelation. But it worried him, too. Where there was such abundant prey, larger predators would surely be lurking.

What kind of monsters did the ocean of Thalassa hold?

He had a flash of memory—hands, gray and decayed, reaching for him in the rising water. Karl thought about his sword, propped up behind his seat. He shouldn't have left it behind the night before.

All unpleasant thoughts, he decided, and tried to turn his mind to other things.

He would see it all for himself soon enough.

After perhaps an hour, Vaelyn switched on a powerful set of floodlights mounted in the craft's nose. The entire area was soaked in a brilliant white light. Here and there, silver glinted as animals sought refuge from the sudden intrusion.

He stared around in disbelief at the ocean floor below them.

"There's nothing here," Karl said.

Vaelyn appeared flummoxed and consulted a small screen on her side of the craft. "This is the bay where we found you," she said.

"Are you sure about that?" he asked sharply.

"I can ascend and show you if you like," she replied, sounding injured. "I am not lying to you, Lord Gyes. This is where your ship went down."

He looked around, confused. And then, out near the edge of what seemed to be some kind of cliff, he noticed deep furrows in the silt, exposing rock underneath. "What is that?"

She looked. "I don't know."

"Can you take us closer?"

"A little," she said, and moved the steering harness, nudging the throttle barely open.

With all the grace of a stingray, the little submersible maneuvered into position, hanging in the open water at the edge of the cliff. Hanging over the crash site. The evidence seemed unmistakable.

"The craft didn't fall over this cliff. It had to have been dragged," Karl said, looking to Vaelyn. "What manner of creature that could accomplish such a thing lives on this world?"

"A kraken, maybe," Vaelyn said, and she too looked disturbed. "They hunt along at the edges of the sea cliffs."

"A kraken? What is that?"

"The largest creature in our seas," she replied. "Nobody is quite sure whether it's a native organism or something made by the early colonists, before..." And she trailed off.

"Before what?"

Vaelyn seemed to visibly shake herself. "Nothing. It's not important. I'm sure it was a kraken. I am sorry."

"Can we go deeper? See where the craft landed?"

"It's three hundred meters to the bottom of these cliffs. I cannot take you there, not without an akker and permission from the Abyssal Clan," she said.

"The who? I don't think I recall a delegate from that clan," Karl said in reply. Vaelyn's face clenched up. He sighed. More secrets. "Alright. I would like to see the surface now."

"Of course."

IN THE FREEZING waters of the depths, Unara burned.

The past infusions had been unpleasant. This was murderous.

It began like any other Unara had received. Lie down in the treatment chair. Strap in. Infusion bag, tubing, needle. That first small prick of pain as a vein was pierced.

And then, fire in her blood.

The pain started locally, centralized around the injection site. But then it spread, spread wide, spread until she could feel nothing else. Not her tail, not her belly, not her fingertips. Her body felt like it was tearing itself apart. She fought her bonds, writhing and thrashing.

Everything but agony ceased to exist.

Still, a few impressions slipped through.

The feel of a hand on her forehead.

Words being murmured in her ear.

A mask, a breathing mask, slipping around her face.

Screaming. Screaming. *Screaming.*

And then her voice fell silent.

For a moment, Unara felt as if she was drifting in some endless dark void. Not water; the comforting touch of even that had fled. But up ahead of her, a line of silver lights burned, and in her mind's eye she thought she saw a figure holding position in the center, a silver-tailed, silver-haired woman watching her with profound sadness in her eyes.

Then even that was gone, and all remaining sense fled.

KARL STARED out across the beach. The bay was ringed by low cliffs set back a few hundred meters from the water's edge, and all that filled the space between was fine white sand. Nothing but sand.

He had been to the Caledon system once as a boy. While the bulk of the population now resided in grand orbital habitats and the title of Caledon Prime had been moved to the main gas giant, humanity's original colony world there had been much like this one: an ocean world, dominated by rough seas and small, rocky islands. Only the wealthiest families and their servants maintained residences there, but the Gyes had been guests of House Willam and had access to that wild, windswept world.

Karl had had the chance there to walk beaches similar to this one.

On Caledon, though, such places were teeming with life. Birds. Scavengers. Grand pinnipeds sunning themselves and nursing pups.

And on the cliffs beyond, blue-green grasses waved in the breeze, and the high sounds of animal calls echoed from the heights.

There was nothing like that here. No sounds but the waves lapping at the beach.

It was strange. Throughout human space, people had found ways to adapt a myriad of environments to the old patterns, almost instinctively reshaping their worlds to the template of the long-lost Old Earth.

He found himself wondering, as he stared out at that blasted landscape, why the people here, with all their bioengineering prowess, had not managed to recreate seals or birds or grass.

"We should be getting back," Vaelyn said, her melodic voice cutting into his thoughts. "I must return the submersible. One of the Amaro delegation has it reserved tomorrow for an inspection of the Oceanfall nacre fields."

Karl looked up at her. In the moonlight, with her pale skin and pale hair, she looked like a ghost. The stars were bright overhead; he saw them every day of his life, of course, but they always looked different from the surface of a planet than they did from space. They felt different down here. More real, somehow.

He grabbed a handful of sand, letting it slide through his fingers again.

Vaelyn watched him for a moment, then sat down next to him.

"This chance to see your planet makes me almost grateful to be back with the main trading fleet," he commented.

"Oh?"

"My father recalled me a few years ago. 'You've had your fun,' he said. 'Time to shoulder the responsibility of protecting the family's wealth.'" Karl snorted. "I was not even heir designate. My older sister was to take up the mantle instead. She died in an accident about five years ago. So it's my burden now."

Vaelyn nodded slowly, her hair falling around her shoulders. "A similar thing happened to a friend of mine recently. Only it was her sister who did not want the role, and when the sister...when she died, my friend's father would not give my friend the role she sought."

"Family," Karl said, shaking his head.

"I wouldn't know," Vaelyn replied, and her voice was quiet now, barely more than a whisper on the sand. "I never knew mine. They left me at Oceanfall as a baby."

For a little while, neither one of them spoke. The moons shone overhead. Quiet waves lapped at the shore.

Something crawled out of the water.

Tentacles.

Cloudy and pale, almost transparent in the moonlight. Yet they were huge and covered with suction cups larger than his head. The water around the base of them was frothing white, more and more and more emerging by the second.

They were both on their feet now, Vaelyn stepping back, a look of horror on her face.

In one of those tentacles, he realized, was something small and dark.

A human body.

A tentacle crashed down between them, the wriggling end of it going for Vaelyn.

The submersible lay only a little way down the beach. Karl was running now, running for the vehicle, dodging another tentacle that was falling toward him. Another crashed down on the submersible as he scrambled up on the winglike outer hull.

Behind him, Vaelyn screamed.

With one great heave, Karl managed to free his sword from behind his seat and whirled around with it, just in time to see another tentacle driving straight toward him, the tip pointed at his chest like a living spear. He swung hard but the flesh gave way with barely any effort at all.

A great screech sounded from below the waves.

Vaelyn was still screaming, and he jumped free of the little submersible. It was dragged under behind him, but he didn't care.

No, he realized. Not screaming. Vaelyn was yelling. A language he didn't recognize. It didn't matter. The tentacles were battering at her. One knocked her face down in the sand, another wrapping itself around her ankle, yanking her down the beach. Karl intercepted that, hacking both off.

That seemed to infuriate the creature more, its arms flailing hard across the beach, slapping down with punishing force, trying to find him. Karl struck every tentacle that got close, but that only led to more making their way toward him. How many arms did this creature have? It seemed endless.

"That one!" Vaelyn yelled.

Karl turned, following her finger. It was the tentacle holding the body. He took off, running, vaulting a wriggling arm thicker than a lander refueling cable and hacking off several smaller ones in an effort to reach the one in question. This tentacle was huge, and it took three blows to completely sever it.

Blue blood splattered the sand. The body dropped a meter down to the sand.

All at once, the screeching stopped. The unseen monster withdrew, back into the white-foamed waves. Bits and pieces of translucent tentacles and suction cups lay scattered across the beach, now streaked a brilliant, glowing blue. The submersible was mercifully untouched.

Karl heard a soft huff.

It was the body that the creature had been carrying.

It was indeed a human. A woman with berry-red hair and that swimmer's build all the Thalassans seemed to have.

"Is she alive?" Vaelyn asked. She was sitting upright now, one knee tucked into her chest, one side of her face rubbed raw from the sand, hair a complete mess.

Driving his sword point-first into the sand beside him, Karl went over to check.

THE STARS.

THE STARS.

That was what Unara noticed first.

There were stars above her. Unara stared up at them in wonder, dashing salt water out of her vision. It burned her eyes like it burned her nose, but she scarcely noticed at the moment. There were stars up there, real and bright and brilliant, unattenuated by water or the mucous membranes that protected a Thalassan's eyes from the deleterious effects of the ocean.

This was the sky as humans were always meant to see it.

She couldn't quite recall the trip out of the labs. Somebody had put a breathing mask and heated wetsuit on her and carried her back into the akker. She remembered that. But the water was so cold, so dreadfully cold, and not even the wetsuit was enough to keep out the chill.

Had anybody come with her? She didn't know. She didn't think so. She had been too weak to move when they'd finally stopped swimming, when she could see the moonlight through the top of the akker's transparent body. So close to the surface. So close.

Then, when she hadn't moved, the akker had shoved one of its own tentacles through the water-locks to get her. Grabbed and squeezed and—

"Are you alright?"

She started to answer and then stopped.

There was no sound to it.

Her voice was gone.

Unara's elation evaporated with that realization, and she pushed up on her elbows, looking back out to sea. Lady Hethra had said there would be consequences to such a rapid transformation, but Unara hadn't cared. Not in the moment.

What could she possibly have lost?

"What was that thing? Was that the kraken you mentioned?" the man asked, looking to somebody behind him.

Unara frowned and tried to sit up. Her arms wouldn't cooperate on her first attempt, but the second was better. She hauled herself up into a sitting position and caught sight of her new lower half. Her tail was gone, her body split and shortened into a pair of human-standard legs. She stared at them for a moment, distracted.

She flexed her toes experimentally. Her new feet tingled. To be expected, no doubt.

She took a deep breath and blew it out again. What a strange thing, feeling air in her mouth. It should have been strange, even panic-inducing, but then, the transformation did come with an extensive set of neural recoding. She tried it again. The air felt strange, but good.

"Those were pretty big tentacles," the man said, and looked back at Unara. "How did that thing get you? What was it doing?"

She tried to speak, but when no words came out, she shook her head and turned to the wet sand. The man came over, kneeling down as she traced a finger through the wet sand. But the man took one look at the line of text—*that was a vehicle, you were never in danger, you shouldn't have attacked it*—and shook his head.

"I'm sorry," he told her, "but I don't understand."

Unara huffed and looked down at the words. They were written correctly. Perfect. Unara had spent years studying the Standard script. Vaelyn had always been so kind as to share her lessons with Unara. She ran a hand over it and tried to start again.

Then she realized her hand was shaking. Her entire body was shaking.

"My name's Karl Gyes," the man told her. "I take it you cannot tell me yours?"

Lord Gyes, she realized with a shock. The man she had rescued the night before. What was he doing here, back at the place where he had almost died? Looking for his fallen ship, perhaps? Thinking about his lost men? She would have saved more of them, if she could have.

When she didn't answer, though, he turned to Vaelyn. "Do you know her?" he asked.

But Vaelyn, who still seemed to be quite stunned herself, shook her head.

"A mystery for another time then," he said. "Can we get her in the submersible?"

"It will be tight, but we'll fit," Vaelyn supplied. "We really should go, before all that blood attracts something worse."

"What's worse than that?" Lord Gyes called.

"Plenty!" Vaelyn yelled back over her shoulder.

For his part, Lord Gyes held out a hand to Unara. "Shall we?" he asked.

She hesitated. There were too many unanswered questions. Why were they here? Why had she been brought to this place, of all places? And most annoyingly, why didn't the words work? It should have been right.

But Unara was exhausted. The transformation had been exhausting and the strange fight with the akker even more so. She would need food and rest and then after that, she could find the right trader with whom to negotiate her passage off-world.

Karl Gyes would be a good candidate. There was a connection here now. She had saved him and he had saved her. In Thalassan culture, such ties made two people as close as blood.

She took his hand.

And walked upon her own world for the first time.

CHAPTER FOURTEEN

Unara woke in full daylight, a brilliant wash of white light that seemingly filled the entire room. For a moment, all she registered was that she was in the air, and she thrashed at the sheets around her.

"Peace, Thalassan."

There was something about the voice that could not be ignored, and Unara found herself relaxing, almost against her own will. She blinked furiously, but her eyes couldn't pick out any details against the harsh white glare of the suns.

A whir, a hiss, and shadows fell in the room. Louvered shutters of some translucent material closed overhead. The light faded enough for her to once again pick out details.

The room was small by Thalassan standards, barely large enough to have fit a full-grown ocean-born. Everything was angular, smooth, like it had all been formed out of one single sheet of glass.

And standing by the door was a figure. Humanoid: head, two arms, two legs, all in proportions similar to a human. But it was too thin, too slender, and its face seemed to be a poured mask of silver.

There was nothing human about it.

Who are you? Unara tried to ask, but no words came out. Just a hiss of air.

"That is what they told me," the strange creature said, coming closer now. "That you could not talk."

Unara just stared at the creature. What was it? What was this place?

"You have not seen one of my kind before," it said. It wasn't a question, but a statement of fact, delivered with confidence. "The feii, we are called in the standard human tongue. I have no idea what the Thalassans might call us. You don't approve of me. I can tell. Although you"—and now the feii came closer, fingers lifting Unara's chin up gently—"are in no position to judge. There is the stink of genomancy about you, girl."

Unara shook her head. What was this thing talking about?

The feii chuckled and took Unara's chin a bit more firmly. "Now, if you shall just relax, I shall see."

Nothing seemed to happen. No words, no movement. And yet, Unara felt a burning, subtle at first, localized to the underside of her chin where the feii was touching her. Then it spread, growing, strengthening, until it was unbearable.

She threw the feii off, collapsing, panting, to the bed. There was moisture on her skin. She stared at her wet hand, confused, then looked back to the feii.

She had pushed the alien harder than she had meant to. The mechanical body had hit the wall with enough force to damage the arm. In the low light, something seemed to shine through the cracks.

The feii caught her staring and calmly began wrapping up the arm. "This form is not me. I am housed within it, Thalassan. Think of it as an environmental suit. Dive gear. I am sure you are familiar with such concepts."

Unara just kept staring.

"A long shot, attempting to read your past, but worth the effort. Lord Gyes wants answers, after all," the feii mused, and then nodded to her. "I am Eyr, healer and advisor to the House of Gyes, in whose drop-craft you now find yourself. After Lord Gyes carried you back here last night, he asked me to ensure your well-being. At least, for the time being."

Carried her back?

The feii, Eyr, continued. "Ah. Yes. Of course. You were unconscious. Vaelyn brought her little submersible in near the aquarium complex and Lord Gyes had to carry you the rest of the way here. You were covered in blood when I examined you."

Unara stared. Blood?

"From your feet, I believe. Lots of little wounds there, like old cuts your skin had not closed over yet. But do not worry, I've attended to it," the feii said. Unara stared at the strange creature. It did not seem to notice or care. "You shall find clothes in the wardrobe here and you are welcome to go anywhere in the drop-craft that you please, with the exception of the command deck, of course. Is there anything you require at the moment?"

Unara wanted to shake her head, wanted this creature to leave her alone, but then her stomach made the decision for her. Rumbled out loud.

Eyr nodded. "I shall give you a few moments to dress, then I shall accompany you to the galley. Perhaps we shall find some way to communicate."

After the feii left, Unara got up to check the wardrobe. With the blanket still draped around her shoulders, she rifled through the clothing. Gauzy dresses and fitted tunics both, good approximations of the clothing that Thalassan women wore. She chose something soft and flowy with a firm over-bodice, something that reminded her of her fish-leathers and nacre breastplate and bracers.

That was all lost now, she thought as she dressed. She had left it behind at Lady Hethra's gene-hallow. Maybe she could have it fetched back from the depths before the trade houses departed.

If she could convince any of them to take her with them.

Struck by the magnitude of that possibility—of being left behind here—she tied up the last few little ties. Unara didn't like a feii being here, much less allowing the thing to be her guide, but if she wanted to get what she had come for, she figured she had better take what she could get.

It took her a moment to open the door. Thalassan construction seldom incorporated the feature, and then, usually in the altered form of a sphincter, opening in the center, fleshy. This one was mechanical and slid back into the wall at a touch of her hand. She wondered at that, looking around at it as she stepped into the hall.

The feii looked her over. "You forgot shoes," she said, and pointed. "May I suggest you wear those? They should fit over the bandages."

Unara followed the creature's finger to a pair of soft boots at the foot of the bed. Cheeks flaring with embarrassment, she went back to grab them. Her new feet protested as she shoved them into their new coverings.

"Shall we find you sustenance now?" the waiting feii asked once she'd finished.

Unara nodded.

She did need to eat.

"Lord Gyes. You seem...rested."

Karl smiled at Vaelyn. She was waiting for him in the shadow of the drop-craft again. "That's kind of you," he said, and stretched a little. "But I'm sure it's a lie."

"Not at all, milord. You do seem invigorated."

"A midnight stroll on the beach with a beautiful woman will do that to you," Captain Thorsen muttered beside him in Rikstag.

Karl shot his bodyguard a look. "There are plenty of sea monsters on this world, it seems. Perhaps you'll get to fight one with me while we're here," he replied in kind, and switched back to Standard. "My apologies, Vaelyn. Captain Thorsen here is quite upset

148

with me for last night. I think he's upset he didn't get to stab a sea monster."

Vaelyn actually smiled at that. It was quite a lovely expression on her, Karl thought.

"What was it, anyway?" he pressed. "One of your kraken?"

She pressed her lips together, that warm smile becoming a cold line in her gray face, and said nothing.

"I understand we have an appointment with the Forest Clan?" Branner asked, coming down the ramp herself. She hadn't slept last night, Karl knew, and her eyes were slightly glassy from stimulants. "Why are we dawdling here?"

"Waiting for you, madame," Karl said with a slight bow. "I wouldn't dream of approaching the negotiating table without you."

"Although you had no problem fighting a kraken without me last night," Captain Thorsen grumbled, again in Rikstag.

"Cheer up, all of you," Karl said. "As my father told me before we came down here, any day we get to stuff the *Vanatar* full of nacre is a wonderful day for the House. Vaelyn, please, if you will. Lead on."

THE DROP-CRAFT, Unara thought, was a marvel.

It was much larger than the craft she had rescued Lord Gyes from. It was of a similar design inside, but on a much grander scale. Utilitarian, perhaps, but quite exotic to her eyes, and she found herself gawking like a child at a clan fair.

The feii led Unara through passages and past doorways and up stairs until they arrived at a wide balcony, covered with glass, overlooking the landing fields and the tall cliffs beyond.

Unara walked over to the edge of the glass, unable to help herself, struck by the sight.

"This is where the humans take meals. I am told your people enjoy looking out across the landscape as you eat."

Nodding slowly, Unara put a hand on the glass. The light was not the harsh sun of her cabin, the burning white of the system's three suns. It was softer here, not tinted but reduced, as if a pleasant twilight resided in the room.

"Self-tinting glass," the feii explained without prompting. "This drop-craft is used on many different worlds with many different environmental conditions. A mobile mansion and operating location for the House. Comfort demands adaptation. Now, if you would join me?"

Unara's legs were aching again. She nodded.

Despite the feii's words, the alien ate and drank nothing. Instead, she sat and talked as a liveried servant brought Unara her meal. It was a local species of meat-fish, which was a kind gesture, but it had not been raised in Thalassa's oceans. Unara could taste the difference, and it was not in the dish's favor. There was a side of vegetables, however, that tasted heavenly.

"Potatoes," the feii said after the server brought a second helping. "Cultivated across much of human space."

Unara absorbed this new piece of information greedily. She felt better about her decision to undertake this change already. She had never heard of this food before, but it was delicious. What other discoveries were out there to be made?

She rubbed at her new legs under the table.

The things would not stop tingling. It was alright now that she was sitting, but walking had been painful. Her body getting used to its new form. That was all.

"Lord Gyes told me that you attempted to write something for him," the feii said, and drew out a book. "I assume you know Standard."

Unara nodded and took the book, paging through it. The design was unfamiliar, the paper thinner and lighter than the kelpskin vellum she was accustomed to. But right away, she could tell there was a problem. The individual letters were familiar. The grouping and spacing was correct. But it was all completely unintelligible.

Not believing what she was seeing, Unara flipped through further.

Nothing. She could read nothing.

She set the book down again, mind spinning. The feii took it from her.

"As I thought," Eyr said. "In other circumstances, I might be able to use my skills to find a work-around. But it seems that we shall have to find a way to muddle through. Unless, of course, you wish to teach me your language."

Unara shook her head, biting her lip. Being unable to make sense of written Standard was not a problem that she had anticipated. It would make securing passage far more complicated, especially considering the loss of her pearl collection.

"I have distressed you," the feii said, and stood. "Not my intention, so I apologize. But allow me to take my leave from you now, Thalassan from the sea. I have much to attend to. Thank you for your company. It has been enlightening."

It occurred to Unara then that this feii had been questioning her. The realization didn't sit well with her. But she was a princess, raised by her father's side as he navigated the fractious politics of their world, and she knew how to keep herself in check. House Gyes was her best chance of getting off-world. There was no point in offending them. So she smiled politely and nodded back.

With the feii gone, Unara picked at her potatoes, trying to plan her next step, distracted.

Her legs hurt.

THE THALASSANS WERE NOT, Karl had noticed, a people who stood much on ceremony.

Last year, he'd accompanied Branner and another of the House's senior negotiators on a trade expedition to Epsilon Merovingia. The Merovingi used pomp like a weapon, every little detail signaling some kind of meaning in the negotiations, right down to the color and number of flowers in table arrangements. It had taken months to get through the negotiations. An exhausting, irritating experience.

By contrast, dealing with the Thalassans was a joy.

A few introductions, a few handshakes or polite bows, and then it was right down to business.

That was how things started at the Forest Hall.

Started.

"It is good to meet you, Lord Gyes. I am meeting with everybody. Out of respect, you understand. It is good to look another man in the eye and speak to him directly," Jarl Yvar said.

This clan representative was young, younger than Karl was himself. Another interesting feature of these negotiations. Karl had not yet seen any old Thalassans. With the exception of the king, everyone here seemed to be under the age of thirty years, Standard. Even with the best regeneratives, there were always telltale signs of a person's age. Perhaps the process was more refined for the Thalassans, so close to an endless supply of the compounds that cost the wealth of entire star systems.

"It is good to meet you too," Karl replied. "I look forward to honoring the contract that our fathers signed together. Your nacre is some of the finest on the planet and—"

Yvar held up a hand. "My nacre is the finest. Some may grow it deeper for a better ablative rating, while others may formulate more artistic color schemes, but ours is the perfect balance of energy absorption and strength."

"Yes, this is true," Karl said. "It is unsurpassed in quality."

"And eighty-five percent of the crop is owed to us," Branner said, going over a stack of kelpskin printouts the Thalassans had provided her when they sat down. "Have you had such a terrible harvest?"

"No," he said. "It has been exceptional."

"Then why are we short six hundred and thirty tons?" she asked, holding up one of the sheets.

Karl looked at her, then back to Yvar. "My advisor asks an excellent question."

The Thalassan delegate shrugged. "The situation has changed."

"The contract still reads the same to me," Branner said.

"I do not speak of contracts. I speak of hard assets. Exchange rates, you might have heard, have changed."

And then Karl understood. He sighed. "How much additional titanium did the Suyarii offer you?"

Yvar smiled. "More than you have, Lord Gyes. Now, we are still providing you the amount of nacre that can be had for the amount of titanium you have agreed to trade. Per the contract, of course."

"That is not how this works, Jarl Yvar," Branner said coolly.

"Then you expect me to sell the hard work of my people at a loss?"

"We expect that contracts will be honored."

"Then please, explain to me how I am not? I am giving you the value that we agreed upon. Current market conditions considered, of course."

Branner laid her thumb on the bio-reader lock on her ledger. "Then why don't we go through the contract line by line, Jarl," she said, flipping open the cover, "and you tell me where your interpretation of terms is supported?"

Karl rubbed his forehead.

It was going to be a miserable day.

After the feii gothi left her, Unara lingered in the galley for a good long while. She was quite thirsty, she discovered, a sensation she was not used to feeling and marveled at. She drank an entire flagon of water as she watched the starport bustle around below her.

The tingling in her legs had become quite sharp, like the sensation of her fins falling asleep, but much more intense. Standing and moving helped somewhat, she found, so that was what she did.

And there could be no better place for it. This craft was fascinating. But more than the engine room or the lower cargo hold or the upper galleries with their fine paintings, Unara wanted answers. Or at least, a path to answers.

What had happened to her written language skills?

She couldn't ask anybody, of course, and nobody seemed to wish to speak to her anyway. But Unara eventually stumbled upon a place she had been hoping to find: a library.

It was a fine place, machinery half-concealed in intricate cases wrought from brass and some kind of blue wood, far harder than anything even the oldest kelp forests could provide. She had no idea how to operate any of it, though. She wandered through the racks, growing more and more frustrated with herself. She had done all the research she could, and she had no idea what these machines even were.

There were holes in Thalassa's knowledge of the outside world, she realized. Holes large enough for a kraken to swim through.

She didn't like the revelation.

But there were books here, at least. Plenty of books.

Unara pulled one out at random, then another. The images on the covers promised many things, but she couldn't understand any of the writing.

Book after book, shelf after shelf, everything was wrong.

She finally found a section of the library that seemed to focus on mathematics. The diagrams, at least, were familiar. Geometry. And she had taken the book over to one of the small reading tables, hoping to glean something from it, when a voice behind her made her jump.

"Found something you like?"

Unara closed the book, startled by the voice. It was so quiet here on the surface, the sudden sound seemed much louder than it was.

Lord Gyes was standing there, an apologetic expression on his face. "My apologies. I've scared you."

Unara shook her head and glanced back down at the cover. At

the title that made no sense. Had something gone wrong in her brain during the change? It was said that could happen sometimes. Neural cells could not be altered to the same extent as other tissues and disconnects between mind and body could form. It was one of the many, many reasons why transformations such as this were normally temporary; there was only so long the human body could suffer the strain of being pulled so far out of its original shape.

"Ah, well, I suppose I am far from the most frightening thing on this world, if that sea monster from last night is any indication," the trader continued. "I was told you were here in the library. I'm afraid we don't have any books written in Thalassan."

No, they wouldn't, Unara thought glumly, and got up from her chair to put the book back into its place. It was an awkward moment, made more so by the fact that she couldn't speak to tell him what was wrong.

"But there is somebody who asked to speak with you. In private, was the request," he continued, almost apologetically.

For a moment, Unara went cold. Had her father found out? Already? It was those surveillance drones, those damn crabs. One of them had gotten inside the drop-craft somehow and spied her and somebody down below had passed it along to Father up here on the surface and—

"Hello again." It was Vaelyn. "Do you remember me from last night? I thought we might have a word together."

Unara raised an eyebrow. Really? They were going to pretend they didn't know each other now? But then, without her voice, there was really nothing she could do but play along. So she nodded.

"Then I'll leave you two ladies to it," Lord Gyes said, bowing a bit. "Vaelyn."

"Lord Gyes," she said, inclining her head.

After they heard the doors shut, Vaelyn sat down at the reading table, throwing her hands wide. "What happened?" she asked.

Unara threw up her hands in frustration. How was she supposed to answer that? Her friend sighed and pulled out a writing tablet. It was a tablet made for temporary note taking, a layer of damp sand pressed in between a hard board backing and a thin retention membrane. A stylus pressed into the sand, leaving the imprints of words, but the sand could be wiped completely clean.

It was something safe to communicate with. No record of their writing would be left behind for the off-worlders to find.

Unara took the stylus eagerly.

Slowly, the story came out. Thalassan runes were complex and the tablet limited; Unara had to write and clear it many times before she finished the whole explanation.

"So that was Lady Hethra's akker at the beach?" Vaelyn asked.

Unara nodded.

"I thought it might have been a juvenile kraken."

Unara glared at her, one eyebrow raised.

"Yes, I understand, they're nothing alike, but it was dark and..." Vaelyn trailed off. "Why did it attack?"

I was unconscious. Perhaps it thought I was food or some kind of invasive organism, Unara wrote.

"Yes, I suppose they have limited memories," Vaelyn sighed.

What were you doing at the beach?

"Lord Gyes requested to see the place where he almost died."

A long way in that submersible.

"He was insistent."

A strange coincidence, isn't it?

Vaelyn didn't answer for a moment. "Perhaps Lady Hethra knew we would be there," she said. "I doubt she anticipated her akker's behavior."

Unara sighed, nodding. That seemed logical. They had been friends for years. Vaelyn wasn't going to start lying to her now, was she?

I am sorry this is not what we planned, she wrote.

Vaelyn shrugged. "It is what it is, Princess."

At least I have my legs now, Unara replied. *But it is strange that my visual language processing has been affected.*

"We are lucky that is all it is," Vaelyn replied. "Imagine what would happen if you couldn't understand any of us at all."

True.

"Don't worry, Princess, I shall help you, as I promised I would. Trust me. All shall be made right."

Thank you.

Vaelyn nodded and carefully wiped the tablet. "Now come. We've left Lord Gyes waiting out in the hall."

But Lord Gyes had not waited out in the hall for them, for he was nowhere to be found when the two Thalassan women emerged from the library. Vaelyn seemed to know where to go, however. She took Unara back up to the command deck, where a low-level officer came out to speak with them.

Apparently, a messenger from the Caledon delegation had made a surprise visit. With an invitation. And Lord Gyes had already left.

"Just my luck," Vaelyn grumbled to Unara once they got the details and were headed away. "The off-worlders tend to receive each other with great pomp. Those two, Lord Gyes and Lord Willam, will be exchanging pleasantries for an hour or more. And I'll have to sit there and watch it all."

Unara looked around to make sure they were alone, then scribbled quickly on the tablet. *What happens after that at these events?*

"A reception," Vaelyn replied tiredly. "Drinking, eating, entertainment. That sort of thing."

What kind of entertainment?

"All sorts, I think. Their party the other night was exceptionally loud and crowded."

Yes, Unara wanted to say, but at least it was an opportunity to see more of the surface world and get to know these people a bit better. She laid down fresh runes. *Can I attend with you?*

"Princess, I can't recommend that. It means going out into the market streets. Somebody might recognize you!"

Unara folded her arms, staring at Vaelyn. Friends they might have been, but Unara was still King Aegyr's daughter. Even now, that meant something.

And Vaelyn seemed to get the message, because she averted her eyes, shaking her head. "I'll find you something to conceal your hair," she grumbled.

Unara smiled.

"Don't thank me yet," Vaelyn said. "You haven't met the Caledons."

CHAPTER FIFTEEN

"So what do you think of my proposal, young Lord Gyes?" Lord Willam asked from his own seat, plucking off a handful of grapes from the cluster in the dish before him.

Karl considered his answer very, very carefully before he spoke again. "I think we would risk the entire kaupang, for all of us, doing what you suggest."

"Something must be done about this Imran! I lost my contract with the Forest Clan today because of him."

"I know, I did as well," Karl sighed. "But my lord Willam, there are practicalities to consider and—"

"There is honor to consider," Lord Willam said firmly, and ripped off another handful of grapes.

Karl sighed and lounged back in his chair.

What was he supposed to say to that?

Caledon was a strange sector. Comprised of one primary star cluster, it was smaller than most. It was also distressingly primitive in its aesthetic: the hall around them, albeit fashioned from the same white corals as the rest of the merchant pavilions, was designed to look like something from one of their great castles, mimicking stone and arched wood beams. Hand-stitched silk tapestries fluttered in the evening breeze. Suits of ceremonial plate armor stood gleaming in niches. The meal tonight was served from communal platters laid out on bare wood tables, and the guests, in their flamboyant doublets and kirtles, ate with their hands.

And yet, the Caledon were the preeminent naval force in the Spiral, famed and feared for their prowess at both navigation and warfare out here in the void. Traders, explorers, adventurers all. If Karl were to set foot on the command deck of any of their ships out on the landing fields, he knew he would find a professional, serious crew, all spit and polish in the modern style, minding their machines with precision and unwavering discipline.

A very strange people.

"The Alamani delegation under Lady Nachtgail are in agreement with my assessment, as is Hektor of the Hellenic League," Lord Willam continued. He was respected, both as a trader and a strategist, but that didn't mean Karl was inclined to ally himself to the man. The antipathy between the Caledons and Suyarii was legendary, and most undoubtedly affecting Lord Willam's better judgement. "Both fleets are willing to position resources against this. Official resources."

That changed things from a military perspective, but it changed nothing from a political one. "If we challenge the Suyarii delegation here, on the ground, the Thalassans will throw us all off-world, and then we get nothing."

"If this Imran is allowed to return home with his holds full—"

"Who says he needs to leave the system at all?" Karl countered, tired. "Deal with him in the void. Not here."

"Here he is but one man. In the void, he is a twelve-kilometer mobile fortress, loaded down with goods desperately needed by the Spiral," Lord Willam said bluntly.

Assassination. That was what Lord Willam wished. An assassination of Imran. And Karl could not fault his motivations. The Suyarii were not welcome in the Occidental Spiral, and for good reason.

And yet, there was a great deal of trade with them. Their own vast empire produced many things of interest to the Occidental Sectors, and they were the gateway to the lucrative markets of the Siam, Nippon, and Zhongguo Sectors. But that trade relied on the Suyarii not having direct access to worlds like this one, precisely so they could not establish their own trade networks and bypass the Occidental Houses entirely. And then, of course, there was the nacre to think of.

By controlling worlds like Thalassa Prime, the Trader Houses of the Occidental Spiral were a key factor in stabilizing and maintaining peaceful relationships with the Orient. A political game that Karl was now a player in, no matter how much he wished he were not.

But being a player didn't mean he had to agree to murder.

"He is one man in the void as well. I will not help you with this," he said.

Lord Willam grunted, clearly about to say something, and then paused. "Ah," he said. "Would you look at that? Seven kaupangs under my belt now, and one of them finally comes to my feast."

Karl looked.

A pair of Thalassan women had just walked in.

A very familiar pair.

Vaelyn had traded her tunic and fish-leathers tonight for something a little more fluid: a steel-gray gown so light and flowy it seemed to be made out of smoke. The color only served to accentuate the paleness of her features. Her skin was almost translucent in the torchlight.

With her was the girl Karl had found on the beach. She was not dressed as her friend was, wearing something cut distinctly in the Rikstag style, complete with one of those fitted caps that hid the hair. All the rage right now, back home.

Lord Willam leaned in. "Who's the other girl, eh?"

"One of ours," Karl lied.

"One of these kaupangs I need to ask the locals for some of their gene-codes," Lord Willam murmured, leaning into Karl now. "Every

Thalassan woman I've seen is exceptionally beautiful. Just look at her. She's your escort, is she not?"

"Yes," Karl said, and pushed back from the table.

"Where are you going?" Lord Willam asked.

"To go save her from the stares of your own women," Karl said, standing. "The jealousy is almost palpable, isn't it?"

Lord Willam laughed and reached for another handful of grapes.

Karl reached them as quickly as he could, holding out his hands to both. "Ladies, what a wonderful surprise. I did not expect to see you attend one of these receptions."

"Neither did I," Vaelyn said, somewhat stiff as she always was.

"Excellent," he said, and looked to the other, the girl from the beach. With her brilliant hair hidden away and dressed as she was, she almost looked like one of his own people. Almost. The Thalassans were a strange people. Like they weren't quite real. "And it is good to see you again as well."

The girl nodded back.

"You came at a good, or maybe bad time," Karl said, sweeping a hand around and gesturing for them to follow him. "The feast is still underway, so eat if you'd like, and later there will be entertainment. Dancing, juggling, maybe a bear."

"A bear?" Vaelyn asked, raising an eyebrow. "If that's an animal, it's not allowed here."

"Well, they do it on their home worlds," Karl laughed, and put a finger to his lips. "Now come, sit, please. Rescue me from a dreadfully boring conversation about politics."

THE STRANGEST THING about the night was how familiar it all was.

Unara had been at the forefront of feasts and celebrations from a very young age. Thalassans loved them, and her father had hosted many over the years, from simple clan gatherings to grand parties where it seemed like all the world attended.

Delicacies would be gathered from near and far: mussels, urchins, reef eel, the salty little fruits of sea flowers. Liquor might be produced as well, heady and strong, harvested from specially grown kelp strains. Singing there would be, and dancing. Stories from the skalds, told to the cheers of the assembly. Politics would be discussed, lovers from different reefs might find one another, children would fall asleep in their parents' arms, lulled by the sagas of the skalds and the motion of the sea.

This was much the same. Food, singing, dancing.

But whereas Unara would normally have had some kind of role in the proceedings, here she was almost invisible. She had sat for a while at the head table, but Lord Willam had only wanted to speak to Vaelyn.

He had quite the reputation among the Thalassans: unpredictable and brash at the negotiating table, able to pull off some of the craziest deals, but always fair in the end. Unara would have welcomed an opportunity to speak with him at length. There was much to learn from a man like that. But she lacked her voice and he lacked interest, and so, she'd wandered off, trying to savor this novel experience.

Not all was well with her. Her legs ached. Unara could feel moisture in the thin slippers that had come with the dress. It was warm and thick, and so she slipped away to a back corner of the grand pavilion to see what it was.

Blood. It was blood, she saw, when she found a safe, concealed place to remove her shoe. Blood, oozing from the skin. Unara stared at it for a moment, trying to figure it out. Something was going wrong with her new skin there. Cleaning off her fingers on the inside of the long dark skirt she was wearing, she wondered what could be done about this. She was just considering the possibility of speaking to Lady Hethra about it when she saw movement.

A human form wrapped in a dark cloak, like the kind the Stone

Clan wore to shield themselves from the suns. Dropping in from a window.

It was so quick, so brief, she wondered if she had imagined it. But then the cloak slipped back and metal glinted on the figure's belt.

Unara quickly shoved her foot back into its slipper and followed.

The figure wound through the dark outer hallway of the pavilion, keeping to the shadows, the cloak obscuring most detail. Unara was not particularly skilled with walking, but she had been on many a hunt before, and knew a few things about concealment and movement, when to step out and how to stay hidden. From column to column, doorway to doorway, she followed the cloaked figure, wishing she had her knife with her.

But soon there was no time for subtlety. As they got nearer to the edge of the hall, the figure dodged behind another column and seemed to vanish. Unara stepped forward carefully, one, two—

And then something glinted in the moonlight.

Unara twisted only just in time, avoiding the knife that came swinging for her face. She blocked a second stabbing thrust with one arm, swinging out with the other in a wide haymaker. Underwater, the motion would have provided her enough momentum to keep turning, smashing her tail into her enemy's face if the initial blow missed. But this was the air, and the rules weren't the same.

Her assailant danced free. Started running.

Running for the head table.

Unara didn't think, didn't consider, just reacted. She tore after the man, pushing her new body into a run that it was not accustomed to. Over a longer distance, she never would have overtaken him. But he was only a few meters away and she reached him just before he got to the edge of the platform. Unara reached out and grabbed his tunic, spinning him around, throwing him back, throwing him down, sending his knife skittering away. He kicked out from the ground, catching her in the chest and leaping over her.

Leaping up on the dais.

And Unara couldn't even call out a warning.

Lord Gyes was dragged out of his chair, narrowly avoiding a knife to the heart. The attacker grabbed him, and the two men crashed down, rolling off the dais in a clatter of plates and spilled drinks. The assailant had a new blade out now, small and strangely shaped. Lord Gyes had both hands around his attacker's wrist, holding the weapon away from him, but the attacker was on top and pressing down with all his strength.

Glancing around frantically, Unara's eyes landed on one of the knives that had spilled from the table. Lord Willam had been cutting his meat with a similar knife, Unara remembered, and she grabbed for it.

Lord Gyes attempted to roll over, but the attacker bore down. The trader yelled as the knife tip dug into his shoulder.

Unara hated fighting. She hated killing.

But like every other Thalassan, she'd learned how to use a dive knife as soon as she could grip it. Hildra may have granted the ocean-born their lives, but keeping it was one's own business.

And Lord Gyes was—hopefully—her ride off-world.

So she didn't even stop to consider the consequences of what she was doing.

She was up, she was moving, she was grabbing the attacker's hair, yanking back, exposing his throat.

Slammed her blade in as far as it would go.

The man immediately let go of Lord Gyes, staggering up, staggering back. Dark red blood was pouring out from around the wound. It should have killed him.

Instead, he stared back at her, eyes glazed and furious, still breathing hard.

Draugr, she thought for a wild moment.

And then the man crumpled, the front of his tunic smoking. Hands clutched at his chest. There was a neat wound there, Unara could see, round and precise. The air smelt different.

She turned around to see Lord Gyes's housecarl standing there, energy pistol in hand and a grim look on his face. He looked at her for a moment and she nodded back, not quite sure what else she should do.

Then the housecarl was moving over to Lord Gyes's side. Lord Willam and Vaelyn were too, the other Gyes men forming a circle to hold back the onlookers already starting to gather.

"I say," the Caledon lord commented, nudging the body with his foot, "next time I'll let you supply the entertainment, young Master Karl."

THE DROP-CRAFT HAD something called a morgue.

The concept didn't make much sense to Unara.

A place to warehouse dead bodies.

What a horror.

She circled this particular corpse, eyeing it. She had never seen a dead human body before, and she found it to be an unnerving sight. Thalassans, ocean- and sky-born alike, tended to break down quickly after death, dissolving in a matter of moments. The stories said that it was a testament to the love between their people and the sea. But beyond the clan hearths, it was sometimes whispered that such things were the price paid for what had been done to the Thalassan genome.

"Came to see your kill?" the feii gothi asked, stepping out of some side room, pushing a tray of tools with her. She had some kind of white garment on over her environmental suit that included integrated gloves and foot covers, like a wetsuit but of a looser, lighter fit. "I hear that some humans like to do that."

Unara shook her head. She had no desire to take trophies like this was a kraken hunt. A man was dead, and she didn't feel good about that. In leaving Thalassa, she hoped to put this all behind her. Find some peace out there in the silence of the stars.

"Well then, Thalassan without a name..." the feii said, and

turned the dead man's head this way and that, forcing the eyelids open. Unara averted her own eyes. "... if you do not wish to gloat or boast or observe your handiwork, then get out of my lab. I have much to do."

Unara cocked her head.

The feii glanced up at her, unblinking. "If you must know, Lord Gyes wishes to know where this one came from and who sent him. I will follow him back through the current of time to find those moments."

Chronomancy? Unara had heard of such a thing but had never seen it done. It was not something done on Thalassa. Such procedures teetered dangerously on the edge between physics and magic. Was that what the feii had been trying to do to her earlier in the day?

"I do not even need to look at you to know you are discomforted by this idea," Eyr said, her hands firmly affixed to the dead man's temples now. "Stay and watch or get out and judge me in the silence of the corridor. I serve the House Gyes in all things. Now, back up."

Unara nodded and backed up, giving the feii the space to work.

The light from the suit's eyes dimmed.

The light in the entire room seemed to dim.

For a moment, just a moment.

A hum began, a sound that was not so much heard as it was felt.

And then a console exploded in a shower of sparks. Unara jumped, scared by the noise, fascinated by the sight.

But the feii just pulled back, flexing her hands, unfazed. "I can't look at you. I can't look at him," she said, almost accusatory. "What power lies on this world to stop me?"

Unara shook her head and spread her hands. *I do not know,* she wanted to say. But before she could figure out some way to communicate that, she caught sight of something behind the dead man's ear.

A smallish bump under his skin, it seemed, but as Unara looked at it, tiny tentacles spread out. Like a coral polyp at twilight, ready to feed.

Before Unara could even point to it, the feii had plucked it out with a pair of tweezers.

"Do you know what this is, Thalassan?" Eyr asked, holding it up, turning it around to examine it.

Unara nodded. It did indeed look like a coral polyp, but the coloring was wrong and the base of it was studded with tiny roots. Her father had once cut one from an assailant's neck after a failed assassination attempt.

A control implant. A parasitic biological device capable of tying into a host's nervous system and overriding their better judgement for the sake of one simple task. The devices were condemned as cowardice, rarely employed, but any apprentice gothi could have grown and programmed one.

"Is this a natural parasite here on this world?" Eyr pressed.

No. Unara shook her head.

"Grown by the Thalassans?"

Yes. She nodded.

"Altered by the Thalassans?"

Another nod.

"To what end?"

Unsure of how to say it, Unara gestured at the body, then pantomimed a stabbing gesture.

"Grown for this very purpose, I assume," the feii muttered. "Which of your clans would agree to something like this?"

Agree? Unara tilted her head.

"What the good healer here is implying is that somebody from one of your clans here provided this to one of the Houses for the purposes of assassinating me."

Both human and feii looked to the door. There was Lord Gyes, his uniform jacket cast aside, bandages visible under the collar of his shirt, dark hair still mussed from the fight. He seemed discouraged to Unara, which struck her as odd. He had survived, hadn't he? Most Thalassans would have been laughing.

"Is this thing traceable? Can we figure out who grew it?" Lord Gyes looked at his housecarl behind him. "Maybe if we figure out who's trying to kill me, Thorsen here will go bother them instead of me."

"This is one of the Suyarii, isn't it?" Captain Thorsen sniffed.

"This was an attempt to frame the Suyarii," Eyr said, "if you want my opinion."

"I do," Lord Gyes said, and turned to Unara. "And yours. You know more about this world and its dangers than anyone in my retinue, and you were quite good with that blade. I should like to keep you on as part of my security detail, if you will consent to it."

Unara almost refused. She was not some mercenary for hire, drifting from reef to reef with no clan of her own. But then, if being under the command of Lord Gyes's housecarl for a little while helped her win the lord's trust, earned her a place in his clan, then the indignity would be worth it.

Any way off-world was a way off-world.

She nodded.

"Good," Lord Gyes replied, and turned his attention back down to the body. "Captain Thorsen, when Healer Eyr is done here, have this body taken back to Imran's drop-ship."

"With pleasure, milord."

"Don't... do anything to it, you understand?" There was a bit of a plea in the young trader's voice. "We're merely returning an individual to his people."

"Wouldn't dream of it, milord."

"And keep that little device, Eyr. No point in sending that back. That's our evidence to hang onto."

Healer Eyr shook her head. "If this was not initiated by the Suyarii, then what good is provoking them with this body?"

Lord Gyes ran a hand through his hair. "Even if he is blameless, I suspect Imran will not be happy to learn that one of his men betrayed him in acting so. Let him investigate his own people. Maybe he'll turn something up."

"It is a fine idea, milord," the healer said approvingly. "Worthy of your father."

"It was my father's idea." Lord Gyes looked even more tired. "Thorsen, get our newest guard set up with whatever gear she prefers. She'll accompany us tomorrow."

"Consider it done, milord."

"Excellent. Now I'm going to go turn in for the night. Then we shall see who intends to kill me next."

A muscle in Thorsen's face twitched. "I don't find that particularly funny, milord."

"Convenient, because neither do I."

CHAPTER SIXTEEN

Unara adjusted the last strap on the unfamiliar armor as she stepped back out onto the main armory floor.

"How's it fit? Alright?"

Captain Thorsen was waiting for her there. He had come by her quarters early this morning. Introduced himself, taken her to the galley, before bringing her down here. He wasn't a man who talked much, which had been a relief. It wasn't that Unara wanted solitude at the moment, but with her voice missing, it made being part of a discussion rather awkward.

Unara looked down at herself.

She'd been provided with the same simple blue and gold uniform that all the House Gyes personnel seemed to wear. The trousers were uncomfortable, tight-fitting and unpleasant, although that could have just been the ever-present ache in her legs. There had been a few different options for armor, at least.

She'd chosen a breastplate. Nacre, with an extruded kevlar-silk undershell, similar to her Thalassan-made one. But the design of this was different, more angular, more minimalistic, grown to off-worlder specifications. Scaled to fit the female frame, though, which she hadn't expected. Lord Gyes didn't seem to have any other women in his personal guard.

"Looks good," Captain Thorsen said gruffly. "A bit more appropriate than that dress you had on last night." And he held out a knife to her. "I'd give you a pistol too, but we'll have to train on that a bit first. You seem like you know how to use one of these."

Nodding, she took the knife and unsheathed it. It was a good design, solid and clean, and most likely made of some kind of steel alloy. Harder than the titanium blades her own people carried. She pushed it back in and buckled the scabbard to her belt. A fishing spear would have been nice, but nobody in the Gyes delegation seemed to carry large weapons like that.

"Like this, you could be a female guard from any of the hundred worlds we've visited over the past few decades, but that hair marks you as Thalassan," he continued. "Not very subtle. You'd be most useful to Lord Gyes, I believe, if we can keep that part of your identity concealed."

Unara nodded, looking around the armory. The walls were hung with all manner of weapons. Utilitarian pieces, she guessed, but still exotic to her. And her eyes fell on a row of helmets on the back wall. Some were quite open, while others had cheek guards or full mouth coverings. Maybe that would be an answer.

Something chimed. Captain Thorsen looked down at his wrist link, then beckoned her to follow him. "We'll have to dye it later. Lord Gyes is wondering where we both are."

Unara nodded but went back to grab a helmet.

"That going to fit over your braid?" he asked, bemused.

She shrugged and handed the helmet to him, shaking her hair loose to replait it. She'd done it up in a style that was often used by her clan when on the hunt: one thick, high braid tight across the scalp, falling loose at the shoulders. Something a bit more subtle seemed to be in order.

Captain Thorsen seemed a bit startled at being handed the helmet, but didn't give it back. Instead, he motioned for her to follow, and she fell into step beside him, working on her hair as they left the armory and headed for the command deck.

The drop-ship was busy this morning, the corridors filled with people rushing to and fro, coming out of compartments in one place only to disappear again into another. Like eusocial crustaceans in the reef sponges, she thought.

The movement of humanity fascinated Unara. It was all quite novel, watching so many people try to navigate around each other while stuck to the floor.

But Thorsen didn't slow his pace at all for her, and she had to run to keep up. It hurt. The boots that came with the uniform were far more cushioned than the slippers from the night before, but she was certain she was going to find blood in there again tonight.

Perhaps Vaelyn could get in touch with Lady Hethra for her. Surely this was a problem that could be corrected.

Daylight filtered by tinted glass illuminated all corners of the central corridor. She looked up at the harsh discs of the trinary suns and wondered what it would be like to see darkness, the stars, out those high windows instead. *Soon enough,* she told herself, and walked on.

The command deck was a semicircle set against a wide, curved bank of windows. Tiered levels of consoles rose up to a flat, broad dais set with several more consoles. There was Lord Gyes up there, a half dozen advisors clustered closely around them, all of them focused on a single figure between themselves and the windows. As they got closer, Unara realized it was a projection, made of pure light.

"Yes, Father," Lord Gyes was saying, "I do believe these are the fairest terms we are going to get for the nacre plating. They were absolutely insistent yesterday."

<I set these orders down fifty-seven years ago,> the figure in light said, his lips unmoving but his voice booming from recessed speakers all around the circular pit above which he lay. <We had agreed to a price then.>

Some kind of projection, Unara marveled. The resolution was far finer than anything even the best bioluminescent larvae could have achieved. She watched it, transfixed for a moment, before she remembered her hair. She started re-braiding it as Thorsen led her up the steps.

"The presence of the Suyarii seems to have changed the basic economics here, Father, and there are three other clans we buy nacre armor from."

<But the Forest Clan's is the most important. The mining investment was vast. Without our full order, our House may leave here bankrupt.>

Unara frowned. Mining investments? Mining was for silica and lime and the other components needed for glass, not...

Ah.

The trade terms offered by Thalassa during the kaupang were deceptive. Metals were useful, of course, but Thalassan society didn't depend on them. The off-worlders seemed to value the stuff and thus it was a good currency, a way of limiting what the traders could and would take. How the off-worlders obtained it was their own concern.

But of course the off-worlders had to acquire their trade goods somehow. Gold and titanium and brass alloys. All of it had to come from somewhere. Unara had no knowledge of where that somewhere might be. She couldn't remember it ever being mentioned. Not in the kaupang archives. Not in the skalds' songs.

When it came to the wider galaxy, Unara's people were incurious. And she felt very foolish for never having wondered about it herself before.

Mining. It was difficult on Thalassa. Was it difficult out among the stars too?

"The Suyarii have more resources than all of us combined. If we push too hard and lose everything—"

<Ensure we have what we need to fill our orders with the Rikstag Navy. Even if it means a reduction in regeneratives.>

"Yes, Father, I will see to it," Lord Gyes said, stiff, tense.

<Good. Now, if there is nothing else, I must rest.>

Everyone gathered around the projection bowed, and the lights shut off.

Lord Gyes turned away from the projection as a more natural light began spilling into the command deck. Huge shutters pulled back from what Unara realized now were windows, revealing a tinted view of the Thalassan sky. He smiled ruefully at both Unara and Captain Thorsen.

"Considering the level of disruption this presents, how likely it is that Lord Imran's expedition here was sponsored by the Caliphate?" Thorsen asked.

"Who knows? There are so many warring factions, so many bored system administrators and petty princes. The Suyarii Empire is far from a united place."

"Until it comes to making war," Thorsen replied.

"Yes, indeed so," Lord Gyes said. "Well, we do not have to deal with the Forest Clan today. They are in talks with House Amaro until the evening hours. We have appointments with the clans of the ice and the other reefs. I do not look forward to telling any one of them that we must cut our orders short. Madame Branner!"

One of the advisors broke away from the rest of the group, a rail-thin woman with the eyes of a shark. "Yes, milord?"

"We leave," he said.

Thorsen looked to Unara, who nodded back. She'd managed to get her hair tamed; it was long but fine and she had gotten it into a relatively small knot at the back of her head. The captain handed her the helmet. Putting it on, she could feel that her hair was concealed neatly under the skirting. Good enough for right now.

"Let's see who tries to kill him today," Thorsen sighed.

Spending the day trailing after Lord Gyes was both boring and exhausting.

They had appointments at three of the clan halls: the Northern Ice, Storm Reefs, and Drift. Unara was particularly nervous as they approached the Drift Clan's trade hall, their last meeting of the day. But even Thalassans, it seemed, saw only what they wished to, and nobody was looking for the princess amongst a trader's entourage.

As to be expected from Jarl Dryagr, the Drift Clan was most hospitable. The Stone Clan members working with them provided seats and brought out platters of fish and pitchers of water for the House Gyes guards, while the delegation no doubt ate within. The fish was cooked in the off-worlders' style, albeit clumsily, and Unara found herself missing the potatoes from yesterday.

How easily one adapted, she mused.

And yet, that ache in her legs was worse than ever.

The talks with the Drift Clan concluded as Brynhildyr began to tip toward the horizon, bringing with it first twilight. Jarl Dryagr came through the door with Lord Gyes, the Thalassan chieftain smiling and talking excitedly, as if they were old friends. And yet, even from here, Unara could tell.

Dryagr's eyes were sad.

It was well after second twilight when Lord Gyes kicked everyone out.

Unara had never been in any of the pavilions before. As a girl, before she had struck upon the idea of gaining a pair of legs for herself, she had looked forward to seeing them flooded and blooming. After the kaupang, the landing fields would be scraped clean of contaminants, the polluted soil sent far into the interior. The grand Oceanfall gates at the mouth of the bay would be closed, sediment-rich water would be brought in from the Inland Sea, and new corals would be seeded throughout the city. Pavilions would be repaired, trade houses expanded, the gates made even more resplendent. Then all would be drained, and once again would the Oceanfall palace rise above the waves.

Swimming through this place would have been a fine thing.

Seeing these structures, dry under the sky, was better. Getting to experience the place the way it was supposed to be experienced was heady.

Even if all the beauty seemed to be lost on the Gyes delegation.

This was just a place of work for them. They'd brought in a huge table of worked wood, set it up in the pavilion's upper story near a broad balcony, and proceeded to pore over the details of the day with clinical efficiency.

Branner was a crafty negotiator and an exceptional mathematician. Unara gathered that much from listening to her talk. She was the one driving most of the House's decisions here, Unara could tell, although Branner was exceedingly deferential to Lord Gyes. As was fitting, Unara thought, vassal to jarl, except that it all seemed to make Lord Gyes more and more miserable.

"I think that's quite enough for one evening," he was now telling Branner, interrupting her mid-sentence. "Could we resume this in the morning?"

"Milord, we have—"

"I know, I know, but things went rather better than expected with Jarl Dryagr today and I trust the figures your team shall come up with," he told her. She just stared at him. "I've had two attempts on my life since we arrived here, three if we count the sea monster. I should like a bit of a break."

Branner eyed him for a moment more, then bowed. "As you will it, milord."

"You too, Captain," Lord Gyes ordered, waving at his bodyguard.

"Milord, I must protest. As you said—"

"I have her here." And he pointed at Unara. "She took care of the last one, didn't she?"

Muttering something under his breath, Thorsen gestured to the two other guards, but Unara didn't miss the look he gave her on the way out.

Keep him safe, that look said, *or I'll gut you myself.*

After the entourage was gone, Lord Gyes flopped back onto the reclining couch set up at the far end of the room. Toeing off his boots, he let his head fall back, face to the ceiling, eyes closed.

"What I would give for a few days' freedom," he sighed, and waved his hand. "Please. Talk to me."

Unara snorted.

"I'm sorry, that was rude of me. I know you can't speak." Lord Gyes sat up a little, looking at her. "You must forgive me, but I need something right now other than politics or trade goods or those damn numbers in Branner's ledgers."

Unara would have been happy to talk numbers with him; she had been rather looking forward to picking over the negotiations with Glaeva every night, watching the flow of wealth and resources, helping ensure that every tribe got the best deals possible for so many decades of hard work.

What could she offer him right now, though?

She couldn't even write properly.

But again, her silence was taken for a problem, because Lord Gyes sat fully upright, a concerned expression on his face. "I didn't... I wasn't trying to imply that I wanted... Perhaps you could just listen?"

What had he thought she had assumed he was—oh. Unara smiled and shook her head. That, she had no interest in. This body was still too strange to even consider such a thing. But if Lord Gyes wanted to her to listen, she could do that easily.

She set her helmet aside and unbuckled her breastplate, letting both drop on the thick carpet, and plunked down in the chair closest to him.

"What do your people do when we're not here?" he asked.

"Farm, I imagine. Nacre mollusks must take some effort to grow. But what else?"

Unara huffed, trying to think of how to show it. She pulled her knife from its sheath, stabbing at the air a few times, pantomiming taking a blow.

"War?" he asked. She nodded. "Each other?"

She nodded and put her hands together, mimicking the movement of a fish.

"And the local sea life, I take it? Like that thing from the other night." Lord Gyes sighed. "Most of the Spiral does consider this a death world, so I do suppose it is quite the struggle to survive here." She nodded again. "What about... Do you ever just go wander? I've seen no boats yet on this world. But I would assume you explore the ocean. Maybe in those submersibles?"

She shrugged. Close enough.

"What about the deserts? Have you ever been there?"

Frowning, Unara shook her head emphatically. Not even the Stone Clan went there, at least not often. There were a few mining operations here and there, mostly for obtaining silica and other components of glassmaking, but even those were as close to the coast as possible and only operated during wintertime. Nobody would be there now, though. All were recalled to the palace during the kaupang.

He gave her a strange look. "Why not?"

She huffed again. Did he think they were idiots?

"I have seen the briefing material, of course, and I know that the deserts here are largely inimical to life. But a few days' or even weeks' journey would be possible with the right setup, I would think."

At that, Unara raised an eyebrow.

"I would prepare ahead, of course. Cache water, food, supplies, before driving in too deep. Moving at nighttime and pitching shelters during the day would help conserve moisture in your own body and prevent things like heatstroke or too much radiation damage from the suns..." He trailed off. "I only saw a little bit from my ship, before I lost her. I am sure it is beautiful out there. And no predators to worry about. Seems a loss, nobody going there."

The man was being utterly ridiculous. Only an off-worlder would entertain the idea of a stroll through the wastes. It was more than a matter of water.

Or perhaps, it was entirely about water.

But he was still looking at her, like he expected an answer. It was a difficult concept to explain, one too tough for mere hand signals. So Unara got back up and went over to the table where the day's ledgers were still scattered. Retrieving one of the sheets, she grabbed a pen and began to draw.

Lord Gyes came over while she was working, looking over her shoulder. "So what's this then?" he asked.

Unara tapped her sketch as she drew. It was a rough diagram showing the continental shelf: sea, cliffs, the rocky interior. Over the ocean she outlined Hildra and Rota. Over the land, she drew the three-sun symbol that was widely used among her people, and one of the only bits of iconography shown to the off-worlders here in Oceanfall.

With Lord Gyes watching, she tapped the moons, then the water, then herself. Then the suns, and the land, and she shook her head.

"Oh," he said, after a moment's thought. "I think I understand. The ocean belongs to the moons, and the land belongs to the suns. And you are the people of the ocean."

She nodded, pleased, and recapped the pen.

"A pity. An adventure into the interior might be fun. But I suppose it doesn't matter," Lord Gyes replied, his smile failing now. "I am stuck here, with all of this, and all too soon, the *Vanatar Deep* will break orbit and head back into deep space and on to the next set of negotiations."

Hearing the regret there in his words, Unara touched his arm. He just pulled away, turned back around to face the windows. "Would you look at that? The last sun is already down. This has been a pleasant conversation, to be sure, but I have another damn party to attend tonight, and we must leave for it soon. Would you step out while I freshen up?"

Unara thought about the last assassination attempt on this man and shook her head. It wouldn't do to let him get killed before she could get her ride off-world. Besides, she was finding she liked this man quite a lot.

He laughed. "I suppose there's no arguing with you, is there? Thorsen's probably put you up to it, no doubt. But if it's a choice between you and him, I'll take you. You're prettier."

She smiled back.

One step closer to the stars.

CHAPTER SEVENTEEN

"It is good to see you like this," the king finally said, strolling along next to Hakon. It was the first he had spoken since leaving the palace. "Out here, in your element, instead of in ours."

The skald bowed his head. "The ocean is mother to us all, my jarl. It does not matter if we are under its waves or above it."

Night had fallen hours ago but Hildra was high in the eastern sky. Several of her little sisters trailed after her in the dark sky like large, luminous stars. Neither King Aegyr nor Hakon had any trouble picking out a path.

They were up along the southern clifftops, high above Oceanfall. The palace was laid out like a village of children's toys below them, twinkling with lights. To the south and west and north, the ocean muttered in its sleep, lapping softly at the stone. But Hakon knew, even now, that life went on, everything hiding or hunting in turn.

There never was truly any peace on a world like Thalassa. But these clifftop paths were far enough removed from it all to make it appear as though there was. Up here was one of Hakon's favorite places to come. The solitude was profound.

Normally.

It was also easy to lock the entrance that led up here, and it was too high for surveillance crabs to climb. It was, therefore, one of the only truly unmonitored sections of the palace. A good place for honest discussion.

"You give a poetic answer, Hakon, but I'm in no mood for songs right now," the king said. His hands were clasped behind his back, his face to the wind. "Honesty is what I require."

"Honesty is all I ever speak," Hakon told him, a little wary. The king seemed to be in a pensive mood tonight.

And indeed, King Aegyr sighed, halting in his steps, eyes cast up at the moon. Rota was ascendent at the moment, a dark shape moving across the stars. "Your mother, Hakon...your mother was a fine woman. She should have returned to the ocean. You should have been born there."

Hakon kept his reaction to those words squarely in check. It was a thought he'd had quite often over the years. But on Thalassa, no human's fate was their own. "It is as Hildra wills it, my jarl."

"Sometimes I wonder if the moons truly have any concern for us at all," the king mused. "My only male descendant and here he is, bound to the surface."

Definitely a pensive mood, Hakon thought. "I serve you better up here."

"I shall be the judge of that," the king snapped, and began walking again. "We live too long here on Thalassa, Hakon. I have watched all my daughters grow and marry and leave me for their husbands' clans. Only Glaeva and Unara were left to me, and now, Glaeva is gone as well. And Unara..." He shook his head.

Hakon sighed. "She would have happily served as negotiator for the kaupang, my jarl. She had a good head on her."

"Her head is in the stars, Hakon. She's always been too interested in the world beyond this. No, I could not allow her to come up here. Can you imagine what kind of trouble she would get up to?" The king chuckled fondly. "She'd probably talk her way onto one of those ships out there."

"Jarl, she loves you," he replied. "I cannot believe she would abandon you."

"I don't know," the king said, stroking his beard. "I have sent for her several times, and she has not come."

Hakon bowed. "Princess Glaeva's death no doubt hit her hard, milord. Let me see if she will speak to me."

"That would be good." The king resumed walking. "Now. Give me your impressions of the kaupang. You have been able to go where I have not."

Hakon nodded. He had indeed been moving through the trade halls freely; as one of the palace skalds, no door was closed to him. His job was to preserve the memories, keep the history. That meant being able to see it all.

"Unsettled, my jarl," he said. "The assassination attempts on young Lord Gyes, coupled with the presence of Lord Imran, seem to have created a great deal of unrest amongst the traders."

"I have heard there have been no further attacks on House Gyes."

"No, Jarl, not for several days now. If we are fortunate, there will be no more before the kaupang is over." Hakon paused, looking out across an ocean that had rejected him. "I remember last kaupang, thick with the off-worlders' scheming against each other. Now, they seem to be plotting together against the newest of their number."

The king just grunted.

"You are considering dealing with the newcomers?"

"Outside our standing contracts, yes. It seems as though they have the resources of a vast stellar empire. If we can replace even a few of the smaller Houses with such a trading partner, it means fewer off-worlders on our soil. Fewer interlopers."

"Sound reasoning. But there is more going on here. Allow me more time to uncover it before you commit to anything, my jarl."

The king inclined his head slightly and kept walking. It was a few minutes before he spoke again. "And your clan?"

"What do you mean?"

"I have noticed at kaupangs past that the sky-born always get restless during contact with the off-worlders. A reminder, perhaps, that humanity's true form is this." And the king waved a hand at his altered body. "Not the one that their rulers wear."

"Jarl, you wear the form that best suits every Thalassan's need," Hakon replied. "Legs or tail, it does not matter, you are still our king."

"I do not fault your defense of your people, but this shift in attitude happens every kaupang. It is expected."

Hakon bit back his sigh. "Yes, Jarl."

"You must understand, Hakon, that most of these children have never experienced those terrible months of Sunwrath. They do not see the need for our way of life because all they know is the ebbing light." He paused. "Give me the names of any who become particularly vocal. And watch for the knife in the darkness, too, that might seek to silence those who are fully loyal. I have no wish to see you as foam on the waves."

"My jarl, who kills a skald?"

"The same people dumb enough to think they can defy the will of those who set the rhythm of our lives," he replied. "Do you suppose I have been king all these centuries because I selfishly cling to power? No, my skald. They"—and he pointed at the sky—"refuse to let me die or grant me the peace of an heir. Instead, they play games with me, giving me only daughters and then taking them away, one by one."

Hakon bowed his head. "I shall find Princess Unara for you."

The king crossed his arms over his chest, staring up at the stars. Sensing that his mood was growing black, Hakon bowed again and took his leave.

Heading back into the palace proper, the skald mulled over his king's words.

There was clearly much weighing on King Aegyr, and it worried Hakon. The king was conducting negotiations not just on behalf of their clan, but for all of Thalassa. He was an intermediary for them all, a source of advice and wisdom. Some—like Jarl Yvar—seemed determined to ignore him at every turn, which likely wasn't helping his mood any. But most, such as Jarl Dryagr, were very communicative, eager for the chance to learn. The Drift Clans would profit greatly this kaupang, Hakon thought, if they continued to cleave to—

Then, voices. In the corridor up ahead. Hakon frowned. This part of the palace was not much used. Remembering the king's words to him, his hand dropped to the hilt of his own knife, and he slipped into the shadows.

He could pick out words now.

"... must be ready, just as... said..."

"It... progress continues..."

"... not fast enough... a few more... and that's all we have to..."

"... I don't know about... if the king..."

Women's voices. And Hakon realized he knew them both. He smiled and stepped out fully, just in time to run into them coming around the corner.

"It's going to be just as promised. All will be made right in the end. All we need to do is—Skald Hakon!"

He nodded to the two Stone Clan women. They both stopped short, looking for all the world like children caught stealing sweets.

"Vaelyn. Leyli," he acknowledged, nodding to them. "Aren't you both on escort assignments?"

"Lord Gyes dismissed me," Vaelyn said, almost defensively.

"As did Lady Amaro," Leyli added. "We're off duty for the night, Skald, we promise."

He looked them over. Hakon had heard a great many rumors over the past few days; discontent among the Stone Clan, as the kind said, had deepened during this time. But he'd never heard anything from or about either of these two. "What are you up here in the ruined reaches of the palace to discuss?"

"Nothing," Vaelyn said.

Definitely defensive, he thought, and sighed internally. "Leyli?"

"We're planning a surprise for Lady Amaro," the other woman said, smiling ruefully. "She had been quite pleasant to us all, and this, she says, is her last kaupang. We wanted to give her something to, umm, remember us by."

Hakon relaxed a little. "I've heard the same rumors. What were you planning?"

"We're still trying to figure it out," Leyli replied. "She is quite fond of music, art, that sort of thing. I was thinking we could invite her to a skald telling, but then, none of those are in Standard."

"Plus the prohibitions, of course," Vaelyn said.

Hakon nodded thoughtfully. "Perhaps an instrumental concert. There is no formal prohibition against sharing our music, although I cannot recall it ever being done. She might enjoy that, and she has certainly dealt with us fairly all these years. I shall suggest it to the king."

Leyli lit up. "That is a fine idea, Skald."

"I shall suggest it," he warned. "But if King Aegyr does not agree, you may have to settle for pearls."

Vaelyn nodded. "That would be wonderful, Skald Hakon. Thank you. Now"—and she took the other Stone Clan woman by the arm—"you must excuse us."

Hakon stepped aside, clearing the path, but then thought of something. "One more thing, Vaelyn!" he called.

She stopped dead. Turned slowly. "Yes?"

"Have you seen Princess Unara recently? I am told that the king's messengers have been unable to locate her on the reef."

"Ah. Yes. She, uhh, decided to take a swim. Princess Glaeva's death was such a blow, she told me she needed some time and space to deal with her grief."

"A swim? To where?"

"The Fjallnar Reefs," Vaelyn replied.

Fjallnar was a six days' swim away, but only two with an akker. It was on the edge of one of the major nacre beds, though, and Unara had always liked going there. How just like the girl to slip away without telling anybody.

"I shall tell the king," Hakon said. "Although I cannot believe she would leave the kaupang. She's been so excited about it."

Vaelyn shrugged. "She said it was far too crowded here for comfort."

"Thank you, Vaelyn," he said sincerely. "I shall let you know about the concert."

She nodded back and hurried away.

Hakon, for his part, headed back up to the clifftops. The news about the princess wouldn't make the king happy, but at least it was an answer.

Vaelyn waited until she could no longer hear the skald's footsteps, then turned on her clanswoman. "A saga? Are you insane?" she hissed.

Leyli shrugged. "What? I didn't see you putting out any ideas to ease his suspicions."

"A saga?" Vaelyn repeated, not believing what she was hearing. "Those are sacred!"

"Only because they're in Thalassan," Leyli replied, and shrugged again. "If it's in Standard, who says there needs to be any kind of prohibition at all?"

"That infusion you got yesterday has scrambled your brain," Vaelyn snapped back. "The king might go for it, but the other ocean-born won't see it the same way. They'll..." And she trailed off, realizing what her friend meant. Leyli was grinning like a cave otter. "Oh."

"Oh yes. It's a wonderful idea, don't you think? I've been just looking for a way to plant the seed somewhere, and where better than with Hakon himself?" Leyli replied gleefully. "The royal bastard. Thinks he's better than the rest of us."

Vaelyn sighed. She liked Hakon, she truly did, and he had always been kind to her. But he couldn't be trusted, not with this. There were other ocean loyalists among the Stone Clan, people who had been quietly pushed out of leadership positions over the past few years, isolated, kept in the dark, but he could not be sidelined. His position, by its very nature, immunized him against politics. It was most problematic. "The king won't be stupid enough to agree to it."

"But what if he does?" Leyli asked gleefully. "It'll be delicious, don't you think?"

"I don't think our culture needs to be a casualty in this war," Vaelyn protested.

Leila's manic smile softened a little. "You should get your infusion, Vaelyn. Stop holding off. You'll see once you get the salt water in your blood. This isn't about songs or food or language or anything else. It's just about the ocean. I can hear her whispering to me."

"Hearing voices isn't going to help me carry out Lady Hethra's will right now," she shot back. "And you haven't transformed yet anyway."

"Of course not," Leyli replied. "The time hasn't come yet for the change to start. But it is coming, Vaelyn. You don't want to be left behind, do you?"

Vaelyn bristled. "I'm the one who recruited you, Leyli."

Leyli just sniffed. "And of the two of us, who's doing a better job carrying out Lady Hethra's will?"

Her friend walked away from her then, leaving Vaelyn standing in the upper hallway alone.

All alone with her fears.

In the shade of the drop-craft, the off-worlders fought.

The surface world limited movement. One flat plane. That was what the air-breathers had to work with. One flat plane ruled over by cruel gravity. And yet, they could still do amazing things.

Unara studied them as she walked up, helmet under her arm. Captain Thorsen was a big man, tall and well built, one whose size almost worked against him out here in the air. Powerful, he moved like a bone-armored shark, direct and aggressive, every movement of his body, every jab and thrust and slice of his sword aiming directly for center mass.

Lord Gyes was quicker, more agile, dodging and twisting away, parrying with his own long blade.

Underwater, you had to use momentum to your advantage. Lots of spins, turns, careful control. Lots of accounting for position. Lots of anticipation, always having to calculate where you might end up or where your foe might go. Here, both men kept their feet on the ground and their attention fixed on each other, never wavering for a second.

The off-worlders moved fast, circling each other, probing

defenses, then moving in for the strike. A flurry of blows, then back again, circling once more. It was a different cadence than that of underwater combat.

There was a lot to learn from these sparring sessions.

Lord Gyes and Captain Thorsen had been doing this every morning since she had arrived. Lord Gyes had confided to Unara that he thought it best he brushed up on his somewhat rusty combat skills.

"Not much use in the expedition fleet," the merchant prince had told her, "but it seems as if it's quite necessary now."

He hadn't seemed happy about it. If Unara had learned anything over the past few days, it was that her benefactor here was a deeply contemplative man, and one who did not particularly enjoy the ebb and flow of trade negotiations.

But just as Unara reached the circle, there came a cry of triumph. Lord Gyes had broken Captain Thorsen's guard. His sword was centimeters from his housecarl's neck.

"Sloppy, old friend," Lord Gyes laughed.

"Was it?" Thorsen replied.

Lord Gyes looked down, as did Unara: the tip of a small dagger, protruding from the closed fingers of Thorsen's fist, was right at his gut. He laughed and backed off, sword flicking back with a simple move of his wrist. "I don't think a sea monster is going to do something like that."

"I'm not worried about sea monsters," Thorsen said. His words were even, but labored. He was breathing hard. He nodded over to Unara. "How do you think our lord here would do against the local fauna down in the water, eh?"

Unara shook her head and spread her hands. Plenty of things here killed through poison, subtle stings or little bites. Even a small blade could be fatal, if one knew what one was doing.

"See? She knows."

"I'm sure we'd all be eaten," Lord Gyes said, a bit more serious now. "Although I wouldn't say no to a dive here. It's been far too long since..." But he stopped himself. "A dive would be nice."

Unara shook her head again. Submersible trips were permitted only because such craft were completely under the control of their operators. Who knew where an off-worlder might go on their own? It was far too much of a risk.

"Is there no way to see the underwater world?" he asked and then snapped his fingers. "The aquariums. I haven't had a chance to visit them yet."

Unara looked at Vaelyn, and Vaelyn cleared her throat. "Milord, considering our schedule for the day..."

"We don't meet Yvar for another three hours. Branner can handle the details with the Seamount Clan," Lord Gyes said. "Why don't we go?"

THE PAST FEW days spent under the sky had been some of the best of Unara's life.

It wasn't that life in the air was easier. In many ways, it seemed to be much more complicated. There were certain tasks, like bathing, that were completely different up here. Movement was far more challenging, stuck to the floor like everyone was, and food was different, and so were a hundred other little things that she should have anticipated but hadn't.

Lord Gyes seemed to be taking her into his confidence, at least, which Unara reveled in.

But these negotiations with Yvar, it seemed, had become quite problematic. Unara could not understand why Yvar was being so difficult about it, nor why Lord Gyes was so focused on it. The Forest Clan's main export was nacre, and not the exotic, beautiful nacres of the deeper ocean. Thick, heavy, utilitarian nacre. It commanded the lowest price per kilo of any grown here on Thalassa, or did, under normal circumstances. Thanks to Yvar's intransigence and Lord Imran's overgenerous nature, however, the price had almost tripled.

It was shortsighted and stupid and Unara wondered why her father had not put a stop to it. But she had to concede that her view on things was somewhat colored by recent knowledge: there was some kind of deep animosity between the other traders and the Suyarii, a fear that she had not quite unlocked yet.

All in good time.

Her main goal right now was securing passage off-world.

Everything else could wait.

"Tell me something, if you can," Lord Gyes said as they strolled along the edge of the great pools on the bronze catwalk. "Why do I see no Thalassans out here? Or anywhere else beyond the trader halls?"

"We dislike the sun, milord," Vaelyn told him. "We do not often come out during the day. If we must perform tasks here, we do it underwater."

"Even now, during the apogee?" Captain Thorsen asked, behind Lord Gyes. He had his rifle slung down in front of him, a ready position, Unara had learned. He never did seem to relax.

"Even now," Vaelyn told him, turning. She pointed at her pale skin. "This was not made for heavy light."

"You live on a desert world and you cannot tolerate the sun?" Thorsen asked, raising an eyebrow.

"We live on an ocean world," Vaelyn replied, and Unara was surprised at the bitterness she heard in her friend's voice. "Attempting adaptations for surface conditions might encourage some of my clan to...attempt to move away, into the interior. And that, of course, would be suicide. The desert has already rejected us."

"Of course," Lord Gyes said. It was polite, but heavy with discomfort.

"Why keep these places?" Thorsen asked as they passed a great glass tower wrapped in brass filigree. "Why maintain aquariums if you do not visit them?"

"We have them for the off-worlders. So you might see parts of our world that would otherwise remain a mystery."

It was a lie, but a well-delivered one. Unara wondered what it was costing her friend to manage such a charade. Thalassans valued honesty; in a world of shifting waters and treacherous beasts, a person's word had to be sound. What else could one trust? And here Vaelyn was, having to deliver untruths to protect her clan.

"A curious thing," Lord Gyes said, stopping. Below them, fronds the size of Unara's body waved in a gentle current, shaded by a great canopy that reduced the sunlight to the proper levels. "What is this place?"

"A section of kelp forest, milord," Vaelyn said.

"Like Yvar's?"

This was indeed where Yvar's clan had stayed before the kaupang began, but Unara wouldn't have told Lord Gyes that even if she could.

"It's an approximation," Vaelyn replied.

"Interesting," Lord Gyes mused, and turned to Unara. "Care to accompany me inside?"

Unara looked at the trader, and then back at the others. Captain Thorsen looked tired, as if he was resigned to Lord Gyes disappearing from his sight. Vaelyn, on the other hand, seemed relieved and slipped away to the eastern shadows of the aquarium's entrance tower.

For her part, pulling open the door in front of Lord Gyes, Unara hesitated. Inside was a shaft. It looked deep, at least thirty meters, with a staircase that spiraled down into the darkness. She felt another new fear bite at the back of her mind. Heights. Heights were very uncomfortable. And the stairs would no doubt get her feet bleeding again.

But that was nothing new. And this, she hoped, might just provide Lord Gyes with some answers as to how to deal with Yvar.

So in Unara went.

DESCENDING into the aquarium's air space was like falling through the neck of a bottle. The cylinder gave way after about ten meters or so to broader, more natural walls, while the stairs continued in a perfectly even downward spiral.

Here and there, metal platforms led away from the central stairs to the sides of the grotto. Windows of polished glass were set into the walls of the space, and every wall was braced with metal. Brass, steel, titanium.

Lord Gyes stopped at one of these reinforcements, looking it over. "So that's what you do with all the metal. Structural reinforcements," he said. "I take it that titanocoral has a maximum pressure rating?"

She nodded. Underwater, it was fine. But in maintaining air space like this, where the inside and outside pressures were so different, reinforcement was necessary. One of the reasons, she assumed, that humanity here had taken so fully to the sea. Without metal, and a great deal of it, it was impossible to sustain safe underwater habitats.

The further down in the underwater grotto they went, the more the light faded, until finally, they were at the bottom. Unara had seen this place from the water before, but never the inside, and marveled at the massive bronze girders and trusses. Lord Gyes wandered over to one of the huge windows, looking out into the depths of the kelp forest's base.

This aquarium was too small to maintain a full-grown forest shark, or a proper colony of cave otters, one of the only mammal species on the planet who survived Sunwrath by hibernating through it. Juveniles of both species were brought in for the kaupang, though, and an otter swam by the window now.

"It's as big as a Caledon seal," Lord Gyes said, watching, fascinated, as the thing plucked an urchin off a kelp trunk. "Does everything grow so large on this world?"

Unara shrugged. There were plenty of small creatures in the sea. The otters had been altered to be larger in order to better reach the bottom of the deep kelp beds. Their presence kept urchin populations from exploding out of control.

"This place is a marvel," he said, and laughed. "Ah, that, that is a nacre mollusk, is it not?"

Unara followed his finger, placed where it was on the viewing window. And yes, it was indeed a nacre mollusk, seeded here at the same time its relatives would have been seeded for harvest at this kaupang.

He stared at it for a moment. "Are the mollusks really grown like this?"

She nodded again.

"I can't let Prince Imran purchase Yvar's harvest," Lord Gyes said heavily, eyes back on the depths. "The chaos it would cause would be incalculable. Lord Willam would most likely ram his entire fleet into Imran's to prevent him from leaving the system with it."

Unara cocked her head, confused as to what he meant.

Lord Gyes looked at her, smiling weakly. "I don't suppose we're entirely honest with you about what we use nacre for."

Industrial purposes, she wanted to say. Plating for electrical systems, energy dissipation. She understood the basic concepts behind such things, even if Thalassan technology had long since left electricity behind.

But she couldn't say anything, so she had to wait for Lord Gyes to continue.

"We say it's for lightweight body armor, machine components, shielding for short-range spacecraft. And that is all true." He sighed. "But the nacre from the forest regions can, for whatever strange reason, withstand even the strongest of directed energy blasts. No other type of shielding gets close. We use it on warships. As armor. Our only remaining strategic advantage against the Suyarii."

War? Unara's heart sank. She walked over to the window, laying a hand on it, staring back out into the water.

"I am sorry," he said, "to talk about such things. For now, the front is many dozens of light-years away from here, and if it ever came to it, the Rikstag Sector authorities would extend protections to Thalassa Prime. They might expect a levy of troops in return, but..." He trailed off again. "Why won't that man honor his clan's agreements?"

Unara huffed, thinking about that. A troop levy? Nobody would go. Nobody could. They were bound to this place. They could not help out there.

But there was something she could do.

Something significant.

Pointing to the ledger folio under his arm, Unara mimed writing. He handed it over wordlessly.

There was a pen and blank paper inside.

She began to write.

Not in faulty Standard, but her own people's runes.

As she did so, Unara burned with guilt. Lord Gyes was watching her with great interest; as far as she knew, no off-worlder had ever so much as seen Thalassan runes, much less watched somebody write them. She could tell herself that she was doing it for the benefit of her people, but in reality, she wanted this man to trust her.

She was doing it for herself.

She was doing it for her way off-world.

Because here, this, was something more valuable than pearls.

Finally, she was done, and she passed the sheet to Lord Gyes, who held it carefully.

"I don't suppose you'll tell me what this says," he asked her.

She shook her head.

"And the Forest Clan won't tell me, either, I assume."

She nodded, then shook her head, then frowned, unsure of herself.

He looked it over again. "I believe this is a significant risk for you, isn't it?"

Hesitantly, she nodded.

He nodded back and folded it carefully, concealing it in an interior breast pocket of his uniform jacket. "Then let us go see what they say."

Karl waited until the rest of the Forest delegation had left the hall before saying anything.

"Jarl Yvar. I would like a word with you."

The Thalassan leaned forward over the back of his chair. "I already told you, there's no deal. You get the minimum amount promised this kaupang, and next, our harvest goes to House Imran."

Karl had tried. Branner had tried. All day, they had been at this. The kaupang was half-over, and because of this man, all of House Gyes's other obligations would have to be worked out on a condensed schedule. But Father had been clear about this: they had contracts with both the Rikstag and Alamani Sector navies. Whatever the cost, the nacre had to be secured.

But Jarl Yvar would not budge. Had not budged.

Karl rubbed his face. "Tell me something, Jarl Yvar."

"If I may," the Thalassan replied.

"Everywhere I go here, I hear the same refrain from your people. They are dazzled by Lord Imran's wealth. They are taken with his promises. Why?"

Yvar laughed. Actually laughed. "After the last four days of bargaining so hard with me, you ask me why we wish to increase our profits?"

"I am asking why you are so eager to deal with a Suyarii nobleman. Their empire—"

"The politics of the stars are not our concern, Lord Gyes. My people wish for one thing and one thing only: to be left alone," Yvar said, his sea-gray eyes hardening. "One group of traders may be preferable to the dozens we suffer now."

There was no arguing with something like that, so Karl reached into his breast pocket. "Always our families have dealt fairly with each other, yours and mine," he said. "I would have liked to continue that relationship." And he pulled out the message from his Thalassan girl. "I am told this may have some kind of meaning to you."

Yvar took it gingerly, as if he thought the paper poisoned. He unfolded it, frown deepening as he took in the writing there. Finally, he looked back up at Karl. "Where did you get this?"

"Does it really matter?"

"It is a capital offense on this world to teach our writing to...outsiders."

"Nothing was taught to me."

"Then you do not know what this says?"

Karl shrugged, affecting an air of unconcern, staring back at Yvar. "Out of deference for the individual who wrote it for me, I didn't ask."

The Thalassan frowned and looked it over. "You hand me something that you cannot read and do not understand, hoping it may... what, sway me?"

"Yes," Karl said simply.

Jarl Yvar stared at him, something flinty in his eyes. And then he sighed. Turned. "Get back in here, all of you!" he yelled at the door, and then glared at Karl.

Karl just stared back. He had the sudden feeling that Yvar's dive knife might find its way between his ribs if he looked away from the Thalassan. The other man's expression was indescribable. A muscle in his jaw twitched.

"Jarl?" Karl asked cautiously.

"You have your wish," Yvar finally replied, as both delegations poured back into the room. "Lord Gyes, my clan will honor our previous agreement without conditions."

Branner, hurrying over, looked shocked. Karl held up a hand to keep her from speaking. "I understand the Suyarii represent an inflationary force here," he said to Yvar, cautious. "As we discussed a few days ago, a five-percent increase is acceptable if you should…”

“Same quantities,” Yvar said.

Not wishing to press his luck, Karl bowed. “That is most generous.”

“In honor of the long-standing ties between your clan and mine,” the Forest Clan delegate said. “And if you will, I would like to return to our discussion about the next kaupang’s orders.”

Branner, having recovered herself somewhat, lifted her chin. “I don’t know, Jarl Yvar. We’ve been here an awfully long time, with no resolution yet. And we do have that appointment to keep tonight, Lady Amaro’s concert.”

“We shall keep it short,” Yvar said. “I still have our proposal from the start of this thing.”

Branner looked even more surprised. “So do we.”

“Let’s see how they align,” Karl said quickly. “Thank you for your generosity, Jarl Yvar.”

“The selfish man drowns in the air,” Yvar said cryptically, and folded up the paper with the runes, tucking it away in a back pocket. “Now, shall we begin?”

“Of course,” Karl replied.

Captain Thorsen and the Thalassan girl were waiting for Karl outside the negotiations hall almost two hours later. Both seemed nervous, especially the girl. He smiled at her approvingly, then nodded his head.

They didn’t speak again until they were out of the trading halls, back out under the open suns.

“I take it your negotiations went well,” Captain Thorsen asked.

Branner grinned. “I have no idea what Lord Gyes said to that man to get him back to the table, but whatever it was, it worked exceptionally well.”

Karl nodded at the Thalassan girl, who just smiled behind her helmet. "I appealed to his better sense."

"Exceptionally well," Branner said. "And now not only have we secured what we need to fill the naval contracts for both this kaupang and the next, but we've managed to retain five tons of our reserve titanium. Milord, if I may suggest—"

"Do whatever you want with it," Karl said. "You know better than I do what would fit best in our holds."

Thorsen snorted. "I cannot understand this insistence the Thalassans have on entertaining the Suyarii delegation. Surely they know about recent events. The incursion into the Hellenic Cluster, for example."

"I do not believe they do," Karl said. "They are most incurious about the world beyond their own star system. And even if they weren't, that main star, Brynhildyr, is so violent that hyperspace communications are all but impossible here. How can they know if we do not tell them?"

And he looked again at the Thalassan girl, walking proud beside him, her features hidden and her hair streaked black with dye. Moving through the world like she wasn't a part of it. Who was she? What, exactly, had she done for him here today?

And what, he wondered, would a man like Jarl Yvar do to her if he found out?

CHAPTER NINETEEN

As the first strains of music began to fill the courtyard, Vaelyn felt guilt squirm in her gut.

It was a sensation she was well accustomed to at this point.

"This shouldn't be happening," she muttered.

"This is by Lady Hethra's design," Leyli replied, voice equally soft. "Are you questioning her now?"

"No, of course not," Vaelyn said, miserable.

She hated this, the mass of humanity around her. It looked like everyone who could manage an invitation to tonight's concert had, and quite a few others had snuck in. House Amaro's pavilion was all arranged around this large central courtyard, ringed with deep, columned porticos that extended up three levels. People were crowded in everywhere, watching from every level, attention focused on the single raised stage down here.

On the Stone Clan musicians, just beginning their performance.

Hakon was here, along with all the other skalds. He had outdone himself, it seemed, and gotten the king to agree to a very truncated translation of the founders' saga, the story of how humanity first came to this world. He was up front, eyes closed, waiting as the musicians warmed up.

Thalassan music was not complicated. Flute and lyre, drum and rebec, horn and pipe. There were other instruments, of course, deep and resonant, that could only be played underwater. Vaelyn suddenly thought of all the nights when both sky- and ocean-born would gather in the Hall of Transformation and play together until one could forget where the air stopped and the sea began.

That did not help her feelings of guilt.

Most of the Thalassan delegates were here tonight. Some, like Lady Ragnyr, had pronounced and unconcealed disdain stamped on their features. Others, like Jarl Dryagr, seemed quite amused by it all.

Vaelyn looked up. Lord Gyes was on one of the upper balconies, Unara by his side, wearing that ridiculous Rikstag dress again. He leaned over to whisper something in her ear, and she nodded enthusiastically.

The Stone Clan woman frowned. That sight stirred something as equally unpleasant, and equally unwelcome, as the guilt. Jealousy perhaps.

But jealousy for what, exactly? That Unara seemed to hold that off-worlder's affections? So what? What did it matter?

In a few days, they would all be—

A conch-trumpet sounded, and all fell silent.

From inside the shadowed depths of the pavilion, a procession. Lady Amaro, lovely in her exotic off-world furs and silks, King Aegyr walking next to her.

Leyli leaned in. "I wish I could be there when that stuck-up skald realizes the consequences of what he's doing. Can you imagine the look on his face when—"

"Shut up," Vaelyn muttered, and looked up at Lord Gyes again. "I suppose I better get up there."

Leyli shrugged. "Suit yourself. I have to stay down here for that air-breathing bitch." And she pointed at Lady Amaro. King Aegyr was offering the old trader his hand to help her climb the steps to the top of their viewing dais.

Shaking her head, Vaelyn broke away from her friend.

The stairs to the upper levels were set well back in the pavilion, and so, Vaelyn only heard snatches of the short speeches that followed. The king said a few words about their world's partnership with the stars, and Lady Amaro thanked everyone for the generous gift of their song and waxed poetic about her time on their world.

If this place mattered to you, you'd leave us alone, Vaelyn thought to herself as she made the upper level, headed for Lord Gyes. He nodded to her as she slipped up against the rail beside him, and then the music organized itself, and the saga began.

Drums. It always started with drums. Drums and voice. At first only Hakon's, the drums quiet, describing the endless silence of the night sky.

Then more voices joined, the pipes rose, the drumbeat became arrhythmic. In a tumult of confusion, the music told of the colony fleet tumbling from hyperspace, pummeled by Brynhildyr's light.

Faster now, swelling now, the music described the panic of their ancestors, their fear. Ships damaged, air leaking, no hope of rescue. Desperate flight down to the surface, and the drums took over again as their landers fell into the storms of the east. The long months of survival.

The music sped up, voices rising. The final landers carried all they could to the surface. The last of the fleet was sent to the Oort. Years it would take. Heroic sacrifice.

Then quiet again, Hakon's voice fell to a murmur, the drums low, all else silent. The long march began, heading west, dragging the gene-vaults, the seeds from which a new world was to grow. The sorrow of it. Equipment failing. Water lost. The dead left along the way.

Brightness. The lute began, the drums faded. Water. Reaching the inland sea, a lifeline at last.

And here, the saga at last deviated.

The full saga told now about an encounter at the inland sea. When the first king received a vision of a woman in silver, showing them the way, giving them the answer.

Hakon did not sing her promise, not for the off-worlders—Hildra's words were for Thalassa alone.

Come to me and be my people.

So much was missing. The final trek from the colonists' desperate settlements through the deep desert, following the dead river away from the inland sea. To Oceanfall. Where the first king of Thalassa walked out into the sea and was transformed.

But there did come the swell from the very end. Everything playing. Everyone singing. The triumph. A white-faced moon, rising above the ocean, home at last.

It didn't matter that the words were in Standard. It didn't matter that the hard facts of history were somewhat different. Vaelyn's eyes were wet as the drums abruptly ended, Hakon's voice carrying the last notes of the song before falling too.

And silence reigned once again.

Lord Gyes leaned in to speak with her, but she did not trust herself in that moment.

She turned away.

And as she did so, she saw Lady Ragnyr fall.

There were cries of surprise, the sound of garments swishing and feet shuffling as people tried to move out of the way.

"What's that now?" Lord Gyes asked. But Vaelyn was already moving, fear in her heart.

Unara was faster, however, and was there at the Ice Clan delegate's side before anyone else. She looked up at Vaelyn, a question in her eyes, and Vaelyn realized the princess had her fingers over something on the ocean-born's leg.

Something silvery, shiny. Something almost like—

Scales, Vaelyn realized.

No. No, not here. Not right now. Not like this.

"What's going on?" Lord Gyes asked, coming over.

"Nothing," Vaelyn said sharply, at the same time that Unara shook her head. "Nothing. Now please, Lord Gyes, if you would just give Lady Ragnyr some space…"

"Is she ill?" he asked.

"No," Vaelyn said, feeling absolutely desperate now. They had to get her out of here. But how? Lady Ragnyr had come alone, and there were no other Thalassans up here on the balcony level. If she was suffering imminent biological collapse, if that was coming…

"She's unconscious," Lord Gyes said softly. "Surely we cannot just prop her up against a pillar and leave her?"

Vaelyn felt like a fish caught in a trap. She looked at Unara, who shook her head and spread her fingers a little. Vaelyn caught her meaning. The scales were spreading.

If Lady Ragnyr reverted to her ocean-born form, here, now, in the middle of this kind of crowd…

"Let me see."

Jarl Dryagr. Where he had come from and what he was doing up here, Vaelyn had no idea. But the Drifter was kneeling down next to them. Unara turned her face away.

"I don't know, milord," Vaelyn said, trying to keep her voice steady. "She just fell."

"I'll take her to the gothi," he said, and began gathering Lady Ragnyr up into his arms. Unara's hand broke away, and Vaelyn moved in to tug the delegate's dress over the patch of skin.

"Surely you shouldn't move her like this," Lord Gyes protested, stepping in.

And for a moment, Jarl Dryagr's normal good humor was completely gone. "Get back, Lord Gyes," he snapped, his eyes flint-cold. "Lady Ragnyr's health doesn't concern you."

"But—"

"Remove yourself from my path, or I shall remove you myself."

Lord Gyes folded his arms across his chest. "I don't appreciate being threatened, Jarl Dryagr."

Then Unara was there, head still down, pulling Lord Gyes back. Jarl Dryagr didn't give him another glance, sweeping past with Lady Ragnyr cradled carefully into his arms, moving as fast as he could for the stairs.

Thorsen watched him go. "What do you suppose that was about, milord?" The question was addressed to Lord Gyes, but Vaelyn realized the bodyguard was staring at her.

The evening concluded without further incident, or indeed, without anybody else in the pavilion seemingly aware of what had happened on the upper level at all. Lord Gyes didn't mention it on the way back to the drop-craft at all, but Vaelyn could not stop thinking about it.

Catastrophic biological collapse up here in the air was not unheard of, but it was rare. Extremely rare. But this early in the kaupang? It was unprecedented. People would be asking questions. Everyone would be wondering.

It had to be intentional. That was all Vaelyn could come up with. Lady Hethra did not miscalculate. Lady Hethra did not make mistakes.

Glaeva's death, Vaelyn could rationalize. A political maneuver, plain and simple. But Lady Ragnyr? What good would killing her do, and in such a public and dangerous fashion? Surely it would only go against their primary objective here of overthrowing King Aegyr and the cessation of the kaupangs, angering the other clans.

Vaelyn could not make sense of it.

She didn't know what to do.

"Thank you for the escort back to the ship," Lord Gyes told her as their small party climbed up the ramp back into the drop-craft, the guards at the air lock entrance waving them through, "and thank you for the wonderful night."

"Lady Amaro has been fair and generous with our world," Vaelyn said. "I hope she enjoyed it."

"I'm sure she did," Lord Gyes said, and then looked to Unara, who had just pulled her cap off and was shaking out her hair. The off-worlders had given her a temporary black dye for it; it worked well but rubbed out over the course of the day. The upper part of her hair was once again its natural berry-red. "If you would join me…?"

Unara nodded but cast one last glance at Vaelyn before following Lord Gyes into the drop-craft proper. Her eyes were haunted. Probably thinking about her sister.

Standing there alone outside of the drop-craft, Vaelyn didn't know how to feel. She kept trying to harden her heart against the princess but couldn't fully manage it. What was Unara doing with Lord Gyes, anyway? Bedding him? It wouldn't have surprised Vaelyn in the least. Unara may have been quieter than the average Thalassan, but there was great determination in the depths of her soul. Vaelyn had no doubt that Unara would do whatever she deemed necessary to get off-world.

The thought did stir more of that jealousy, though, and Vaelyn stamped on it hard.

There was nothing else to do here tonight.

She turned on her heel and headed back to the palace.

"Skald Hakon? I wanted to congratulate you on a wonderful performance."

The skald paused in his work, polishing the last of the flutes from that night's performance. It was busy work and nothing he needed to be doing himself; he should have left it to the apprentices for their morning's labors. But the news about Lady Ragnyr was distressing to the extreme, and he needed something to occupy his mind.

"Thank you for the suggestion, Leyli. An artist always enjoys the challenge of something new," he said, nodding to his clanswoman who had just entered his storage space, "although the music does sound different without the water to add its harmony."

"I was thinking much the same thing," she replied, and smiled at him a little. Then her face fell.

"I am told Lady Ragnyr will make a full recovery, even if she will do it under the waves instead of on the surface," he told her gently, and placed the flute back down on the workbench. "If that is what you are worried about."

Leyli nodded. "It is a relief to hear, Skald Hakon, but that isn't what I wished to speak with you about."

"Oh?"

She pulled something out of a pocket, a piece of paper, the bleached white stuff used by the off-worlders. "Jarl Yvar reversed course today," she said. "Not just for House Gyes, but he has said he intends to revert back to the original terms for all his contracts."

"And?"

"And I believe this is why." She handed over the paper. "Lord Gyes gave him this, I am told. Jarl Yvar ripped it apart, of course, but I gathered the scraps I could and repaired it for you."

Looking over the paper, Hakon frowned. It was the name of one of the sagas, the runes drawn in their high official style. *The Faithless Man Drowns in the Air*. A somber story, a cautionary tale, about a clan chieftain who tried to hoard far more than what his people needed, until Hildra withdrew her favor and Rota destroyed all with a tidal wave, leaving him alone and dying on the desert shores.

"I could see how this might motivate him to reverse position," Hakon replied, and looked at it carefully. "Do we know who gave this to Lord Gyes?"

"No, Skald, but I can find out."

And then Hakon realized where he had seen this handwriting

before. "No," he told her, a chill running through him. "No, I think I can answer this question myself. Hildra forgive me for saying so, but Jarl Yvar has a harsh and binding temper. When he got carried away by his own foolishness, he likely needed some way to reverse course. So, he fakes some secret message. Ridiculous, wouldn't you agree?"

"Of course, Skald."

"You may go, Leyli," he said. "But thank you for bringing this to my attention."

"For Thalassa," she replied, and nodding a little, left him to it again.

Hakon waited until she was gone before sagging a little. He tossed the paper aside.

Unara.

This was Unara's handwriting.

But Unara wasn't on the reef right now, or so he'd been told. So what was she doing, violating Thalassan law like this? She could have gone to Yvar directly, demanded his presence in a boundary pool. Why give this to an off-worlder? And how?

There was only one way to find out the truth of it.

So Hakon headed down into the bowels of the palace. Down to the water-locks, dive gear in hand.

Even here in Oceanfall Bay, night dives weren't the safest thing in the world, but Hakon made it to the outer akker paddocks without incident.

The outer akker paddocks.

Where Unara's akker bobbed with the rest, sleeping away.

She wouldn't have left for the Fjallnar Reefs without the thing, he knew. Too far, too risky, to swim alone. But she wasn't on the reefs here; he had verified that himself.

So where was she?

And what, exactly, was she doing giving advice to House Gyes?

THE NIGHT WAS calm and quiet, Rota high in the sky, a dark shadow against the stars. Vaelyn didn't bother looking up at the moon.

The grand square was empty now, most people having drifted back to pavilion or ship for the night after the conclusion of Hakon's song. Working, no doubt, or resting up for another busy day tomorrow. Everyone in Oceanfall right now had business to conduct, the work of months crammed into days. But even so, there were a few figures here and there, lit by the soft glow from Lady Amaro's wonderful trees. What a marvel those were, Vaelyn found herself thinking, that there were places where such plants could grow, proud and unafraid, under their world's suns.

But even as she found herself drifting closer to them, she stopped.

Something had just broken off from the shadows. Two-legged, human-shaped, but shambling, stumbling.

Corroded bronze glinted in its hand.

Vaelyn stopped cold. Looked around. More shadows moved. More shapes detached. And she remembered what Unara had said about the assault on the submerged spaceship.

"Draugr," she breathed, and looked around desperately. There was a pair of off-worlders under the trees, laughing with each other, heedless of the monsters creeping up behind them. "You there!" she yelled in Standard, her dive knife out, advancing fast. "You two, watch out!"

The couple looked up at her. But before they could even yell a response, hands grabbed them from behind. Hands on mouths, hands on shoulders. Blades flashed. Bodies fell.

Vaelyn stepped back, whirling around. There were more. More of the corrupted creatures. Climbing over the edge of the cliffs, shambling across the square. A few broke off, headed for the pavilions, but most seemed to be headed in one single direction.

East.

East, to the landing fields.

Vaelyn stood rooted to the ground for a moment, heart racing. Why was no alarm raised? Why were the conch-trumpets not sounding out? Why was the king not rallying forth?

She turned to look at the palace gates, questions pounding at her skull, wanting to—

She screamed.

Behind her, not ten centimeters from her face, was a draugr, a corrupt parody of a human being. Barnacles and polychaete worms hung from its slack gray flesh. The blue light of the depths glowed in its eyes. Its breath stank of death.

But the thing didn't attack. Instead, it almost seemed to sniff at her, then turned away, ambling around her with its decrepit, shuffling gait.

Vaelyn put a hand over her chest, gasping for air. There were others now, all of them moving around her, as indifferent to her presence as they might have been to a hunk of dead coral. The nightmares from a hundred lurid sagas, made manifest here tonight.

Then something touched her foot.

She looked down, mute with terror. But it was just a crab. One of the surveillance drones. As she looked at it, its eyes lit up.

One of Lady Hethra's little messengers.

"Do you see this?" Vaelyn hissed, enraged now. "Do something!"

A front claw extended. Pointing to the east. Pointing to the landing fields.

The command was clear.

And yet, for the first time since pledging herself to the abyssal chieftain's mission, Vaelyn hesitated.

Draugr, *draugr*, real and walking out of the sea. She couldn't... she couldn't...

Then the crab began to move.

Then the crab began to write.

Then Vaelyn understood what was being asked of her.

She stood still, watching the draugr pass her by, and didn't move again until they were gone. Vaelyn poked the expired drone, looking at its last words, and then east to the landing fields.

The screaming had started.

Gritting her teeth, she pushed herself up off the ground.

The saga tonight had reminded her. She was a daughter of the ocean.

She was going home.

Whatever the price.

CHAPTER TWENTY

Unara woke first. She hadn't been sleeping well on land. Too still, too quiet. Any little disturbance seemed to be enough to stir her here.

With bleary eyes, she glanced at the clock glowing in the upper corner of the room. It wasn't late yet, not even midnight. She couldn't have been asleep more than twenty minutes.

Nothing was wrong.

And yet, something had woken her.

Unara looked around her small quarters for a moment more, trying to determine the cause of her restlessness, figuring it was nothing.

She tried to settle back down.

Then she heard it again.

The padding of feet.

But not the steady, even steps of the off-worlders.

These were uneven. Shuffling.

Unara was up in a flash, shoving her bare feet into her boots, grabbing for her knife, buckling armor on over her sleep dress, rushing out into the corridor.

She had to reach Lord Gyes.

The ache in her new legs had not subsided, not all week. It seemed to be something wrong with the skin, for that frequently oozed blood. Slower, careful steps were less painful than fast movement. But it didn't matter tonight.

She ran.

The light was poor; most of the drop-craft's lamps were out as she raced through the central corridor. Only the grand windows above, open to the stars, offered anything to see by. Unara's other sense had been compromised somewhat by the transformation, but eyes were a delicate and difficult organ to alter; she still retained much of her ocean-born night vision.

She reached Lord Gyes's chambers, expecting to see his guards on duty. Two of them were there, yes, but one was already clearly dead, body discarded on the floor like a broken toy. The other was fighting for his life, overwhelmed by three black shapes hunched over him, long fingers scrambling for his eyes, clenching down on his throat.

Unara didn't hesitate. Diving in, she slashed one monster's throat open to the bone. Another turned on her. Too slow. She rammed her knife straight into its eye socket.

The guard, legs free now, kicked the third one off of him and grabbed for his energy pistol. It took three shots to put the draugr down.

Already, the bodies were dissolving.

The other guard looked at her questioningly, then stiffened.

Unara had heard it too.

It was the unmistakable sound of a blade being drawn from a sheath.

Bursting through the doors, Unara's heart went cold at the sight before her. The expansive room had at least half a dozen dark shapes within it, one even upon the dais where Lord Gyes's bed lay, an ugly bronze knife in hand.

The first of the monsters turned to look at her, then the others followed. In the nighttime darkness, lit only by starlight, its eyes glowed a deadly blue.

She bared her teeth.

Fortunately for her, her companion was not limited by flawed vocal cords and yelled a warning. "Lord Gyes!" he cried, at the same time firing his pistol.

The energy blast blew a hole the size of a fist clean through the nearest draugr's chest.

And then, they had the full attention of them all.

In her life, Unara had fought sharks, octopus, kraken. But the worst things, the absolute worst things to kill were reef eels. They weren't large and they didn't naturally hunt in swarms, but if you got bit by one, you could be assured a mass of them would soon be upon you, ripping, tearing, fighting for mouthfuls of flesh. It didn't take long for the Thalassan body—whole or in pieces—to break down, but eels could swallow fast enough that the process happened in their stomachs. They still got fed. And that led to a frenzy.

These draugr moved like eels.

No finesse. No concern for any other factors. Focused totally on the kill.

All five of the remaining monsters rushed Unara and the House Guard all at the same time. The guard began firing, standing his ground even as the monsters came on.

That was not the way you fought eels.

Unara, by contrast, kept moving. She whirled and twisted, knife in a backhanded grip, the upper flat edge laid back along her forearm, striking out when she could, dancing away when she couldn't. Two of the draugr came apart under the assault.

The guard went down, three of the draugr falling on him. His energy gun spat deadly light, blowing through one of their chests, reeking sea-foam crashing on the floor. One of the remaining draugr ended the guard and the other got up on all fours toward the bed, where Lord Gyes was just waking up.

Unara was there, throwing herself down for a strike. But movement here in the air was all different from the water, and she misjudged the impact of gravity. in the water, she could have grabbed the thing by a limb and use her own momentum to throw it away. Here. she just left herself vulnerable.

It roared at her, scrambling over her, clawed hands tearing at her breastplate, trying to reach her throat. She got a knee up between herself and the monster, kicking the draugr off of her, kicking it away.

Before she could get her knife up and through its neck, though, a long blade flashed in the starlight, swinging down hard. It sliced clean through the vertebrae of the draugr's corrupted neck and its head rolled away.

She looked up to see Lord Gyes in nothing but a long sleep shirt, pulling his sword free with a grunt. He had swung with such force, the tip had embedded itself in the deck beneath the carpet.

"I need my trousers, boots," he muttered, looking around, finding them. "What are these things?"

Unara had no idea how to explain a draugr to him. But she tried, pointing at him, then making a little ship with her hands, diving it down, pantomiming a brief little fight and a swim up.

"Are you saying these are the things that attacked my ship?" he asked, incredulous, as he dressed rapidly.

She nodded.

"But how would you know about..." Trousers up and fastened, he jammed down his left heel into its boot and stood, loose linen shirt billowing. He seized the other boot. "Never mind. I take it such monsters are endemic on this world?"

Unara shook her head.

"At least they die," he said grimly, and retrieved his sword. "Come. We must reach the command deck."

THE TRIP up through the drop-craft was surreal.

The draugr seemed to be everywhere. Their stink. Their knives, crooked and corroded. Lord Gyes had the better reach with his sword, and Unara, guarding the rear, found herself wishing once again for a fishing spear. In the distance, they could hear screaming, yelling, the distinct crack of energy weapon discharges.

"There's too many of them," Lord Gyes panted after they'd finished off a small cluster encountered at a corridor junction. He looked around in disgust at the bodies. They were already falling apart like sandcastles in the ebbing tide. "What's happening to them?"

Unara shook her head and pulled at his arm, pointing behind them. Her legs were on fire, sensation fleeing as waves of pain pushed it away, and she was afraid of losing her footing. But only speed would save them.

More draugr were coming, so thick now they filled the entire corridor.

Unara and Lord Gyes fled.

As they approached the final junction in the hallway, they ran headfirst into a group of draugr coming up the opposite way. Unara grabbed Lord Gyes and pulled them both around the corner. Only just in time.

Something in the hallway seemed to explode, a sound louder and more painful than anything Unara had ever heard. She almost dropped her knife.

"To us!" somebody yelled.

She looked up, half-dazed from the sound.

Captain Thorsen, waiting for them inside the main air lock, him and a half dozen of the House Guard. He had a smoking gun in his hand, a design she had not seen before.

Lord Gyes pulled her to her feet, and she glanced back. The draugr were so thick now that there was no space between them.

"We'll cover you!" Captain Thorsen yelled again and raised the gun. Another deafening shot. Another draugr falling.

Together, Unara and Lord Gyes closed the distance to the

command deck in a few seconds. Every guard was firing now. Running into that strange gunfire seemed suicidal to Unara, but there was no choice. They kept a straight line through the center of the hallway and did not waver from it.

Lord Gyes stumbled at the edge of the air lock, but Captain Thorsen was there to pull him in. One of the other guards hit the controls to shut the doors.

The door began sliding shut. Several of the guards stood in the breach and kept firing. The draugr were here now, arms and knives reaching through the closing gap, and, inexplicably, the doors stopped. Began opening again.

"It's the safety protocols! It won't close with bodies in the way!" somebody yelled. Unara glanced behind her. One of the guardsmen had a control panel torn open, desperately yanking and stripping wires. "Attempting manual override!"

"Drive them back!" Captain Thorsen shouted. He tossed Unara the guard's gun, and she smashed it into the face of one of the draugr. "Clear the doors!"

With the butts of energy guns and a cacophony of explosions that left the air lock smoky, Unara, Lord Gyes, and the House Guard battered the draugr advance. The creatures were mindless, heedless of anything like their own survival, so all the defenders could do was hold.

Finally, after what seemed like an eternity, just as a draugr grabbed her gun and tried to wrest it away, Unara saw the doors move.

They smashed down fast, so fast the arm grabbing for the gun was cut off and lay like a beached fish, flopping for a moment or two before falling to scraps of flesh and bone.

The silence that filled the air lock, just for a moment, was profound.

Then the inner doors dinged open. Back to chaos.

All around the command deck, people were at their stations, reading off reporting, calling information up to the captain.

"What were those things?" Lord Gyes demanded as they strode over to the captain's station. It was all Unara could do to keep herself from limping as she followed.

"Unknown, sir. We can't seem to get a read on where they came from or what they are," the captain reported, and brought up a projected view of the landing field. "Right now, they seem to be attacking three delegations. Us, the Caledons, and the Suyarii."

"Confirmed?"

"We have visual confirmation of muzzle fire. Radio reports are garbled. You know how bad communications are here on this planet."

"Muzzle fire," Lord Gyes muttered, and looked to Captain Thorsen, who was still holding that strange gun of his. "Why are you using a projectile weapon on my drop-craft?"

Captain Thorsen patted it. "Should I have left you out in the hall to die, sir? Over a couple little holes in the hull?"

Lord Gyes stared at him for a moment more and then seemed to remember himself. "Of course not. Forgive me." He turned to Unara. "Is there anything you can tell us?"

She shook her head, casting around for something, anything.

And then she saw it.

A draugr. Inside the bridge. Knife up, right behind one of the radio operators.

Unara pointed desperately, shaking a little as she did so, but it was too late.

The radio operator screamed, and then screamed no more.

Draugr were suddenly everywhere, falling on the crew.

People began running, yelling. Some fought, but most didn't have weapons. Lord Gyes brought up his sword, even as the guard formed a circle around him. They were firing at will now, but Unara could see that it wasn't going to be enough.

"Captain Thorsen!" he yelled.

"Seal the entrance!" the captain bellowed.

But then, Unara watched in horror as one of the creatures, seemingly as solid and bony as a human, squeezed up through a narrow space under a console, like a reef octopus after a crab. She grabbed Thorsen's arm and pointed.

He looked at it for a moment, then put a bullet through the draugr's head. "Death world indeed," he muttered to himself.

THE FIRST TIME Unara had visited the Drift Clan, she had been ten years old. Dryagr was a strong boy of fifteen then, already taken with Glaeva, who had giggled and teased him, the two chasing each other through the akker habitats when they thought nobody was watching.

One day, though, as Father worked out whatever deal he'd gone there to work out, their shoal of akkers had drifted through a bait ball, an enormous group of small silver prey-fish, being pursued by a pack of fast-swimming hunter-thunnus. The prey-fish hadn't had a chance. Over the course of a half hour or so, the thunnus devoured them all, one by one, until nothing was left but a cloud of glinting scales, drifting in the currents.

A wholesale slaughter.

That was what Unara witnessed on the bridge that night.

The draugr were nowhere near as elegant as the thunnus, nor nearly as fast. But there were many of them and more kept coming. As before, on the *Gylfy's Delight*, they breached the air lock doors. As before, the crew formed a tighter and tighter circle around Lord Gyes, seemingly heedless of their own safety as they fought to keep their House scion alive.

Unara fought with them, fought as hard as she could. Stabbing, slashing, striking, smashing. She used her knife until it broke, then she grabbed up a rifle from a fallen guard, firing and striking. What she would have given for a fishing spear! It wasn't enough. For every rotten skull she caved in or dark body she knocked off the captain's platform, more kept coming. Her body was a mass of pain, and her muscles ached, but it was all very distant.

Lord Gyes was there too, as was Captain Thorsen. Then the bodyguard was grabbed and hauled away, down into the melee, and Lord Gyes was pulled down, banging his head on a console, and then it was just her.

The draugr were all advancing on the downed lord. Too many to fight hand to hand. But no other option was open to her.

She tried to pick up Lord Gyes's sword, but it was too heavy for her. She let it fall and grabbed her half-shattered rifle instead, the barrel cracked apart and razor sharp.

As if from a great distance, she wondered what her father would have said about all this.

One of her legs was grabbed, then the other. The draugrs' hands were like ice. She hit the deck hard, weapon knocked aside. She kicked out, desperately trying to reach her gun. Unara got one leg free and pulled herself to a knee, even as a pair of draugr clumped toward her, carrying half a command console in their hands.

There. An energy pistol.

Grabbing it, she shot one of the oncoming draugr in the face. At this range, she couldn't miss. It collapsed, the console falling with it.

But those were only two. Two out of what seemed an endless shoal. Too many to fight, too many to beat back. Icy-cold hands tore at her, yanking her down the steps. She kicked, she writhed, but the creature wouldn't let go. No longer was she even fighting to save Lord Gyes. All reason had fled. The only thing left was a single over-riding desire to live.

And then, just as hands grabbed her hair, forcing her head back and her throat out, a light.

A blinding, overwhelming light.

Hands loosened. Screams, inhuman, echoed around the room.

The draugr was screaming.

And then Unara was free.

More guards were rushing into the room now. The draugr were dying. The draugr had lost.

Unara sagged, falling down next to Lord Gyes's side, and let others finish the fight.

"YOU SHALL LIVE," Healer Eyr was saying as she bound a bleeding gash on Unara's arm. "Superficial wounds like this, I might knit back together outright. A very simple temporal manipulation." Unara glared at her. The feii shook her head. "But not here. My skill with such things fails me on this world. Tell me, Unara, do you know why?"

The princess ignored the alien's provocation, looking around instead. Beyond the feii, it seemed that the drop-craft had a human medical team as well. Right now, they were all on the bridge, helping the ones they could. Black cloths were draped over others. Unara didn't understand the significance of that, but assumed it was some sort of funeral custom.

"It looks worse than it is," Eyr assured her. "Most of the crew survived. Not most of the bridge crew, of course, but others elsewhere."

Unara nodded, closing her eyes for a moment. When she opened them again, she saw Thorsen across the room, talking to one of his men. The man was propped up against a console while a medic fitted some kind of device over the stump of his left leg. The captain had a bandage wrapped around his own head and one of his uniform sleeves was shredded, the rags remaining stained red with blood, but he didn't seem to notice.

"What strange things I noticed, burning my way from Medical up here to the bridge. These things had the feel of the abyss about them," Eyr replied, and picked up a small scrap of flesh from the deck plates. "So tell me, Thalassan, who on your world practices this kind of black genomancy?"

Unara thought about Glaeva. About Ragnyr.

Both of them beneficiaries of Lady Hethra's improvements to the normal transformation process.

But before that dangerous thought could go any further, a projection field glimmered on, harsh light coalescing into the shape of a man. The effect on the crew was immediate; everyone who could stop what they were doing had, their attention fixed on it.

"Lord Gyes," Captain Thorsen said, standing immediately, saluting. "It is good to see you, even just like this."

<Healer Eyr told me what happened,> a voice boomed from concealed speakers around the room. <Is my son alive?>

"Yes, Father," Lord Gyes coughed, pulling himself painfully to his feet. He gestured vaguely. "Thanks to her."

<Thalassan,> the man of light said, looking around at the carnage. It was a hologram, and yet it acted as if it could see. Maybe it could. Off-worlders did strange things with their technology. <What a mess you've made of my ship.>

Everyone on the ship was looking at her, Unara realized. The figure in the projection was looking at her.

With a great deal of effort, she got to her feet.

<Your actions have saved this craft tonight, Thalassan, and more importantly, you saved my son, without whom there is no future for this House,> the projection of the old Lord Gyes said. <What gift can the Gyes bestow upon you for this act?>

Unara didn't hesitate.

This was her chance, wasn't it?

She pointed up.

<I don't understand,> old Lord Gyes said.

"Milord, with respect," Captain Thorsen said, stepping painfully toward the projection, "she cannot speak."

<So what is she asking?>

Unara made a few more little gestures before Captain Thorsen nodded and turned back to the projection. "I believe she is asking to come with us when we leave. Is that correct?"

She nodded emphatically.

A murmur went up around the command deck, but the man in the projection held up a hand and all fell silent. <That is a serious request, Thalassan.>

She nodded again.

<None of your people leave this world,> he said, and seemed to sigh. <But a promise made is a promise kept. When we depart for the stars, you shall be with us.>

The princess couldn't help the smile that spread over her face, slowly, then all at once. Not even the carnage around her could dim her joy.

At last.

Everything she had worked so hard for, sacrificed for, given up... her plan was all coming to fruition. Just as it was supposed to. Just as she knew it would.

But then, Unara caught sight of movement, over there by the door. Vaelyn. With an expression on her face that Unara had never seen before. An expression she couldn't quite place. Something about it cooled her mood, like being plunged into deep water. What was that about?

Vaelyn noticed her then, and, nodding back, made a quick hand gesture.

She wanted to talk.

Unara looked around. All attention on the command deck was back on the projection of old Lord Gyes now. He was talking, talking in Rikstag now. Nobody was paying attention to her. And with one last look back at Lord Gyes, Unara slipped away.

CHAPTER TWENTY-ONE

Vaelyn was almost disappointed by how easy it was to get Unara down to the boundary pools.

She had grabbed the writing slate from Unara's shipside quarters on her way up to the command deck, but so far, they hadn't used it much. Vaelyn had simply explained that a Thalassan security detachment was on the way—which it was—and it would be better if Unara wasn't there—which was also true—and might it not be a good idea to pick up her pearl collection before departing the planet?

That last one may or may not have been necessary. Vaelyn had no idea how finances worked off-world, but House Gyes seemed to pride itself on its word. If old Lord Gyes had promised Unara safe passage, then he would provide it. The younger Lord Gyes seemed quite fond of Unara as well.

It irritated Vaelyn, how easy everything seemed to come to the ocean-born woman, and how little she seemed to notice. Wasn't being a princess good enough? Did she really need to defy law and tradition and all rational sense to take an excursion out to the stars?

At least the trip down to the pools was uneventful. No encounters with any other Thalassans; nobody was out in the tunnels. Everything was eerily quiet.

And so it was that they reached their old boundary pool, one of the little-used and oft-forgotten ones, where the two of them had talked and laughed and—

Get yourself together, Vaelyn admonished herself silently. *You always knew this was coming.* And she swallowed her emotion down. Forced herself to be cold about it.

"As promised, Princess," she said, gesturing to a small collection of things near the edge of the water. "Your effects. I brought them up a few days ago for you."

It was a lie, of course. Vaelyn had had nothing to do with this. But it scarcely mattered at this point. What was one more lie now?

Unara smiled, happiness clear, and she swept back her long hair as she knelt down to open the things. She was dressed only in some thin, gauzy shift and her breastplate, making her look like some primordial water nymph from one of the creation sagas. She carefully inspected the contents of the clamshell case.

Vaelyn had never seen Unara's collection before, but the princess had talked about it before. She'd seeded a fair number of pearls back when she'd first had the idea of escaping Thalassa, and she'd found others, old and forgotten. She'd been secretly tending them for years.

Effort well spent. The contents of that chest were exquisite. All colors, all shapes, some larger than a human fist, growing for years or even decades in some distant corner of never-visited reefs. Vaelyn watched her count them, guilt warring with anger inside of her.

"Everything is there," Vaelyn said, hesitating. "I didn't take anything if that's what you're..."

And she stopped cold.

Because there Unara was, holding out an iridescent pearl the color of second twilight, one so large that she had to use both her hands to hold it.

Vaelyn stared at the thing. "It's lovely, I agree, but..."

Unara shook her head and held it out, a little closer this time.

"For me?" Vaelyn asked, still hesitating. Pearls were the most valuable commodity on Thalassa, the closest thing to currency they had; most trade, both above and below the waves, was conducted with such things as this. But this, this belonged in the royal treasure vaults. "I can't take that, Unara. That's worth a fortune."

Unara nodded and placed it in her hand nonetheless. Vaelyn, still stunned, almost dropped it. And then Unara was holding out something else.

Her akker's control bracer.

Vaelyn backed up at that, clutching the pearl to her chest. "I can't take that, Unara. Akkers barely listen to the sky-born. If anybody finds out I'm riding yours, I'm dead."

Unara shook her head and pulled out the writing tablet. *Take care of it for me, at least. It'll need a new rider or it'll go feral and then the palace guard will have to kill it. You can pass it along to whoever you feel deserves it.*

"Unara..."

I raised it from a juvenile. I can't leave knowing it'll die. Please.

And there was such an honest, earnest look on Unara's face that Vaelyn almost broke. All the lies, all the sneaking around and plotting and manipulating. All the guilt.

"Unara, you need to—" she began.

Something moved in the water.

Too late.

Because the inner door burst open then, Leyli and three other Stone Clan members all holding off-world energy guns. Vaelyn looked back at Unara, half-risen from her crouch on the sand. She looked at Vaelyn, a terrible realization dawning in her eyes.

Suddenly ashamed, Vaelyn looked away.

<Hello, Princess,> a voice said.

Lady Hethra was here.

<Unara,> Lady Hethra said from beyond the acrylic panel. <How good of you to join us. Vaelyn, thank you for getting her down here so readily.>

Unara glanced back at her friend, who had turned even more gray than usual, but spoke with a clear voice. "Yes, Lady Hethra, as you asked."

<Excellent.> Lady Hethra laid a hand on the glass, peering in like she was considering some wary fish trapped in her net. Her attitude was strange. <How did this start between you and I? 'Oh please, Lady Hethra, I didn't get what I wanted, please give it to me.' What a selfish, worthless little thing you are. I wonder, will the stars be enough for you?>

Unara frowned, looking back at Vaelyn. What in hell and high water was going on here?

Lady Hethra rapped on the glass. <Don't you look at her, daughter of Aegyr. You look at me,> she snarled.

Never in her life had anybody spoken to Unara like that. It was like a slap to the face. Unable to retort the way she wanted, Unara was forced to use the writing slate. *What is going on here?*

<Oh, I'm sure you'd love answers to that, wouldn't you?> Lady Hethra replied, a cruel smile on her lips. <I am...returning balance to the seas.>

Balance?

<Yes, little spoiled princess. Balance. The balance your father and all his kind have discarded for too long, selling the treasures of this world to the stars, inviting the detritus of the human race here to steal it all away.>

Treasures? What treasures? Everything traded to the stars was grown, farmed, hunted. All could be remade. All was renewed.

And then Unara realized what was going on here.

This is a coup, she scribbled hastily on the tablet.

<Far more than a coup, little princess, although your father's death will bring me great satisfaction. No, you think too small! Vaelyn, tell her.>

Unara looked back at her friend—former friend?—but the other woman wouldn't meet her eyes. "Just kill her and be done with it, milady."

<Kill her! What a fantastic idea. Unara, do you hear that? Kill her! Lovely.> Lady Hethra swam this way and that, driven by tiny movements of her tail. She was smiling. <Just like I'm going to kill your father, and all the rest of you who defy the will of the moons. But death is never enough. What we need is a little...chaos first.>

Chaos? That was Rota's realm. Unara bared her teeth. *You sent the draugr tonight!*

<I did,> Lady Hethra said, still smiling. <For the music alone, it was deserved. But no, Princess Unara, just killing your father isn't enough. He must be exposed!> She turned to Vaelyn. <Do you have proof that she requested to leave the planet?>

Unara stared at Vaelyn, mind racing. She could see her mistake now. She could see what was happening. Lady Hethra had helped her assume this form all for the goal of humiliating her father. Already the people said that Hildra had withdrawn her favor from him. Bad harvests on the reef, no male heirs, and now, a daughter who dared to buck a thousand years of tradition...

Vaelyn, looking miserable, just nodded and held up a small recording crab. "It's here, Lady Hethra."

<Excellent,> the abyssal chieftain purred, and gestured to one of the Stone Clan with guns. <Kill her. Somewhere Hildra won't see you do it, as we discussed. Vaelyn!>

"Yes, milady."

<Go back to the Gyes pavilion. Seed the Trader Houses with the information that King Aegyr is trying to wipe them out in order to ensure exclusive contracts with the Suyarii. That seems to rile them up. I want them at war with each other before the end.> And she smiled at Unara. <Then I'll kill your father myself, and the Abyssal Clan will remind Thalassa of what true ocean power looks like.>

Unara couldn't even scream as they dragged her away.

ACT THREE
WASTES

CHAPTER TWENTY-TWO

Things were already in an uproar by the time Hakon got to the Hall of Dreams that morning.

For a moment, Hakon just took in the scene, trying to process what he was seeing. The Hall of Dreams was deep inside the palace caverns, underwater, with only a very minimal amount of airspace in its single dry gallery. This morning, however, so many people were crammed into that space that additional ventilation had been brought in to ensure an acceptable oxygen level in the air. And it was noisy too, everyone talking, shouting, yelling.

"Where is the king?" he demanded of the nearest person.

"Over there, Skald," his clansman said, pointing to the space near the glass.

Hakon looked. There the king indeed was, standing stock-still, arms crossed over his chest. Staring at the scene drawn in bio-lights in the dreamer pool.

It took Hakon a moment to realize what he was looking at, but when he did, his blood ran cold. Unara. It was Unara. With legs. On the deck of a spaceship.

What in all the blackwater was going on?

Nobody stopped Hakon as he pushed his way through the crowd. Indeed, most moved aside the moment they saw him. He was a skald, the court historian, and this, it seemed, was a moment that would need to be remembered.

Hakon finally reached a bit of open space; Jarl Dryagr was standing near the window with the king, all the kaupang representatives in a semicircle around them. Every clan chieftain on the Oceanfall reefs was assembled outside in the water. Lady Hethra was senior among them, and even she looked uncomfortable.

There was only one sky-born up there. Vaelyn, kneeling. Kneeling beside King Aegyr, who was standing at the wall, one hand on the glass. He was dressed in nothing but a rough tunic, as if he had been dragged from his bed.

"My apologies, my king," she said, head bowed and hair falling over her face and shoulders, obscuring all expression. "I am sorry to bring such news."

"When did you find out about this, Vaelyn?" he asked softly.

"Only after last night's draugr attacks, milord, I swear it."

Draugr. Hakon had heard that word whispered around the palace today, and now it started a new uproar, both in the air and out in the water.

"Silence!" Jarl Dryagr yelled. "I will have silence for this proceeding! Or would you all condemn our king out of hand?!"

<The evidence seems clear enough.> That was Jarl Ranar, the chieftain of the northern seas, beyond the glass, out in the ocean. His wife, Lady Ragnyr, leaned on him. <What else needs to be said?>

Hakon stepped into the open space, moving over to Jarl Dryagr. The chieftain of the southern currents looked exhausted but noticed Hakon and waved to him. "Skald," he said as Hakon approached. "I am glad to see you. I would have your counsel on this."

"What is happening?" Hakon asked.

"Princess Unara stands accused of violating Hildra's law, and with her, the king."

Hakon thought of the handwritten note that Unara had given to

Jarl Yvar. His blood ran cold. Did they know about that too? "The princess's actions, whatever they are, are her own." He waved a hand at the scene out in the water. "This is not our king's fault."

"I know. But there are quite a few voices among the ocean-born upset about the music given to Lady Amaro last night," Dryagr sighed. "And then, of course, there is the matter of the draugr attack."

"Was that confirmed to be draugr?"

"Nothing's confirmed yet," Dryagr replied, and then raised his voice again. "My fine people! I must have silence!" A disgruntled calm fell in the airspace. Dryagr breathed out. "Thank you. Now, we must know. Is this authentic?"

<It is, milord,> the master of the pool said from beyond the window. <I have examined the drone that recorded this scene. It is indisputably real.>

"Then how did such a thing come to pass?" Dryagr demanded, looking around. "Sire, was this action by Princess Unara approved in some way? Perhaps some new tactic for negotiating this kaupang?"

It was an out, Hakon recognized. A way for the king to save face, to save his daughter. But King Aegyr had always been a serious man, honest to a fault. Now, the king shook his head. Stroked his beard. "I have no idea how this came to pass. It was not authorized by me." He stared at the image, eyes narrowed. "I do not know why she would do this."

<But what gene-hallow would be so foolish as to facilitate something like this without your express permission?> Jarl Ranar asked. <Do these warm seas addle the minds of your gothi?>

<I may provide some insight into that,> Lady Hethra replied. <Gothi Strygr. He was excommunicated from the abyss for...unsavory practices. He has been making his home up here, I understand, over the past decade or so, out in the wild reefs that no clan claims as territory. Perhaps Princess Unara went to him.>

"How long has the princess been up here?" Jarl Yvar suddenly demanded. "And what has she been doing? Helping this whelp manipulate the other traders?"

<You were ready to betray them all for the contents of the Suyarii's holds,> snapped Lady Ragnyr. <Who are you to speak now?>

"Wanting to increase my clan's profits is betrayal? Then what do we call this?" Yvar demanded, thrusting a hand at the scene in the water. "Unara must be dragged back here and made to answer for this affront! Is it any wonder that the depths sent its demons to attack these off-worlders?"

That sent off a fresh round of yelling. Dryagr had to pound the floor with his spear this time to silence it.

As it dwindled again, Hakon stepped forward, hands out. "May I speak?" he asked.

Dryagr sighed. "Of course, Skald Hakon. I think we are all in need of a little wisdom."

"I understand that the singing of our songs for the Lady Amaro was pushing the boundary of what we may reveal to the outsiders, the ones who do not ride the ocean, who do not live in the light of our moons," he began, looking around, gauging his audience as he always did. "But it was my crime, for I am the one who translated the words, and I am the one who sang them."

<But the king permitted it,> one of the clan chieftains, outside in the water, protested.

<And you are his grandson,> another pointed out. <Why would you not defend him?>

"My mother was his daughter, that is true. But I was born under the sky," Hakon said, bowing a little. "I am Stone Clan only. If I have erred in my dedication to the ocean, it does not mean that our king has."

<And what of this blood connection?> Jarl Ranar said. <Some might say Skald Hakon's life is proof that Hildra's favor has withdrawn from our king.>

"No," Hakon said hurriedly, seeing where this was headed. "It is my crime. Put me to death if you must. Judge the princess when she returns to the sea. This is not—"

<You misunderstand, Skald Hakon,> Lady Hethra said, and her voice was sad. <The princess has requested passage off-world, and House Gyes has granted it.>

For the first time in a long time, Hakon had no idea what to say. Stunned, he looked over at the king, hoping for some kind of insight, guidance, anything. But the man's eyes were fixed, his jaw set. Silent.

Jarl Dryagr held up both hands before the yelling could resume. "Please, please, my good people. You elected me to adjudicate this proceeding, so allow me to do so." Hakon saw nods of agreement, and Dryagr sighed. "We cannot hold a full trial now. That requires all the chieftains of all the clans to be present, or at least, all that can be gathered. Such a thing will take weeks to prepare." A few voices called out, but he waved them down again. "But clearly, Princess Unara must not be allowed to carry out her plan. Vaelyn, is she still with House Gyes?"

The Stone Clan woman finally looked up. She had been crying, Hakon could see, but she straightened and wiped her face. "I don't know."

"I shall go out to their drop-ship myself to collect her when we are done here," he decided. "And if they do not wish to turn her over for trial and judgement, we shall force the issue. The off-worlders are greedy. They will not risk their regeneratives for a single woman, even a princess."

There were a few chuckles, a few whispers.

Dryagr continued. "If, as has been suggested, we are facing the ocean's wrath right now as a result of the king's actions or anything else, we must take steps to ensure our safety."

"Yes," Yvar snapped. "Executions."

Dryagr whirled on him, spear snapping out. "There will be no blood shed here until I am satisfied as to whose blood it should be!"

Yvar stared back, heedless of the blade at his throat. "What are you afraid of, Dryagr? Finding out that your precious Glaeva is dead because her family is cursed?"

For a moment, Hakon thought that Dryagr might strike the other jarl down. But the Drift Clan chieftain didn't move. "Lady Hethra, bring me that gothi."

<With all haste.>

"We shall have answers, Yvar, not blood," Dryagr said. "We are not sharks or kraken to be driven mad by the scent of death in the water. If the moons have brought down draugr on us as punishment for the king's actions, then we shall turn him over to the depths as tradition demands. But not until I have proof." He looked around at the rest of the room, at the ocean-born assembled outside. "Do I make myself clear?"

Nods came, murmurs of agreement. Dryagr nodded back and looked to the king. "Sire, my apologies, but you will need to be confined."

He nodded back. "I understand."

"Have you nothing to say to us, my jarl?" Yvar sneered.

The king fixed him with a furious glare, and some of that bravado seemed to melt away. "The truth will come out," he said. "As it always does. Whatever force was behind last night's attacks, we shall see its true face soon enough."

"I think I'm looking at it," Yvar shot back.

"You overstep!" Dryagr snapped and turned to the Stone Clan behind him. "Please find a place for the king. Make it comfortable, at least. We shall need to hold him until the kaupang is over."

The guards nodded, and the king was led off without protest. The sight of him being escorted out of the room under armed guard made Hakon's heart ache.

<What of the kaupang?> Lady Ragnyr asked.

"We finish it, of course," Jarl Dryagr said wearily. "All contracts must be finalized today, of course, and material exchange begins the day after tomorrow. I see no reason why any of that must be interrupted."

<I nominate Jarl Dryagr to assume the king's duties,> Lady Hethra said.

<Let's put it to a vote,> Lady Ragnyr agreed.

There were no dissenting voices, Hakon noticed. Dryagr was well-liked and well trusted and had no enemies here. Even Yvar was a yes vote.

"I accept the decision of my peers," Dryagr said, and sighed heavily. "Skald Hakon, please make a written record of this proceeding."

Hakon bowed. "An unusual step, Jarl, but it shall be done."

"Good. Now I must go speak to Lord Gyes and all the rest of them. Vaelyn, tell your fellow escorts to offer little information today. I want them uncomfortable."

"Milord, if I could speak to you in—" she began.

<Vaelyn knows what to do,> Lady Hethra said, outside the glass, cutting the sky-born off. <The ocean demands a reckoning.>

<Yes, milady.>

"Then this gathering is adjourned," Dryagr said. "Go about your business, please, and do not talk about this to others who were not here. The rumors shall be bad enough without speculation about curses and monsters."

Hakon stayed behind as the room emptied, air and water both. When everyone was gone, he looked back to Jarl Dryagr. The man was leaning hard on his spear, still staring out at the image of Unara on the spaceship bridge. It was falling apart now, the dreamer crab dropping her influence, her larvae once again floating freely in the room's soft currents.

"Jarl," Hakon began.

But Dryagr cut him off with a hard sweep of his hand. "Don't, Skald. I know that you were only doing as ordered last night, but we both know you should never have sung that song."

Hakon hesitated. "Do you truly believe that is what caused the draugr attack?"

"I don't know," Dryagr said, and his hand tightened on his spear shaft. "But it doesn't matter what I believe. Or even what I can prove. There is fear here, and fearful people do foolish things." Then he shook himself. "If I can get the princess back, perhaps we can avoid war."

"If there's anything I can do, Jarl, please—"

"Stay out of my way," Dryagr told him.

And then Hakon was left alone, considering the ocean beyond the glass.

Draugr? The ocean's wrath? Hakon had sung of it many times, but that did not mean he took the stories at face value. Humans were most often the cause of their own misery, not some supernatural force watching them from the sky or lurking in the blackwater. Something else was going on here.

But what?

CHAPTER TWENTY-THREE

"Do we have any idea where she might be?"

"None, sir. She departed the drop-craft last night with Vaelyn, but that's all we know."

"Has Vaelyn turned up yet?"

"No, sir. I haven't seen her, either."

Karl rubbed a hand over his face, looking out at the bright daylight just cutting through the command deck's windows. The scene inside the drop-craft was bleak. While most of the equipment had survived the night intact, the human cost had been high. Dozens of crew were either seriously injured or dead; extra medical staff had been flown in from orbit to deal with the crisis. Bloodstains were still being scrubbed from the deck.

The Thalassan girl was the least of his problems. And yet, he worried.

"I don't like it. Something's happened. Activate whoever you can to find out what's happened. An action by a rival House, perhaps."

"Or the Suyarii."

"It's a possibility, of course, but—"

"Milord!"

It was one of the crew, the day's shift lead.

"What is it?" Thorsen asked.

"Somebody's coming," the crewman said. "Main entrance. Thalassans."

Karl raised an eyebrow. Beyond the escorts and his girl from the beach, the Thalassans almost never came out to the landing fields. Not even last night. "I shall go see who it is. Maybe they can help unravel this mystery," Karl told him, already moving.

"Mystery indeed," Captain Thorsen grunted, and fell into step next to him.

KARL WAS HALF EXPECTING it to be the king again—the man had seemed quite perturbed by the attack, despite his silence on the cause of it. But it was not the king who was waiting for him in the broad entrance hall of the drop-craft, but Jarl Dryagr. He looked more martial than he had in his trading hall, wearing a nacre breast-plate over fish-leather armor, instead of his usual gray tunic and leggings, and carrying a wicked-looking spear. His silver-blue hair was braided back tightly against his head.

"Weapons are not permitted on board!" Captain Thorsen snapped as they approached. "Guards, who let them in like this?"

"Peace, Captain," Karl said, and stepped in front of him, hand extended to Jarl Dryagr. "I am sure there is no problem here. The landing field was attacked last night. We should all be armed right now."

"Yes," Jarl Dryagr said. Gone was the jovial nature and easy smile that he had worn at their previous encounters. He was on edge, watching everything keenly, like he was expecting some hidden enemy to spring a trap on him. "So this is what a star-akker looks like on the inside. Not so different from the habitat-akker my own clan cultivates."

"Those are your living submersibles, correct?" Karl asked.

The jarl eyed him. "And who told you that?"

"Vaelyn mentioned it to me."

"Ahh yes, Vaelyn. Of course." Dryagr looked around a bit more. "Not what I expected at all."

It was a strange conversation. Strange enough that Karl was on edge now. What did this man want? Why was he here? Why now, when his crew had been slaughtered last night without a single shred of help from local security forces? Karl forced himself to smile. "Allow me to give you a tour, Jarl Dryagr."

"Regretfully, I cannot. I have much to attend to this morning and must keep this brief." He produced a roll of kelpskin paper, passing it along to Karl. "Do you recognize this woman?"

Karl unrolled the paper. It was a fine sketch, rendered in some kind of colored pigment, so bright it was almost glowing. And it was all Karl could do to school down his reaction.

It was an excellent likeness of his Thalassan girl, the one from the beach.

"I don't know," he lied, and tried to hand the scroll back. "All your women are so beautiful, it's hard to tell them apart."

Dryagr refused to take it. "Look again, Lord Gyes. Are you sure you don't recognize this one?"

"I have seen very few of your people since making planetfall last week," he said, wary now. "Why should I know this one? And what does it matter?"

The Thalassan sighed. "I have heard that she might be attempting to leave the planet."

"Is that so?"

"Yes, it is."

"That hardly seems a reason to be asking me about her."

"Perhaps you do not understand, Lord Gyes. For a Thalassan to leave this world is death."

Karl glanced over at Thorsen, whose face had hardened. He was tensing, as if anticipating action. "You would execute her for that?"

"I use the wrong word, maybe. We would not be the ones to kill her, but she would die nonetheless."

"And why is that?"

Again, Jarl Dryagr hesitated. "Are you sure you have not seen this woman, Lord Gyes?" he pressed. "For if any House was to even attempt to smuggle this woman off-world, they would not only leave here with their holds empty, but they would find no welcome for themselves here next kaupang. And who knows, they might even find themselves sharing in her fate."

Karl folded his arms. "Is that a threat?"

"A promise, Lord Gyes. There are consequences for breaking our law, even for her. But if you turn her over to us, however, you help both yourselves and her."

"I don't know where she—"

And suddenly, there was a spear in his face.

At the same time, Karl was dimly aware of rifles coming up. Thorsen's detail, all aiming right at the Thalassan lord. He held up a hand, signaling them to stop.

"I shall grant you one last chance to be honest with me, Lord Gyes," Jarl Dryagr growled. "I know she was here. I know she was with you. I know your father promised her off-world passage. You will turn her over to us, or tides help me, you will suffer for it."

"Drop the weapon, Jarl Dryagr," Captain Thorsen snapped.

Karl waved him back, eyes fixed on Jarl Dryagr. "If you know that, then you know she saved my life last night. During that little attack by whatever monsters lurk under the waves here. Surely you understand that?"

Jarl Dryagr's expression wavered, but his spear did not. "I understand a blood debt, Lord Gyes, and I am sorry you cannot fulfill it, for Unara will not be leaving this world, no matter what lies between you."

Karl heard the sound of more guns being primed. He glanced up. More guards had arrived, ringing the upper levels of the dropcraft's rear atrium. "My men will cut you down the second you draw my blood, Jarl Dryagr. And then what is accomplished? How does that help your Unara?"

The tip of the spear moved a fraction closer to his throat. "Where is she?"

"I don't know. She left here last night after the attack, and I have not seen her since."

"And she said nothing to you?"

"She has said nothing at all. She doesn't have a voice," Karl told him honestly. That seemed to catch the Thalassan off guard. Interesting. "What is she to you? Family?"

The Thalassan lord's face twitched, and he finally withdrew his spear. "You have until this time tomorrow to hand her over to us. Do not come to the final ceremony without her tomorrow, or I shall declare all negotiations with House Gyes null and void."

Karl folded his arms. "Who are you to enforce such a thing? Where is the king?"

"Tomorrow," Jarl Dryagr warned. And with that, the Thalassan lord swept out of the drop-craft, silent.

After a moment, Karl followed him to the main entrance, watching him descend the ramp, the man vanishing back into the morning mist.

Thorsen joined Karl out there, rifle still in his hands. "What in all the void do you suppose they want with her?"

"I don't know," he said, "but even if I had her, I wouldn't turn her over while they're threatening to execute her."

"That risks the House, sir."

"I am not going to make deals over the bodies of dead friends, Thorsen," he replied.

"And what if it comes down to the fleet or a girl, sir?"

Karl rubbed his face, trying to think. "We don't have her, so it's all theoretical anyway. Find her."

"Yes, sir."

"And find out how they knew about what happened last night."

"Yes, sir." Thorsen sounded more irritated that time.

"And find Vaelyn, if you can," Karl added. "I have a feeling there's more going on here with the Thalassans than we can see."

After the meeting in the Hall of Dreams, Vaelyn didn't know what to do with herself. She needed to think, to be alone, to gather herself.

So she went out where she always did, out on the paths that ringed the cliffs, to the entrance to the grotto. It was daytime and the sea was rough, but the tide was low, and Vaelyn knew the way well enough. She sat in the grotto's shadow for a long time, watching the waves, morose. Unara had not exactly been a friend, but she had never been an enemy. Not truly. And Vaelyn had betrayed her.

For what?

For this, she told herself, staring out at the ocean. For a chance to live life the way all Thalassans should have been able to live. The song of the sea was in all their blood; being without it was like a physical pain.

And maybe that was why she had hated Unara so. Unara, the princess who had everything Vaelyn had ever wanted and turned her back on it.

Now she was dead. Dead, just like Glaeva, for no greater crime than simply being King Aegyr's daughter.

This wasn't what Vaelyn had signed up for.

Except it was, wasn't it? She had always known it would end here, in blood. And more people were going to die soon—a lot more. Lord Gyes and Captain Thorsen and Branner and all the other off-worlders Vaelyn had met. Fine people, pleasant people, people who had committed no crime, no offense, other than to take what was offered here, and at such extreme risk to their own fortunes...

Vaelyn squinted up at the sky. Hildra was high. The tide was calm. Then she looked back into the shadowy depths of the grotto.

Shedding her heavy outer fish-tail skirt and boots, Vaelyn

jumped into the water. She had no lantern, and the suns were on the other side of the cliffs right now, but it scarcely mattered. She knew the way enough by touch.

While sky-born Thalassans lacked many of the adaptations given to the ocean-born, some things, like the manner in which the body disseminated oxygen in deep water, were still present. And even the Stone Clan had to gather food, hunt for meat, out on the reefs. Dive gear wasn't always practical or possible to have with you, and it often broke.

Treading water in the pool, she gulped air the way she had been taught as a child, by Hakon, nonetheless, and she pushed the sudden, unwelcome memory aside. Quick harsh inhales, filling her lungs, and then she was diving, kicking out as hard as she could.

Without fins, propelling herself downward with lungs full of air was difficult, but not impossible. It took her six minutes to clear the tunnel. No time to spare.

Vaelyn kicked her way up to the airspace at the top of the strange little gene-hallow, grabbing a fresh lungful of air, breathing hard to clear the carbon dioxide from her body.

"Free diving here. I'm impressed."

Ducking back under the water, Vaelyn looked around. It was indeed Lady Hethra, and the woman was holding out a medical breathing mask for her.

Vaelyn took it gratefully. <Thank you,> she said after she secured the thing over her face.

"What brings you down here?"

What brings you? Vaelyn wanted to ask but held her tongue. Lady Hethra had an uncanny ability to find her at the most inopportune times. "I suppose I needed to see it," she said lamely.

"Yes, the salvation of your clan. Have you come to finally accept it yourself?"

<I... I don't know,> she said. It was a deception, but not a lie. Something had been holding her back all these months, preventing her from taking that last step. <I keep seeing Glaeva in my mind,

coming apart. Or Unara, suffering so badly from the maintenance infusions to hold the change at bay.>

"And you fear that for yourself?" Lady Hethra asked gently. "Don't. Their agony was intentional."

<Lady Ragnyr collapsed too, and...>

"Oh, Vaelyn, don't worry, I have tested this extensively. It was not without...error, at first, but even such mistakes have been... useful. They break down quickly, at least, so the off-worlders have no flesh to extract our secrets from."

What did... Oh no.

Vaelyn's blood ran cold.

The draugr. Were they...had Lady Hethra...

"It will work on you, I assure you of that," Lady Hethra continued, and smiled at her fondly. Almost like— "I guaranteed that before I sent you ashore."

It was a strange phrase. <What do you mean?>Vaelyn asked slowly.

"Children are hard to grow, in the abyss. It is cold, energy limited. It can take years to conceive, if you can conceive at all. And then, to force the change so early, so young, all to ensure the success of a plan that..." And Hethra sighed. "It will be good to finally bring you home, daughter."

Vaelyn choked on her air supply, coughing into her regulator.

Lady Hethra watched her sadly, carefully. "I am sorry I never told you, Vaelyn. But it is time you knew the truth, my daughter, my only heir. Half the ocean is yours, Vaelyn. I shall make a gift of it to you, and you shall understand."

<No,> she said. <No, I'm not—>

But Hethra was swimming away from her, watching as an eel tucked into the bottom of the chiller sponge caught an unwary passing fish.

"Do you know why Thalassa spawns such terrible monsters?" she commented softly. "It is because of us. Because of what we have forced upon it. Because it hates us for disturbing its peace. For the moons. For forcing the evolution of the surface world before its time. Whatever we must do to make amends, we must do."

<I—>

"Do not worry, my daughter. When this is all over, I shall take you home and we will build a new world, with any who are deemed acceptable to serve." Lady Hethra smiled at her, indulgent, kind. "I know you are afraid now, but all will be well in the end. You will see. The depths are beautiful, Vaelyn, and in time, you will learn to hear their whispers as well."

Vaelyn was in shock.

Absolute and utter shock.

But Hethra—her mother, oh tides, her mother—was watching her, expectant, something vicious behind the concern in those pale eyes. Yet, refusing anything right now would end in her death. Swift and merciless. Or make her part of some mindless, shambling horde.

A horde that would drown the entire world.

"Come home, Vaelyn. Take the infusion and reclaim yourself," Lady Hethra said, reaching out a hand. "Don't worry. I will make everything right. We will make everything right."

The sea. Vaelyn had always wanted the sea.

Not like this, though. Not the abyss. Not the cold. Never had she thought...

But Lady Hethra was watching her. Lady Hethra was testing her.

This was where Unara was wrong.

There was no escape from this world.

Vaelyn took her mother's hand.

"Alright."

CHAPTER TWENTY-FOUR

Darkness.

Only once had Unara seen such darkness. On the way to Lady Hethra's vent fields. But even that way had been illuminated by the living lights of Thalassa's seas. There was nothing here. Nothing.

She wanted to ask the guards, but they were up front, talking, laughing. They were happy.

Unara didn't know how to feel about that.

Unara didn't recognize the men who had grabbed her. Leyli she knew, not well but in passing at least. She had remained behind, as had Vaelyn, as the others had grabbed her and dragged her up to a lower pool, where a four-person submersible had been waiting for them. They'd thrown her into the back water-lock, gone up to the cockpit, and dived.

At some point in the journey, she'd fallen asleep, although when and for how long she didn't know. Sleep looked the same as the world outside. Blackness. Nothing but blackness.

The guards had laughed at her when she pounded on the window. Laughed. Unara had never encountered anything like it in all her life. And in the growing chill of the water-lock, staring out at all that dark water, she was forced to consider why this was happening.

A coup, assuredly. Driven by Hethra, perhaps, but facilitated by the Stone Clan. She thought of Vaelyn. Thought of the friendship she'd thought she had there. What kind of anger would drive a person to lie, to manipulate another for years? And if Unara had learned anything over the past week, it was how different life was here under the sky.

Perhaps the ocean-born didn't truly understand what the Stone Clan endured.

That still didn't mean she had to die for their bitterness. All life on Thalassa Prime was hard. All of it. The sea was no kinder to humanity than the land.

Their jealousy, if that indeed was what this was, was woefully misplaced. Lady Hethra's plan was likely to drag Thalassa into a bitter war that it could not win. Not a clan war, either, but a true war with the stars. There would be no defense, no recovery, from orbital bombardment. The seas would be left dead and barren. Or the off-worlders would land troops and machines, not wanting to risk the nacre plating growing in Thalassa's waters. Unara's people would hold out a little longer in that case. But clan by clan, bay by bay, they would fall.

Become a subjugated people, farming armor for some far-off overlord, unable to leave the ocean to fight back.

No. It had to be stopped. Hethra had to be stopped.

But how?

Unara mulled that over during all the long dark hours of the ride.

But no answer would come to her. And she despaired.

She had looked to the stars for peace, for respite, but it seemed as if there was conflict everywhere. That, even more than the knowledge of her own imminent execution, brought Unara low. She was going to die, her people were going to die, and thanks to her own selfishness, there was nothing she could do.

FINALLY, the submersible stopped. It was impossible to discern position or depth or anything else. Only the engines falling silent gave any indication that they had arrived somewhere. The water-lock opened.

"You sure about this?" the first guard asked as he entered the space.

"Where else is there? The desert?" the second guard replied. "The damn off-worlders can see it all from orbit. So can any of the moons, and you know they'll pass it along. No, it has to be this way."

"I wish Aegyr could see this," the first said. "His youngest daughter, drowning to death."

The second guard chuckled a little and yanked Unara to her feet, roughly pulling her around. For a moment, his body was between herself and the other guard, and she felt something press into her hand. "That would be something, wouldn't it?" he replied, words light.

Unara closed her fingers around the object.

"Did you really think the Stone Clan was going to accept the ocean-borns' rule forever?" the first asked.

"Long live Thalassa," the second replied, and the water-lock snapped shut once more.

Unara lifted her face, trying to adopt as much dignity as she could, and turned to face the outer doors. She looked down at the thing in her hands.

It took her a second to recognize it. A rebreather organism, a small biological device meant to pull oxygen from the water. The Stone Clan used them when diving, a backup to their air tanks or lung capacity. Once awoken, the things were short-lived; they supplied oxygen to the user at the cost of their own biological function.

A light in front of her dinged green, and the outer doors hissed.
Hell rushed in.

The small submersible had been built for access to the ocean, but it seemed like the guards had disabled the safety features that let water in slowly, or else just didn't care what happened to her. The water knocked her off her feet, the sudden current tearing at her, and she grabbed at the wall. She held on as long as she dared, breathing deep, not knowing what to do. The water was freezing cold, and she lacked the adaptations of her ocean-born body. Hypothermia would set in, and quick.

The rebreather would only give her a little bit of time.

It would have to be enough.

She shoved the thing into her mouth at the last possible second and let go.

Unara drifted in the ice-cold void, unable to tell which way was up, unable to discern anything at all. She held onto her last breath as best she could, hoping to preserve the rebreather's functions. Her lungs burned.

And then, a light.

A light?

Not the submersible. That was already gone. So this had to be...

She kicked out, trying to move herself in a familiar environment with unfamiliar limbs. No good. She had no idea how to swim with legs. But her arms still remembered what to do, and she began to move—slowly, too slow—toward that faint illumination.

Twice during that endless dark swim, she bumped herself against rock.

Finally, Unara felt her head break the surface of the water.

Air.

Stale, thin, but breathable.

Keeping her head above the water was unfamiliar and uncomfortable, but she soon realized she could take quick breaths and put her face back under. After that, she swam quicker.

Eventually, after what seemed like an endless swim, Unara's fingers touched something solid. Rock. Vertical. A wall. She surfaced for a better look.

The light was stronger now, a weak blue glow under the surface of the water, enough for her to discern where she was. She had come up in a tight cave, one with a sloping ceiling that touched the top of the still water in all directions around her.

Fear gripped Unara as she realized what was going on. The light was coming from underneath the water, which meant that there was an underwater tunnel she would have to swim through. A flush of heat ran through her. Her limbs started shaking. Panic. She was panicking. And that, she knew, was going to get her killed.

"Stop it," she muttered to her altered body, looking around at the still water, doing her best to tread in place. "Stop it."

She took a deep breath of the stale air and pushed herself under, looking.

A passage through the rock. Maybe six, seven meters long. With her tail, she could have done that in a few seconds.

You don't have your tail, her mind whispered to her as she surfaced, trying to catch her breath, *just this pair of legs that can't do a damn thing. You're going to die in there.*

But then, what was the alternative? Dying here in this pocket of air? Dying with the knowledge of Hethra's coup?

No. No.

Unara may have wanted to leave Thalassa, but that didn't mean she wanted to see the planet razed by war.

She took another breath, fixed the rebreather in her mouth, and pushed down.

It wasn't far.

She could do this.

She had to do this.

Unara had grown up in the oceans of Thalassa. She had hunted rock eels through coral canyons as a child, she had tamed her akker and survived the season of storms, when cyclones hit even the most sheltered coves on the western coast, she had fought kraken and defeated reef sharks, and she was not going to die in her own waters.

But she realized she had never known real, true fear until this day.

Distances could be deceiving underwater. The tunnel was long, longer than she had imagined, and tight. It squeezed down and down and down, until she was no longer swimming but pulling herself forward with her arms, skin scraping over the rock.

And then she got stuck.

The panic was back. She could feel it. A deep-seated fear of the water, of drowning, long suppressed in the Thalassan genome, waking up now with a vengeance. She was going to die here, she was going to—

No.

It was just her chest. She had gotten her shoulders through. Her chest.

With her last bit of self-control, her very last shred of logic, Unara exhaled everything left in her lungs and pushed through the hole.

Unara cut herself on the rock, pulling herself along the last meter, but it scarcely mattered. She was out of the tunnel. She was headed for the light, for the air. Her head broke the still surface of the water, and this time, the air was fresh. Harsh, dry, scratching at the back of her throat, but full of life-giving oxygen. She gulped greedily, letting herself float for a moment, taking in her position.

Brilliant noon light danced across the surface of the still water. Unara had emerged in the end of the cave, a huge space, as big as the biggest halls back at the palace. Ripples made by her sudden surfacing lapped against a set of stairs cut from the raw, wind-chewed rock of the cave, and she noticed a depth gauge carved into the wall nearby.

On a flat stretch of rock nearby, a great construct sat. A construction crab, used across the western coast for building or excavating rock.

What was it doing here?

What was this place?

"You would threaten me in my own house?" Karl asked in disbelief, leaning hard on the balcony railing.

"My dear boy," Lord Willam replied, "I would threaten the High King himself, should his actions be leading us to the total loss of this year's nacre harvest. And to the Suyarii nonetheless! You must turn this girl over or I will be forced to take action."

Karl sighed, already weary of this conversation. It had been a difficult day. Yvar had rescinded his previous agreement, demanded to renegotiate once again. The terms were worse now. The other major Houses had all sent representatives to talk to House Gyes; they had all gotten visits from Jarl Dryagr, it seemed, although none of the others had been accused of harboring this Princess Unara.

That told Karl that there was most definitely hard evidence on the Thalassan side that his father had, in fact, promised her safe passage off-world. The question of how they knew it was still unanswered.

Lord Willam was only the latest in that parade of anger. He had been more blunt than the others, though.

"The Suyarii do not have enough titanium to buy the entire planet's harvest," Karl sighed. "You will get yours."

"The Suyarii can purchase it all if they purchase nothing else," Lord Willam replied.

"You speak without knowledge, Lord Willam," Karl replied, and held up a hand as his fellow trader bristled. "We have passive surveillance drones drifting through their fleet even as we speak. I shall soon know the full extent and composition of their ships, once we can collect them again. Then we can assess just how much titanium they are likely to have."

"Truly?" Lord Willam asked sharply, and Karl nodded. The Caledon lord relaxed a bit. "All my probes were shot down."

"I suspect the Suyarii are quite good at detecting Caledon hardware by now," Karl replied.

"Quite," Lord Willam conceded, and poured himself another glass of wine from the decanter on the table. The ruby liquid glinted in the light of the last setting sun. "But Karl, my point still stands. The Thalassans want that girl back and they don't care if it means handing the entire Occidental Spiral over to the Suyarii Empire in the process."

"The situation is not that dire, Lord Willam."

"It is."

Karl sighed and rubbed his temples. "Why him?" he asked quietly, looking out to sea. "Why did Dryagr deliver that message and not the king?"

"Thalassans are a strange people. Who knows?"

"Does it not seem significant to you?" Karl pressed.

"Meddling in the affairs of royalty, even royalty of a world so small as this one, will inevitably lead to your destruction," Lord Willam said, and then smiled a little. "Or theirs. But it all depends on who the victor is, of course."

"Are you suggesting King Aegyr has been deposed?" Karl asked.

"I am suggesting nothing," the Caledon trader replied. "Just a little drunken musing. Now, I must thank you for the company and for the wine, but I'm afraid I must attempt to salvage my own House's position in things." And before Karl could protest, he came over, clapped him on the shoulder, and leaned in. "Look to the crabs," he murmured in perfectly accented Rikstag. Karl stared at him; he didn't know the other trader knew his home sector's language. Lord Willam grinned back, wide and disarming. "Pretty women are as common as the stars in this galaxy. Don't damn us all over this one," he added, once again in Standard.

He left his unfinished wine on the table.

For a few moments, Karl wondered what Lord Willam had

meant. The crabs? The crabs were seemingly ubiquitous up here, one of the only creatures that crawled out of Thalassan's seas, as common and present as gulls on Caledon, or—

And then he noticed one. Only a few feet away, hiding in the shadow of the railing, stock still. Even its mouth-parts were still. Watching him.

A thought seized him, and he walked over, slowly, ambling, like he wasn't paying attention to where he was going at all. He leaned once again on the railing, right next to the picket where the crab was attempting to conceal itself, and before the thing could scuttle away, he quite deliberately stepped down.

He lifted his foot away again, feigning surprise, just in case there were any more of the things around. Scooping it up with the tray the wine had been brought in on, he called for Thorsen.

Who appeared instantly.

"Is there a problem, milord?"

"No, just a little encounter with the local wildlife," Karl said, brandishing the tray. "I think I should like to go back to the drop-craft now."

"The drop-craft?" Thorsen asked, confused. "Lord Imran is hosting that reception tonight in the market square and—"

"Yes, to force us all to come and drink his wine pretend that we are all friends, but I do not feel like participating in any more political charades today." *Or ever,* Karl added silently. "Besides, I'm afraid my boot has been quite ruined by this thing."

Thorsen had a questioning look in his eyes, but whatever he was thinking, he didn't give it voice. "We shall leave right away then, milord."

"Yes," Karl said, considering the dead crab. "Yes, we will."

UNARA WAS TRYING to figure out her next move—which had to

include getting out of the water; she was freezing cold—when she heard it.

Movement.

Voices. Too quiet for her to catch any but a few echoed words.

"... coming along..."

"... need to...faster..."

"... push...beyond tolerances..."

"... it done..."

The voices were soon drowned out by the sound of the huge construction crab getting to its feet. It strode forward into the water, slipping into it with unexpected care.

It wouldn't be going through the narrow entrance she had barely squeezed through, she knew, and she slipped beneath the water after it.

Underwater, it became clear that they were on a large promontory of rock jutting out into the inky black depths. There was a narrow passage, and then, open water.

While deep, the water was clean and clear. She could see the crab falling down through the water, descending almost peacefully. Below it, the floor of the inland sea was rocky and bare, but silt stirred up in huge clouds as the crab touched the bottom. Where it went after that, she couldn't see.

Unara surfaced again, closer to the voices this time. They were above her on a small cliff; she plastered herself against the stone, listening.

"And our families?" one, a man, asked.

"It will be as Lady Hethra promised," the second voice said. Female, this one. "She's offering the change to us all. Thanks to her, we'll have what's ours here soon."

"I don't know. It didn't work on the ocean-born."

"Because it wasn't supposed to! How many times do I have to tell you that? She altered their infusions on purpose. We, on the other hand, we get the real ones."

And Unara realized what they were talking about.

Glaeva. Ragnyr. Everyone. Her father.

Lady Hethra had poisoned their transformations.

Hethra had killed her sister.

The voices started moving away again, fading into the distance again.

Suddenly filled with rage, Unara swam after them.

She got to the steps and pulled herself up. Her hands wouldn't work right, numb from the swim, but she didn't care. Hethra had killed her sister, and these two were helping her.

That could not stand.

Unara was practically naked, and she needed to secure some way to get back to the palace. They were her best chance at that. She needed their vehicle, their supplies, some kind of clothing. Unara crept up the stairs, trying to think of a plan, trying to—

"Well, what do we have here?"

A voice. Right above her. She'd misjudged the distance, some trick of the acoustics in the cave, she realized.

"It's one of the ocean-born," the man said, the one who'd been arguing, now surprised.

The woman, wrapped in a full desert cloak, snorted. "Look at her, wearing legs like she's a real person. Which one of them are you, huh?"

Unara looked between them.

The man was already reaching for an energy pistol at his waist. Off-world tech, nothing a true son of the ocean should have been carrying.

Maybe, when she made it off-world, Unara thought, she could lay down her blade forever. But until that happened, while she was still trapped here on Thalassa Prime, she had to fight. Unara was cold and tired from the long swim, but she was desperate, and that lent her strength.

She bared her teeth and lunged.

Unara went for the man first. He was bigger and stronger than her and if it came to a protracted fight, she wouldn't survive it. So speed was all she had. She launched herself up, grabbing his knees and using her body weight to swing him around, throw him to the ground. His head made a sickening thud as it hit one of the stairs. Scrambling over his body, she grabbed the pistol and fired it at point-blank range into his chest. The cavern filled with the scent of scorched flesh and ozone.

The woman was standing there, obviously stunned, like she couldn't process what had just happened.

Unara shot her through the face before she could move. The body crumpled, rolling down the steps, and the princess caught it only just in time to keep it from falling into the water.

After hauling the body back up, Unara collapsed. She lay there on the steps, in a pool of light for a few moments, trying to catch her breath. Her shivers had turned into a full-body shake now; she was trembling almost uncontrollably.

The warmth helped, though. Slowly, after what seemed like forever, she felt good enough to move again. Good enough to get to her aching feet and do something useful.

By that time, the bodies had broken down. The task of searching the remaining effects was an unpleasant but necessary one. Unara sorted through the mess, looking for anything useful. Clothing, boots, equipment. A set of vehicle keys. Food in the dead woman's pack, fish jerky and dried seaweed.

Only after finding that did Unara realize how very hungry she was.

Unara took her haul and stepped out into the cave entrance, chewing on a kelp strip and drying her hair. She was careful. Anything could be out there. Unara half expected a squad of heavily armed guards to greet her.

Instead, there was...nothing.

Nothing at all.

The cave entrance was located in a rocky outcropping at the top of a small rise. From here, Unara had an unobstructed view of the desert. And it was desert, desert in all directions. Windswept rock and sun-bleached sand and no signs of life. No sea in sight.

Except... There, out to the east, far in the distance, Light glinted off the water. Water.

The inland sea.

Far to the south, a great finger of the ocean pushed dozens of miles into the continent before curving north and west and filling a basin with stagnant water. The same water she was looking at now. It wasn't very large, perhaps two kilometers across at its widest point. As was told in the saga, a small river, barely more than a stream, had once connected the inland sea to the ocean proper.

To Oceanfall.

While the aboveground river had long since dried up, there was an underground river connecting the inland sea to the bay at Ocean-fall. It was the means by which the bay was filled, the grand gates shut at the king's command to allow mineral-rich water to flood the entire basin.

An underground river.

That Unara had just swum out of. Where construction crabs were working away.

What was Hethra doing here?

Unara mulled it over as she ate, trying to figure out what the plan might be.

But there would be time enough to think on the way.

The suns were starting to move now, dipping west toward the horizon, toward night, when temperatures would fall by nearly twenty degrees.

She needed to get moving.

Working her way down the hillside, in the dead woman's boots that were slightly too small for her, Unara spotted her first bit of luck.

A sandcrawler.

These were fully mechanical vehicles, some of the very few on

Thalassa, equipped with broad, fat tires to navigate the coastal deserts. It was a small thing, barely enough room in the cockpit for two people, with the back area taken up by storage lockers. One contained camping gear and some type of machine that she guessed could cool the air in a small space, and the other boasted food, water bladders, and other sundry items, like a knife and thin rope and the like. A desert survival kit, she guessed, although her knowledge of such things was poor.

She tried to take the sandcrawler. She did. She tried everything she could think of. But clearly, it wasn't enough, and she wasted nearly half an hour on the task of turning it on.

Finally defeated by the mechanical monster, Unara slid back out of the cockpit to take stock of her situation. She knew roughly where the underground culverts ran. It was thirty-five, maybe forty kilometers from the westernmost shore of the inland sea to the palace. She had the suns and the moons for guides, she had food, and she had some water. If she moved fast enough, she might make it back in time to warn everyone of the danger.

If you still had your tail, she thought bitterly to herself, *you could swim back.*

But the thought of moving through that strange underground river filled her with trepidation, and it wasn't something she could do anyway. If she wasn't too far from the palace...

Unara looked out across that barren land, emptier than the abyssal plains of the blackwater. She most likely would die out there.

But there was no other choice.

So, legs aching with every step, exhausted from the past twenty-three hours, Unara, princess of the ocean, set out across the lifeless desert.

CHAPTER TWENTY-FIVE

First sunset, under the water, was always a pleasant thing. With the brilliant white of Brynhildyr and the harsh orange of Hyrja below the horizon, only quiet red Thogyn was left in the sky. She lingered far longer than her sisters, creating a quiet, cool twilight where the titanocorals could feed and fish darted about in coppery-gold shoals.

Out here, under the open sky, the effect was more pronounced. The horizon was a deep purple, the bare rock of the land washed with pale red light. This time of year, Thogyn lingered a long time in the sky, and Unara would have sunlight for a long time.

The air was cooling. Already she could feel the first chills of night in the faint breeze. She pulled the dead woman's desert cloak around her and tried not to think about the stains on it.

While Unara had emerged from the subterranean sea on top of a hill surrounded by flat land, she soon realized she was in something of a bowl. The going was easy for the first few kilometers, and despite the ever-present pain in her altered legs, she made good time. But then the land turned hard, the hardpan giving way to rock formations carved and twisted by the screaming winds whipped up by Brynhildyr. Unara struggled to pick a path through those, and it was only after she was deep into the maze that she realized what this barrier meant.

The sandcrawler could not have come this way from the palace.

But then, she reasoned, stopping for more jerky and a sip from her pack, that might not mean anything. She had no idea what the sandcrawler's route had been, whether it had stopped at many such little caves or come from some other location. There were no guarantees it had come directly from the palace.

As long as she kept walking west, she figured, she would make it back.

The other side of the rocky ridge was a bewildering maze of boulders, rocks ranging from the size of her fist to the size of houses, scattered about the land like the discarded shells of molting crabs. True night fell as she picked her way through them. It was exhausting, difficult work. She missed the sea; if this was underwater, she would have been able to swim over these obstructions, make good time. And then what was that ahead, rising like the waves near shore?

It didn't matter. There was only one direction to go.

She kept the polar star to her right and kept moving.

Dunes.

There were dunes.

Dunes stretching on forever, rising and falling like waves across the barren land. Unara tried at first to walk straight through them, but some of the great crests of sands were taller than the Hall of Transformation, and it was an impossible task. Instead, like with the ravines, she settled for picking a path around their bases. But even that was exhausting. Every step sent sand skittering away from her feet. Every little movement hurt.

Finally, she could stand it no more.

Stopping on the western side of a dune, Unara eased one of her feet out of the stolen boots. Clear pus oozed from blisters on her ankle. There were such things all over her feet.

She sighed. Feeling rather foolish for not understanding there was a problem beyond the effects of the transformation, she started patching herself up with the first aid kit.

Unara didn't know anything about the intricacies of human footwear but thought the entire thing stupid. If feet were so delicate that they couldn't survive contact with the ground, why not readapt them to do their job? Tweak the genes, make something more useful? But then, none of the off-worlders she'd met at the kaupang displayed much modification beyond regenerative treatments and perhaps a few cosmetic surgeries.

Were such things frowned upon in the wider galaxy? Illegal?

Impossible to know.

It was something to think about as she fixed the footwear. With the knife from the pack, Unara cut the boots down and apart, poking holes through the tough fish-leather sides and re-lacing them with the old ties. It took her a few tries to get something that stayed on her foot, and it was far from ideal but comfortable, at least, and her blisters felt better.

Sand clung to her wounds, but that was something the gothi could help her deal with later.

Unara got back on her feet and kept walking.

STEPPING into the lab later that night, Karl felt his skin crawl. He had grown up around medical equipment, especially this kind, the esoteric and often baffling machines that Eyr built, but he had never liked it. Being the last son to a man who could not play with him, embrace him, even smile at him, had been profoundly disturbing for him as a child. Back then, Karl had blamed the equipment for that physical separation. Now, as an adult, he recognized that it was the equipment—the tank, the life-support systems, Eyr's constant modulation of blood chemistry and nerve function—that had given him and his father any contact at all.

He still hated Eyr's workspaces.

"You wanted to see me?" he asked.

The feii did not look up from her bank of screens, but waved him over nonetheless. "Yes. I have finished the gene-sequencing and function-patterning for this specimen you brought me, and I thought you might like my report."

"What is there to see?" Captain Thorsen asked. Perhaps stung by the events of the night before, he had steadfastly refused to leave Karl's side, even at the drop-ship. "It's a crab."

"It is crab-shaped, yes. Its underlying DNA is that of a crustacean, the same as one might find on a thousand other human worlds. But this is not a crab," the feii said. "This is a surveillance device."

"Surveillance?" Karl asked, surprised.

"I suspect it transmits imagery back to some kind of control hub," Healer Eyr said, indicating a few of her screens. Models of the crabs rotated there, along with a series of complex read-outs both in Standard and the incomprehensible glyph-language of the feii. "Not surprising that they have such things. But there are large sections of this thing's genome that are defying even my attempts to model it."

"What does that mean?"

"It means that while Thalassans are masters of gene-craft," she said, "there are other powers at work here as well. This transmission organ"—and she indicated a protrusion on the back of the crab—"was not created by conventional genetic engineering."

"What then?" Karl asked. "Are you talking about...?"

"Genomancy, yes. Magic, I believe it is called in Standard."

"That's not possible."

"I think it is," she said. "The sample of DNA from the strange assailants last night models as a baseline homo sapien, with absolutely no modifications at all, which they certainly were not. But the blood I took from your Thalassan girl—"

"Unara," Captain Thorsen said gruffly. "She has a name."

Healer Eyr inclined her head. "Unara, then. Her DNA shows all kinds of things. Modifications to the hands, the eyes, the fat cells and distribution thereof, the lungs, interestingly enough, and some very disturbing alterations to the pelvis, legs, and feet, although I have not gotten a clear view of what has gone so desperately wrong there."

Karl frowned. "What do you mean?"

"Much like this crab, there are gaps in her genetic pattern that I cannot account for. She shouldn't be able to breathe air, per these models. In fact, she shouldn't be alive at all. The fact that she is indicates to me that something else is sustaining her. I suspect that is the influence of the moons."

"The moons?" Thorsen asked, raising an eyebrow.

"Hildra, most likely," Eyr continued. "When my people first came here, we found a world rich with potential but badly unbalanced. The axial tilt was unpredictable, wild. So we brought the first moon here. Rota. She calmed the tilt but enraged the seas, and eventually, we were rejected wholesale."

Karl thought about the song that the skalds had sung the night before, the story Vaelyn had told him. "So the colonists captured Hildra."

"Yes, and all the other minor bodies that came along in her wake. This settled the tides. Complex life could now flourish here, as it does. All because of the moons."

"What does this have to do with crabs?" Thorsen asked again.

"What does this have to do with magic?" Karl pressed.

"Everything," Eyr said, spreading her hands. "I submit that the entire Thalassan gene-code is dependent upon it."

Stunned into silence, Karl didn't speak for a little while.

"What does that mean for this crab?" Thorsen asked.

"Some kind of psychic link, most likely," Eyr said. "A spy network that they operate when the Trade Houses are here, in order to keep themselves informed. It is interesting, but of little consequence. However, it does provide me a datapoint for examining the other tissue samples.”

“How so?”

“Magic leaves traces of itself behind,” she replied. “Imprints, whispers, a lingering scent. My people sense it in different ways. To me, this crab is suffused with a kind of silver tint. Unara’s blood contains the same thing. But there is darkness in this,” Healer Eyr said, and tapped the stasis container. “I can feel it, like sand in my teeth.”

“Do you have teeth?” Captain Thorsen asked.

She ignored him. “It is not from a moon, that much is clear to me.”

“Then what?”

“There are many powers in this galaxy that are not well understood, not even by my people. The verrater that have plagued the Alamani for so long, for example, or the djinn of the core Suyarii worlds. Ember-sprites said to roam the Caledon and Merovingian Sectors. Things of that nature. Not all are evil, of course, but who knows what their true objectives are?” Eyr tapped the stasis container again. “There has always been something dark in the Thalassan seas. The presence of the guardian moons calmed the chaos here, and in so doing, likely drove it back into the deepest depths, where currents and tides do not matter. But it is angry about what the moons have created, milord, very angry.”

“Angry oceans and talking moons,” Thorsen snorted. “Next you’ll be telling us those things last night were ghosts.”

Eyr clearly wasn’t paying him any attention. “Now the question is, what fool decided to channel the rage of the depths into living flesh? What human is insane enough to infuse black magic into Thalassan gene-craft?”

“Black magic?” Karl asked.

“Of the worst kind,” Eyr said.

And Karl was still trying to formulate a response to that when he received a notification from the bridge.

The spy craft sent out into the Suyarii fleet had finally drifted back to the *Vanatar*.

He thanked Eyr for her diligence, pulled Thorsen away, and headed back to the bridge.

Fairy tales and skald songs could wait.

He had more pressing matters to attend to.

UNARA WAS NOT YET out of the dunes when the fog began to gather.

Fog. It scared her and delighted her at the same time. The presence of fog meant she was at least somewhere near the ocean; it only went a few kilometers inland. But it would also block out the sky, destroy all chance of navigation. Visibility would be cut to nothing. She would have to stop, rest, begin again when the suns burned it all off again in the morning. But Unara had no idea how much time she had. The kaupang ended tomorrow evening. Whatever Hethra was planning, no doubt she would spring the trap before then.

Unara had to get home.

She kept moving, putting one bleeding, aching foot in front of the other. Over and over. Crawling through the sand, little better than an echinoderm looking for food in the vast wastes of the abyssal plain.

The dunes subsided. The fog thickened. Sand gave way to hardpan, the change both welcome and unpleasant, the footing more solid but more painful. Cuts began to appear in the ground, small at first, then widening. Shallow ravines they seemed at first, a sandstone plateau worn apart by the winds, but they grew deeper quickly. Rock walls soon rose high around her, filling with fog. The stars were gone. But then, perhaps it didn't matter. In these ravines, there was only one way to go.

The fog thickened. Subtle air currents made open spots at first, patches where she could still see well, still move with confidence.

But soon even these closed in. The floor in the ravine grew tortured, uneven. She had to pick her way up and down obstructions she could barely see, even her eyesight straining to make any sense of it. Unara had dealt with these night fogs over the past week or so back at Oceanfall, but that had been when she was rested, well fed, uninjured. When there had been light and markers and people around.

Now, there was only silence.

And as she was picking her way down a steep incline, nearly blind, her foot slipped.

She fell, hitting the ground hard.

The gray world around her went black.

Dawn.

It was dawn. But not the dawn Unara had seen this week at Oceanfall, rendered dull and uncertain by the fog. It was dawn as it might be, as it could be, clear and open to the eastern sky, a wash of color so brilliant it seemed unreal.

Unara was standing on a spit of land, the sea raging around her, foaming and swirling and crashing on the rocks. So close it was, she could feel the spray on her skin.

"The world as it was," a voice said.

Unara started. A woman was there with her, a woman with the long, graceful tail of the Drift Clans, cast in silver scales and draped in a dress of silk like any ocean-born might wear at a clan ceremony. Her garments, her hair, all moved as if caught in some gentle underwater current, and yet she hung, suspended in midair.

"What do you mean?" Unara asked, and was surprised to hear her lost voice.

The figure in front of her smiled and turned slightly, looking down at the waters below. "This is a strange world. Your ancestors could not terraform it, and thus, changed themselves instead. But

274

they also changed the sea as well, and there are things here that have never forgiven you for it."

"Who are you?" Unara asked.

The woman ignored her. "The suns give this world light, but little can exist here without the moons," the strange woman said, and reached out, laying a hand on Unara's cheek. There was something so gentle about it, so enormously dangerous, that the princess felt tears start to well in her eyes. "The little that can... How were we to know it would be made so angry by our own children? And now you will all suffer for it."

"I don't understand."

"Hethra has made her choice. And you, Unara, you've made your choice as well. You have another to make before the end," the strange woman said, "for the transformation you have undertaken is not yet total. Does this world live or die? It hinges on you."

She shook her head. "I don't want such responsibility."

"And I did not ask to be dragged from the quiet of the Oort and bound to this world, but sometimes, we find our purpose where we least expect it."

"Hildra?" Unara asked, eyes widening.

But it was too late.

Unara woke with a gasp. Her entire body hurt and her hands were rubbed raw, but she was alive.

She looked up.

The fog was lighter here, light enough for her to see some distance around. Through the curling tendrils of mist, she saw the place from where she had fallen. Five meters up.

How had she survived that?

But there was a light above the mist now. Hildra, taking her turn in the sky.

Thank you, Unara tried to whisper, but once again, her voice was gone. But then, it had never really come back, had it? It was all just a dream.

Her pack had taken the brunt of the fall, it seemed; the kelp sheets were smashed to crumbs, jerky soaked, water bladder burst. All her supplies.

And then, in her despair in the deep night, Unara noticed something.

Something that looked...constructed.

It was a wall. A low wall of stacked stone, obviously laid by human hands. She looked around. More walls, rooms built up against the steep scarp she had fallen down.

She thought of Skald Hakon's song.

The journey from the east.

The settlements.

Along the river. The only river. The river that led from the inland sea...

... straight out to Oceanfall Bay.

Right to the palace.

Unara looked down the landscape.

It was sloping, falling. And far, far in the distance, lights glittered.

Once again, Hildra had come to her people in their time of need.

Unara would not disappoint her.

CHAPTER TWENTY-SIX

The morning fog was just burning off as Unara stumbled back out of the desert onto the edge of the landing fields.

So tired was she that she barely realized she was back at civilization. Dark, boxy shapes rose like more cliffs from the failing fog; the ships, ships from a dozen other human worlds. Between them, from out of the fog, shapes moved. Humans, walking about, carrying equipment or patrolling with weapons. She bumped into such a pair, but they just stood back and let her pass. A maintenance crew tending to one of the landing craft stopped their work to stare. She kept walking, ignoring the words one of the men spoke to her.

Unara's legs were on fire now. Her muscles burned. Her feet were once again bleeding freely. She scarcely noticed. She had to get through the fields. She had to get to the palace. She had to find her father, throw herself down at his feet, beg for his forgiveness.

If her body would allow it, her broken, exhausted body.

Finally, her legs gave out. She stumbled. She collapsed.

But she didn't hit the ground.

No, instead, a strong hand bore her up.

"A Thalassan woman walking in out of the desert?" Lord Imran asked, voice bemused. "Now I have seen everything."

THE SUYARII TRADER brought her back to a shaded pavilion made of brightly colored textiles, with cushions scattered about the floor and low wood furniture all around. He reclined back as servant girls with shaved heads brought brass flagons of water and a platter of strange terrestrial fruits.

"I have much to attend to today," Imran said, handing her a silver goblet of water, "but I am curious about you. You are the female guard from the Gyes delegation, are you not? Your hair is a little different now. I didn't realize you were Thalassan. Fascinating."

She focused on gulping the water down. Unara had never tasted anything sweeter in her life. A servant girl automatically refilled her goblet.

"The mute one, I presume?"

She nodded again.

"I know your people have some form of accounting system, mathematics, perhaps even a written language, despite the fact that you do not share it with outsiders," he said, considering her. "Can you write Standard? I should like to have a full conversation with you."

She took another sip of water, then held out her hands, imitating writing. The prince snapped his fingers, and another servant girl was there, a notebook and pen on a tray.

"Show me," he ordered.

Despite a tremble in her hands that would not go away, Unara wrote out a short paragraph. She had given this some thought on her long walk back from the inland sea. The letters were correct; this she had been able to determine. But somehow, she was putting them together in the wrong order.

Prince Imran took the paper once she was done, examining it.

"Standard is my second language as well," he told her, and handed her back the sheet. "Write the name of this world. In Standard, please, not your own tongue. Thalassa Prime."

Confused, she did so and then handed it back.

He nodded. "As I thought. May I?" He held out a hand for the pen. Confused, Unara passed it to him. He rewrote the words directly below hers, letters spaced apart equally to hers. "See?"

And yes, she saw it. Both words had the same number of letters. Both words had letters reused and repeated. But the actual letters used were different.

She breathed out, seeing it, and reached for her water to hide her discomfort.

Prince Imran gave her another sympathetic smile. "Whoever taught you this, taught you wrong. And considering that the difference between your understanding and the correct usage is both simple and yet consistent, I take it that it was intentional. Some sort of cypher, easy enough for your tutor to employ. But who, Thalassan, taught you wrong? And what did they wish to gain from it?"

Vaelyn, Unara tried to say. Vaelyn had taught her. Agreed to share—no, wait, had volunteered to share her daily lessons after she had won the position in the delegation.

Vaelyn.

Her friend, her best friend. Her friend...

The traitor.

Unara realized then that this was a scheme going back years. Hethra had known Unara would come to her begging for help. Hethra had planned for her to lose her voice. Hethra had deliberately warped the final transformation infusion to produce this exact effect.

Had she killed Glaeva too?

And if that was true...

"I see this brings you grief," Prince Imran said, "and I am sorry for that. But this seems to be an easy error to unlearn. If you would accept my hospitality and remain here with my house, then perhaps tomorrow we can begin to give you back your voice. And we shall see what secrets you have been forced to leave unsaid."

Unara nodded, too tired to argue.

Lord Imran rose, shaking out his robes. "Now then, Thalassan, I must take my leave from you. There is some official meeting in a little while, which I am forced to attend." He smiled at her. "Rest yourself now. I grew up on a world such as this. A journey through the desert is nothing to undertake lightly. We shall talk more when I return."

Unara watched him go, gulping more water.

One of the servant girls shook her head almost imperceptibly. Another pointed at the door.

Unara nodded back and got up, moving as quietly as she could toward the exit.

Nobody bothered her. She grabbed a scarf and a set of mechanics' fatigues on her way out through the broad maintenance bay.

She had to get back to the palace.

"AND WE ARE SURE OF THIS?" Karl asked, not believing what he was looking at.

<It is unmistakable,> the fleet's lead intelligence officer replied. The projection field had been tuned to show the man sitting at the table with the rest of them. <I can send you the entire report, milord, for context.>

"Do that," Karl said, staring at the images hanging over the table's polished glass surface. It was a high-definition rendering of the entire Suyarii fleet. "What has my father said about this?"

<With Healer Eyr's absence, we've had to place him back in stasis.>

"So it's my decision," Karl sighed.

<Milord, we are not positioned to move on this.>

"So you recommend doing nothing? What will Sector Command say when they find out?" Thorsen asked.

<I assure you, Captain, they will understand. Sometimes preserving knowledge for action later requires us to refrain from action in the moment.>

"Spoken like a true spy," Thorsen said derisively.

"We do nothing in the void. Not yet," Karl said, thinking of his words to Lord Willam a few days before. "Here, on the planet, we're just men, and we may still be able to settle this as men."

<Aim for the space between his eyes, if you do anything, milord. You'll want to kill him on the first shot.>

"I'll keep that in mind," Karl said dryly, and terminated the link. He tossed the tablet across the table, looking around. "Void take it. This was supposed to be a simple week."

"It's Thalassa Prime," Branner said, hands folded in front of her. "Nothing is simple here."

"Report is uploading, milord," the communications officer in the corner announced.

Karl rubbed his temples. Weighing politics and fleet actions and the fate of everything in his hands. What he would give to be back in the expedition fleet, unburdened by all of this nonsense.

Thorsen leaned in. "I just got a notification from the guards at the entrance, sir. Vaelyn is here."

"Vaelyn?" Branner asked. "So she finally decided to show her face?"

"I'll meet with her on my way out," Karl decided, and pushed back from the table. "Load that fleet projection to my tablet."

"Yes, milord."

"And wake my father at once," Karl said, straightening his jacket and going for his sword. "I am not committing this House to an impossible fight without his opinion."

Vaelyn was indeed waiting for Karl at the main air lock. She was leaning hard on the wall, breathing heavily, but pulled herself upright when she saw him.

"I need to speak with you," she said.

"It must wait, Vaelyn. I have business with the other traders right now."

"But this is—"

"Tell me on the way."

"I'm not sure...going there...would be a good idea."

And at that he stopped moving. Really looked at her. She didn't look well. Her skin was more gray than usual, her eyes bloodshot and her lips tinged blue. Her clothing was damp, her hair stiff with salt. Her expression was haggard and her movements tired. It looked as if she had spent the entire night out in the open ocean. Maybe she had. He knew so little of how the Thalassans lived.

"What happened to you?" Karl asked, a little less certain of himself now.

"Doesn't matter," she said, shaking her head. "Lord Gyes, you must get back to orbit. Now. You must leave and not come back."

He stared at her in disbelief. "That's not possible, Vaelyn."

"You all must leave, as soon as possible." She coughed. "You're all in terrible danger."

There was blood on the back of her hand, and she staggered. Karl caught her before she fell, and she clung hard to his hand. "I'm alright."

"You don't look alright."

She shook her head, coughing again. "It would take too long to explain. Please, you have to listen—"

"I have urgent business with the other traders," he said, holding up his folio case. "We have a problem up in orbit, and I must handle it before we lose this world."

"You'll lose it anyway if you stay here," she replied and coughed again, doubling over.

Torn between wanting to help this woman, this strange, beautiful woman, and his need to speak with the others, Karl wavered.

But she stumbled again, and this time, he went down with her, catching her as she fell to her knees.

"Milord." Thorsen's voice intruded on the moment. "Milord, we have to go. This cannot wait."

Karl looked at the woman in his arms. What had Thorsen asked him? One girl or the entire fleet? He wasn't sure what choice he truly would have made, had he been able to make it freely. But then, that was the entire problem, wasn't it?

There was no freedom anymore.

"I won't be long," he told her. "Stay here. Healer Eyr can attend to you while I'm gone, and then we can talk."

Vaelyn shook her head. "You don't understand."

"Then tell me," he said, gentler this time. "Where have you been? Where is your kinswoman, umm, Unara, I heard her name was?"

Vaelyn shook her head, tried to speak, then started coughing again, doubled over this time. Blood flecked the deck.

"Guards!" he yelled.

But it was Healer Eyr who arrived at the air lock first. "I shall take her," the feii said. "Go, milord. I have her."

"Wait for me here," Karl told Vaelyn, squeezing her hand.

The Thalassan woman stared at him for a moment, then hung her head, red-gray hair falling around her shoulders, obscuring her face. "As you wish."

Unable to spare any more time, Karl stood, waving to Thorsen, and the entire detail swept out of the air lock, back down toward the strange coral city below.

CHAPTER TWENTY-SEVEN

Striding into the upper palace that morning, through the great water-lock, Karl made directly for the king's own hall.

The doors were not open. No guard had been posted. Strange. But a small crowd had gathered in front of it.

"All traders," Thorsen murmured as they approached. "Only one Thalassan. Where are they?"

"We shall see," he muttered back, and raised his voice. "Where is the king? I need to speak with him immediately!"

Lord Willam turned first. "Ah, young Master Karl! We were just wondering when you might show up. Tell me, do you have the girl with you?"

"Where is the king?"

"Regretfully he cannot be here right now," that sole Thalassan said.

It was the green-haired skald, the one who had sung at Lady Amaro's pavilion. Strange. "Jarl Dryagr then," Karl said.

"Also indisposed," the Thalassan replied.

"When will the king be here?"

"Regretfully, I can't answer that."

Void take it, Karl thought. "Fine," he ground out, looking around the circle until his eyes settled on the one he was searching for. "You, Imran! We must speak, here and now."

The Suyarii lord raised an eyebrow, turning his attention away from Lady Amaro, with whom he had been talking. "Still bitter about losing the next kaupang's nacre contract?"

"Order anything you like. You'll never return here to retrieve it," Karl replied, and held out his tablet. He turned on the tablet's projection lens, causing a miniature hologram of the Suyarii fleet to appear above it. "Your very presence here is an act of war."

All talking ceased, every trader there looking at the fleet rotating slowly in the field.

"That's an Achaemenid-class capital ship," Lord Willam finally said, breaking the shocked silence. He turned to Imran. "Clever work, Suyarii. You did a good job of concealing the gunports, but the hull configuration is unmistakable."

"I deny it wholeheartedly," Imran said coolly. "The Achaemenids are the Suyarii Empire's most fearsome warships. What would a simple trader be doing with one?"

"A trader wouldn't have one," Karl replied. "But a lesser son of the Sultan might, especially one who was on some kind of infiltration mission."

"I don't like the accusation I hear in your tone."

"Then hear it in my words," Karl said, taking a step forward. "You are no trader. At least, trade is not your primary mission here. What, exactly, are you planning on doing here? Killing us, or killing this world?"

People who had been laughing and joking a moment before had now gone quiet, grim-faced.

And Imran laughed. "Did you truly think the Empire wouldn't eventually find the source of your irritatingly effective shield material? Really, Lord Gyes, the only reason why this planet isn't already a boiled husk is the regeneratives grown here. I have no idea how my father might look upon the loss of that resource. And besides, if we can corner that market for ourselves, why wouldn't we?"

The skald looked around. "Who is this man?"

"An enemy," Lord Willam said flatly. He fingered the pommel of his sword.

Lord Imran smiled coldly. "You really think you can take me, old man?"

"One man on the surface, or a twelve-kilometer floating fortress in the void," Lord Willam said with a smile. "I fancy my chances here."

Imran shifted his stance, reaching for the jeweled knife on his belt. "You take my head off, my men will kill you before it hits the ground."

"No matter," Lord Willam replied, voice as cold as the void, hand closing around his sword's hilt now. "Your fleet will never leave this system alive."

Beside him, Thorsen tensed.

A silence fell over the trader group.

Until one single voice broke it.

"Princess?"

THE PALACE AVENUES were all crowded with people; every off-worlder on the planet seemed to be out in the streets right now, all working feverishly. Pavilions being emptied. Last-minute minor deals being hashed out. A few stolen moments between friends or lovers from different fleets, different Houses.

Today was the last day of the kaupang. All negotiations would be ratified this morning down in the trading halls. By midnight, every off-worlder in this city would be back up in orbit.

Tomorrow, bulk lifters would be landing at their designated zones to make the final exchange of goods. Tomorrow, and for the next two weeks or so. But those lifters were largely automated, any human crew forbidden from opening cockpit shutters or exiting the craft in any way. It had happened a few times over the centuries. No House had ever survived such a breach of contract.

Thalassa kept its secrets.

With one last wistful glance at the riot of humanity around her, a galaxy she had wanted so desperately to be part of, Unara passed under the grand coral arch that marked the palace's water-lock and headed for the trading halls.

The inside was as busy as the outside, albeit with the balance tipped well in favor of the Thalassans. Unara pulled her scarf tighter around her face.

Up ahead, at the end of the grand open atrium, clustered in front of the trading hall doors, she could see the traders. They all seemed to be in some kind of argument. Lord Willam was reaching for his sword.

Frowning, Unara made for them, moving as fast as her exhausted body would allow. She had to find her father, had to tell everyone about—

"Princess?"

The voice brought her up short.

Hakon.

Standing there with the off-worlders, a terrible sense of recognition stamped on his features.

"Princess?" That was Captain Thorsen, a bemused smile on his lips.

"Princess," Hakon repeated, rushing over to her now. "Where have you been? You look terrible, like you got caught outside the shield coral during Sunwrath. What..."

He trailed off, watching as she tried to trace the runes for *desert* on her palm.

"She can't speak," Lord Gyes said. "She's mute."

"She wasn't a week ago," Hakon snapped back, but pulled a kelpskin book and squid-ink pen from his pocket, handing them both over to Unara. She immediately started writing.

288

"So this is the girl for which you were willing to sacrifice not just your House, but ours as well?" Lord Willam asked. "She's a good fighter and pretty in that Thalassan way but—"

"She's King Aegyr's youngest daughter. Mind your tone!" Hakon said in a voice Unara had never heard him use before. Even Lord Willam seemed taken aback.

In the silence that followed, she held the book up for Hakon, runes hasty but legible.

I need to see Father.

"Impossible," he said, still in Standard.

The change? Already?

"No. The king has been...confined."

That caused a stir amongst the traders

"What?" Lady Amaro demanded.

Why? Unara wrote.

"There was surveillance footage taken of you on the bridge, the night of the draugr attack," Hakon told her. "Did you not think there would be consequences?"

"Excuse me," Lady Amaro asked more forcefully this time. "What is going on?"

Then Unara heard a noise. Quiet. Far in the distance. But unmistakable to anyone who had grown up on an ocean world.

Lord Willam heard it too. Turned to her, a question in his eyes.

She couldn't answer.

It would have done no good.

Her warning wouldn't come in time.

It was already too late.

CHAPTER TWENTY-EIGHT

"You need urgent medical attention," the feii gothi was saying, one long-fingered hand resting on Vaelyn's forehead. "Something very strange is happening within you."

Vaelyn had no idea when her transformation would happen. Hethra had promised them it would be delayed until the right moment, but it would likely be soon; Vaelyn's insides felt like they were being ripped apart. Coming here had been a risk. Huge. Too much. And with Lord Gyes gone now... What had she been thinking?

"No," she said. "No scans."

"Death is coming for you," Eyr announced.

"Of course it is," Vaelyn gasped.

Movement. Off in the shadows, under the drop-craft ramp. Crabs. Dozens of them. Staring up at her. The ones that Hethra had commandeered, Vaelyn realized.

Was her mother watching her right now? And what would her mother make of this? What would Hethra do to her for coming here?

Vaelyn thought about Unara, staring in disbelief at Vaelyn's betrayal.

Vaelyn thought about Glaeva, coming apart.

All Vaelyn had wanted was to go home.

Not this.

Not like this.

Anger suddenly flooded her, and she tried to stand, grabbing for the wall. Eyr stopped her. "You are going nowhere. You need medical attention."

"Are there radios on this ship? A way to talk to the other ships on the ground?"

Eyr regarded her with blank eyes. "Yes, of course."

"I need to send a message," she said, and when the feii didn't move, she grew desperate. "Right now!"

Finally, Eyr responded. She helped Vaelyn up, letting the human lean on her as she led Vaelyn, limping, over to a bulky equipment panel. The mechanical tech that the off-worlders used was unlovely in Vaelyn's eyes, but it did its job well. A few buttons pushed and a voice came on.

<What is it, Eyr?>

The alien gestured at the panel, and Vaelyn leaned in.

"Captain," Vaelyn said. "This is Vaelyn. I'm sure you remember me. You need to get off the ground right now. Everyone needs to get off the ground right now. I don't know how you facilitate that, but—"

<There is no facilitating that, Vaelyn. Do you know how complicated it is to—>

"I don't care!" she snapped, and something squeezed in her chest. She pitched forward, only barely stopping herself from smacking face-first into the speaker. "Everyone still on the ground is going to die. Get in the air! Now!"

"Sir!" somebody yelled from down the ramp. "Something is happening out here!"

The drop-craft was oriented so that the nose, the main

command deck, was facing west. Out to sea. Which meant that the back end, where Vaelyn now stood, faced east. Toward the desert.

So she had a perfect vantage point to witness the flood begin.

Vaelyn had taken a submersible out years ago, back through the ancient underwater tunnels. Those ways were limited, intentionally narrow with old mechanical gates that were easily closed and only opened with extreme difficulty. Those ways were opened after the kaupang, used to gently fill the bay with mineral-rich waters that would nurture new titanocorals, grow new buildings and repair the old.

It had not been possible to capture those, dig them wide enough for Lady Hethra's purposes.

So these had been cut instead. The work of decades, employing both Stone Clan technicians and Abyssal Clan overseers and the strange gene-crafted crab constructs.

A catastrophic flood. That was what Hethra wanted. Something cataclysmic. Enough force, enough water, to sweep even starships from their moorings.

The two broad mesas that straddled the old riverbed, the dead river that had once guided the first colonists to Oceanfall, had been hollowed out as fully and completely as was possible while still maintaining some kind of structural stability. Year after year, the underground rivers were dug. Year after year, the hills had been gnawed away. For years, for decades, the water had been building up.

And now, they were breached.

A small puncture, barely visible, but Vaelyn was Thalassan; she recognized the sea.

"By Hildra," she gasped.

The first rumblings began. The ground started to shake. People outside the craft stopped to look.

Then the mesas simply ceased to exist, exploding outward in a deafening cacophony of collapsing rock and tumbling water. A twenty-meter-high wall of white foam roared toward the off-worlders' ships, throwing up boulders the size of akker-habitats, the rubble of the mesas being dragged along, tossed in the rage of the sea. A tsunami, captured and imprisoned and unleashed from the desert.

Klaxons sounded, mechanical screeching rising from every craft on the landing fields. Engines flared into life. People began running.

Vaelyn almost fell, trampled under the rush of people flooding into the drop-craft now. Strong, certain hands caught her, steadied her, and space opened up around them.

Eyr, she realized. The feii was holding her as easily as she might have a child.

"This world, it seems, finds new ways to kill us," Eyr commented almost casually. "But not today."

Light flared from her hand, burning through Vaelyn, even as the feii stood and strode to the back of the ramp.

Vaelyn fell to her knees, clutching at her chest. She couldn't breathe, she couldn't move, she couldn't think.

All she could do was watch as the wall of water bore down on the field, tossing up ships, throwing boulders, coming to murder them all.

But the feii was still walking forward, walking down the ramp even as terrified people streamed up around her. Her entire body glowed, ribbons of stronger light flaring out. Her hands were outstretched by her side, fingers wide. The first wave was almost upon them, the furious water arcing high, and then—

Then nothing.

The wave hung there, frozen in midair, daylight streaking through the water.

Everyone else around her was staring as well, Vaelyn realized. Even the people down below, who surely should have been dead, were standing, staring up at it with slack mouths.

Eyr trudged back, slower now, as if greatly burdened.

"I cannot maintain this for long," she panted, looking at the nearest guard. "Get this ship off the ground."

The guard nodded and ran for the radio.

And Eyr looked at Vaelyn, light like Sunwrath itself burning inside of her eyes.

"Something is attempting to rewrite your genetic code, Thalassan. I have stopped it for now. Isolating that process while allowing your cells to still function is quite difficult."

Vaelyn stared at the feii and looked back at the wave. Now she understood. The feii had slowed time. Selectively. Somehow. "Chronomancy," she breathed.

"I will extend my apologies to Rota and Hildra and the rest of your planet's guardians later," the feii said. "Now, you, go."

"Go where?"

"The palace," Eyr replied, pointing. "Move with speed, Vaelyn. As I said, I cannot hold this forever."

Vaelyn stared up at the arching bow of water. It was higher than the drop-craft. If it had fallen as it should have, it would have undoubtedly swept them all away. If she got caught out there when the feii's chronomancy failed, Vaelyn would absolutely die, killed by the ocean.

But then, she thought to herself, how would that be different than any other day on Thalassa?

Steadying herself, she strode down the ramp and, in the shade of the frozen wave, began to run.

THE RUN BACK to the palace's main water-lock was something out of a dream.

The landers were not so tightly packed as submersibles in their grottos; none were closer to each other than a hundred meters or so. But the floodwaters had already penetrated deep into the field by the time Eyr had stopped them, and those waters seemed to be flowing faster the further Vaelyn got from the feii. The roar of engines and downdrafts from the vertical takeoff jets seemed to disrupt the effect further, leading to some very strange sights,

To her right, one of the House Amaro landers flew through the top of a frozen,cresting wave as it took off. The water fell, all together at first and then splashing free, knocked loose from the feii's effect, hitting the ground and rushing out in all directions, water returned to the proper flow of time.

Vaelyn ran on.

Past the landers. Past the control tower. Into the market streets. Downhill now, downhill to the inner gates, the lower levels. The market streets were just ahead. She made the main avenue and heard screaming around her. She looked back over her shoulder and nearly stumbled.

Behind her, the way she had just come, was a huge wave of water, bearing down now at full speed.

There were Thalassans around her now, her own people. She yelled at them in their own language, urging them on. Not that anybody needed any encouragement. The water-lock wasn't far. Everyone—Thalassans and off-worlders alike—was headed that way, as fast as they could go.

Vaelyn pushed her flagging body, lungs screaming, legs burning; even among the sky-born, swimming was a far more common pastime than running.

The water-lock was closing, the great doors pushing shut under the influence of the awakened muscle fibers concealed within the walls. "Wait!" she shouted. How fitting it would be if she died here, she thought wildly, if it ended with her being dashed to pieces by her mother's own flood. "Hold the gates!"

She reached them only just in time, barely enough room between them for a human to fit. Vaelyn threw herself through the opening and the doors slammed shut behind her, sending a fountain of water spraying out around the hall.

The wave had hit. Only centimeters behind her, the wave had hit.

Vaelyn collapsed on her hands and knees on the floor, panting, trying to plan her next move as she caught her breath. Perhaps she could find Jarl Dryagr now, tell him what was happening, tell some-body, anybody…

But she looked up to find a spear in her face.

Held by Unara. Glaring down at her. Furious.

KARL DIDN'T KNOW what to think of any of this.

Vaelyn was there, on her knees, Unara with a spear on her. She'd grabbed one of the strange wide-bladed things away from a guard and had it leveled right at the other woman the second the gates had slammed closed.

"I know, I know. But Unara, we've got to stop her," Vaelyn said.

Nothing but silence. Unara's entire body was tense.

"This isn't you, Unara, and we both know it. Isn't that what you wanted? No more killing? Please. Let's stop it. Let's stop it together."

The other woman's face contorted, but she pulled back, spear up. She looked back at Hakon, who was there by her side with the book in a second.

"Are we safe?" Lady Amaro asked.

"Most likely," the skald replied. "The seals on water-locks and windows alike are rated for the maximum depth to which the bay can be flooded. The bay will drain before it reaches anywhere near that level, however."

"You sure about that?" Thorsen called from one of the windows.

Karl looked. He was indicating the gap, that narrow gap, in the encircling cliffs.

It was filling up now. Filling up with crabs, strange crabs, crawling atop one another. They looked small at this distance but had to be huge, the size of the off-worlders' war engines and glinting with nacre coatings, and they fitted into one another like inter-locking blocks. A living dam, sent to stop up the bay. So odd was the sight that Karl couldn't make immediate sense of it.

"Void beyond," Lord Willam breathed. "They're blocking us in."

Karl turned back to Hakon. Unara was holding up the book to the skald. "The princess says our number one goal is find her father, and with that, I concur."

"There'll be more draugr coming," Vaelyn said, hanging on to Karl's arm as if she would collapse without it. "Hethra... She told me...that these things are..."

"Hethra?" Hakon asked sharply. "What does she have to do with this?"

"I think...she may have sacrificed her entire clan."

"To what, to make those things?"

Vaelyn nodded. "She may have thousands of them to send after us."

"To what end?" Karl asked. He had no idea who this Hethra was, but judging from the expression on the skald's face, she was somebody of some importance on this world. There was shock there, and anger. Deep anger.

"To ensure your death, Lord Gyes, and the death of everyone else," Vaelyn replied, her face a mask of shame. "Hethra tried last kaupang to destroy your House, bring down the whole trade system. When that failed, she... I don't know, she's gone insane."

Unara gestured at the book again, indicated more hastily written runes, and Hakon sighed. "I know, Princess. But how do you suggest we unplug that gap? We have nothing large enough."

Karl looked back over his shoulder. "Lord Imran!" he called. "Do your void-to-surface bombardment cannons function?"

"Of course," the Suyarii prince said. "But they are useless here. I can't drop anything on this bay. Even our smallest ordnance would destroy this palace and everyone in it."

"Energy strike then," Lord Willam said thoughtfully. "Focus the beam as tightly as possible."

"The water may prove a problem. And those crabs are coated with nacre."

"It's our best chance. How do we make it happen?"

The Suyarii looked around at everyone, as if suddenly realizing this wasn't some theoretical discussion. "I shall need a clear view of the sky and preferably, a shipside radio. Hand units can't cut through all the interference on this world to reach orbit."

"I've got a line to our lander," Thorsen said, "but we'll need a spot to rendezvous with it."

"We can go to the clifftops," the skald said, and looked at Unara. "Above maximum pool depth. You'll be safe there, Princess."

Unara shook her head and wrote something.

"Absolutely not," he replied, watching her hand move. "We don't even know if the king is still—"

She shut the book and took back her spear, already moving across the atrium.

"Wait," Karl said, stopping her. "Where are you going?" She stared at him, and he looked back to the skald. "Where is she going?"

"Into the under-palace to retrieve the king," Hakon said. "But I don't think it's a good—"

"I'll go with you," Vaelyn said, getting to her feet. She swayed a little.

Hakon eyed her. "What exactly did Lady Hethra promise the clan, Vaelyn?"

Straightening, Vaelyn wiped tears from her eyes. "It doesn't matter now. Unara, please, let me come with you. Let me help."

Unara looked furious but nodded anyway.

Karl followed.

"Milord!" Thorsen said. "I must protest!"

"If this began with my family, then I must end it," Karl said, and clapped Thorsen on the shoulder. "Take the guard. Protect the other traders. I'll be fine."

"Milord..."

"What good is all that combat practice if I don't actually get to fight a sea monster?" he yelled and was off to catch up with the women.

CHAPTER TWENTY-NINE

Unara wasn't familiar with the sky-facing sections of the palace, but Vaelyn was. The Stone Clan woman led them on, down stairs and through corridors, descending ever deeper.

As they ran, Unara caught glimpses of the Stone Clan's life: enclosed halls, walls smudged black from soot, apartments whose only light came from glowing tanks, sprawls of living ventilation tubing, breathing out sour air. It was similar in many ways to the areas below the water that were carved into the rock: the same style of architecture, the same sinuous, twisting design. But it all functioned differently here. Optimized for the sea, the design failed utterly in the air.

Seeing it, Unara realized how easily Hethra might have fanned the flames of jealousy and resentment into...well, into whatever her plan was.

The palace halls were filled with panicked civilians, many of them clutching children. Vaelyn stopped to talk to several groups of them, explaining as quickly as she could, urging them to make for the clifftops.

"Draugr," one woman gasped, holding a squalling baby to her chest. "There are draugr in the lower levels."

"I know," Vaelyn said, grim. "Keep moving!"

"What was she saying?" Lord Gyes asked as they moved on again. Standard wasn't spoken outside of official trade negotiations; all those brief exchanges had been in Thalassan.

"She was saying draugr have been spotted in the palace depths," Vaelyn explained.

"The monsters?"

"Yes, Lord Gyes, the monsters."

Finally, they came to a spiral staircase leading down to what Vaelyn claimed was the level of many of the water-locks. For whatever good that would do. Water was leaking from ventilation units. The stone steps were slippery, the hallway at the bottom flooded ankle-deep.

"What's happening?" Lord Gyes asked as Vaelyn paused to take stock of their location.

"There are several species of biological piping that pull air in from above," she said, looking back and forth down the hallway. "Something must have been injured, gotten breached. Pipes meant for air are now bringing in water."

Unara tapped her on the shoulder, held up the pad. *Where is my father?*

"I'm not sure," Vaelyn said. Her voice was shaking, like she was fighting for breath. "I'm sorry, everything looks different right now, I'm all turned around."

Unara brought her spear up.

"I'm not lying to you!" Vaelyn said, desperate.

Down the hall, movement. Unara whirled. Lord Gyes already had his gun out.

A group of people, an old woman with a gaggle of children, running toward them, a pair of draugr close behind.

"They're moving too slow," Lord Gyes said grimly, striding out.

Unara was already moving too, but the going was hard. The

water, once her friend, was holding her back. Too shallow to swim in, too deep to run through. The children were screaming now. The old woman turned around, knife out, yelling for them to keep moving as the draugr bore down.

But before either of the creatures could grab her, someone else careened around the corner, knocking the draugr down. Dark blood raced through the water ahead of the children, and the first one of them, a little boy no taller than Unara's knee, threw himself into her, trembling.

The rest were soon on her as well, along with the old woman.

"We were down at the aquariums...having a swim..." she panted, leaning on Unara for support.

Unara didn't know what to do and just held on to the woman before she could fall.

"Honored grandmother, are you alright?" Vaelyn asked. "Can you walk?"

The old woman stared at her for a moment, then slapped her across the face. "You young ones who wanted your revolution! You've killed us all!"

Vaelyn stepped back, clutching her cheek.

"I think we have a problem!" Lord Gyes called from down the hall.

Unara poked Vaelyn, and Vaelyn shook herself. "The level above this is dry, Grandmother. Make for the clifftops. I'm sure others will help."

The old woman spit at her feet, then gathered up the children and made for the stairs. Vaelyn watched them go, sadness on her face. Unara had to grab her by the arm to drag her away, down to where Lord Gyes was talking softly with the one who had saved the children.

It was Yvar, Unara noticed with a start. Yvar who had collapsed against the wall, sweating profusely, head bowed.

Unara touched his shoulder, and he looked up. Nictitating membranes slid over his eyes as he blinked at her. "Unara," he said, voice thick, and grunted. "It was you, wasn't it, that message from Gyes?"

She nodded, looking him over. *How long?*

"It's coming too fast," he said, head still in his hand. "Drowning in the air now. I was trying to reach...the king..."

We need to get you in the water.

"You think?" he asked and then groaned. "I can't stand. By Hildra, this hurts."

Where is my father?

He pointed. "Third water-lock that way." He looked at Lord Gyes. "I hate to impose on you, but—"

"We can talk about your terrible negotiating style later," Lord Gyes said, and pulled Yvar to his feet, draping the man over a shoulder.

The four of them trudged through the ever-deepening water. Vaelyn went ahead into the water-lock Yvar had indicated, peering through the porthole. "The king is here," she announced. "Get inside. You'll need to close the outer doors before the inner will open."

Unara glanced through the porthole herself. Yes, there her father was, propped up against a rock wall, eyes shut.

Behind them, movement. Vaelyn had stepped out into the hall. Unara brought the spear up, preventing her from moving any further.

"I know you want to kill me," Vaelyn said. "And I don't dispute that I deserve it, after what...what Hethra did to you. But I need to find Dryagr, get him in the water."

"The water's getting deeper," Lord Gyes observed. "Fast."

"It's not far," she told him. "I'll be alright." She looked at Unara. "I'm sorry," she said, and then she hit the controls from the outside.

The door muscles contracted, locking them in.

Yvar coughed. "You are going to tell me what's going on, Princess," he said.

"Some woman named Hethra's trying to kill us all, apparently," Lord Gyes said.

"Hethra?" Yvar asked and groaned. "No wonder everything's wrong. That bitch had her hand in everybody's infusions."

"Infusions?"

But the inner door finally opened, and only just in time.

Yvar collapsed.

Water gushed out across the rocky floor, carrying with it blood and shredded fish leather and not a little bit of skin.

Yvar had changed back and was now gasping for breath. Drowning in the air.

Unara threw down her spear and grabbed her fellow ocean-born's hands, pulling him toward the pool. After a moment of hesitation, Lord Gyes jumped to help her. Yvar was heavy, the footing treacherous. Unara almost slipped down the stairs to the sunken conversation area, but Lord Gyes pulled her back. Between the two of them, they got Yvar to the pool.

The Forest Clan delegate pulled himself the rest of the way in, diving headfirst to the bottom in a swirl of shredded clothing and castoff skin. As that swirled away, Unara could see him lying on the bottom, his dark red tail swishing slightly.

"What's going on?" Lord Gyes asked. Unara looked back at him. He looked completely lost.

"Another word and it'll be your last."

Father.

Standing between Unara and Lord Gyes, face pinched, clearly in pain himself, holding Unara's discarded spear.

The trader shook his head, confusion on his face. "I... I didn't mean to—"

"Not another word," Father growled, and then looked to Unara. "Oh, my daughter. What have you done to yourself?"

"She can't talk," Lord Gyes said.

Unara put her hands together in a pleading gesture and then

scrambled back to the water-lock for her notebook. *Please spare him,* she wrote quickly.

The king looked between them and then down in the water. "You still alive in there, Yvar?"

<Yes, my jarl,> came his voice through the speaker-conch.

"The three of you. Explain what's happening. I can hear the ocean screaming."

VAELYN SLOSHED DOWN THE HALL, growing more chilled with each step. There was a current to the water now, a strong one. She wished she had a wetsuit. She wished for many things.

It didn't matter.

Jarl Dryagr's clan kept no mansion here, too used to the open ocean to feel comfortable in the confines of rock and coral and glass. Instead, when they were here, they kept a small habitat-akker anchored outside the bay. So Dryagr would be at one of the outfacing water-locks, surely one of those.

There were many water-locks that faced out, however, and Vaelyn checked five of them before she found one that was open. The water was above her knees now, and she had to fight for every step. Vaelyn grabbed for the door, pulling herself around the threshold.

There he was. Inside. Pulling on dive gear.

"Jarl Dryagr!" she said, running up. "I have urgent..."

And then Vaelyn trailed off.

Because Leyli was there. Leyli. Helping him get his gear on.

"Vaelyn? Yes. I have very little time," he said. "But you'd best get in here and get suited up. There won't be any going back that way, not at the rate the water is coming in."

"Was there something you needed?" Leyli asked. Her voice was sweet, but her eyes were hard.

Vaelyn moved cautiously, pulling down a wetsuit and stripping to the skin. "Where are you going, Jarl?"

"Lady Hethra calls for my clan's aid. We have many people here on the reef to protect," he said. "I can feel the change coming, but it's not sufficient yet for me to breathe in the ocean. This shall have to suffice to rally my warriors."

Vaelyn looked again at Leyli. "You can't," she said. "You can't help her. Jarl, Lady Hethra—"

"Is only trying to save us from King Aegyr's folly. Draugr in the palace!" Leyli said. "Just think of it, Vaelyn!"

Vaelyn glanced between them. "Do you know who they are?"

"The damned, Vaelyn, come to take their vengeance on the king for—"

"They're the people of the abyss. Hethra turned her entire clan into monsters!" Vaelyn snapped.

"She wouldn't do something like that, Vaelyn."

"Yes, she would, Leyli. She's been listening to the voices from the depths! They've convinced her to kill the entire surface world, everything the sun touches! Everything Hethra promised us is a lie."

Leyli narrowed her eyes. "Don't do this, Vaelyn."

"What choice do I have?" she snapped back and turned to Jarl Dryagr. "Please, Jarl, please, you must understand..."

"The Abyss and the Drift have been allies for centuries," he said, a warning in his voice as he drew his own knife.

"She killed Glaeva, my jarl," Vaelyn said, and bowed her head. "She told me so herself. Strike if you must but I speak the truth."

His knuckles turned white around the hilt of his knife.

Vaelyn braced herself.

But the blow didn't come from him. Instead, Leyli let out a strangled cry and threw herself at Vaelyn.

All Thalassan children, born to the sky or to the ocean, grew up learning to fight. The reef eel, the shark, the great clams that produced the wealth of the seas. Underwater, always underwater, and always against murderous wildlife.

Never before had she had to fight one of her own kind, her own clan, in the air before.

The two women thrashed around the room, tearing, stabbing, pulling. Under normal circumstances, they might have been evenly matched. But Vaelyn was cold from the water and Leyli had a wetsuit on and that gave her the advantage. She fell on her, knocking her down into the water. Vaelyn managed to kick the other woman's knife away but to no avail: Leyli jammed the bone of her forearm down on Vaelyn's throat and drove her under the surface, bearing down with her full weight.

For a few terrifying moments, Vaelyn thought she might drown, right then and there. She couldn't get Leyli off of her. Finally, just when she thought she couldn't bear it any longer, the pressure on her neck lifted away. Vaelyn surfaced with a gasp.

And there Jarl Dryagr was. He looked at her and then shoved Leyli out the water-lock and into the treacherous flood beyond, shutting it behind her.

"Thank y—"

"Don't," he warned, a vicious light in his eyes.

"Jarl, please, Lady Hethra…"

He didn't listen. Pulled on his regulator and mask instead, stepped into the water, and was gone.

Vaelyn stood for a moment in the flooded chamber, alone, chilled to the bone.

What was she supposed to do now?

But then she felt something in her tunic pocket, something she had almost forgotten, and an idea struck her. A crazy idea that would probably get her killed.

She waded over to the wall of gear and grabbed a wetsuit.

It was still better than drowning to death in here.

"Looks similar to what we used in the expedition fleet," Lord Gyes was saying, examining the row of wetsuits on the wall. "I don't recognize all the components."

"Biologics," Father coughed. Unara helped him ease down into the pool. He had refused to put on a wetsuit or even take an air tank; his only concession to his current condition was a rebreather Unara had pressed on him. The change was close. "Do you know how to use it?"

"Close enough," Lord Gyes replied.

<Jarl, we don't know what will happen to you out there,> Yvar said. <If what the princess says about poisoned infusions here is true, then it is likely that Hethra planned for you to—>

"The ocean isn't going to let me die, Yvar. Not now. Not today," her father growled. "Have you killed it yet?"

<Working on it, my jarl.>

"What is he doing down there?" Lord Gyes asked. His tone was deceptively light; his hands were shaking as he pulled on dive gear. Unara was watching him closely, copying his movements, working on her own as fast as she could. It was necessary, it seemed; they were flooded in, and the ventilation sponge was no longer breathing in fresh air. What oxygen was still in the room would be used up quickly. The only place to go was the water.

"Getting the door open," Father replied. "The organism that seals the exit was injected with hyperadrenaline to induce a paranoid state. It won't listen to my commands."

<So we have to—ah! There you are!> Yvar crowed happily.

"Blood in the water," Father said disapprovingly, watching the red plume swirl out below them. "You'll bring every shark in the reef down on us."

<I'll try to not stab it so hard next time, my jarl. Might make ending its life a bit difficult, though.>

Father shook his head and slipped fully under. <Give me that trident of yours, Yvar.>

Unara looked back at Lord Gyes, who was getting his tanks

strapped on. He gave her harness a once-over, nodded, and grabbed a pair of fins off the wall. "Do you need these? Or are you going to… change…too?"

She made a grabbing gesture. He retrieved a second pair. Sounds were echoing out of the pool's speakers, distant and strange.

<Unara, when you get in, take the off-worlder and find a place to hide. I must see to our people.>

"King Aegyr, I must—"

<Do not put yourselves in the middle of this, do you understand me? For once in your life, Unara, listen to your father,> the king said.

Stung by the rebuke, Unara pulled on her breathing mask. The world narrowed.

<How far back must we stay from the mouth of the bay?>

It seemed to take Lord Gyes a moment to realize the question was aimed at him. "At least a hundred meters, I believe. More would be better."

<Doesn't give me much room. Yvar, we make for the central seamount, rally there. We must find and stop the draugr advance and be ready to evacuate our people once the barrier is down.>

<Your command, Jarl.>

"What about this Hethra?" Lord Gyes asked.

<What's been set in motion will continue, regardless of whether or not that woman dies. Survival first, then revenge.>

And then they were gone.

The water was deep on the floor now, deep and rising fast. They couldn't stay here. But Unara found herself suddenly unable to move.

Lord Gyes held out a hand. "Come on."

Unara looked down at the dark water in the pool with not a little bit of trepidation, remembering the long trip through the underground river. But that was ridiculous, Unara told herself. She was a princess of this world, a daughter of the ocean.

She picked up her fishing spear.

Time to go home.

CHAPTER THIRTY

Hakon led the off-worlders to the clifftops. Through the Stone Clan's private spaces. Hall and gallery, hearth and home. Guilt still smoldered in the skald's heart, lit by Jarl Dryagr's anger. Off-worlders had been killed for less than this in the past. Entire fleets had been wiped out.

He tried to tell himself it was all in the name of the greater good. Without Lord Imran's warship, the day would be lost; nothing else would dislodge those crab constructs.

This was in the service of Thalassa and her people.

But the guilt still burned.

Up, up, up they went, gathering more people along the way. Children, families, mostly. Stone Clan who had not thrown in with Hethra mostly, but even a few who had. One such man tried to slip his knife between Hakon's ribs. Hakon opened the man's throat in response, leaving the body to dissolve into sea-foam behind him, driving the astonished off-worlders on.

Draugr emerged, here and there, shambling out of back halls or forgotten chambers or passages from the lower levels. Most of the traders had at least one or two warriors with them; the Gyes housecarl had a detail of six men. Hakon was grateful for them all. Their energy guns possessed great range and accuracy, and many lives were saved.

But the draugr disappeared soon enough, and they emerged from the Stone Clan's halls into daylight once again, out onto the clifftops. The plateau up here was narrow, the drop precipitous, but there was room for hundreds. Women gathered frightened children back from the edges, corralling them as best they could, while anyone with the means and ability to fight said goodbye to their loved ones and friends and headed back inside.

"Where are they going?" Captain Thorsen asked Hakon, coming up alongside him.

"Back down to cover our exit," Hakon replied. "It is when the octopus disappears that you must be the most wary, for it has likely driven you into a trap."

"How big do the octopus get here?" the housecarl asked.

"Big," Hakon said flatly, and went to speak with the traders.

The off-worlders had all clustered together at the opposite end of the plateau, looking east, despair stamped on their features. Hakon could see why.

Across the bay, the devastation was clear to see. The landing fields had been hit hard. Boulders the size of kraken had been ripped loose from the cliffs and sent tumbling across the field. Wrecked starships lay on their sides or in piles of twisted metal. Water continued to pour from Fjorgyn's wounds, gushing like blood across the landscape. The market streets were all within that flow now. If the main water-lock doors did not hold, the entire palace might flood.

"My ships were closest to the cliffs," Imran muttered, fury in his eyes. "I can see their hulls amongst the wreckage."

"As are some of mine," Lord Willam agreed. "I hope the missing ones are in the air."

"I don't see ours on the ground at all," the Gyes housecarl said, and raised his wrist to his mouth, speaking into the bracer he wore there. "Gyes, Gyes, does anybody copy? This is Captain Thorsen. We are in need of immediate assistance."

A crackle, a hiss, and then a voice.

<... read, Captain Thorsen. Where are you?>

"The southern clifftops of the bay," he said, voice steady but relief on his face. "Can you establish a link to orbit?"

<Yes. We are discussing the crisis with old Lord Gyes now.>

"Good. Get here." He glanced at Prince Imran. "We need that link."

IT SEEMED A LIFETIME, but it only took a few minutes for the Gyes ship to reach the cliffs. Hakon was in the middle of telling a funny little story to the assembled children when it descended to the level of the cliffs, engines roaring.

All the Thalassans stared at the star-akker. It was a monster of a thing, all metal and fire and some scent that he could not quite identify. It was nothing that belonged here, hanging in the sky like a manta ray.

But the wonder of it all seemed lost on the off-worlders. The Gyes housecarl simply strode up the ramp as soon as it was lowered to the rock, followed closely by Prince Imran.

"What are you doing, Thalassan?" the housecarl demanded as Hakon joined them inside the craft, walking with them toward some unknown goal.

"My duty," he said simply, looking around. What a wonder this ship was. Hakon hoped that there would be a chance to see it better, otherwise his song would be lacking.

"Your duty doesn't extend to my ship."

"It's a skald's right to go wherever he sees fit. How else can I weave the songs that save our history?"

"You're wasting time with this protest, Thorsen," Imran said. "The deeper the water gets in the bay, the worse for all of us."

The housecarl gave Hakon one more sideways glance, then shook his head. "Fine. Let's go."

THE JARL of the star-akker was immediately on edge when the men walked onto the bridge, pulling Captain Thorsen aside to talk to him. Hakon strained to listen. It wasn't Standard, that much he could tell, but several of the sounds were similar to their own tongue. Interesting.

And then there was Imran. Imran who was pretending to be aloof from it all while he and his men were clearly studying everything in the room. Like the jarl of a rival clan invited for a feast, assessing his enemies' defenses.

This, too, would not go into Hakon's saga. But the king would surely be interested.

If he still lived.

Finally, the two men from House Gyes broke off their discussion and the jarl nodded. "Our communication setup is right here," he said, patting the back of a console. Imran began moving toward it. "We will need your fleet codes and a transmission cypher."

"I don't think so," Imran said, looking over the console. "Operator, send my words on an open channel, wide broadcast." He looked at Thorsen. "This is no time for stealth."

"Probably for the best. Everybody's going to see it anyway," Thorsen replied with a vindictive smile. "Wouldn't want somebody else misinterpreting your actions and...doing something about it."

Imran just grunted.

"Channel open, milord."

"Good." And Imran began to speak.

CHAPTER THIRTY-ONE

Underwater now, Karl realized that the ocean was indeed screaming. Loud noises filled the water. But he had no time to consider what was causing it. Unara was moving already. Karl went after her, suddenly worried about what she might do.

Karl remembered looking down from the pavilion marveling at how clear, how blue, how shallow it seemed. He remembered the view from the submersible, the nighttime ocean dark and occluded. But here was his first true glimpse of the world under the waves. Of the Thalassa that her people knew.

There was an entire city down here in the bay. Buildings wrought from stone and coral, organic and twisting, scattered throughout the reef, tucked in, grown from the same stuff that nurtured eel and fish, crab and octopus.

And through it all, people were dying.

The draugr had overrun everything. They were slow but they were endless, a dark plague spreading across the reef. Where they went, Karl noticed with mounting trepidation, corals and anemones and sea stars, too slow to move away, died. Everything fled before them. People—all of them with tails—fled into the open water, but to no avail. The draugr swam, undulating through the water like sea snakes. Pushed by the movement of the water, groups of them drifted into knots of Thalassans.

The Thalassans fought. Knives and spears, tridents and bare hands. There were a few, here and there, wearing something that looked like armor. It was a world of a thousand little battles. A thousand little losing battles.

Then, a cry. Words Karl didn't know, words that still managed to tug at something deep inside of him.

It was King Aegyr, small in the distance, hovering above a rise in the middle of the bay, like a hill. Light seemed to shine from his trident. People turned. People began streaming toward him, fighting their way free of situations that only moments ago had seemed hopeless. The water was filled with cries answering the king's.

Karl looked to Unara, trying to gauge her reaction to all this. She was holding position just inside the cave's mouth. There was some kind of fleshy growth here, embedded in the rock near the exit, bleeding profusely into the current.

<The door organism?> he asked. The suits lacked integrated radios, but his voice translated well enough out into the water.

Unara nodded, swirling a finger through the blood and then pointing out. Her meaning was clear: they couldn't stay here.

But where could they go?

This was a killing field.

And then light lanced down from the heavens, filling the entire reef with its fury.

"Direct hit!" Imran called from the bridge's main windows.

"Milord, sensors indicate beam dissipation at ten meters under the surface!" one of the Gyes crew called.

"Flagship, hold," Prince Imran snapped, rushing over to the woman who had just spoken. "That can't be right."

"The chemical composition of the ocean is strange here. It interrupts scanning, after all," Thorsen replied.

"Surveillance scans utilize far less powerful forms of electromagnetic radiation," Imran snarled, and snapped his fingers. "You, Skald. Any insights?"

Hakon was by the window, watching the scene unfold. The light had been painful. A solid column of white-blue light slamming down from above, like Brynhildyr's own illumination had been drawn from all the rest of the sky and concentrated here; all had gone dark. For a moment, it had seemed as if the endless night of the depths had risen up to overtake the sky. Just a moment, just a heartbeat, and then there was nothing but the boiling sea. What a sight. What a song this would make.

"About our oceans?" Hakon said, addressing the off-world housecarl's question. "None that I'll offer you even now."

"Captain! Movement in orbit! Craft on an intercept course to the Suyarii fleet!"

Hakon turned, curiosity piqued by the edge of fear he heard in the crewwoman's voice. Whatever was happening, it was not expected.

"Show me!" Imran snapped, and with a nod from the captain, a projection came up in the middle of the bridge.

That, Hakon thought, was truly fascinating. A sculpture of light. It took him a moment to figure out what he was seeing. The blue curve there was Thalassa. The white points of light were ships. The scale was impressive; how large his world was, and how insignificant the star-akkers were against it all. A red line snaked through it. A path of travel, he realized. And it was moving.

"It's changing course. Accelerating!" one of the other crew said. Thorsen was staring now, like he couldn't believe what he was seeing.

"What is that?" Imran demanded. "Whose fleet is that coming from?"

Hakon had spent a lifetime, several lifetimes, studying the sky. Rota and Hildra were easy to observe. Their smaller sisters—Guthr,

Olrun, quiet Sygrun, Hyrja in her lonely route from pole to pole—
were harder to become acquainted with. But it was Hakon's duty to
his clan, to his king, to gather and save all the knowledge that he
could.

So Hakon knew which moon it was.

"By Hildra," he breathed.

The light-guns of Imran's star-akker would never speak again.

For five thousand kilometers above the surface of Thalassa's
ocean, the moon Svythir, tiny next to her sisters but massive
compared to anything made by human hands, smashed through the
heart of the Suyarii fleet.

DEAD AND DYING crab bio-constructs drifted in the current,
tumbling away from the pile in blue-gray clouds. The beam from the
energy cannon of the Achaemenid-class warship had lanced through
the upper layers of the living wall. The nacre might have held in the
void, Karl knew, but in the atmosphere, there were other factors to
consider. The things had no doubt been flash-boiled inside their
protective shells.

But it wasn't enough. The water had scattered the beam; only
the first ten meters underwater seemed to have been affected. And
already, new crabs were crawling up into position.

<What—> Karl began to ask.

But he never got a chance to finish his sentence.

Because Unara grabbed him.

Turning, Karl saw a shark, head armored in bone, coming right
for them.

IMRAN SAID nothing to anyone on the bridge.

Nothing at all.

He stood at the glass, watching as the light faded above. Explosions. Up in orbit. Like watching a star being born in the daylight. Beautiful, even though Hakon knew that thousands of lives had just been lost.

"Lord..." Captain Thorsen began.

But the trader prince just growled deep in his throat, drew his strange, curved sword, and started to move. Striding, then running. Out the bridge. Down the hall.

"Void take it," Thorsen groaned, and took off after him.

Sparing one last glance around at the bridge, Hakon set off as well.

Imran went directly for the back of the craft. Some of the off-world traders and their retinues had come aboard. Chief among these was Lady Amaro, who had collapsed in a heap of silk and was being attended to by that feii creature.

"Lord Imran!" Thorsen was yelling. "Lord Imran, stop!"

But there was no stopping the furious prince. Not breaking stride for a moment, he strode down the ramp and back out onto the clifftop, making straight for Lord Willam, who was deep in conversation with his own entourage.

"You! You honorless son of a dung beetle!" Imran roared and swung for him.

Hakon was there in an instant, grabbing Imran's sword arm and hauling him back, even as Thorsen's men rallied, guns out, and the Caledon guard drew swords. The Thalassans, clearly unsure of what was going on, backed away.

"You coward!" Imran yelled, desperately trying to fight his way free. "You killed them! You killed them all!"

"You want me to say that the death of that monstrosity brings me no joy?" Lord Willam taunted back. "I cannot, for I am quite pleased right now."

Imran swore in a language Hakon didn't know and tugged again at his sword arm. "Let me go!" he snarled at the skald. "Let me kill the man who killed my fleet."

"It wasn't him," Hakon replied.

Imran stared at him for a moment, then his eyes narrowed. "Then who?"

"Who cares? An ocean of ale to the one who did it," Lord Willam replied. "But you can be assured I didn't give the order, for I would have waited until after we cleared the bay. Look! It only knocked down the top of the barricade!"

Hakon did look. Out to the mouth of the bay, where the gigantic crab constructs, burned and bubbling from the assault, were nevertheless attempting to reconstruct the barrier, crawling up over the dead to lock their living bulk back in place. But the skald's keen violet eyes also caught something else entirely.

Out from the open water. Under the surface. Swimming fast.

Oh, no.

ON THE MADDENED SHARK CAME, slamming into the entrance so hard that rocks fell from the walls inside. Unara yanked Karl back, as far as they could manage. Jaws snapped, body writhed. It backed up, readying itself.

But before it could charge them again, a pair of metal-tipped tentacles came out of nowhere, slicing into the creature. The shark whirled in the water, fighting even as it died, but one of the strange blades slashed down through its head. It was flung off, into the reef, a strange screeching filling the air.

Karl looked around, stunned, and then a voice cut through the confusion.

<You'd better take over, Unara, before it eats us all!>

And there Vaelyn was. On the back of a creature that was all arms and blades and glowing, moving light. It was—

<Akker,> Vaelyn explained as they swam toward it. <I thought you might need it.>

The princess nodded. Held out her hand. The thing, the akker, slid a tentacle around her wrist, tightening down, one of its blade-tipped appendages raised above her. For a terrible moment, Karl thought it might eat her or something.

The thing instead turned a brilliant, undulating blue and loosened its grip. Unara, more graceful now, grabbed on and swung herself around into a prone position on its back. She tapped it, and something like a seat appeared in its side.

Karl hesitated. Vaelyn laughed. <I told you you wouldn't like them,> she replied.

And then the akker whirled around, nearly knocking him into the coral, tentacles up and tense, the entire body now a dark, flashing red.

Through the gap, tentacles the size of starship refueling cables were forcing their way through the dying, falling crabs.

"Kraken!" somebody in the distance roared.

CHAPTER THIRTY-TWO

From her underwater vantage point, Unara could only watch the scene in horror.

Kraken. More than one. At least three of the things were attempting to force themselves into the bay, drawn in by the scent of the dying crabs and driven to frenzy by the abundance of prey within. Everything, from the smallest fish to the largest shark, was fleeing away from those grasping, reaching tentacles, desperate to avoid being shoved into one of the creatures' many beaked mouths. No juveniles, these, but full-grown adults. Armored, vicious, implacable. The sound of rocks crashing spoke to the damage the monstrous things were inflicting on the other side of the bay wall. There could have been dozens out there, Unara realized with a chill, an entire deepwater swarm. Coming straight for them.

<By the void,> Karl said, shock registering even through the regulator.

<Look!> Vaelyn cried and pointed.

The abyssal manse sat away from the others, on the north side of the bay. And now its gates were opening.

Pouring out was what was left of the Abyssal Clan.

Unara's blood ran cold upon seeing them.

When she had visited the depths, she had wondered at the empty city, the dark pressure-habitats. She had wondered why nobody had been there.

Because here, here they all were.

The draugr were bad enough, twisted mockeries of old humanity, visions of drowned men come back to haunt the living. These were worse. This mob bore the signs of severe gene-manipulation, nightmares of the depths. There was a group who had the tails of sharks and the heads as well, an individual who resembled a giant polychaete worm, every arm ending in a human hand, another whose tail had been replaced with the long, spindly spikes of an abyssal urchin. Others, too many others. All horrible. All screaming with voices that were no longer human.

And up through the center floated a bloated, monstrous, strange akker. A cephalopod genetic template, as so many were, all tentacles and hard-edged shell plating. But the head narrowed instead of widening out, and within that column of flesh was Hethra, embedded up to her waist.

The abyssal chieftain was swimming hard. Swimming directly for Unara's father, for the ocean-born.

Rage filled Unara at the thought of proud Thalassan gene-craft, the gifts of the moons, being twisted so.

Hildra give me the strength to end this, she thought, and without a second thought, pushed the akker into a furious dive, headed right for Hethra.

Right past the kraken incursion.

And so, for the last time in her life, Unara rode into battle against Thalassa's monsters.

Imran and Willam were fighting now, yelling at each other. It was taking all of Thorsen's men to restrain them.

Then a woman screamed.

Draugr were spilling out on the clifftop. Shambling, shuffling draugr. Slow, but then, they didn't need speed. Foam dripped from their corroded knives, their bare hands, clung to their legs. Everyone was backing up, backing into each other, backing toward the edge. Small children, the ones too young to understand, were wailing. Hakon saw one boy pull out his own little dive knife, even as his mother shoved the boy behind her. Hundreds of civilians, Hakon's entire clan, everyone who was still alive perhaps, everyone he had ever known...

Imran and Willam had ceased their fighting. Staring, too, like all the rest.

Then, the sound of metal scraping over metal. Lord Willam drawing his sword, the blade murmuring its metal song as it was pulled from its sheath. "Interesting monsters you have here," he commented to Thorsen.

From the drop-craft, Thorsen's men began firing.

UNARA'S AKKER flew through the water. Jets pumping, fins twisting, she buried herself in the pilot's position and steered as best she could.

Vaelyn had the spear Unara had taken from the guard above and Lord Gyes had his sword out. It was awkward in the water, slow and clumsy, but powerful.

Nobody knew how big the kraken could get. The size of habitat-akkers, the Drift Clan claimed. A hundred meters from fins to tentacle-tip. Bigger, even. Absurd proportions, but nobody knew for sure. Nobody had ever lived through such an encounter to tell the tale.

But with these, Unara could almost believe the stories.

The current in the bay was brutal, thanks to the cascade of water still pouring from the clifftops. Visibility was low, confused by ink and blood and the foam from the dying. All was obscured. But Unara and her akker swam hard and true.

Through the lead kraken's arms, diving and dodging through a forest of deadly suckers and impenetrable mollusk-armor. They were small, but they were food, and the kraken's lesser tentacles smacked and jabbed around them, seeking to bring them into one of the secondary mouths.

Vaelyn and Lord Gyes struck when and how they could. The off-worlder's sword was slow in the water, but brutally effective, cutting through the kraken's tough skin like it was nothing. Vaelyn jabbed and stabbed where she could, balancing in the saddle, extending her reach further than Lord Gyes could. Unara left them to their fight, focusing only on making it through to clear water. So close, right there...

A massive tentacle, one of the huge primary ones, swept down through the water in front of them with such force that Vaelyn was almost thrown from her saddle. Lord Gyes reached out, grabbing her back, slashing out at the arm at the same time, as Unara urged the akker into a hard dive. It was fighting her now, its own instincts wanting to go back, tear, rend, capture, feed.

She slammed a fist against its back, hitting it as hard as she could. It took the order. Only just in time.

They went vertical, hurtling below the kraken, and as Unara pulled it up again, a great cry went out from the seamount.

The front line of the Abyssal Clan had reached the base of the hill, swimming—or crawling, or slithering—up the seamount. Unara could see that Father already had his hands full, battling both the kraken and the draugr, up in the shallower water. To allow this band of monstrosities to crash over them as well would overwhelm them completely.

<Make for Hethra!> Vaelyn yelled, but she didn't need to. Unara yanked hard, pulling the akker left, and they slammed into the back of the abyssal line.

Blades flashed. Foam filled the water. Taking targets of opportunity, Lord Gyes and Vaelyn striking anything that came within range. Vaelyn was yelling out now, trying to warn the people above of the danger from the depths. Lord Gyes was silent, utterly focused.

Then, Unara lost sight of the abyssal akker. It was gone. Just...gone.

Camouflage, she thought desperately, and pulled her own akker up, trying to get some distance to see where the rocks might be moving, trying to see in the darkness.

<What are you doing?> Lord Gyes called, hacking away at a questing tentacle cast down by the kraken above.

Unara's akker brought its bladed arms up, ready to strike.

<There!> Vaelyn yelled, pointing.

Unara couldn't see it, but her akker did. Without any prompting from her, it jetted forward again, diving to the sea floor.

Falling right onto the back of Hethra's akker.

The two gene-wrought vehicles collided so hard Unara heard coral snapping, bits of the reef crushed as the bigger akker was driven down into the sea floor. The bigger one immediately dropped its camouflage coloring, flashing red, streaming with bio-lights, turning to attack.

They had seconds at best, and they used it. Vaelyn stabbed. Lord Gyes swung. The akker flashed a triumphant white and rammed both its blades deep into the other akker's fleshy back, rending hard.

Seconds spent. Seconds lost.

Huge tentacles, the primary ones, reared up above them. In the glinting sunlight from above, Unara could see rows and rows of titanium blades shining.

Unara tried to urge the akker on. It wouldn't move, intent on killing the foe underneath it. She punched the back of the akker's head—the command to disengage—but it would not. Cursing internally, she wrested a leg free of the saddle and kicked at Lord Gyes, holding out a hand to indicate the abyssal akker's tentacle.

It was all the warning she could give.

The arm slapped down.

Lord Gyes swung out.

The tentacle floated free in the current.

The akker screamed then. Screamed. And not the scream of the animal whose genetics had been taken to create the thing.

It was a woman's scream. Hethra's scream.

The akker whirled, throwing them off, sending them flying out into open water.

<She's coming!> Lord Gyes yelled.

And Unara suddenly had a plan.

She turned her own akker, flying under an arcing arm from one of the kraken, and started swimming south.

Away from the seamount. Away from the people there.

The akker of Unara's clan were built for agility, for rapid bursts of speed, just like any other reef-dweller. But even wounded, Hethra's akker was larger and faster, and it was on them in seconds.

One of Hethra's tentacles slid around Unara's akker, squeezing, yanking them around. The akker flashed orange, alarm streaming down its side in neon light.

Lord Gyes was hacking at the other main tentacle. Another tentacle smashed Vaelyn out of her seat. The abyssal akker rose.

Hethra loomed over Unara now, dark glee on her face. "Die, last daughter of Aegyr," she hissed, and aimed a trident right at Unara's heart.

"To the akker! Get in the star-akker!"

Hakon was yelling it at his people in their own language, hoping they were listening to him. He didn't have any time to spare for a glance. It was all he could do.

The clifftops were running with foam, the kind of scum that got churned up on storm waves, the rocks slippery with it. The draugr came on and died and came on again.

Everyone who could fight did. The off-world warriors from

House Gyes were pouring their deadly light into the draugr advance. Lord Willam and his personal guard had formed up together, cutting deep with their long, straight swords. Lord Imran was everywhere, his curved blade flashing in the harsh sunlight. Hakon had his knife out, but closing with these things was dangerous. This was not the kind of combat he was used to, and it was endless.

A whirl, a strike, another draugr gone. But the skald had overextended himself. He slipped, fell, hitting the rock below hard. Hakon shook himself, barnacle-encrusted faces gathering around him, hands pawing at him. Disgust filled him, and he kicked one creature down, rolling over to drive his knife through its eye socket. It fell apart, dissolving in moments. But there were others, more, too many.

A glorious song, Hakon thought, and wondered if any would be left to sing it.

CHAPTER THIRTY-THREE

From out of the churning blood-streaked waters, Unara heard a cry. The Thalassan battle cry, as old as the ocean-born themselves.

"Drown your foes!" one voice roared.

"Win the seas!" dozens more answered.

Dryagr. Hunched low over his akker. Back in his ocean-born body. Most likely in great pain from the change, he was throwing himself headlong into the battle nonetheless.

The Drift Clan charged. Up through the mouth of the bay, over the crabs that still remained, under the krakens, their akkers moving with such speed against the tumultuous currents that it was almost impossible to believe. They had always been a people that depended on speed. Speed for hunting. Speed for survival.

The Abyssal Clan, even as changed as they were, were no match for them, and scores of the wretched creatures were cut down in the first charge.

"Excuse me," Hethra sneered, and flung the akker away, all attention suddenly on her oldest ally, her newest enemy.

There was nothing Unara could do. The akker tried desperately to right itself, but its outer muscle layers had been shredded by the other's blades, its port jet torn apart. None of the touch controls were working. Blue blood streamed out around them as they hurtled toward the cliff face.

Only just in time, Unara slithered forward out of the saddle and grabbed the first tentacle she could reach, yanking up hard. The akker's dying brain seized onto this and obeyed, using the last of its strength to flip around, belly to the wall.

It contacted the wall with a sickening thud and moved no more.

The force of the impact threw Unara free, and she shot her arms out wide, arresting her movement as best she could. She turned, looking back at the cliffs. The akker floated there, limp, red lights cycling down its length. Then nothing.

Out in the current, Unara saw Vaelyn floating, limp, limbs loose. Bubbles streamed from the tank on her back. Cracked, it seemed, and for a second, Unara thought about leaving her there. Her false friend, the one who had betrayed her.

For a moment, Unara considered leaving her there to die.

Who would ever know?

Then Hethra was on her. Hethra's strange akker mount, rising up, tentacles out, trident up.

"You betrayed me," the chieftain of the Abyssal Clan growled. Her voice had taken on some strange cadence, like the sound of lava cracking open on the sea floor. "I shall show you what true pain is, daughter."

Before she could land a killing blow, something silver tore between them. Blue blood fountained out of Hethra's akker. It turned an enraged red, thrashing.

"You've killed enough Thalassans today, old friend!" Dryagr sneered, his spear streaming blue in the current as he tore around them, swinging out in a wide arc through the turbulent waters.

"Fool!" Hethra roared.

A feral smile on his face, Dryagr spurred his own mount into a direct charge, spear forward.

Unara realized what he was doing. Attempting to distract Hethra, so that Vaelyn would have a chance.

But it was a feint that cost him everything.

He came at Hethra as hard and as fast as any shark might have. But it wasn't quick enough. Almost too fast to see, Hethra turned aside at the very last second, and speared him through the chest. The middle tine of her trident coming clean out of his back, the woman smirking at him for a moment. Then she hurled his body away.

For a moment, Unara thought she saw a smile, contented, happy, on the face of the man her sister had loved. And then he, too, was gone, his body turning into a mist of bubbles that were lost to the sea.

And Hethra set about to slaughtering the rest of his clan.

HANDS CAUGHT HAKON'S LEGS, yanking him down. He kicked out, smashed the draugr's face in, then rolled over to finish the thing off with a slash of his knife.

It wasn't enough. Nothing was going to be enough.

The draugr kept coming. An endless wave of them, like a horde of lobsters come up from the depths. Only these monsters were here to kill, not to breed, and none would benefit from their presence.

Draugr fell, crawling and squirming toward him, moving like eels across the ground, grabbing at him, holding him down. Others had fallen like this, Hakon knew, and struggled to his knees. But then a hand caught his hair, yanking him down again, and the monster's whole weight landed on him.

The creature sitting on his chest brought its head close, the jaw opening, stretching far wider than any humanoid face had the right to. Its gums were set with shark's teeth. Its breath stank of death. Hakon bared his own teeth and tried to free his arm from underneath the thing's knee. He had seconds, he knew, mere seconds to save his life, and the strength in this thing, by Hildra, the strength of it...

A glittering silver arc above him.

Foam, falling around him.

A hand was extended. Lord Imran. The man was bleeding from a gash on his arm but hardly seemed to notice.

"Interesting monsters you have on this world!" Lord Willam hollered as Hakon let himself be pulled up.

Behind him, the skald could see that his people were evacuating. The drop-craft was huge but the ramps they were using now were narrow, slowing the flow. Children were panicked, the elderly unsure of their footing. The Gyes clan had people just inside the air lock, helping others in, urging them on—or pulling them across wholesale. There was screaming as somebody slipped on the ramp and nearly fell.

It was not something Hakon could afford to be distracted by.

All they had to do here was hold out a little longer.

But the circle of defenders was getting smaller. One of Lord Willam's men was dragged down. One of the Gyes men who had joined them was thrown off the cliff. Captain Thorsen's blade had broken, and with one hand he was stabbing out with what remained, firing an energy pistol with the other. A few of the Stone Clan women had stayed behind, their children handed off to others to be carried across the ramps, and had rushed to Hakon's side, adding their own dive knives to the fight.

"A good fight!" Lord Willam roared as he put his blade through another leering draugr.

"Speak for yourself, Caledon!" Lord Imran yelled back. Hakon was unfamiliar with the Suyarii's weapon, some type of curved sword that cut wide arcs through the air, but it was effective.

"The High King would approve!"

"Your king's a barbarian!"

Lord Willam started laughing.

Hakon saw Thorsen grin just as he stabbed his broken blade into another draugr face.

"What are they saying, Skald?" one of his clanswomen asked.

Hakon smiled grimly. "It's the battle-joy talking."

She made to respond but took a broken bronze shaft to the chest.

He couldn't even reach her before she fell apart on the cliffs.

The sight of it caught Lord Imran up short, and he stopped mid-strike, staring.

"Prince!" Lord Willam roared and moved.

The Caledon blocked the next draugr, throwing it back, sword out, standing in front of the Suyarii. Hakon hacked a draugr down and pulled the off-worlder up. Imran had a strange expression on his face but threw himself back into the fray anyway.

The evacuation progressed faster now, driven by fear. The draugr had overrun almost the entire clifftop; the ship was the only escape. Lord Willam lost the rest of his guard, his men pulled down by draugr while protecting the rear of the evacuation. The Gyes men fell back to help the last stragglers across. Hakon pulled his two surviving clanswomen close to him and they fought together, striking out at anything that came close.

The draugr seemed to have no sense of themselves, no concept of danger. Always, always, Hakon had fought things that cared for their own survival. Reef eel or man, it made no difference. There were pauses in such fights. Reprieves, hesitations, feints.

There was none of that here. The draugr were mindless.

"Aboard! My lords, get yourselves aboard!"

Hakon turned. There were no civilians left. He pushed the women behind him and struck out at a draugr with a face like a shark. "Go!" he ordered them.

They ran.

The four remaining men on the clifftop—Hakon, Thorsen, and Lords Willam and Imran—drew closer, backing up as best they could, fighting even as they withdrew. Lord Willam was roaring, still striking out even as Thorsen grabbed at him.

"Milord!" he yelled. "You must go!"

But Hakon could see the signs. The battle-joy was hot in his blood. There would be no retreat for him, not now.

"Lord Imran!" Thorsen tried. But Imran ignored the housecarl, a sneer on his face and his eyes fixed on the foe.

Somebody was yelling at Thorsen from the drop-craft. Their own language again. Hakon saw that the draugr had overtaken one of the ramps. It was being withdrawn, the creatures still clinging to it, climbing up. The House Gyes guard poured their killing light down onto the things. Thorsen yelled something back and then was running back up the last ramp. A few moments later, a fresh round of light lanced into the draugr front.

Hakon didn't even consider getting aboard. Never let it be said, he thought, that a Thalassan ran while an off-worlder fought on.

Not that there was any chance of winning here.

Then Lord Willam lashed out at a pair of draugr that got a little too close but missed one coming in from the left. Imran leapt in, sword arcing out.

And took a knife to the left ribs.

Hakon grabbed for Imran as he stumbled, catching him before he hit the ground. Lord Willam turned, taking in the situation in a moment. His face contorted, then he hauled Imran up, throwing the man over his shoulder, running for the only remaining ramp.

Hakon, alone for a moment, smiled at the draugr horde, spit on the ground before following Willam into the ship. The draugr streamed after him. Ice-cold hands almost caught him.

Thorsen grabbed him, though, hauled him on board. Energy rifles barked. The ramp was pulled in, dripping with foam.

A shift. Movement. The cliff withdrew. Hakon looked back to see draugr tumbling off the edge of the rockface, falling like a water-fall. As tightly packed as they were, the mindless motion of the ones behind was pushing off the ones in front.

"I thought you were a poet," Thorsen panted, looking at Hakon. The housecarl's face was bruised, his uniform shredded.

"Nothing lives on this planet that can't fight for itself," Hakon replied.

"Eyr! You damned feii, where are you?!"

It was Lord Willam's voice.

Hakon hurried back into the main hall, looking for the man. There were people everywhere, his people, all in various states of shock. There was very little talking; the prohibition against speaking their language in front of the off-worlders held strong. One old woman, murmuring to the group of children huddled around her, glared up at him. As if daring him to condemn her.

He nodded. Kept moving.

"Eyr!"

"I'm here, I'm here. Let me work."

Lord Willam was kneeling in the middle of the hall, Lord Imran on the floor in front of him. The Caledon had taken off his cloak and shoved it under the Suyarii's head and was talking to him, trying to get him to respond. Lady Amaro was next to Imran as well, seemingly heedless of the blood soaking into the hem of her dress, a cloth pressing to a seeping wound on Imran's forehead. Imran's eyes were open, but Hakon could tell, they saw nothing.

The alien had a hand over the off-worlder's wound. Light glowed from between her fingers, then faded.

"I'm sorry," she said and stood. "He's already gone."

The Caledon trader sat down heavily on the deck, sword cast aside, head in his hands.

Hakon spared him one last glance, then went to see to his own people.

The moons gave life, and the ocean took it.

Such was the way of Thalassa.

CHAPTER THIRTY-FOUR

Pain shot up Karl's leg.

He reached down, wincing. Broken, at least. Shattered, most likely. It was trapped in the akker's saddle, the shell casing crushed when the thing had smashed into the underwater cliff. Karl wasn't sure how or why the strange bio-ship had turned at the last moment, but he was grateful for it; it likely would have killed him. As it was, his leg was trapped.

He sucked air through his regulator. Something was glowing yellow in his mask: a warning light. His air supply was running low. The battle seemed far distant, his mind wrapped in insulation blankets.

Movement in the current.

A bone-armored shark, two, three, swimming right for him.

The sight jolted him back to full awareness. He reached for his sword—still there, miraculously—and with only a moment's hesitation, hacked into the body of the akker, cutting his way free. It released a torrent of brilliant blue blood into the water around him, obscuring the world around him, but it did the trick. The pressure on his leg let go.

Karl tore out of the saddle, falling down in the water as the sharks slammed into the akker's body. Forgotten by the mega predators, he kicked out hard with his good leg, trying to leave the creatures behind.

On his own, injured, the sword was far too heavy to hold. With only a moment's hesitation, Karl let it go, watching as it disappeared into the dark waters below. By the void, it had to be fifty, sixty meters deep here, and he just stared down, wondering what other nightmares might be lurking there.

Then...

Something grabbed him. He struggled for a moment but saw berry-red hair floating around him. Unara, her braids all loose now. She had Vaelyn in her arms. The other Thalassan wasn't moving, and for a moment, Karl feared the worst.

Unara pointed at her mask, then up to the surface. Karl took her meaning. Air. They all needed air. Why Unara hadn't changed back to that ocean-going form, like the king or Yvar, he had no idea. Not the time for questions. But he shook his head.

<We've been too far down. If we surface too quickly, we'll get decompression sickness and we'll be dead anyway,> he told her, but then saw the pressure indicator on his air tank. It was low. Too low for decompression stops on the ascent.

Void take it, he thought, and hoped his drop-craft had escaped the floods above. They were all going to need a stay in Eyr's hyperbaric chamber when this was over. If they survived.

There was no use trying to keep his broken leg stable. The water was worse than free fall, constantly in motion, constantly tugging and pushing, and the chaos of the battle beyond made it all worse. The water was filled with scales, sand, blood. Drifting bits of things Karl couldn't identify. People were shouting in the distance, but there was no way of knowing what was happening.

Didn't matter.

Vaelyn stirred as they ascended the cliff face. <Too far west,> she muttered. <Too far. No need to worry about the bends. The waves will dash us apart if we go up here.>

<Save air. Don't talk,> Karl said.

Unara tapped them both and pointed. There were lights up there, glowing deep inside the cliff.

<As good a place as any,> Karl said, and they swam for it.

The space turned out to be an underwater tunnel, narrow, tight. Unara took a now-unconscious Vaelyn and swam ahead. It took six minutes for her to return, during which time Karl's tank indicator went from yellow to red. His flow rate was starting to drop, the equipment clearly trying to conserve what was left.

The swim was tight, the underwater cave quite unpleasant. But it was only a few minutes before it opened up again. He found himself in a circular room, one of the strangest Karl had seen here on Thalassa. It was filled with biological growths—sponges, maybe, or some type of local coral he didn't recognize—that ringed the walls and rose up in the center. There were flat areas, large enough to fit a human body.

In the central column was the source of the light.

Small sacks set into deep recesses, glowing.

Karl went over to one, tugging on it gently. It came free easily enough. A bag with raised runes on the side, made of some rubbery material. It was connected to the inside of the recess via some kind of tubing. Whatever it was, it was being grown here. Deliberately.

<What is this place?> he asked, curiosity overwhelming all other concerns for a moment.

But Unara took the bag from him, placing it back in its recess, and pointed up. There was a shimmer there, movement.

Air space, above the water.

They surfaced, Karl yanking off his mask and regulator to take a deep, grateful breath. The air was stale, still, but breathable. There was a flat shelf of rock here, only a few meters wide, and Unara had placed Vaelyn there.

Karl swam over to the unconscious Thalassan woman. Carefully, he pulled himself up onto the rock to sit next to her. His broken leg was swelling up inside the wetsuit, and the motion made it throb horribly. The rapid ascent from the bottom of the bay had been dangerous as well. Karl could already feel a headache starting. But in that moment, he didn't care.

He brushed a bit of hair out of Vaelyn's face. She looked drawn, paler than normal, and her breath was coming in harsh gasps. The sight tore at him, an unexpected feeling, but even under the circumstances, not an unwelcome one.

She was still alive, at least.

That was something.

It was everything.

"Is there any way back up into the palace from here?" Karl asked hopefully, looking back at Unara.

Still in the water, the princess shook her head. Pointed. There was a water-lock at the back of the small cavern, but the water was past the top of the window.

"No way out and no spare tanks," he said, looking around. "I don't fancy a free dive out through that tunnel. So how do we get out of here?"

Unara bit her lip, shrugged, looked around again. The ceiling of the cave was almost touching the water here, and glowed blue from ever-present plankton. It made Vaelyn's face look even more ashen than it already was.

"There has to be a way," Karl said.

Unara shook her head, like she was considering it, and then she was gone.

And before Karl could even process what had just happened, tentacles flopped out onto the rock.

Grabbing him and Vaelyn both.

Dragging them under.

CHAPTER THIRTY-FIVE

Unara barely had time to process what was happening. One moment she was at the surface, watching Lord Gyes stroke Vaelyn's hair. The next, she was underwater on the gene-hallow's floor.

Tentacles pressing down on her. Tentacles. Tentacles like...

Hethra's akker. Half-dead and yet on it came, its skin painted a furious red. The thing was far too big for the space it was forcing itself into, its tentacles curling, thrashing, sliding around each other as they rippled toward Unara.

She tried to fight, but she was pinned. Legs tied up together, arms forced down by her sides. Another arm curled around her, beginning to squeeze.

Vaelyn and Lord Gyes were here now, pulled down and bound up in the same way Unara was. Vaelyn's eyes were open again. Lord Gyes was struggling, but he'd managed to pull his mask and regulator back on. Vaelyn had nothing.

"Ahh, my little rebels."

Unara's head shot up. Hethra.

The abyssal chieftain came swimming through the forest of

cephalopod arms. Smiling. "Look at you," she purred, moving between them, finally settling on Vaelyn. "My daughter. My only child. What a disappointment you are."

Unara kept her eyes on Hethra, moving her right arm slightly. No response. Carefully, slowly, she began sliding her arm down her side.

"Ironic. I wait for you this long, then offer you your rightful place here in the ocean with me, and this is how you repay me?" Hethra sneered, but Vaelyn just looked away, blinking. Unara was close enough to see nictitating membranes close down over her friend's eyes.

Sky-born didn't have those.

And this place, this place was undoubtedly a gene-hallow, the chiller sponge holding infusion bags of some sort. *Transformation formula*, the bags had read.

Unara suddenly realized why the Stone Clan had thrown in with Hethra.

What must have been promised.

She moved her arm again. There. The hilt of her dive knife.

"No words?" Hethra taunted, looking between them. "Of course not. But don't worry. Even if I die, the depths won't. There are things down there, beautiful things, eternal things, and they will have their due."

<You're insane,> Lord Gyes snapped, casting a desperate look at Vaelyn. <Listening to whispers from shadows never ends well. Not on any world, anywhere in the galaxy.>

Hethra was on him in a flash, grabbing the front of Lord Gyes's mask. "Little son of a dead man. How did your father survive that poison?"

"Magic." Lord Gyes spat the word at her.

"How cute," she said, and tore the mask off.

Vaelyn thrashed at her bonds, using the last of her air to scream into the water.

Unara's fingers, creeping slowly down her side, finally reached her knife.

Seizing the hilt, she tore it up and out of its sheath, the razor-sharp titanium alloy blade slicing clean through the tentacle around her chest. That, the akker did respond to, thrashing around the small room, smashing itself apart, ripping living equipment from the walls and ceiling and beating loose the chiller sponge.

But it let go of Vaelyn and Lord Gyes, and as they swam for the surface, Unara braced herself back on the wall and launched herself at Hethra.

It was nowhere near the speed that she could have managed in her ocean-born form, but it was enough.

Enough to bury the knife in Hethra's chest. Up to the hilt.

The abyssal chieftain screamed. A tentacle caught Unara in the chest, smashing her against the floor and holding her there. Bubbles streamed from her air tank.

<An end for you, Princess,> Hethra snarled, advancing. The blood streaming out around the knife wound was cephalopod blue.

A terrible realization hit Unara then: the thing wasn't a mount at all. It was part of Hethra. She had merged with it somehow. What kind of black genomancy was Hethra engaged in?

Revulsion filled Unara as the abyssal chieftain advanced on her. Slowly, chuckling. Unara was buried under a forest of tentacles, each piling down on her, driving her further into the sand. All she could do was glare.

"You know," Hethra said, almost conversationally, "when you stop worrying about the limits that moons put on our gene-craft, it's amazing what you can do." She reached Unara, hand descending almost gently to the front of her mask. Unara began sucking air, little breaths all at once, like she'd seen Vaelyn do before, like what had saved her life in the underground river. "Others will hear the call of the depths. Others will avenge them. And all you've done here will be for naught."

And the abyssal chieftain ripped Unara's mask off, all the tentacles squeezing Unara's chest with enough force to crack ribs.

Unara only just managed to hold on to a mouthful of air. But it was hopeless. She was going to drown, she thought, going to die with water in her lungs.

Hildra, help me, she thought.

And then the weight on her body went slack and a terrible scream rent the waters.

Hethra, screaming.

A fishing spear protruding from the front of her rib cage.

Lord Gyes was holding it. He nodded to Unara, and with the last of her breath, she pushed up, wrested her knife free of the abyssal chieftain's chest, and sliced Hethra's throat open to the spine.

For a moment, nothing happened.

And then the thing that Hethra had made herself into, or joined with, or become, fell apart.

For a moment, one terrible moment, Unara was reminded of Glaeva. She couldn't see anything else. She hated the dying. She hated the killing. She just wanted it to stop, wanted—

Lord Gyes grabbed Unara's arm then. She shook herself out of the sudden reverie and kicked up with him.

They broke the surface as the water boiled around them. It smelled foul now, some stench released by Hethra's dissolving form, but it was still air, and Unara gulped it in greedily.

Exhausted, Lord Gyes and Unara pulled themselves up onto the narrow shelf of rock, above the waterline but hardly dry. Vaelyn was slumped back over where she had been before, working on stripping herself out of her wetsuit.

"You don't have to ask," she panted, trying to pull the zipper down. "It's the change. I can feel it. It's not far away. I'll be alright. You need air." She touched Lord Gyes's face. Pulled back. Looked at Unara with those altered eyes. "And Unara, you need one of those bags down there. It'll work on you. Seems to be working on...on me. Then we'll get him up. Up to the air."

Unara stared at her friend for a moment, unsure what to do with all of this. But Lord Gyes was already there, pulling himself painfully over to sit next to Vaelyn. He wound his fingers through hers and she smiled at him, Unara's presence all but forgotten.

Something unpleasant roiling in her chest, Unara took the deepest breath she could and slipped back under the water.

The scene was grim. The gene-hallow had been completely destroyed, smashed apart in Hethra's death-throes. The chiller sponge was cracked open, its bladders burst, all lost. Gone was the gene-craft that could turn an air-breather into an ocean-born.

Unara surfaced, filled her lungs, dived again. The air was definitely going bad. She could taste it. She found nothing. Another breath, another dive. Three more. And just as her body was about to give up Unara finally caught sight of a glow.

A bag. An intact infusion bag.

Quickly, she rummaged through the ruins of the room. Found tubing, a needle, all the necessary components for setting up an infusion. She brought everything to the surface to assemble it there.

Vaelyn had moved closer to the water, prone now, eyes closed. Lord Gyes was sitting beside her, still holding her hand.

"Did you...find it?" he asked, eyes closing.

Unara nodded, holding it up.

"Good," he said, trying to rouse himself, sinking back further against the rock. "Wake me... when... time to..."

And nothing.

Unara looked at the bag.

One dose.

Only one dose.

There was always the possibility that Hethra had been lying. That she had planned on killing Vaelyn, just like she had killed Glaeva. But it was common knowledge that Lady Hethra had no children, no heirs, no successor. And if Vaelyn truly was her daughter, it was very likely that Hethra had planned on bringing her home.

If Unara didn't do this, she would die here.

And yet…

She looked over at Lord Gyes. Unconscious in the failing air, or from battle fatigue, or the effects of the hard, deep swim they'd just endured. Decompression sickness. She felt a stab of guilt.

He was another human being. Why did his life matter less than hers?

Unara sat there, head aching, thoughts growing foggy. She needed to act. But she didn't know what to do.

And then, with perfect clarity, Hildra's words came back to her.

You've made your choice. You have another to make before the end.

Unara had thought it would be something grand, some huge, sweeping thing. Why else would one of the planet's guardians involve herself?

But it was a simple thing. The smallest thing.

Save herself, or save somebody else.

Painfully, Unara scooted over next to Lord Gyes, unzipping his wetsuit and peeling it off. She did this quickly, fingers increasingly clumsy. She hung the infusion bag up on a hook that must have been for dive gear, unwound the tubing, had everything ready to go. But then she hesitated, needle to his skin.

What if he didn't want this? What if it killed him? What if—

They were both dead anyway. This, at least, gave him a chance.

Unara plunged the needle in.

The water in the room was rising rapidly now. The water-lock seals had cracked. Unara crept over to the corner furthest from the deluge, shivering uncontrollably. Her vision was graying. Her head, her entire body, ached. She pulled her arms tightly around herself and tried to breathe as slowly and deliberately as she could.

Choice made, she thought to herself. *Hildra, choice made.*

And perhaps it was the lack of oxygen, perhaps it was her own desperation, but Unara thought she heard footsteps, soft and gentle, coming across the water. Thought she saw a silvery-white hand held out to her. Thought she heard soft words, whispering to her, telling her—

ACT FOUR

HEIGHTS

CHAPTER THIRTY-SIX

<S o this is the true face of Thalassa. Not what I was expecting.>
    <I could say the same of you, old friend.>

Skald Hakon could not help but be struck by the strangeness of this particular encounter. Already, his mind was working on how he would describe the events of the past few weeks. The depths rising up, the moons protecting the Thalassan people once again.

It would make a fine saga indeed.

Hakon looked to the old Lord Gyes. Gone was the vital and crafty trader Hakon remembered from the last kaupang. Instead, here was a man brought low to the point of death by Thalassan genomancy, confined to a medical tank borne up by an anti-grav sled and accompanied only by a feii healer.

Her presence was inexplicable. The seas had not risen up to strike the alien down yet, as the stories claimed. And yet, hadn't one of the guardian moons taken out the Suyarii fleet? Hadn't Hildra herself intervened here on the surface? For now, Thalassa permitted this alien to walk their world for reasons he could not discern.

Or perhaps it wasn't complicated at all. Perhaps it was for this, this moment. So all truths could finally be spoken.

Were they really so different, off-worlder and Thalassan?

Here were two of the most powerful men from each group, staring at each other across a divide that neither could cross. Such a small distance, and yet, so utterly profound. Both caught behind barriers they could not cross, their survival dependent upon the conditions in which they floated. So different and yet—

Watch, observe, then spin the song, Hakon admonished himself. He was already getting lost in his poetry.

<I must admit, King Aegyr,> old Lord Gyes was saying, <I did not expect to find anything like this in the heart of the oceans here. A people of the water, yes, but not—>

<We are the people of the moons,> King Aegyr said evenly. <But yes, the ocean is our home and our salvation, just as the waters of that tank are yours.>

<Perhaps not for much longer,> Lord Gyes said.

"With the death of your sea witch, the effects of her poisons seem to be fading," Healer Eyr said, bobbing her head a little.

<May it be so for all her evil works,> King Aegyr said, a flicker of a smile crossing his thin face.

Lady Hethra. Ah, how Hakon would enjoy singing of Lady Hethra. Especially the part where the young Lord Gyes and Princess Unara slew her together. He had heard the story, of course, but the details weren't suitably heroic. A last mad scramble in the confines of a tight little cave? No, it needed to be a grand battle out in the open water, perhaps against the backdrop of the orbital strike, and—

<And you, my son. How are they treating you?>

Lord Gyes's face turned slightly, fixing on another beyond the glass boundary wall. For while King Aegyr had ordered the hall emptied for this, he had not come alone.

Beside the king was another man, younger, stronger, his newly scaled tail flashing silver-blue in the shafts of light from the suns above. It was an auspicious color, the color of Hildra's favor, although Hakon wasn't going to tell Karl Gyes that.

<I am well, Father,> the younger Lord Gyes said, looking down

at himself, expression somewhere between fascination and fear. <Even if this does take a bit of getting used to.>

The tank emitted a strange sound. <It does, doesn't it? At least you have a bit more freedom than do I, my son.>

<I regret that it affects the fleet. If I could—>

"You cannot," Hakon said, speaking up for the first time since this strange audience began. "Hildra chooses her people. If she extended her protection to you in this way, then you can never leave this world."

<I have had this explained to me but I still don't understand it.>

"And yet, it seems that I shall be able to depart." The words, soft though they were, startled the skald. He turned to see Princess Unara, standing there with a smile on her lips. "Or will Hildra strip my life away from me too, when we leave orbit?"

Hakon had lived ninety-five punishing Standard years on the surface of Thalassa and had spent much of that time as a nocturnal creature. Singing for the evening feasts and nighttime gatherings, writing his sagas, teaching the younger skalds. But watching the moons was a favorite pastime of his as well. While he never would have said it to any of the ocean-born, he felt that his place under the sky was a fortunate one, for it let him study the moons. Allowed him to know them as well as any mortal man could.

But even he had been surprised at the tale Unara had told.

Under normal circumstances, it took nearly a year to fill Ocean-fall Bay, and even with the fury unleashed from the inland sea via Hethra's tunnels, the water level had not risen anywhere near that high. The flow had been stopped, at least. For the past few days, several of the trader fleets—Amaro, Hellenic, Gyes—had been working diligently to help them stem the flow, block up the underground tunnels. The old river was now flowing again, but the flood had stopped.

But it hadn't mattered. The landing fields were littered with boulders. The market streets above the palace were ruined. Cleanup would take years, decades, perhaps.

The palace's exterior remained mostly intact, although appearances didn't tell the whole story. Saboteurs from the Stone Clan had opened seals, killed water-locks, broken windows. Much of the palace lay below the waterline, or near it, and with the rising water in the bay, much of the interior had been flooded.

Getting an accurate death count was difficult. There were no bodies to account for, not among his own people.

Many people had made the cliffs, but many had died inside, killed by the draugr or the rising water. Others—Thalassans and off-worlders alike—had been swept out to sea. Several of the trade delegates who had not changed back had drowned.

Drowning in the air. It would certainly add a tragic poignancy to Hakon's saga.

When questioned about what they had been thinking, one captured saboteur admitted that Hethra had promised them the change. But very few of the ones who had taken her infusions were anywhere to be found; drowned, no doubt, or as whispered rumors now held, changed into draugr.

Hakon doubted they would ever know the truth of it.

The death toll was not as high as it could have been. Even now, days later, search and rescue operations were still underway, releasing people trapped in flooded ships. These were being undertaken with the greatest care to avoid any further exposure of the ocean-born to the off-worlders, of course, but there were many who had been saved from the depths.

And in the palace many people had clung to life in pockets of air scattered in storerooms, water-locks, and elsewhere.

Every able-bodied Thalassan over the age of ten had been enlisted to aid in the search. Many of the Stone Clan who had bought into Hethra's lies had begged to help as well. King Aegyr would decide their fate later. For now, they dove.

Hakon had taken to the water as well. Swimming through the flooded halls of his home brought him grief, and he'd found himself wandering further and further from the palace core. Further and further, until something grabbed him in the dark.

He'd almost killed the offender, on edge, on alert as he was, but a human voice had delivered one desperate plea.

"The princess! Needs air! Immediately!"

She was unconscious when Hakon had reached her, her head being held up in the last little bit of air by another ocean-born. The air was absolutely foul, unbreathable. He didn't have much hope.

Without even a glance at the other man, Hakon had broken the surface to slip his spare face mask on the unconscious princess. <Is there a quicker way to the surface?> he'd asked in their own language. <This backup tank's only good for a half hour, and I fear it may not be enough time.>

<What?> the ocean-born had asked in Standard.

Unara shouldn't have lived. Air samples, taken later at the king's behest, showed a lethal amount of carbon dioxide in the space. She should have been dead long before Hakon reached her. And when she had finally woken again, she'd grabbed Hakon's wrist and spoken.

"Hildra," she'd gasped. "Hildra! Where is she?"

"I have conferred with Gothi Injyr," Healer Eyr said, shaking Hakon out of his recollections, "and we have reviewed your genetic code together, Princess. There is no sign of any Thalassan adaptations in your current DNA pattern, nor any sign of the previous alterations you underwent. No doubt this is the reason why your voice has returned. The body you wear now is beyond the moons' ability to control."

<And this is why you cannot remain,> Gothi Injyr added from below the glass. <Even if you wished to.>

<We shall take good care of her,> old Lord Gyes said, and in his tank, he nodded once, slow. <As if she is my own daughter.>

"Milord," Captain Thorsen said, a way back from the small party. "We have reports from orbit that the moons are shifting paths again. We need to leave soon, if we're to avoid a collision."

<They're angry about the strike,> Father said. <But they won't hurt any of you now. The threat has been neutralized, and they know this.>

<Still, I will take no chances,> old Lord Gyes said. <Eyr, we withdraw!>

Unara stood by the glass wall for a moment more. She laid a hand over her heart, looking between her father and Hakon, then stepped forward, touching an open palm to the cool surface. Beyond, the young Lord Gyes swam forward. He laid his own hand over hers. Smiled at her.

She nodded back and began to walk away.

"Unara," Hakon said softly, walking with her. "Your father has granted your request."

"Oh?"

"None of the off-worlders will lose their life for this," he murmured to her. "Everyone leaves from here with their memories of that day."

She bowed her head. "That is most generous of my father."

"Thank the moons," he said, waving an arm around at the statues in their niches. "They fought for Thalassa. A bit of indulgence is in order."

The princess looked at him for a moment more, then threw her arms around him, hugging him tight. "Thank you, Hakon."

He held on to her for a moment before pushing her back again. "Never forget this world, Princess. It will be a fight of a different kind out there, but I believe you shall win it." He laid a hand over his heart. "Drown your foes."

"Win the stars," she whispered back, and dashing tears from her eyes, turned to follow old Lord Gyes from the hall.

Hakon watched her go. A bittersweet thing, this. But Unara burned too bright to stay here. She would be a star caught in the darkness of the Stone Clan's existence. She needed to go, needed to ascend.

Hildra's will, Hakon thought.

CHAPTER THIRTY-SEVEN

"Where will you go?"

Karl paused. Movement was in many ways easier now, but almost more difficult. He had woken up his first morning in this new state in a panic, unable to separate his legs, certain he was going to drown. Those sensations were subsiding now. It was common even among the ocean-born during their return to the ocean, the palace gothi had assured him, and would fade with time.

He wasn't so sure.

Such a strange thing this was.

"I don't know," he said, turning around. This place, he was told, was the royal armory. Unara had sent him a note before she left, telling him she had left him a gift here. To Karl, it seemed more like a coral grotto with a few weapons placed haphazardly inside, but then, that seemed to be the way with all of Thalassan construction. "King Aegyr has graciously offered to let me find a place that suits me before pledging to his, or any other, clan. What about you?"

Vaelyn awkwardly rubbed her arm. She looked much the same as she had before, albeit with subtle changes. Silver skin, instead of gray. Dark red hair, striping on her tail to match. Whole, somehow. Karl remembered his first impressions of the Thalassan delegates, how they appeared to be missing part of themselves. Vaelyn had found that part of herself now, but it hadn't seemed to help her unease.

"My appearance marks me as one of the abyss," she said, waving at her altered body, "and I am certain that my mother's people are not much welcome anywhere right now. If any of them still live at all."

"You might be surprised," he told her gently. "You are here, are you not? If...Hildra chose you, who is anyone else here to say otherwise?"

She smiled, a brittle expression, but shook her head. "I don't know, Lord Gyes."

"It's just Karl now," he said.

Her smile grew a bit stronger then, and she swam over to him. Unlike him, she seemed to have no issue with her new state. But then, she was Thalassan. She had grown up in the ocean. It must have been like second nature for her. "What do you have here?" she asked.

He gestured at the weapon. "Unara left this for me. I gave her my sword, once they pulled it from the reef, but I fear it's not so well balanced for a woman's hand."

Vaelyn picked up the trident, hefting it experimentally. "She wouldn't have been worried about the weight. She won't use it. She always did want to get away from the death here." Vaelyn set it down again, fingers resting on the shaft. "She never was at peace with the nature of this place."

"I don't see death on this world," Karl said. "I see struggle and pain, but I see freedom as well, a chance for a new life."

Vaelyn looked at him then. "What kind of life are you looking for, Karl?"

"I don't know yet," he said, and then, seized by a sudden idea, held out a hand. "Come with me."

"I told you, I—"

"And I told you, people might surprise you," he replied, and smiled sheepishly. "Besides, I think you may have more knowledge of how to hunt in these waters than do I. I wouldn't like to starve on my journey."

Closing her eyes, Vaelyn shook her head. Her long hair, tied back in its complicated braid, moved like a second tail in the water. "If you need somebody to teach you to hunt, there are far better instructors here among the ocean-born than I."

"Then perhaps I should be more blunt," Karl said. "You are beautiful, Vaelyn, and whatever you think of yourself, you have earned the right to see the world that you helped save."

She looked at him for a moment more and then back to the trident. "These are effective weapons, but highly personalized. You shall need a different one, more suited to your length and tail configuration."

"Then why don't you have this one?" Karl said. Vaelyn hesitated. He laid his hand over hers. "I think Unara would be happy to see you wield it."

"I don't—"

"Come with me, Vaelyn. Come with me, and we'll find out who we really are. Together."

Vaelyn hesitated a moment more, then sagged, as if released from some gray burden. She wrapped an arm around his chest, laying her cheek right above his heart. "I have always been alone," she murmured.

"Not anymore," he replied, smoothing back a bit of her hair that had come loose in the current. Karl laid his other arm around her shoulders and held on.

"WE SHALL NEED to close the blast shutters soon. Protection, you know."

"Protection? From what?"

Unara knew she probably looked like a child on her first akker ride, but she couldn't help herself. The world beyond the observation dome was so vast her mind had trouble comprehending it. It made her feel like laughing uncontrollably. And there was no gravity up here, allowing her to float as easily as she might have in still water.

Swimming out among the stars.

What a wonderful feeling.

Captain Thorsen didn't laugh at her, though, nor scold her as he pushed up to grab the rail beside her. His was the same steady, calm presence from the surface. Something familiar in all of this strangeness.

"The void looks empty," he told her, "but it is far from it. Radiation, micrometeors, debris, gas clouds, all manner of things exist up here. Why, there are solar winds from your stars, if you can believe that. Like currents."

Solar wind. "What a wonderful concept," she said. "But they aren't my stars anymore."

He smiled at her. "In fifty-seven years, we shall come back here, and I would bet good money that you will be delighted to see this planet again."

"Perhaps. In fifty-seven years." Unara pushed herself closer, laying a hand on the glass. She knew she sounded giddy. She didn't care. "But I want to see other things first."

Captain Thorsen laughed. "There's an entire galaxy out there to see. And I know Lord Gyes is quite eager to show you the ins and outs of House operations, if you are so willing."

"I'm honored. It is a great deal of trust to place in me."

"It is. But if you don't mind me saying, he sees the utility in you."

Unara looked around again at the stars. "It is still a great trust."

"He also has great fondness for your father, even if he won't say it aloud," Captain Thorsen replied, and offered Unara a hand. "Now come. The pilots are eager to begin accelerating."

Unara nodded but didn't yet move, entranced by the star field, the endless sky.

It was so quiet.

"I'm afraid the old man has much for you to learn," Captain Thorsen continued. "Our own language, of course, and history and finance, and the finer points of interstellar politics, for we never truly escape that, and—"

"I'm up for the challenge," she replied, and took Thorsen's hand.

Time to go.

Time to fly.

AFTERWORD

Retellings might be my new favorite thing. Seriously, these are so much fun to write.

Fairytales and science fantasy go together really well. At least, the original fairytales. These are stories about danger and courage, magic and will, virtue and vice. And *The Little Mermaid* is a particularly complicated story, with an ending that divided critics even back in the 1800s when it was first written.

One big challenge for fairytale retellings is giving the side characters their own stories, to make them fully fleshed out people, while still staying true to the original tale. Unara is a woman looking for something more than what her world offers her. So it just made sense that the other main characters—Karl, the prince, and Vaelyn, the girl who finds him on the beach—had parallel journeys.

All three long for the life they can't have, but they all have different reactions. Karl is trying to resign himself to his fate. Vaelyn allows herself to get caught up in something terrible. And Unara, of course, has to scramble for a Plan B when her carefully constructed Plan A doesn't work out.

The other thing I always want to do with retellings like this is ensure that the culture that the story comes from is represented. Stories are so often grounded in their time and place and fairytales are no exception, even if *The Little Mermaid* has become somewhat universal.

So here, with this being a Danish fairytale, I opted to reference two different periods; an Enlightenment vibe with House Gyes and a bit of Norse flavor with the Thalassans. Underwater Vikings with biotech? I had fun writing it and I hope you had fun reading it!

If you did enjoy the book, there's no greater compliment a writer can receive than a review! More importantly, it helps other readers find and enjoy it as well. Even just giving a star rating is a great thing. (And hey, if you hated it, thank you for reading this far and I'd love to hear your thoughts too). Thank you so much for reading!

If you'd like to subscribe to my newsletter for some free short stories, future release information, and the occasional Embarrassing Cadet Tale, please head over to my website and sign up!

https://rensingwrites.com/

Cheers,

Eryn